THE COMPLETE
MAHABHARATA
Santi Parva and Anusasana Parva

THE COMPLETE MAHABHARATA

Volume 10

Santi Parva (Part III)
and
Anusasana Parva (Part I)

Anjuli Kaul

RUPA

For Richa, naturally.
And for Akshay, necessarily.

Published by
Rupa Publications India Pvt. Ltd 2017
7/16, Ansari Road, Daryaganj
New Delhi 110002

Sales centres:
Allahabad Bengaluru Chennai
Hyderabad Jaipur Kathmandu
Kolkata Mumbai

ISBN: 978-81-291-4513-0

First impression 2017

10 9 8 7 6 5 4 3 2 1

The moral right of the author has been asserted.

ANJULI KAUL grew up in Mumbai, lives in Goa,
but dreams of Kodaikanal. She has been
a teacher for thirty years. More recently, her
love of language and literature has drawn her
into editing and writing. She is passionate
about education, organic farming,
sustainable living and sunsets.

RAMESH MENON was born in 1951
in New Delhi. He has also written modern
renderings of the Mahabharata, Ramayana,
Srimad Bhagavad Gita, Siva Purana,
Devi Purana and Bhagavata Purana.

THE MAHABHARATA of Veda Vyasa is
the longest recorded epic in the world.
With almost 100,000 verses, it is many times
as long as the *Iliad* and the *Odyssey* combined
and has deeply influenced every aspect
of the Indian ethos for some 4,000 years.

The main theme of the epic is the Great War in
Kurukshetra, but it teems with smaller stories,
and other stories within these, all woven
together with a genius that defies comparison.
As its heart, it contains Krishna's immortal
Bhagavad Gita, the Song of God.

The Mahabharata embodies the ancient
and sacred Indian tradition in all its earthy
and spiritual immensity. Famously, 'What is
found here may be found elsewhere. What is
not found here will not be found elsewhere.'

Many believe this most magnificent epic
to be the greatest story ever told. Yet, the only
full Indian translation of the Mahabharata into
English is the one penned in the 19th century
by Kisari Mohan Ganguli. More than a hundred
years have passed since Ganguli accomplished
his task, and the language he used is now,
sadly, archaic.

THIS NEW TWELVE-VOLUME SERIES
RETELLS THE GREAT EPIC, LINE BY LINE,
IN FRESH, EASILY READABLE ENGLISH PROSE.
WITH IT, WE HOPE TO BRING
THE MAHABHARATA ALIVE AGAIN
FOR THE CONTEMPORARY AS WELL AS
THE FUTURE READER.

❋

CONTENTS

PART III
Santi Parva

CANTO 302

"Yudhishtira says, 'Rajan, you have recommended to me the judicious path of yoga as a loving guru does for his sishya. I now ask about the principles of the Samkhya yoga. Speak to me about those doctrines, in their entirety. You are erudite about all the knowledge that exists in the three worlds!'

Bhishma says, 'Listen now to the subtle teachings of the followers of the Samkhya yoga established by all the great and puissant Yatis beginning with Kapila. There are no errors in that philosophy. Its merits are many. Truly, it is flawless. I understand that all things are imperfect. Manavas, Pisachas, Rakshasas, and Yakshas, Nagas, Gandharvas and Pitris, intermediate orders of beings like birds and animals, great avians like Garuda, the Maruts, royal and enlightened sages, Asuras and Viswadevas, divine Rishis and yogins, the Prajapatis and Brahma himself are all enmeshed with these objects that are difficult to discard, and they all strive to free themselves.

The Samkhyas understand the limits of one's time in this world. Aware of the highest, transcendent truth as well, they also know the truth about what is called happiness in this world, and the sorrows that befall those concerned with transient objects of desire. Aware of the grief of those who have fallen into the intermediate orders of being and of those who have sunk into hell, they see the merits and shortcomings of swarga, O Bhaarata, and all the merits and flaws of the Vedas, and the yoga and the Samkhya systems of philosophy. They realise also that the sattva guna has ten properties, that rajas has nine, and that tamas has eight, that the intellect, Buddhi, has seven properties, Manas, the mind, has six, and Akasa, space, has five; they discern that the understanding has four properties and tamas has three, and the rajas has two and sattva has one.

Knowing the path that is followed by all creatures when death overtakes them and the course of Atmagyana, self-knowledge, the wise and experienced Samkhyas, exalted by their discernment and awareness of causes, and acquiring true wisdom thorough auspicious living, attain the bliss of moksha like the rays of the sun or the wind taking refuge in Akasa.

Vision is attached to form, the sense of scent to smell, the ear to sound, the tongue to taste, and the skin to touch. The wind is housed in space. Dark stupor harbours in tamas. Greed takes refuge in the objects of the senses.

Vishnu is the Lord of the organs of motion; Indra that of the organs of strength; Agni of the stomach, and Bhumi of the waters.

The waters have heat for their haven. Agni has Vayu; and the wind has Akasa; Akasa has Mahat for its refuge, and Mahat has the understanding. The understanding is housed in tamas, tamas in rajas; rajas is founded in sattva and sattva is attached to Atman.

Atman has the glorious and puissant Narayana for its refuge. Narayana resides in moksha. Moksha has no need for any dwelling. The followers of the Samkhya yoga know that this body, imbued with sixteen attributes, is the outcome of sattva. Fully understanding the nature of the physical organism and the character of the Chetana that dwells within it, they recognise the one existent Being that lives in the body, the Atman, detached and sinless, and realising the nature of the actions of persons attached to the objects of their senses, they also know the character of the senses and the sensual objects which have their refuge in the Atman.

The Samkhyas appreciate the difficulty of moksha and the sacred texts that describe it, and recognise the nature of the vital breaths called

Prana, Apana, Samana, Vyana and Udana, as also the two other breaths: the one going downward and the other moving up. Indeed, they know those seven breaths ordained to carry out seven different functions.

Parantapa, establishing the nature of the Prajapatis and the Rishis and the many high paths of righteousness, and the Saptarishis and the countless Rajarishis, the great Devarishis and the other Maharishis radiant like the sun, they see all these falling away from their power in the course of many long ages.

Hearing of the destruction of all the mighty beings in the universe, the Samkhyas understand the inauspicious end of sinful creatures, and the miseries of those that fall into the river of hell, Vaitarani in Yamaloka.

They grasp the ill-fated wanderings of beings through diverse wombs, housed in the unholy uterus in the midst of blood and water and phlegm and foul-smelling urine and faeces, and then in bodies, resulting from the union of blood and the vital seed, of marrow and sinews, supplied by hundreds of nerves and arteries, forming an execrable abode of nine doors.

O Lord of the Bharata vamsa, the followers of the Samkhya yoga, fully conversant with the Soul, know what produces good, and they clearly see the vile conduct of those whose natures are characterised by tamas, rajas or sattva—darkness, passion or goodness—and their sins that prevent them from attaining moksha.

They see the eclipse of the moon and the sun by Rahu, the falling of stars from their fixed positions and the deflection of constellations from their orbits, and recognise the sad division of all that was once united, the diabolical behaviour of creatures in devouring one another, the absence of all intelligence in the infancy of human beings, and the deterioration and destruction of the body.

The Samkhyas observe how little men value the sattva guna because they are overcome by anger and confusion. They see that only one among thousands of human beings struggles to achieve moksha; indeed they understand the difficulty of attaining moksha in accordance with the shastras, the scriptures.

They recognise the great anxiety that creatures have for unattained objects and unfulfilled desires and their comparative indifference to those that have been attained and gratified; son of Kunti, they mark the sins that result from the pursuit of the senses, the lifeless repulsive bodies of those who live miserably even in the midst of spouses and children.

The Samkhyas know the end of terrible dissolute men who are guilty of killing Brahmanas, and of evil Brahmanas addicted to intoxicants; they are also aware of the equally wretched death of those who lust after the wives of their acharyas, and of those who do not revere their mothers and the Devas.

After studying the diverse declarations of the Vedas, their knowledge helps them to understand how evil men will die; and also what will befall those who are born in the intermediate varnas.

Establishing the recurrent pattern of seasons, the passing of years, months, fortnights, and of days, they see the waxing and the waning of the moon, the rise and ebb of the seas, the increase and diminution of wealth, and the separation of unified objects, the end of yugas, the destruction of mountains, the drying up of rivers, and the degeneration of the purity of the varnas and also the end of that deterioration, repeating endlessly.

Beholding the birth, decay, death and sorrows of creatures, knowing truly the weaknesses of the body and the anguish of human beings, and their vicissitudes, the followers of the Samkhya philosophy, understand all the flaws of their own souls and bodies, and attain moksha.'

Yudhishtira says, 'O you of immeasurable tejas, what are those faults that you ascribe to one's body? Dispel all my doubts on this matter.'

Bhishma says, 'Listen, O Parantapa! The Samkhyas, followers of Kapila, who are wise and conversant with all paths, say that there are five faults in the human body. They are desire, anger, fear, sleep and breath. All mortals have these faults, which are found in their bodies.

The wise cut the root of wrath with the help of forgiveness. Desire is destroyed by giving up all goals. By cultivating sattva sleep is defeated, and fear is conquered by honing mindfulness. Breath is vanquished by an abstemious diet, Rajan.

They truly understand gunas aided by hundreds of gunas, hundreds of flaws, and diverse causes through hundreds of causes. They realise that the world is like the foam of water, cloaked in hundreds of illusions flowing from Vishnu, like a painted edifice, and as fragile as a reed, and they see it as a terrible dark abyss, as unreal and as short-lived as bubbles on water when compared to the duration of eternity.

The sagacious Samkhyas discard even tenderness towards their own children, knowing the world to be devoid of permanence and joy, with inescapable destruction for its end, sunk in rajas and tamas, and helpless like an elephant stuck in mire.

With their comprehensive yoga of knowledge, and the power of their penances, these Yatis sever and bludgeon all inauspicious vasanas born of rajas and those from tamas, and indeed all auspicious vasanas arising from sattva, and all pleasures of touch and the other bodily senses arising from the same three gunas, and in doing so, these Yatis cross samsara, the illusory ocean of life.

That terrifying ocean has sorrow for its waters. Anxiety and grief constitute its deep lakes. Disease and death are its colossal crocodiles. The great fears that pierce the heart at every step are its massive serpents.

The deeds inspired by tamas are its tortoises. Those inspired by rajas are its fish. Wisdom is the raft for crossing it. Sensual desires are its marshes. Decay constitutes its region of sorrow and turmoil.

Parantapa, knowledge is its island. Deeds make up its great depth. Truth is its shores. Pious practices form the lush weeds floating on its breast. Envy constitutes its swift tide. The emotions of the heart make up its mines. The diverse kinds of gratification are its precious jewels. Grief and fever are its winds. Misery and thirst form its mighty eddies. Agonising and fatal diseases are its colossal tuskers.

The collections of bones are its flights of steps, and phlegm is its froth. Gifts form its pearly banks. The lakes of blood are its corals.

Deafening laughter constitutes its roars. Diverse sciences make it impenetrable. Tears are its brine. Solitude is the high refuge of those that seek to cross it.

Children and wives are its countless leeches. Friends and kinsmen are the cities and towns on its shores. Non-violence and truth are its shorelines. Death is its last tempest.

The knowledge of Vedanta is its island that can harbour those tossed upon its waters. Compassion towards all creatures constitute its buoys, and moksha the priceless treasure offered to those voyaging on its waters seeking merchandise.

Like a horse spewing flames of fire, this ocean too, has its fiery terrors. Having transcended the limitations of dwelling within the gross body, so difficult to transcend, the Samkhyas enter into Akasa.

With his rays, Surya then bears those righteous men, followers of the Samkhya yoga. Like the fibres of the lotus-stalk sending water to the flower into which they all converge, Surya imbibes all things from the universe, and delivers them to those good and wise men.

Son of Kunti, these Yatis are carried by a gentle, cooling, fragrant wind, their attachments destroyed, animated with tejas, filled with the treasures of penances and crowned with success. That wind, the best of the seven winds, and which blows in blissful lands of great felicity, bears them, son of Kunti, to that which is the highest end in Akasa.

Then Akasa conveys them to the highest end of rajas. Rajas then bears them to the highest end of sattva. Sattva then lifts them to the Supreme Narayana.

Through himself, the puissant and pure-souled Narayana at last bears them to the Paramatman. Having reached this, Rajan, those pure ones attain immortality, and they never have to return from that condition.

That is the highest goal, O son of Pritha, which is achieved by those Mahatmans who have transcended the influence of all the contradictions and pairs of opposites.'

Yudhishtira says, 'O sinless one, after attaining this puissance and bliss, do these men of firm vows have any recollection of their lives including birth and death? O you of the Kuru vamsa, it is fitting that you tell me the truth about this, even as it is appropriate for me to ask none other but you this question.

On the subject of moksha, the scriptures are inconsistent and seem flawed, for some declare that consciousness disappears in the emancipated state, while others hold the very opposite.

If in this exalted condition the Yatis continue to live in consciousness, it would seem that the religion of Pravritti is superior. If, again, consciousness disappears from this state and the liberated one only resembles a person sunk in dreamless slumber, then it is wrong to say that there is no consciousness in moksha for of all that happens in dreamless sleep is that one's consciousness is temporarily eclipsed and suspended, but never lost, for it returns when one awakes.'

Bhishma says, 'However difficult to answer, your question, my son, is proper. Bharatarishabha, this kind of question unsettles even the most learned. For all that, hear the truth about this as I tell it to you.

The high-souled followers of Kapila have set their lofty intellects to this subject. The senses of knowledge, planted in the bodies of embodied creatures, are used for perception. They are the instruments of the Soul, for it is through them that subtle Being perceives.

Separated from the Atman, the senses are like bits of wood, quickly consumed, vanishing like the froth on the ocean's breast. When the Jiva, the embodied creature, along with his senses, sinks into sleep, the subtle Atman roams among all the realms of perception like the wind through ethereal space.

During its slumber, it continues to perceive all the fields of the senses just as well as it does when awake. However, without their ability to act during sleep, the senses are stilled in their places, losing their powers like snakes deprived of poison.

At such times, the Atman moves into the respective place of all the senses and fulfils all their functions.

All the qualities of sattva, all the attributes of the intellect, as also those of mind, and space, and wind, and all the characteristics of water, and of earth, the senses with these qualities, Yudhishtira, which adhere to Jivatman, along with the Jivatman itself, are engulfed in Brahman, the Paramatman.

Pious and evil karma, deeds, also overwhelm that Jivatman. Like sishyas waiting upon their guru with reverence, the senses too, wait upon the Jivatman; it reaches Brahman, which is Narayana, the highest, changeless, beyond all the pairs of opposites, and transcends Prakriti.

Freed from both punya and paapa, the Jivatman enters the Paramatman which is nirguna, without all attributes; from this abode of all auspiciousness, it does not return, O Bhaarata. What remains, O son, is the mind with the senses. These have to come back once more at the appointed time to do the bidding of their great master.

Soon after the sloughing off of this body, the Yati striving for moksha, endowed with knowledge and wishing for freedom, succeeds in achieving that eternal peace of mukti, which is his who becomes bodiless.

The Samkhyas, Rajan, are exceedingly wise. They succeed in attaining to the highest end through this kind of knowledge. There is no knowledge that is equal to this gyana. Do not doubt this.

The knowledge described in the system of the Samkhyas is regarded as the highest. That gyana is immutable and is everlasting. It is eternal Brahman in fullness. It has no beginning, middle and end. It transcends all contradictions.

It is the cause of the creation of the universe. It is complete and stands in fullness. It is without any kind of change or decay. It is uniform and perpetual. Thus the wise sing its praises.

From it flow creation and destruction, and all change. The great Rishis speak of it and laud it in the scriptures. All learned Brahmanas and all righteous men regard it to flow from Brahman, supreme, divine, infinite, immutable and undiminishing.

All Brahmanas that are attached to sensual objects adore and praise it by ascribing illusory attributes to it. The same is the view of yogins so observant of tapasya and dhyana, and of the Samkhyas of fathomless insight.

Son of Kunti, the Srutis declare that the Samkhya yoga is the very form of that Formless One. According to it, all cognitive knowledge is the knowledge of Brahman.

There are two kinds of creatures on Bhumi, Lord of the earth—the moving and the immobile, of which the mobile are superior. That supreme gyana which exists in persons conversant with Brahman and that which is contained in the Vedas, that which is found in other scriptures and that in yoga, that which is seen in the diverse Puranas, is all found in Samkhya philosophy.

Whatever knowledge exists in the itihasas and in vigyana, pertaining to the acquisition of wealth as approved by the wise; whatever other knowledge exists in this world—all flows from the lofty gyana of the Samkhyas.

Serenity, puissance, all subtle scriptural knowledge, tapasya of spiritual force, and all kinds of felicity, Rajan, have all been duly ordained in the Samkhya yoga. If they fail to achieve that complete knowledge recommended in their system, the Samkhyas attain the status of deities and pass many years in pleasure and happiness. Reigning over the celestials at will, at the end of the allotted time of their punya, they fall among learned Brahmanas and Yatis.

Like the Devas who ascend into the sky, the truly regenerate Samkhyas cast off this body and enter into the superior state of Brahman by devoting themselves entirely to their philosophy which is revered by all wise men. Faithful to the acquisition of Samkhya gyana, even if they fail to reach that eminence, they never fall among intermediate creatures, or sink to the status of sinful men.

That Mahatman who is fully conversant with the ancient, vast, ocean-like and profound Samkhya doctrines that are pure and tolerant and agreeable, becomes equal to Narayana. I have now told you the truth about the Samkhya yoga. It is the embodiment of Narayana, of the universe as it exists from the earliest time.

When the time of creation arrives, He causes the generation of life, and when the time comes for destruction, he swallows everything. Having withdrawn everything into his own body he falls into sleep, that inner Atman, Soul of the universe.'"

CANTO 303

"Yudhishtira says, 'What is that state known as Akshaya, the immutable, attaining which no one has to return? What, again, is that which is called Kshaya, decaying, from which one has to return once more? O Mahabaho, tell me the distinction between the two so that I may truly understand them both.

Delighter of the Kurus, Brahmanas who know the Vedas speak of you as an ocean of knowledge. Highly blessed and Mahatman Rishis and Yatis do the same. You now have but very few days to live.

When the sun turns from Dakshinayana, the southern path, to enter Uttarayana, the northern, you will attain to your high end. When you have left us, from whom shall we hear of all that benefits us? You are the lamp of Kuru's race. You shine with the light of knowledge. Perpetuator of the Kuru vamsa, I want to hear all this from you. Listening to your discourses, sweet as amrita, my curiosity in never satisfied but only increases!'

Bhishma says, 'In this regard, I will tell you the ancient story of the conversation that took place between Vasishta and King Karala of Janaka's race.

Once upon a time when that foremost of Rishis, Vasishta, effulgent like the sun, was seated undisturbed, King Janaka asked him about that highest knowledge which is for our supreme good.

Erudite in the domain of Atmagyana and having vast learning in all branches of that science, as Maitravaruni Vasishta was seated at his ease, the king approached him with folded hands; in humble words, sweet and well-spoken and lacking in all contentiousness he asked, "Holy one, I want to know about the Supreme and Eternal Brahman by attaining to which men of wisdom do not have to return.

I also wish to know that which is called Kshaya, destructible, and that into which this universe enters when destroyed. Indeed, what is that which is said to be indestructible, mysterious, beneficial and free from all evil?"

Vasishta said, "Lord of the earth, listen to how this universe is destroyed, and about that which was never and can never be destroyed. According to the measure of the Devas, twelve thousand years make a yuga; four such yugas taken a thousand times, make a kalpa which measures one day of Brahma. Brahma's night, also, Rajan, is of the same duration.

When Brahma himself is destroyed, Sambhu of formless soul, in whom the attributes of Anima and Laghima are inherent awakens, and once more creates that First, most primeval of all creatures, having vast proportions, of infinite deeds, imbued with form, and identifiable with the universe. That Sambhu is also called Isana, the Lord of everything.

He is pure effulgence, and transcends all decay, his hands and feet stretching in all directions, with eyes and head and mouth everywhere, and with ears also in every place. That Being exists, pervading the entire universe.

The eldest-born Being is called Hiranyagarbha. In the Vedanta this Holy One has been called the Buddhi. In the yoga scriptures he is called Mahat, Virinchi, and Aja, the unborn. In the Samkhya scriptures, he is indicated by diverse names, and regarded as having Infinity for his Soul.

With many forms, constituting the soul of the universe, he is regarded as One and immutable. The three infinite worlds have been created by him alone and filled also only by him. In all these forms, he is said to be of Viswarupa, universal form.

In all these variations he creates himself by himself. Filled with great energy, he first creates Consciousness and that Great Being Prajapati endowed with Chit, Consciousness. The manifest, Hiranyagarbha, is created from the unmanifest. This the wise refer to as the creation of knowledge. The creation of Mahat or Virat, and Chetana, by Hiranyagarbha, is the creation of ignorance.

This gives rise to the assigning of attributes worthy of worship and their destruction, what interpreters of the Srutis call avidya and vidya, ignorance and knowledge; after these two, arose, the other of the three— known as Akshara, Hiranyagarbha, or Virat.

Rajan, know, then, that the creation of the subtle elements from consciousness is the third. In all kinds of consciousness, the fourth creation flows from the modification of the third. This fourth creation comprises wind and light, space and water and earth, with their properties of sound, touch, form, taste and smell. This aggregate of ten arises simultaneously.

The fifth creation arises from the combination of these primal elements. This comprises the ear, the skin, the eyes, the tongue, the nose, and speech, and the two hands, the two legs, the anus and the organs of generation.

The first five make up the organs of knowledge, and the last five the organs of action. All these, with the mind, arose simultaneously. These twenty-four exist in the bodies of all living creatures.

By understanding these properly, Brahmanas with insight into the truth never have to yield to sorrow. In the three worlds a combination of these, called the sarira, body, is possessed by all embodied creatures.

Indeed, Rajan, this combination is known as such in Devas and Manavas and Danavas, and Yakshas and Gandharvas and Kinnaras, and Nagas, and Charanas and Pisachas, in divine Rishis and Rakshasas, in biting flies, and worms, and gnats, and vermin born of filth, rats and dogs, and Swapakas and Chaineyas, and Chandalas and Pukkasas, in elephants and horses, donkeys and tigers, and trees and cows.

All creatures that exist in water or space or on earth, for there is no other place in which creatures exist as we have heard, have this combination. All these, the manifest, are destroyed every day, and day after day. Hence, all creatures produced by a union of these twenty-four are said to be Kshaya, destructible.

This then is the Akshaya. And since the universe, made up of Vyakta and Avyakta, decays, it is said to be destructible. The very Being called Mahat who is the eldest-born is always spoken of as Kshaya.

I have now told you, O king, all that you asked me. Beyond these twenty-four, is the twenty-fifth called Vishnu. That Vishnu, because he is nirguna, is not a subject of gyana though, as he pervades all the tattvas, he has been called so by the wise. Since that which is destructible has created all that is manifest, all this has form.

The twenty-fourth, Prakriti, is said to preside over all that has sprung from her variations. The twenty-fifth, which is Vishnu, is formless and, therefore, cannot be said to activate or enliven the universe.

That unmanifest Prakriti, which, in union with Chit, is endowed with a body dwells in the hearts of all creatures with bodies. Eternal Chetana, the Akshaya, although he is without attributes and without form, assumes all variations as a consequence of a union with Prakriti.

When he unites with Prakriti, which has the attributes of birth and death, he, the Purusha, also assumes these qualities. From such a union he becomes an object of perception even though in reality he is without all attributes.

It is in this way that the Mahat, Hiranyagarbha, fuses with Prakriti and suffused with avidya, ignorance, undergoes changes and becomes conscious of selfhood, ahamkara. As a result of his forgetfulness and becoming involved in ignorance, uniting with the gunas of sattva, rajas and tamas, He becomes identified with diverse creatures belonging to diverse orders of being.

As a result of his birth and death arising from the fact of his dwelling with Prakriti, he thinks himself to be what he seemingly appears to be. Regarding himself as this or that, he assumes and follows the attributes of sattva, rajas and tamas.

Under the influence of tamas, he attains those states that are shaped by tamas. Under the influence of rajas and sattva, he similarly acquires the conditions influenced by rajas and sattva.

There are three colours in all—white, red and black. All these colours pertain to Prakriti; according to the nature of Prakriti he is identified with for the time, he becomes white or red or black.

Through tamas one goes to hell. Through rajas one acquires and remains in the state of humanity. Through sattva, people ascend to Devaloka and share in great felicity. By sinning continuously one sinks into the intermediate order of beings. By acting both righteously and immorally, one attains the status of the gods.

Thus, the wise say, Akshara, the indestructible, by union with Prakriti, the unmanifest, is transformed into Kshara, destructible. By means of gyana, knowledge, however, the indestructible is once more apparent in his true nature.'"

CANTO 304

Bhishma continues, 'Vasishta said, "As a result of his forgetfulness, the Atman pursues ignorance and obtains thousands of bodies one after another. He attains thousands of births among the intermediate orders and sometimes even among the Devas because of his union with particular gunas and the power of those attributes.

From the state of humanity he goes to Swargaloka, and from heaven he returns to humanity, and again from humanity he sinks into Yamaloka for many long years. Just as the worm that spins the cocoon shuts itself completely within the very threads it weaves, the Soul, too, though nirguna, free of all attributes, in reality, acquires these gunas and deprives himself of freedom.

Though in his real nature he transcends both joy and sorrow, in this way he subjects himself to pleasure and despair. Thus, although he is beyond all disease, the Soul regards himself to be afflicted by pain in the head, eyes and teeth, suffering in the throat and abdomen, and by burning thirst, and enlargement of glands, and cholera, and vitiligo, and leprosy, and burns, and asthma and phthisis, and epilepsy, and all other diseases that afflict the bodies of living creatures.

He considers himself to be born wrongly among thousands of beings in the intermediate orders, and sometimes among the Devas; he bears suffering and also enjoys the fruits of his good deeds.

Steeped in ignorance, he regards himself as robed sometimes in white cloth and sometimes in a full dress of four pieces, or as lying on floors instead of on beds, or with hands and feet contracted like those of frogs, or as seated upright in the yogic posture of dhyana.

At other times, he sees himself as covered in rags or lying or sitting under the canopy of the sky, or within mansions built of bricks and stone or on rugged stones or on ashes, or on the bare earth or on beds or on battlefields, or in water or in swamps, or on wooden planks or on diverse kinds of beds.

Goaded on by desire of benefits, he sees himself as clad in a kaupina made of grass or totally naked, or robed in silk or in the skin of the black antelope, or in cloth made of flax, or in sheep-skin or in tiger-skin, or in lion-skin or in fabric of hemp, or in barks of trees or in cloths made from the skins of prickly plants, or in attire made of threads woven by worms, or in torn rags or in other countless kinds of garments, too many to describe.

The Soul regards himself also as wearing a variety of ornaments and jewels, or as eating diverse kinds of food. He regards himself as sometimes eating at intervals of one night, or once at the same hour every day, or at the fourth, the sixth and the eighth hour every day, or once in six or seven or eight nights, or once in ten or twelve days, or once in a month.

He also sees himself as eating only roots, or fruits, or surviving on air or water alone, or on cakes of sesame husk, or curds or cowdung, or the urine of the cow, or herbs or flowers or moss, or raw food, or just on leaves fallen from trees or fruits that lie on the ground, or other kinds of food—driven by the desire of achieving ascetic success.

The Soul regards himself as observing Chandrayana according to the scriptural rites, or other vows and ceremonies, and the duties prescribed for the four asramas of life, and even derelictions of duty, and the duties of other subsidiary modes of life included in the four principal ones, and the many kinds of practices that are signs of the wicked and sinful.

The Soul regards himself as enjoying secluded places and delightful shades of mountains, and the cool banks of streams and fountains, and solitary riversides and sheltered forests, and sacred groves of the gods, and lakes and waters withdrawn from the busy haunts of men, and isolated mountain caves providing the shelter that houses and mansions do.

The Soul regards himself as employed in the recitation of different kinds of hidden mantras or as observing various vows and laws and different kinds of penances, and a variety of sacrifices and rituals.

The Soul sees himself as sometimes assuming the ways of traders and merchants, sometimes the practices of Brahmanas and Kshatriyas and Vaisyas and Sudras, and also making many kinds of gifts made to those that are destitute, blind or helpless.

As an outcome of being affected by ignorance, the Soul adopts the attributes of sattva, rajas and tamas, and dharma, artha and kama. Influenced by Prakriti, the Soul himself undergoes modification, observes, adopts and practises all these myriad forms and changes, and regards himself as being them all.

Indeed, the Soul recites the sacred mantras Svaha and Svadha and Vashat, and bows to his superiors; he considers himself as officiating at the sacrifices of others, as teaching sishyas, making gifts and accepting them, performing sacrifices and studying the scriptures, and engaging himself in all other karmas and kriyas of this kind.

The Soul regards himself as concerned with birth and death, disputes and killing. All these, the learned say, constitute the paths of dharma and adharma. It is the Goddess Prakriti who causes birth and death.

When the time for the Pralaya, universal destruction, approaches, all existing objects and attributes are withdrawn by the Paramatman which then exists alone like the sun withdrawing his rays at dusk; when the time for creation arrives, he once again creates and sends them forth as the sun his rays at dawn. Thus the Atman at play repeatedly regards himself invested with all these conditions, which are his own infinite forms and aspects, his maya, his leela, so pleasing to himself.

In this way the Soul, though really transcending the three gunas, becomes attached to the path of karma and creates Prakriti invested with the attributes of birth and death and identical with all deeds and works characterised by the three gunas of sattva, rajas and tamas.

Once on the path of karma, the Atman knows that particular acts have special characteristics and produce specific results. Rajan, the whole of this universe, with all things in it, has been blinded by Prakriti and overwhelmed by rajas and tamas.

The Soul, being invested by Prakriti, repeatedly gives rise to these gunas that produce all the pairs of opposites, dvesha and advesha, joy and suffering, pleasure and pain, and the rest. In consequence of this ignorance, the Jiva considers these sorrows to be his and imagines them as pursuing him.

Through that ignorance the Jiva imagines he should somehow move beyond those sorrows, and, finding Devaloka, enjoy the felicity that awaits all his good deeds. It is through ignorance that he thinks he should enjoy these delights of heaven and endure the woes here in samsara, this world.

Through ignorance the Jiva thinks: I should secure my happiness. By continually doing good deeds, I may have happiness till the end of this life and I shall be happy in all my future lives. My sins, though, may earn me unending anguish.

The human condition is fraught with great misery, for from it one sinks into naraka. From naraka, it will take many long years before I can return to a human condition. From being human I shall once more rise to attain to swarga. From that superior state I will have to come back again to being human only to sink again into hell.

One who always regards this combination of the primal elements and the senses, with the reflection of Chit in it, to be thus invested with the characteristics of the Soul, repeatedly wanders among the gods and men and sinks into demonic tenures in hell. Filled with the ideas of me and mine, the Jiva is forced to make an interminable round of such births.

The Jiva must endure millions upon millions of births in the successive forms he assumes, all of which are mortal. He who lives and acts in this manner, the way fraught with good and evil consequences, has to take successive births, forms and deaths in the three worlds, and to enjoy and endure the fruits of his good deeds and his sins.

It is Prakriti that generates good and evil karma; and it is Prakriti that enjoys and suffers their consequences in the three worlds. Indeed, Prakriti follows the course of karma.

The state of the intermediate beings, of humans, and of the gods as well, originate in Prakriti, she who is regarded as nirguna, without attributes. Her existence is affirmed only because of her doings, beginning with Mahat.

In the same manner, the existence of Purusha, the Soul, though without qualities himself, is affirmed by his reflection in the acts of the body. Although the Soul is not subject to any kind of change and is the active principle setting Prakriti into motion, yet he enters a body with all its senses of cognition and action, and regards all these as his own.

The five senses of knowledge begin with the ear, and those of action begin with speech—these unite with the attributes of sattva, rajas and tamas to become engaged and embroiled in their numerous objects. The Jiva imagines that it is he who is the doer, and that the senses belong to him, though in reality he has no senses.

Without form, he imagines he has a body. Though bereft of gunas, he thinks he is imbued with them, and though transcending time, envisions himself to be under time's control.

Though lacking in cognisance, he regards himself as filled with it, and though transcending the twenty-four subjects of the senses and the mind, he considers that he is one among them. Though immortal, he deems himself mortal, and though motionless believes himself to be an active being.

Without a material body, he still thinks he possesses one, and though unborn he regards himself as endowed with birth. Though transcending tapasya, he sees himself engaged in penances, and though he has no goals to strive for, he still thinks that he must achieve a variety of ends.

Without birth and movement, he deems himself to have both, and though beyond fear, believes that he is subject to it. Though indestructible, he sees himself as mortal. Invested with ignorance, the Soul thinks thus of himself.'"

CANTO 305

Bhishma says, 'Vasishta said, "Thus, as a result of his ignorance and his association with others who are shrouded by ignorance, the Jiva has to take millions and millions of births, each one ending in dissolution. The consequence of his transformation into Chit invested with ignorance is that the Jiva is born into millions of bodies, among intermediate beings and men and the gods, all of which will end in being destroyed.

On account of avidya, ignorance, the Jiva, like Chandramas, the moon, has to wax and wane thousands and thousands of times. This is truly the nature of the Jiva when invested with ignorance.

Know that Chandramas has in reality sixteen parts. Of these only fifteen increase and decrease. The sixteenth, that portion which remains invisible and appears on the night of the new moon, remains unchanging, constant.

Like Chandramas, the Jiva too has sixteen parts. Only fifteen of these, namely, Prakriti with Chetana's reflection, the ten senses of knowledge and action, and the four inner faculties, appear and disappear. The sixteenth, that is, Chit in its purity is not subject to any change.

Endowed with ignorance, the Jiva is repeatedly and continually born into these fifteen portions. With these births, the eternal and immutable portion in the Jiva, the primal essence, becomes united with the fifteen, and this union takes place repeatedly. That sixteenth portion is subtle. It is also known as Soma, eternal and immutable. It is never upheld by the senses. On the other hand, the senses are sustained by it. Rajan, since those sixteen are the cause of the birth of creatures, no creature can be born without them. They are called Prakriti. The final end of the Jiva's propensity to be united with Prakriti is called moksha mukti.

The Mahat-Soul, which is the twenty-fifth part the unmanifest, must repeatedly assume bodies of the sixteen divisions. The Soul, which is pure, becomes sullied since it is embroiled in avidya, dark unknowing that which is in reality pristine and untainted, becomes impure from being involved with what is both pure and unclean...

Devoted thus to ignorance, the Jiva, though essentially characterised by knowledge, becomes repeatedly associated with ignorance. Though free from every kind of flaw, yet in consequence of its bonding with the three gunas of Prakriti, it becomes itself steeped in them.'"

CANTO 306

'J anaka said, "O holy one, it has been said that the relation between the male and the female is like that which exists between Purusha, the indestructible, and Prakriti, the destructible.

Without a male, a female of any species cannot conceive. Without a female, a male also cannot create form. The forms of living creatures flow out of their union with each other. This is so with all orders of living beings.

Living creatures are born through sexual union, each depending upon the attributes of the other, and in their fertile seasons. I shall tell you about these. Listen to which are the traits that belong to the sire and which to the mother.

Bones, muscles, sinews and marrow, O regenerate one, we know to be derived from the man. Skin, flesh and blood, we know are drawn from the mother. We read about this in the Vedas and other scriptures.

What can be read as stated in the Vedas and other scriptures can be taken on authority. The authority of the Vedas and other consistent scriptures is eternal. Moksha cannot exist if Prakriti and Purusha are always joined in this way by both opposing and depending on the other's attributes.

Holy One, you have a spiritual vision that enables you to see all things as if they are present before your very eyes. If you know of any direct evidence of the existence of moksha, speak to me about it. We desire to attain it. Indeed, we wish to realise that which is auspicious, formless, not subject to decay, eternal beyond the reach of the senses, indeed, supreme."

Vasishta said, "What you say about what the Vedas and the other scriptures say in this matter is true. You have understood as they should be.

However, you are only familiar with the texts of the Vedas and the other shastras. You are not, Rajan, truly conversant with the real meaning of those scriptures.

One who understands merely the texts without knowing with their inner meaning, knows them in vain. Indeed, he who memorises the contents of a work without comprehending their meaning bears a useless burden.

On the other hand, he who gleans the true meaning of a treatise is said to have studied it with actual purpose. Questioned about the meaning of a text, it is fitting for him to explain that meaning acquired by careful study.

It is an unintelligent man who refuses to elucidate the meanings of texts in an assembly of the learned; indeed such a man never succeeds in expounding them properly. An ignorant person trying to explain the true meaning of treatises incurs ridicule. Even those who have knowledge of the Atman are mocked on such occasions if they try to explain something that has not been acquired through proper study.

Listen now to me, Rajan, on the subject of mukti that has been expounded by gurus to sishyas since the most ancient times among Mahatmans with the gyana of the Samkhya and the yoga systems of philosophy.

What the yogin beholds is that which the Samkhyas attain. He who knows the Samkhya and the yoga systems to be one and the same is deemed wise. Skin, flesh, blood, fat, bile, marrow, and muscles, and the senses of both knowledge and action, about which you speak, do exist. Objects flow from objects; the senses from the senses. From the body one acquires a body, as a seed is obtained from a seed.

When the Paramatman, the Supreme Being, is without senses,

without seed, without matter, without body, He must be without all attributes, nirguna.

Akasa and the other elements arise from the gunas of sattva and rajas and tamas, and disappear ultimately into them. Thus they are born from Prakriti. Skin, flesh, blood, fat, bile, marrow, bones and muscles, these eight arisen from Prakriti, may sometimes be produced by the vital seed of the male alone.

The Jiva and the universe both partake of Prakriti characterised by the three gunas. The Paramatman, the Supreme Soul, is apart from both the Jiva and the universe. Just like the passing seasons may be inferred from the appearance of certain fruits and flowers, Prakriti, too, though formless, can be inferred from the attributes of Mahat and the rest that spring from it.

The existence of Chaitanya in the body allows the Paramatman, without any gunas and perfectly pristine, to be inferred. Without beginning and without end, the foremost and most auspicious, that Paramatman is endowed with these elements as a result of its apparently identifying itself with the body and other gunas, as if in play.

Those who truly know these gunas recognise that only the ephemeral objects can be invested with sattva, rajas and tamas. That which transcends all attributes can have none. When the Jiva overcomes all the gunas born of Prakriti, only then does it gaze upon the Supreme Soul.

Only the highest Rishis conversant with the Samkhya, and true yogins know the Paramatman, which all the diverse philosophies and their adherents agree is beyond the Buddhi, the intellect which is regarded as the knower. He is endowed with the highest wisdom for he has cast off all consciousness of identification with Prakriti.

He transcends ignorance, is unmanifest, is nirguna beyond all attributes, and is called the Supreme. Dissociated from all gunas, he ordains all things, and is eternal and immutable. He surpasses Prakriti and all that is born of Prakriti; indeed transcending the twenty-four subjects that constitute enquiry, he forms the twenty-fifth.

When the wise, who stand in fear of birth, of the many conditions of living consciousness and of death, succeed in knowing the unmanifest, they gain understanding of the Supreme Soul at the same time. An intelligent man regards the union of the Jiva with the Paramatman as due and fitting, and consistent with the scriptures; the foolish man regards the two as being distinct from each other. This is the difference between the man of intelligence and he who lacks it.

The indications of both Kshara, the destructible, and Akshara, the indestructible, have now been expounded to you. Akshara is Oneness or unity, while Kshara denotes multiplicity, diversity. When one studies and properly understands the twenty-five subjects of enquiry, only then does one comprehend that the Oneness of the Atman is in accord with the scriptures, while its multiplicity is in opposition to them.

These are the many signs of what is included in the account of the created and what transcends that account. The wise have stated that there are only twenty-five themes to the entire tale of creation. Transcending these, and beyond those, forms the twenty-sixth.

The comprehension of these twenty-five created subjects, according to their aggregates of five, is the study of material elements. Transcending these is that which is eternal.'"

CANTO 307

'Janaka said, "O foremost of Rishis, you have said that unity is the attribute of Akshara, the indestructible, and variety or multiplicity is the attribute of Kshara, the destructible. I have not yet clearly understood the nature of these two. Doubts still lurk in my mind.

Ignorant men look upon the Atman, the Soul, as imbued with the phenomenon of multiplicity. Wise men know it to be one and undivided. My intellect is dull, and so I am bewildered and unable to comprehend all this. My restless intellect has made me almost forget the causes you assigned for the unity of Akshara and the multiplicity of Kshara. I want you to once more instruct me on unity and multiplicity, on him who is knowing, on what is without knowledge, on the Jiva, vidya, avidya, Akshara, Kshara, and on the systems of Samkhya and yoga, in detail, individually and frankly."

'Vasishta said, "I will tell you what you ask. Listen to me, Rajan, as I expound to you the practices of yoga separately. An obligatory practice with yogins, dhyana, contemplation, is their highest power. Those conversant with yoga say that contemplation is of two kinds. One is the concentration of the mind, and the other is pranayama, the regulation of breath. Pranayama is said to have physicality while the pure concentration of mind is without it.

Except for the three times when a man urinates, defecates and eats, he should devote all his time to dhyana. Withdrawing the senses from the objects of their perception, through the mind, an intelligent man, having purified himself with the twenty-two ways of pranayama, unites the Jivatma with that which transcends the twenty-fourth subject, namely Prakriti, which is also ignorance, the Paramatman which, according to the wise, dwells in every part of the body, and thereby transcends decay and death.

We have heard that it is through those twenty-two methods that the Soul may always be known. Only one whose mind is free of sinful passions can engage in this practice of yoga. No other may.

Detached, abstemious in diet, and controlling all the senses, one should fix one's mind on the Atman; O king of Mithila, during the first and the last part of the night, having subdued the senses, quieted the mind by Buddhi, the understanding, one should assume a posture as still as a stone.

When men of knowledge, who know the laws of yoga, become as fixed as a post of wood, and as immovable as a mountain, they are said to be in yoga, communion. When one does not hear, or smell, or taste, or see, when one is not conscious of any touch, when one's mind becomes perfectly free from every purpose, when one is not conscious of anything, when one cherishes no thought, when one becomes like a block of wood, then one is in perfect yoga.

In this state one burns like a lamp where there is no wind, steadily; at such a time one is freed even from one's sukshma sarira, one's subtle form, and perfectly united with Brahman. When one has achieved this, one no longer ascends or falls among intermediate beings.

When we say that there has been a complete identification of the knower, the known, and knowledge, then is the yogin said to behold the Supreme Soul. While in yoga, the Paramatman reveals itself in the yogin's heart like a blazing fire, or like the irradiant sun, or like dazzling lightning in the sky.

That Supreme Soul which is unborn and which is the essence of amrita, nectar, that is seen by Mahatman Brahmanas, endowed with wisdom and knowers of the Vedas, is subtler than the subtle and greater than the great. Though dwelling in all creatures, that Atman is not perceived by them.

The Creator of the worlds is seen only by one who is rich in the intelligence guided by the lamp of the mind. He dwells beyond tamas, darkness, and transcends even Iswara. Those acquainted with the Vedas and imbued with omniscience call him the dispeller of darkness, transcending darkness, pure, and nirguna.

This is what is called the yoga of yogins. What else marks yoga? Such practices allow yogins to glimpse the Supreme Soul that transcends death and decay.

I have told you about the science of yoga in detail. I will now discourse upon that Samkhya philosophy by which the Paramatman is seen through the gradual destruction of darkness, ignorance and faults.

The Samkhyas, whose system is built on Prakriti, say that Prakriti, which is unmanifest, is foremost. The second principle, Mahat, arises from Prakriti.

We have heard that from Mahat flows the third principle called Chit, Consciousness. The Samkhyas blessed with vision of the Soul say that the five senses of sound, sight, touch, taste and smell flow from Consciousness. All these eight, together, they refer to as Prakriti.

The modifications of these eight are sixteen in number. They are the five gross or material essences, of Akasa, Agni, Bhumi, Jala and Vayu—space, light, earth, water and wind—and the ten senses of action and of knowledge including the mind. Wise men devoted to the path of Samkhya, and who know all its laws and dispensations, regard these twenty-four subjects as encompassing the whole range of Samkhya enquiry.

That which is created is merged into the creating. Created by the Paramatman, one after another, these principles are destroyed in reverse. With every new creation, the gunas come into existence in the order I have told you, and with destruction they merge, each into its Creator, in a reverse order, like the waves of the ocean vanishing into the very ocean that gives them birth. Rajan, this is the manner in which Prakriti is created and destroyed.

The Supreme Being is all that remains at the time of Pralaya, and it is he that assumes multifarious forms when creation breaks into life. This is what men of knowledge have established.

It is Prakriti that causes Purusha to assume diversity and then revert to unity. Prakriti herself also has the same indications. Those who know the nature of the themes of enquiry know that Prakriti also assumes the same kind of diversity and unity; when destruction is at hand she reverts into unity and when creation flows she assumes diversity of form.

The Atman makes Prakriti, which contains the principles of creation or growth, and acquires manifold forms. Prakriti is called Kshetra, the field in which karma is sown, also identified as the body. Transcending the twenty-four principles of nature is the Atman, Soul, which is great. It, the Kshetrajna or knower of the field, presides over Prakriti or Kshetra.

Thus, the foremost of Yatis say that the Soul is the controller. He is so regarded as he presides over all kshetras. Aware of that unmanifest Kshetra, he is also called Kshetrajna, the Knower of Kshetra. And because the Atman enters into unmanifest Kshetra, the body, he is called Purusha. Kshetra is distinct from Kshetrajna. Kshetra is unmanifest.

The Soul, which transcends the twenty-four subjects, is called the Knower. Knowledge and the object known are discrete. Knowledge has been said to be unmanifest, while the object of knowledge is the Soul which transcends these principles.

The unmanifest is called Kshetra, sattva, Mahat, and also Iswara, the Supreme One, while Purusha is the twenty-fifth, unsurpassed, principle; though regarded a subject, it is not one, for it transcends them all. This, Rajan, is an account of the Samkhya philosophy.

The Samkhyas see the cause of the universe, and merging all the grosser principles into the Chit, gaze upon the Paramatman, the Supreme Soul. Studying the twenty-four subjects properly, along with Prakriti, and determining their true nature, the Samkhyas succeed in beholding that which transcends these twenty-four principles.

In reality the Jivatma is that very Soul which transcends Prakriti and is beyond the twenty-four principles. When he succeeds in knowing that

Paramatman by dissociating himself from Prakriti, he then merges into that, the Supreme Soul.

I have now told you everything about the Samkhya yoga, in all its aspects. Those who know these doctrines succeed in attaining direct cognisance of Brahman. They achieve peace and tranquillity.

Indeed, as men whose understanding have direct awareness of Brahman, reach that state from which they do not have to return to this world after the dissolution of their bodies, those that are said to be emancipated in this life, they attain the great power and ineffable felicity of Samadhi, and immutability, through attaining the nature of Akshara, the indestructible.

They who perceive this universe as many instead of as one and unified are said to see falsely. These men are blind to Brahman. O Parantapa, such men have repeatedly to return to the world and assume bodies in the diverse orders of being. Those who realise the Brahman become omniscient, and when they pass from this body they are free forever of all physical forms.

All things, the entire universe, are said to be the result of the unmanifest. The Atman, which is the twenty-fifth tattva, transcends all things. They who know it, the Soul, have no fear of returning to the world.'"

CANTO 308

'Vasishta said, "I have discoursed to you thus far on the Samkhya philosophy. Now I will tell you what is vidya, knowledge, and what is avidya, ignorance. The learned say that that Prakriti, which is fraught with the attributes of creation and destruction, is called avidya; while Purusha, who is free from these and who transcends the twenty-four tattvas, is called vidya.

Listen to me first as I speak to you on the nature of vidya among the other successive concepts in the Samkhya philosophy.

Among the senses of knowledge and those of action, the senses of knowledge are said to constitute vidya. We have heard that vidya comprises the senses of knowledge and the objects of their perception. The wise say that of the objects of the senses and the mind, the mind constitutes vidya. Between the mind and the five subtle essences, the latter make up vidya. Of the five subtle essences and Consciousness, consciousness is vidya. Of Chit and Mahat, the latter, O king, is vidya. Of all the principles beginning with Mahat and Prakriti, it is Prakriti, unmanifest and supreme, that is regarded as vidya.

Of Prakriti, and that called Vidhi which is Supreme, Vidhi should be known as vidya. Transcending Prakriti is the twenty-fifth principle, called Purusha, who should be known as vidya. Of all knowledge that which is the object of knowledge has been said to be the unmanifest, Rajan.

Again, knowledge has been said to be unmanifest and the object of knowledge to be that which transcends the twenty-four. I repeat, knowledge is unmanifest, and the Knower is that which transcends the twenty-four.

I have now told you the true significance of vidya and avidya. Listen now as I tell you about the indestructible and the destructible. Both the Jiva and Prakriti have been said to be indestructible, and both of them have been said to be destructible. I will tell you why this is so, as I have understood it.

Both Prakriti and the Jiva are without beginning and without end, without birth and without death. With regards to creation, both are regarded as supreme. As a consequence of its attributes of repeated creation and destruction, the unmanifest Prakriti, is called Akshara, indestructible. That unmanifest is continually modified, in order to create the evolutes. And because the principles beginning with Mahat are produced by Purusha as well, and also because Purusha and the Avyakta are mutually dependent upon each other, therefore is Purusha also, the twenty-fifth, called Kshetra, Akshara, indestructible.

When the yogin withdraws and merges all the principles into the unmanifest Brahman, then along with all the others, the twenty-fifth evolute, the Jiva or Purusha, also dissolves into it. When the principles merge, each into its Creator, then the one that remains is Prakriti.

When Kshetrajna too, O son, vanishes into what produces him, all that remains is Brahman; thus, Prakriti along with all its evolutes becomes Kshara, is destroyed, and becomes nirguna, and attains to the condition of being without attributes, from becoming detached from all the tattvas.

We have heard that Kshetrajna, when his knowledge of Kshetra disappears, becomes devoid of gunas, attributes. When he becomes Kshara he takes on gunas.

When, however, he attains to his own real nature, he succeeds in understanding his own condition of truly being nirguna. By casting off Prakriti and beginning to realise that he is different from her, the intelligent Kshetrajna comes to be regarded as pristine and taintless.

When the Jiva no longer exists in a state of union with Prakriti, then he becomes identifiable with Brahman. While he remains united with Prakriti, he remains distinct from Brahman. Indeed, when the Jivatman shows no attachment for Prakriti and her tattvas, he then succeeds in beholding the Supreme; having once beheld him he wishes that he not fall away from that felicity.

When the knowledge of truth dawns upon him, the Jiva begins to lament: Alas, my ignorance and foolishness have made me fall into this mesh of Prakriti, like a fish entangled in a net.

Through ignorance I have migrated from body to body like a fish from water to water thinking that this in the only element in which it can live. Just as a fish does not know anything other than water to be its natural element, I also have never known anything other than my own family, my children and wives. Shame on me that through ignorance I have been repeatedly wandering from body to body forgetful of the Paramatman.

The Paramatman alone is my friend. I have the capacity for friendship with him. Whatever be my nature and whoever I may be, I am able to be like him and to merge with him. I see my similarity with him. I am indeed, like him. He is pure, untainted. It is clear that I am of the same nature.

Through ignorance and torpor, I have become associated with inanimate Prakriti. Though really detached, I have passed this long time in a state of attachment with Prakriti. Alas, without being aware of it, I have so long been subdued by her.

Prakriti assumes various forms: high, middling and low. Oh, how will I dwell in those forms? How will I live conjointly with her? It is on account of my ignorance that I repair to her companionship.

I will now immerse myself in Samkhya or yoga. I will no longer keep her companionship. When I consider how long I have been with her, I think that I have been too long deceived by her, for being really unchanging and free myself, how could I keep company with one that is subject to constant change?

But she cannot be held responsible for this. The blame is mine, since turning away from the Paramatman I freely became attached to her. In consequence of that attachment, though in reality formless I have had to live in multifarious forms.

Though formless by nature I am endowed with forms because of my sense of me and mine, and thereby disturbed and agitated. As a result of my false sense of selfhood in Prakriti, I am forced to take birth in diverse orders of being.

Alas, though without any true sense of ego, yet in consequence of affecting it, I have sinned in a myriad of ways in those orders in which I took birth while I remained in them as a Jivatman who had lost all true knowledge. I will no longer have anything to do with her whose essence is consciousness, who divides herself into many and who seeks to bind me with these many.

Only now have I been awakened and have understood that I am by nature without any sense of ego and without that consciousness which creates the forms of Prakriti that appear all around. Discarding that ego, with respect to her and whose essence is made up of consciousness, and casting off Prakriti herself, I shall take refuge in him who is auspicious.

I shall be united with him, and not with Prakriti which is essentially without reality. It will be to my benefit if I unite with him for I share no true similarity of nature with Prakriti.

The twenty-fifth principle, which is the Jivatman, when he thus succeeds in understanding the Paramatman, is able to cast off the Kshara, the mortal, and merge with that which is Akshara, immortal, the essence of all that is auspicious. In reality, the Jiva is nirguna and Avyakta, without attributes and unmanifest, but becomes invested with what is Vyakta, manifest, and assumes gunas.

O lord of Mathura, when he succeeds in gazing upon that which is nirguna and which is the source of the unmanifest, he achieves union with it.

I have told you the indications of what is indestructible and what is destructible, according to the best of my knowledge of what has been expounded in the scriptures. I shall now speak to you about what I have heard as to how knowledge that is subtle, stainless and certain arises. Listen to me.

I have already discoursed to you on the features of the Samkhya and the yoga systems of philosophy as described in their respective texts. Indeed, the science that has been explained in the Samkhya treatises is identical with what has been laid down in the yoga shastras.

Rajan, the knowledge which the Samkhyas preach can enlighten everyone. In the Samkhya doctrines that knowledge has been explicated for the benefit of its disciples. The learned say that this Samkhya system is extensive. Yogins have great regard for this system as also for the Vedas.

In the Samkhya philosophy no subject transcending the twenty-fifth is accepted. I have duly described to you the highest principles of the Samkhyas. In the yoga philosophy, it is said that Brahman, the essence of knowledge without duality, Advaita, becomes the Jiva only when suffused with ignorance. The yoga scriptures speak of both Brahman and Jivatman.'"

CANTO 309

Bhishma says, 'Vasishta said, "I will now discourse to you on Buddha, the Supreme Soul, and Abuddha, the Jiva which is the dispensation of the attributes of sattva, rajas, and tamas.

Under the influence of maya, illusion, the Paramatman, becoming the Jiva, assumes myriad forms and comes to regard them all as real. As a consequence of regarding himself indistinguishable from such transformations, the Jivatman fails to understand the Supreme Soul, for he bears the gunas of sattva and rajas and tamas, creating and drawing into himself what he creates.

O Rajan, the Jiva undergoes ceaseless changes for his sport, and because he is capable of understanding the action of the Avyakta, the unmanifest, he is called Buddhyamana, the comprehender.

The unmanifest or Prakriti can never comprehend Brahman which is, in reality, nirguna, without attributes, even when it manifests itself with gunas. Hence Prakriti is called unintelligent. The Srutis declare that if ever Prakriti does succeed in knowing the twenty-fifth tattva, the Jiva, Prakriti will then be identified and united with the Jiva, instead of being apart from It.

However Prakriti can never comprehend the Paramatman, which is ever detached and which transcends the twenty-fifth evolute. As a result of his attachment to and union with Prakriti, the Jiva or Purusha, who in his real nature is unmanifest and not subject to change, comes to be called the unawakened or ignorant.

Indeed, because the twenty-fifth tattva can realise the Avyakta, the unmanifest, that he is called Buddhyamana, or comprehender. He cannot, however, easily grasp the twenty-sixth, which is stainless, which is knowledge without duality, immeasurable and eternal.

The twenty-sixth tattva, however, can know both the Jiva and Prakriti, who are the twenty-fifth and the twenty-fourth principles respectively. O radiant son, only the wise succeed in knowing that Brahman which is unmanifest, which inheres in its real nature in all that is seen and unseen, and which is the one independent essence in the universe.

When the Jiva considers himself distinct from, and other than what he truly is, when he thinks of himself as fat or lean, fair or dark, a Brahmana or a Sudra, it is only then that he fails to recognise the Supreme Soul and himself, and Prakriti with which he is united.

When the Jiva succeeds in understanding Prakriti, and knowing that she is something apart and different from him, only then is he restored to his true nature and attains to that exalted knowledge which is pure and untainted and which is of Brahman. When the Jiva reaches that highest understanding, he then attains to that pure and non-dual knowledge, which is the twenty-sixth principle, Brahman.

He then casts off the manifest, Prakriti fraught with the attributes of creation and destruction. When the Jiva recognises Prakriti, unintelligent and subject to the influence of sattva, rajas and tamas, he then becomes nirguna, without attributes himself.

When he understands that the unmanifest is different from him, he acquires the nature of the Paramatman, the Supreme Soul. The learned say that when the Jiva is freed from the attributes of sattva and rajas and tamas, and united with the Supreme Soul, he becomes identified with that Soul.

The Paramatman is called tattva as well as atattva, and transcends decay and death. O bestower of honours, the Soul, despite resting in the body, with its manifest principles, cannot be said to have acquired the nature of those principles.

The wise say that there are in all twenty-five principles, including the Jivatman. Indeed the Soul does not possess either Consciousness or any other principle. Invested with pure intelligence, it transcends the tattvas. It quickly discards even that principle which is the indication of the knowing or awakened one.

When the Jiva considers himself as the twenty-sixth being, not subject to decay and death, he succeeds through his own light in attaining identity with that twenty-sixth. Though awakened by the twenty-sixth, pure intelligence, the Jiva still becomes subject to ignorance. This is the cause of the Jiva's myriad forms as explained in the Srutis and the Samkhya scriptures.

When the Jiva, endowed with Chetana and unintelligent Prakriti, loses all consciousness of a distinct or individual self, then he discards his multifariousness and resumes his oneness. When the Jivatman who lives in joy and suffering, seldom free from the consciousness of self, succeeds in merging with the Paramatman which is beyond the reach of the understanding, he is then liberated from virtue and vice.

Indeed, when the Jiva attains to the twenty-sixth tattva, which is unborn and puissant and apart from all attachments, comprehending it thoroughly, he himself becomes possessed of infinite puissance and entirely casts off Prakriti. Once he understands the twenty-sixth tattva, the first twenty-four lose all significance and worth.

I have now narrated to you, according to the indication of the Srutis, the nature of the Abuddhya or Prakriti, and of the Jiva; I have also told you about that which is pure knowledge, the Paramatman, the Supreme Soul. Guided by the scriptures, variety and oneness are to be thus understood.

The difference between the gnat and the udumbara, or that between the fish and water, illustrates the difference between the Jivatman and Paramatman, the Supreme Soul. The multiplicity and unity of these two are then similarly understood.

This is called emancipation, mukti, this comprehension or knowledge of oneself as something distinct from unintelligent Prakriti. By making him know the unmanifest, the Paramatman, which transcends Buddhi, intellect, the twenty-fifth tattva, which dwells in the bodies of living creatures, is emancipated.

Indeed, that twenty-fifth is capable of achieving moksha in this manner only and by no other means. Though really different from the Kshetra in which he dwells for the time being, he partakes of the nature of that kshetra as a result of his union with it.

Uniting with what is pure, he becomes pure. Merging with the intelligent, he becomes Intelligent. By joining with one that is emancipated, he is liberated. By uniting with one that has been free from every attachment, he too, is freed from all attachment.

By uniting with one striving for mukti, imbibing the nature of his companion, he himself strives for emancipation. By mingling with one of pure deeds he becomes pure, of pure deeds himself, and blazes with effulgence. By uniting with one of unstained Soul, he becomes of unstained Soul himself.

By fusing with the one immaculate and independent Atman, he becomes one and independent. Uniting with the one that is dependent on its own self, he acquires the same nature and attains to freedom.

Rajan, I have duly told you this that is perfectly true. I have honestly discoursed to you on the subject of the eternal and stainless and primeval Brahman. You may impart this high knowledge, able to awaken the Soul, to that person who though not conversant with the Vedas is nevertheless humble and has a keen desire to acquire Brahmagyana, the knowledge of Brahman.

It should never be given to one who is false, or cunning or roguish, or is weak-minded or devious, or to one who is jealous of learned men, or one who gives pain to others. Listen to me as I speak of those to whom this knowledge may safely be divulged. It should be given to one who has faith, who is meritorious, who abstains from speaking ill of others, who is devoted to tapasya from the purest of motives, who is wise, and who knows the sacrifices and other rites laid down in the Vedas.

This knowledge may be revealed to one with a forgiving disposition, who is compassionate and kind to all creatures; or one who is fond of dwelling in solitary quietness, who lives and acts in accord with the scriptures, or to one never given to quarrels and disputes, or one possessed of great learning or one endowed with wisdom, forgiveness, self-restraint and tranquillity of soul.

This high knowledge of Brahman should never be imparted to one who does not possess such qualities. It has been said that there can be no advantage or punya when such knowledge is given to one who is not suited to receiving it. This high knowledge should never be revealed to one who disregards any vows and restraints even if, in exchange, he gives all of Bhumi, the earth, brimming with jewels and diverse wealth as dakshina. However, without doubt, this knowledge should indeed be given to one who has conquered his senses.

O Karala, let no fear be yours any longer, since you have listened to what I have said about the high Brahman. I have told you about the holy Brahman, without beginning, middle and end, and who can dispel all kinds of grief.

Seeing Brahman can dispel both birth and death, O king, the Brahman full of auspiciousness that removes all fear, Brahman who bestows true weal. And having acquired this essence of all knowledge, cast off all error and stupor today. I acquired this gyana from the eternal Hiranyagarbha himself, Rajan, who divulged it to me when I had gratified that great Being of the most superior soul.

Asked by you today, I have imparted to you the knowledge of eternal Brahman, just as I myself acquired it from my guru. Indeed, I have given you this highest knowledge, the Brahmagyana, which is the refuge of all conversant with mukti exactly as I once received it from Brahma himself.'"

Bhishma continues, 'I have now told you what the great Rishi Vasishta said to King Karala of the Janaka vamsa, about the twenty-fifth tattva, attaining which the Jiva has never to come back into the world. It is only when the Jivatman does not truly recognise the Paramatman, the Supreme Soul, which is not subject to decay and death that it has to frequently leave and return to this world.

When the Jiva attains to that high knowledge, he has no longer to come back. Having heard it from the Devarishi, I have, O son, discoursed to you on this Brahmagyana from which arises the highest good.

This knowledge was obtained from Hiranyagarbha by the high-souled Rishi Vasishta. From Vasishta, it was acquired by Narada. From Narada I have learnt it, the knowledge that is indeed the eternal Brahman.

O Kurusattama, foremost of Kurus, having heard this discourse of high import, filled with sacred wisdom, do not grieve any longer. That man who knows Kshara and Akshara is free from fear. Only he who is bereft of such knowledge is obliged to cherish fear.

As a result of this ignorance of Brahman, the soul of the foolish man has to repeatedly come back into this world. Dying, he has to be born into thousands upon thousands of orders of being, every one of which ends in death.

Now in the world of the gods, now among men, and now among intermediate orders of being—he must appear again and again. In course of time, if he succeeds in crossing samsara, the ocean of ignorance in which he is plunged, he then succeeds in avoiding rebirth altogether and merges with the Paramatman, the Supreme Soul.

The ocean of ignorance is fearsome and terrible. It is bottomless and called the unmanifest. O Bhaarata, day after day, creatures fall and sink into that sea. Since you, Rajan, have been freed from that eternal, boundless ocean of darkness, you are also liberated from both rajas and tamas.'

CANTO 310

"Bhishma says, 'Once upon a time a king of Janaka's royal house, while hunting for deer in the uninhabited forests, saw a superior Brahmana, a Rishi of Bhrigu's vamsa. Bowing before the Rishi who was seated at his ease, King Vasuman approached him and, when he also sat, with the sage's leave, asked him this question:

"O holy one, tell me what is of the highest benefit, both here and hereafter, to a man who has an unstable body and is the slave of his desires?" Thus questioned, and properly honoured by the king, that Rishi of profound ascetic merit replied with these most beneficial words.

The Rishi said, "If you desire what is agreeable to you both in this world and the next, be self-restrained and abstain from injuring all creatures. Righteousness is beneficial to the virtuous. Dharma is the refuge of those who are good.

The three worlds with their moving and still creatures flow from dharma. You who so eagerly wish to enjoy all pleasures, how is it that you are not yet satiated with the objects of desire? You see the honey, O you of small understanding, but are blind to the fall.

As one who wants to earn the fruits of knowledge should set himself to the acquisition of knowledge, so also one who desires the fruits of dharma should set himself to the acquisition of righteousness.

Desiring virtue, a wicked man finds it impossible to fulfil his desire despite striving to act in a pure and taintless manner. On the other hand, if a good man is impelled by the desire to earn punya, he accomplishes even a difficult deed with ease. Living in the forest, if one acts in a manner so as to delight in the pleasures of a dwelling among men in towns, he is regarded not as a forest recluse but as a townsman. Similarly, while living in towns, if a man desires the felicity enjoyed by a forest recluse, he is considered not a town dweller but a vanaprastha.

Know then the merit of performing and abstaining from religious karma; concentrate on and be devoted to the practices of dharma in thoughts, words and deeds. Ascertain the propriety of time and place, purify yourself by rituals and vows, and when entreated, without malice make endowments to the virtuous.

Acquiring wealth by righteous means, one should offer it to the deserving. One should bestow gifts, discarding anger; and having made these offerings one should neither regret nor extol those gifts with one's own mouth.

The Brahmana who is full of compassion, honest, and whose birth is pure, is one regarded as deserving of gifts. A man is said to be pure in birth when he is born of a mother that has only one husband and who belongs to the same varna as her husband.

Indeed, such a Brahmana, conversant with the three Vedas—Rig, Yajur and Sama—learned, and who observes the six duties of performing yagnas himself, of officiating at those of others, of learning, teaching, offering dana and receiving gifts, is regarded as being worthy of receiving gifts.

Dharma becomes adharma, and unrighteousness becomes righteousness, according to the character of the doer, of time, and of place. Sin is washed away like the dirt on one's body, with a little exertion and more when the effort is greater.

After purging his bowels, a man should take ghee, a tonic which makes his system healthy. In the same manner, having cleansed oneself of all faults, if one sets oneself to acquire dharma, such righteousness will produce the highest happiness in the next world.

Good and evil thoughts exist in the minds of all creatures. Withdrawing the mind from evil thoughts, it should always be directed towards those that are pure. One should always revere one's svadharma, the practices of one's own varna. Strive, then, to act in a manner that you may have faith in the duties of your varna.

O you of impatient soul, undertake the practice of patience. You of small understanding, seek to become endowed with intelligence. Bereft of serenity, seek to be calm; and lacking in wisdom as you are, try to act wisely.

He who moves in the company of the righteous succeeds, through his own efforts, in acquiring the means of accomplishing what is beneficial for him both in this world and the next. Indeed, the root of this benefit is unwavering steadfastness.

The Rajarishi Mahabhisha fell from heaven through want of this firmness. Yayati, also, was boastful and arrogant, exhausted his punya, and was cast down from swarga; he succeeded in regaining the realms of felicity through steadfastness. You will surely attain to great intelligence and your highest good by paying heed to virtuous and learned men of ascetic merit.'"

Bhishma continues, 'Hearing these words of the sage, King Vasuman, possessed of a good character, withdrew his mind from the pursuit of desire, and set it upon the acquisition of dharma.'"

CANTO 311

Yudhishtira says, 'It befits you, Pitamaha, to discourse to me on that which is free from dharma and its opposite, which is free from every doubt, which transcends birth and death, as also virtue and sin, which is auspiciousness, eternal fearlessness, indestructible and immutable, which is always pure, and which is ever free from the toil of exertion.'

Bhishma says, 'In this regard I will narrate to you the ancient story, Bhaarata, of the discourse between Yajnavalkya and Janaka. Long ago, the famous King Daivarati of Janaka's royal house, fully conversant with the import of all questions, asked this question of Yajnavalkya, that foremost of Rishis.

Janaka said, "O regenerate Rishi, how many kinds of senses are there? How many kinds are there of Prakriti? What is the Avyakta, unmanifest and highest Brahman? What is higher than Brahman? What is birth and what is death? What are the limits of age?

O Dvijottama, instruct me on these subjects; I am ignorant while you are an ocean of knowledge. Truly, I wish to hear you speak on all these matters."

Yajnavalkya said, "O king, listen to my answers to these questions of yours. I shall impart to you the supreme knowledge valued by yogins and especially that which the Samkhyas possess.

Nothing is unknown to you; still you have asked me. And, on being questioned, one should answer. This is the eternal practice.

Eight main principles, tattvas, have been named as being of Prakriti, while sixteen have been called indriyas, modifications. Of the Vyakta, the manifest, there are seven. These are the views of those conversant with the science of Adhyatma.

The unmanifest, or original Prakriti, Mahat, Consciousness, and the Panchamahabhutas—five suksma or subtle elements of Bhumi, earth; Vayu, air; Akasa, space; Jala, water, and Agni, fire—these eight are together known as Prakriti. The indriyas are certainly manifest or gross, sthula. Listen now to the enumeration of those called indriyas. They are the ear, the skin, the tongue and the nose; and sound, touch, form, taste and scent; as also speech, the two arms, the two feet, the anus and the organs of pleasure and generation.

Amongst these, the ten beginning with sound, and having their origin in the five Panchamahabhutas, the great evolutes, are called Visesha. The five senses of cognition, are called Savisesha. Those who know the Adhyatma vigyana regard the mind, Manas, as the sixteenth.

This is in consonance with your own views and those of other learned men who know these truths.

From the unmanifest, Rajan, springs the Mahat. The wise regard this to be the first Prakriya, creation relating to Pradhana or Prakriti: From Mahat is produced Chit, Consciousness. This has been called the second Prakriya, having Buddhi, the intellect, for its essence.

From Consciousness has sprung Manas, the mind, which is the essence of sabda, sound, and the others that are the attributes of Akasa and the rest. This is the third creation, related to Chit. From Manas have sprung the five great elements. Truly I say, know that this is the fourth Prakriya called sukshma, subtle or spiritual.

Those who know the primordial elements say that sabda, sound, sparsa, touch, rupa, form, rasa, taste, and gandha, scent, are the fifth creation, related to the great primal elements. The creation of the ear, the skin, the tongue and the nose, forms the sixth; this is regarded as having multiplicity of thought for its essence.

After this arise the senses that follow the ear and the others, those of action, karma, O Rajan. This is called seventh Prakriya and relates to the senses of cognition. Then comes prana, the breath that rises upward, followed by samana, udana and vyana, those that have a transverse motion. This is the eighth creation and is called Arjava.

After these breaths that course transversely in the lower parts of the body—samana, udana and vyana—comes that called apana flowing downwards. This ninth creation is also called Arjava, O king.

These nine Prakriyas, and these twenty-four tattvas, I have expounded to you according to what has been laid down in the sacred shastras. Now, O Rajan, listen to me as I tell you about the durations of time as indicated by the learned in respect of these tattvas."'

CANTO 312

'Yajnavalkya said, "Listen to me, O foremost of men, as I tell you about the duration of time with respect to the unmanifest, the Supreme Purusha. Ten thousand kalpas are said to constitute his single day. Equal is the duration of his night.

When his night passes, he awakes, and first creates herbs and plants that sustain all embodied creatures. He then creates Brahma who springs from a golden egg.

We have heard that Brahma is the form of all created things. Having dwelt for a whole year within that egg, the great ascetic Brahma, also called Prajapati, Lord of all creatures, emerged from it and created Bhumi, the earth, and swarga, the heavens above.

Brahma, then, it is said in the Vedas, placed the sky between; heaven and earth separated from each other. Seven thousand and five hundred kalpas comprise one day of Brahma. Those who know the science of Adhyatma say that his night also is of an equal duration. Brahma, called Mahan, then creates Consciousness, Bhuta, which is unsurpassed in essence.

Before creating any physical bodies out of what are called the Mahabhutas, the Great Elements, Mahan or Brahma, imbued with tapasya, created four others referred to as his sons. They are the sires of the original Pitris.

Rajan, we have also heard that the senses of knowledge along with the four inner faculties, have sprung from the Pitris, the five great elements, and that the entire universe of mobile and immobile Beings has been filled with those Panchamahabhutas.

The puissant Consciousness created the five Bhutas. These are Bhumi, earth; Vayu, air; Akasa, space; Jala, water, and Agni, fire or light. This Consciousness, this Great Being, from whom springs the third Prakriya, creation, has five thousand kalpas for his night, and his day is of equal length.

Sound, touch, form, taste and smell—sabda, sparsa, rupa, rasa and gandha—are called Visesha. They inhere in the five great elements. All creatures are continually pervaded by these five; they desire one another's companionship, become subservient to one another; they challenge and transcend one another; led by these immutable and compelling urges, creatures kill one another and wander in this world entering into numberless orders of being.

Three thousand kalpas represent the duration of their day. Equal is the measure of their night. Manas, the mind, roves over all things, Rajan, led on by the senses. The senses do not themselves perceive anything. It is Manas that perceives through them.

The eye sees forms when helped by the mind but never by itself. When Manas is distracted, the eye fails to see even the objects directly before it. It is commonly held that the senses perceive. This is not true, for it is the mind that perceives through the senses.

When the activity of Manas, the mind, ceases, the cessation of the activity of the senses follows. That is the end of the activity of the senses, which is the end of the mind's activity. One should thus know that the senses are controlled by the mind. Indeed, Manas is the Lord of all the senses. O illustrious king, these are all the twenty Bhutas in the universe.'"

CANTO 313

'Yajnavalkya said, "I have, in succession, told you the order and duration of the Prakriyas, the creations, and the total number of their various tanmatras or evolutes. Listen now to me as I tell you of their destruction. Listen to how Brahman, who is eternal and undecaying, and who is without beginning and without end, repeatedly creates and destroys all created things and beings.

When his day ends and night comes, he desires sleep. At such a time the unmanifest and Holy One urges the Being called Maharudra, who is conscious of his great powers for destroying the world. Compelled by the Avyakta, Maharudra assumes the form of Surya of countless rays, and divides himself into a dozen amsas each resembling a blazing fire. With his tejas, he then swiftly consumes the four kinds of created beings, the viviparous, oviparous, bacterial and vegetable.

Within moments all mobile and immobile creatures are annihilated, and the whole of Bhumi, the earth, becomes as bare as a tortoise shell. Having burnt everything on the face of Bhumi, Rudra of immeasurable power then inundates it with water of immense force.

He then creates the fire of dissolution, which dries up that Jala into which Bhumi has been dissolved. The water disappears, leaving the Mahabhuta Agni, the fire, to burn fiercely.

Then arises the mighty Vayu, wind of immeasurable force, in his eight forms, who swiftly swallows that inferno of transcendent force, with seven flames, and which is indeed identifiable with the heat existing in every creature. Having consumed that Agni, Vayu courses in every direction, upwards, downwards, and transversely.

Then Akasa, immeasurable space, swallows that wind of transcendent energy. Then Manas, the mind, effortlessly swallows Akasa. Then Consciousness, Chitta, the Soul of everything, consumes Manas.

In his turn, Chitta is swallowed by the Mahat who is and knows the past, the present and the future. The incomparable Mahat, or universe, is then swallowed by Sambhu, that Lord of all things, in whom the attributes of yoga, anima, laghima, prapti, and others, naturally inhere. He is the supreme and immutable light.

His hands and feet extend over every part; his eyes and head and face are everywhere, his ears reach every place; his existence overwhelms all things. He is the heart of all creatures and his measure is of a digit of the thumb!

That Infinite and Supreme Soul, Paramatman, that Lord of all, thus swallows the universe. After this, what remains is the undying and the immutable. That One is flawless, immaculate, the Creator of the past, the present, and the future, and is perfect.

I have thus, O Rajan, told you about the Pralaya, the great destruction. I will now tell you about Adhyatma, Adhibhuta and Adhidaivata.'"

CANTO 314

'Yajnavalkya said, "Brahmanas conversant with these subjects of enquiry speak of the two feet as Adhyatma, the act of walking as Adhibhuta, and Vishnu as Adhidaivatam of those two limbs. The anus is Adhyatma; its function of ejecting faeces is Adhibhuta, and Mitra, or Surya, is its Adhidaivata.

The organ of generation is called Adhyatma. Its gratifying function is called Adhibhuta, and Prajapati is its Adhidaivata. The hands are Adhyatma; their function as represented by doing is Adhibhuta; and Indra is the Adhidaivata of the hands.

The organs of speech are Adhyatma. The words uttered by them are Adhibhuta; and Agni is their Adhidaivata. The eye is Adhyatma. Rupa, form, is its Adhibhuta; and Surya is the Adhidaivata of that organ. The ear is Adhyatma. Sabda, sound, is Adhibhuta; and the points of the horizon are its Adhidaivata.

The tongue is Adhyatma. Rasa, taste, is its Adhibhuta; and Jala is its Adhidaivata. The nose is Adhyatma. Gandha, scent, is its Adhibhuta; and Bhumi is its Adhidaivata. The skin is Adhyatma. Sparsa, touch, is its Adhibhuta; and Vayu is its Adhidaivata.

Manas has been called Adhyatma; that with which it is exercised is Adhibhuta; and Chandramas is its Adhidaivata. Consciousness, Chitta, is Adhyatma. Conviction in one's identity with Prakriti is its Adhibhuta; and Mahat or Buddhi is its Adhidaivata. Buddhi is Adhyatma. That which is to be understood is its Adhibhuta; and Kshetrajna is its Adhidaivata.

Rajan, I have thus truly expounded to you, who fully know these original tattvas, in detail, one by one, the puissance of Brahman, the Paramatman as he manifests himself in different forms, in the beginning, the middle and the end.

Prakriti, as if for sport, O king, of her own accord, by undergoing modifications, playfully produces thousands upon countless thousands of combinations of her original transformations that are called gunas. As men can light countless lamps from a single one, Prakriti, too, transforms herself and multiplies the three gunas of Purusha—sattva, rajas and tamas—into numberless creations.

The qualities of sattva include patience, joy, prosperity, and satisfaction, the lustrousness of all faculties, happiness, purity, health, contentment, faith, liberality, compassion, forgiveness, steadfastness, benevolence, equanimity, truth and the acquittance of one's svadharma.

Mildness, modesty, calmness, outward purity, simplicity, observance of obligatory customs and practices, dispassion, fearlessness of heart, disregard for the appearance of banishment of good and evil as also for past deeds, accepting only what is offered as a gift, the absence of greed, concern for others, compassion for all creatures: these have been said to be the qualities ascribed to the sattva guna.

The tale of the qualities of rajas include pride of personal beauty, assertion of power, war, the absence of munificence and compassion, indulgence in kama, and so enduring of happiness and misery, delight in speaking ill of others, and an eagerness for fights and disputes of every kind.

Arrogance, rudeness, anxiety, indulgence in hostilities, sorrow, usurping what belongs to others, shamelessness, crookedness, disunions, roughness, lust, wrath, pride, assertion of superiority, malice and slander are also said to spring from rajas.

I will now tell you about the assemblage of qualities which spring from tamas. They are the torpor of judgement, obscuration of every faculty, darkness and utter, blind darkness. By darkness is implied death, and blind darkness is great wrath, kali.

Besides these, the other indications of tamas are greed with respect to all kinds of food, an insatiable appetite for both food and drink, taking over much pleasure in perfumes, royal attire, sporting events, luxurious seats and beds, and sleep during the day, lies and reckless deeds springing out of heedlessness, delighting in dancing and music on account of ignorance of purer sources of joy, and an aversion for every kind of religion. These, indeed, are the indications of tamas.'"

CANTO 315

'Yajnavalkya said, "O best of men, sattva, rajas and tamas are the three gunas of Prakriti. These attach to all things of the universe and always inhere to them. The unmanifest Purusha invested with the six attributes of yoga, by embracing these trigunas, transforms himself by himself into millions and millions of forms.

Those who know the science of Adhyatma say that to sattva is assigned a high, to rajas a middling and to tamas, a low place in the universe. With the help of pure dharma, righteousness, one attains to a high position, alongside the Devas and other divinities.

Through righteousness tainted with sin one attains to the condition of humankind. Finally, through unmixed sin, one sinks into depravity, a vile end, by becoming an animal or a vegetable. Listen now to me, Rajan, as I speak to you about the mixture or compounds of the trigunas of sattva, rajas and tamas.

Sometimes rajas is seen existing with sattva. Tamas also exists alongside rajas. With tamas may also be seen sattva. Sattva and rajas and tamas can exist together and in equal proportions. They constitute the Avyakta, the unmanifest, or Prakriti.

When the unmanifest Purusha is suffused with only sattva, he attains to the regions of the gods. Imbued with both sattva and rajas, he takes birth among human beings. And with rajas and tamas, he takes birth among the intermediate orders of beings. With all three, sattva, rajas and tamas, he attains to the condition of humanity.

Those Mahatmans that transcend both righteousness and sin, attain to that place which is eternal, immutable, undecaying and immortal. Gyanis, men of knowledge, attain to births that are unrivalled, and their place is immaculate and undecaying, transcending the realm of the senses, free from ignorance, above birth and death, and full of light that dispels all kinds of darkness.

You asked me about the nature of the Paramatman that dwells in the unmanifest Purusha. I will tell you, Rajan; listen to me.

Even when dwelling in Prakriti, Purusha is said to dwell in his own nature without partaking of the nature of Prakriti. Prakriti is without reality and inert. Only when presided over by Purusha can she create and destroy."

Janaka said, "Wise one, both Prakriti and Purusha are without beginning and without end. Both of them are without rupa, form. Both are undecaying. Both are, again, unfathomable. How then, Maharishi, can it be said that one of them is inanimate and unintelligent? And how can the other be said to be animate and intelligent?

And why is the latter called Kshetrajna? O foremost of Brahmanas, you know the entire dharma of moksha. I want to hear in full and in detail about emancipation.

Speak to me then of the existence and oneness of Purusha, of his separateness from Prakriti, of the deities that attach to the body of the place to which embodied creatures repair when they die, and that place to which they may go ultimately, in the course of time.

Tell me also of the knowledge described in the Samkhya philosophy, and of the yoga system, separately. O best of men, it befits you also to speak of the premonitory symptoms of death. All these principles are as well known to you as the lines and signs in the palm of your hand!'"

CANTO 316

'Yajnavalkya said, "That which is without gunas cannot be explained by ascribing gunas to it. Listen to me and I will expound to you what possesses attributes and what is nirguna. High-souled and wise Munis, who know the truth about all the tattvas say that when Purusha seizes attributes like a crystal catching the reflection of a red flower, he is said to be imbued with gunas; but when freed from them, like the crystal freed from reflection, he can be viewed in his true nature, that is, nirguna, beyond all attributes.

Unmanifest Prakriti is by her nature filled with gunas. She cannot transcend them. Inert by nature, she becomes attached to attributes. Avyakta, she cannot know anything, while Purusha, by his nature, possesses gyana, knowledge.

There is nothing higher than myself—this is what Purusha is always conscious of. For this reason the unmanifest or Prakriti, although inherently without reality and inert, becomes animate and intelligent in consequence of her union with Purusha who is eternal and indestructible.

When Purusha, through ignorance, repeatedly becomes associated with gunas, he fails to realise his own true nature and thus he fails to attain moksha. As a result of Purusha's reign over the tattvas that flow from Prakriti, he is said to partake of the nature of those evolutions. In consequence also of his agency in the matter of Prakriya, creation, he is said to possess the attribute of creation. In consequence of his agency in the matter of yoga, he is said to possess the attribute of yoga. For his lordship over those particular tattvas or tanmatras known as Prakriti, he is said to possess the nature of Prakriti.

For his agency in the matter of creating the seeds of all immobile things, he partakes of the nature of those seeds. And because he causes the several principles to initiate life, he is as subject to decay and destruction as are these principles themselves.

Since he is the witness of everything, and besides him there is nothing else, and for his consciousness of identity with Prakriti, Yatis crowned with ascetic success, knowers of Adhyatma, and freed from fever of every kind, regard him as existing by himself without a second; he is immutable, Avyakta, unmanifest, in the form of cause, unstable, and Vyakta, manifest, in the form of effects.

This is what has we have heard. The Samkhyas who depend upon gyana alone for their Liberation, and the practice of compassion for all creatures, say that it is Prakriti which is One while Purushas are many.

In fact, Purusha is different from Prakriti which, though unstable, still appears to be stable. As a blade of a reed is different from its outer sheath, even so is Purusha different from Prakriti. Indeed, the worm that is ensconced within the udumbara tree is distinct from the udumbara. Though existing with the udumbara, the worm is not to be regarded as forming a part of the tree.

The fish is distinct from the water in which it lives, and the water is separate from the fish that lives in it. Though the fish lives in the water, it is never drenched by water.

The fire that is contained in an earthen pot is distinct from the pot, and the pot is distinct from the fire it contains. Although the fire exists in and with the pot, it is not to be regarded as forming any part of it.

The lotus-leaf that floats on the surface of some water is distinct from the water on which it floats. Its co-existence with water does not make it a part of the water.

The perennial existence of these things in and with other things is never correctly grasped by ordinary people. They who behold Prakriti and Purusha in any other light are said to possess a flawed vision. It is certain that they have to repeatedly sink into naraka, terrifying hell.

I have now instructed you in the philosophy of the Samkhyas, that excellent science through which all things have been correctly ascertained. Knowing the nature of Purusha and Prakriti in this way, the Samkhyas attain moksha. I have also told you of the systems of those others who are conversant with the great principles of the universe. I will now describe to you the vigyana of the yogins.'"

CANTO 317

'Yajnavalkya said, "Rajan, I have already spoken to you of the science of the Samkhyas. Listen now as I discourse on the way of the yogins as heard and seen by me. There is no knowledge that can compare with that of the Samkhyas. There is no power that compares with that of yoga. These two ordain the same practices, and both are regarded as leading to moksha.

Men who are not blessed with intelligence regard the Samkhya and the yoga systems to be distinct from each other. We, however, look upon them as one and the same; we have arrived at this conclusion after study and reflection.

That which the yogins say and do is the very same which the Samkhyas have in view. He who sees both the Samkhya and the yoga systems to be one and the same is to be regarded as truly conversant with the principles that ordain the universe.

O Rajan, know the vital breaths and the senses are the chief means for practising yoga. Just by regulating those breaths and the senses, yogins can go everywhere at will.

Sinless one, when the gross body is destroyed, yogins endowed with subtle bodies, possessing the eight siddhis of yoga, such as anima, laghima and prapti, among others, wander throughout the universe, enjoying in that body all kinds of bliss.

In the shastras, the wise have spoken of yoga as conferring eight kinds of powers. They have spoken of yoga as having eight limbs. Indeed, O king, they have not spoken of any other kind of yoga.

It has been said that the excellent and effective practices of yogins are of two kinds. These, according to the indications in the scriptures, are those with attributes and those free of them: saguna and nirguna.

Dhyana, the concentration of the mind on the sixteen named objects, with the simultaneous regulation of the breath, is of one kind. The concentration of the mind in such a way as to destroy all difference between the contemplator, the object contemplated, and the act of dhyana, along with subjugation of the senses, is of another kind.

The first kind of yoga is said to be that possessed of gunas, attributes; the second kind is said to be that free of them.

Pranayama, regulation of the breath, is yoga with attributes. In nirguna yoga, the mind, freed from its functions, should be still. King of Mithila, at first, only saguna pranayama should be practised, otherwise if the inhaled and suspended breath is exhaled without mentally focusing upon a definite image furnished by a limited mantra, the increase of wind in the neophyte's body will cause him great injury.

In the first yaama of the night, twelve ways of holding the breath are recommended. After sleep, in the last yaama of the night, another twelve ways have been laid down. Without doubt, one who is calm, of subdued senses, living in solitude, rejoicing in his own self, and fully conversant with the import of the scriptures, should focus his Atman on the Paramatman by regulating his breath in these twenty-four ways.

Dispelling the five faults of the five senses, by removing them from their objects of sabda, rupa, sparsa, rasa and gandha, and dispelling the conditions called Pratibha and Apavarga, all the senses should be fixed upon Manas, the mind. Manas should then be fixed on Chitta, Consciousness; Chitta should be set on Buddhi, intelligence, and Buddhi should then be fixed on Prakriti.

Thus merging these, one after another, yogins contemplate the Supreme Soul which is One, which is freed from rajas, which is stainless, immutable and infinite, pure and perfect; who is the eternal Purusha, who is unchangeable, who is indivisible, without decay and death, who is everlasting, who transcends diminution, and who is the immutable Brahman.

Rajan, listen now to the indications of one that is in yoga, communion. All the indications of cheerful contentment of one who rests in perfect peace are seen in him who is in Samadhi. The wise say that the man in Samadhi looks like the still flame of a lamp full of oil and burning in a windless place.

He is like a rock which cannot be moved even slightly, not by a torrential cloudburst. He cannot be shaken by the blasting of conches and beating drums, or by songs, or the sound of hundreds of musical instruments played together.

These are the signs of one in Samadhi. Like a poised, brave and determined man who, while climbing a flight of stairs with a vessel full of oil in his hands, does not spill even a drop even if threatened by armed men, the Yogin, when his mind has been concentrated and when he beholds the Paramatman in Samadhi, remains unmoved, for he has entirely stilled his senses.

These are the signs of the yogin while he is in Samadhi. While in Samadhi, the yogin beholds Brahman, supreme and immutable, and which is a blazing light in the midst of deep and heavy darkness. By these means he attains, after long years, to moksha, after casting off this inanimate body.

This is what the eternal Sruti declares. This is called the yoga of the yogins. What else is it? They know it, they that are enlightened with wisdom, and regard themselves as crowned with final success.'"

CANTO 318

'Yajnavalkya said, "Listen now to me attentively, Rajan, as I speak of the places to which those who die will go.

If the Jivatman escapes through the feet, it is said that the man goes to the region of Vishnu. If through the calves, we have heard that the man goes to the regions of the Vasus. If through the knees, he attains to the company of the divinities called Sadhyas.

If through the anus, the man attains to the realms of Mitra. If through the back, he returns to Bhumi, and if through the thighs to the world of Prajapati. If through the flanks, the man attains to the realms of the Maruts, and if through the nostrils, to the realm of Chandramas.

If through the arms, the man goes to Indraloka, and if through the chest, to that of Rudra. If through the neck, he goes to the excellent loka of the great Rishi Nara. If through the mouth, the man attains to the world of the Viswadevas, and if through the ears, to the world of the Lokapalas.

If through the nose, the man attains to the realm of Vayu, and if through the eyes, to that of Agni. If through the brows, the man goes to the loka of the Aswins; and if through the forehead, to that of Pitris. If through the crown of the head, the man repairs to the world the puissant Brahma, greatest of gods.

Janaka, I have thus told you about the several realms to which men attain according to the manner in which their Jivatmans escape from their bodies.

I will now tell you the premonitory indications for those who have but one year to live, as laid down by the wise. Having previously seen Arundhati, the fixed star, or the other called Dhruva, one who fails to see it, or one that sees the full moon or the flame of a burning lamp to be broken towards the south, has but a year to live.

Those men who can no longer see images of themselves reflected in the eyes of others have but one year to live. One, who, though radiant, loses lustre, or being endowed with wisdom loses it, indeed, one whose inner and outer nature are thus changed, has but six months more to live.

He who disregards the gods, or has altercations with Brahmanas, or one who, being naturally of a dark complexion, becomes pale, has just six months to live. One who sees the moon as having many lacunae like a spider's web, or one who sees the sun with such gaps, has but one week more to live.

On smelling fragrances in temples, if a man perceives them to be as being offensive like the smell of corpses, he has but one week more to live. The depression of the nose or of the ears, the discolouring of the teeth or of the eye, the loss of consciousness, and of all bodily heat, are symptoms indicating death that very day.

If, without any perceptible cause a stream of tears suddenly flows from his left eye, and if vapours are seen to issue from his head, that is a sure indication that the man will die before that day ends. Knowing all these premonitory symptoms, the man of cleansed soul should, day and night, unite his Atman with the Paramatman in Samadhi.

Thus should he go on till the day for his dissolution arrives. If, however, instead of wishing to die he desires to live in this world, he can cast off all pleasures of gandha and rasa and live on in abstinence. In this manner he conquers death by fixing his Atman on the Paramatman.

Indeed, the man who is blessed with knowledge of the Atman practises the way of life recommended by the Samkhyas and conquers death by uniting his soul with the Supreme Soul. At last, he attains to what is entirely indestructible, which is without birth, auspicious and immutable, eternal and stable, and which is incapable of being attained to by men of impure souls.""

CANTO 319

'Yajnavalkya said, "You have asked me about that Supreme Brahman which resides in the Avyakta, the unmanifest. Your question relates to a deep mystery. Listen to me with close attention, O Rajan.

Having conducted myself with humility according to the ordinances laid down by the Rishis, I obtained the Yajuses from Surya. With the austerest penances I earlier adored the sun god.

The mighty Surya, pleased with me, said, 'Ask, O twice-born Rishi, for the boon upon which you have set your heart; however difficult it may be to obtain, I will gladly grant it to you. It is not easy to incline me to grace!'

Bowing and paying obeisance to him, I addressed that supreme heat-giving luminary in these words: 'I have no knowledge of the Yajuses. I want to know them without delay.'

Thus solicited, the divine one told me, 'I shall impart the Yajuses to you. Made up of the essence of speech, Goddess Saraswati will enter into your body.'

Surya Deva then commanded me to open my mouth. I did as I was told. Devi Saraswati entered into my body, O Anagha. At this, I began to burn. Unable to endure the pain I plunged into a river. Not knowing that what the high-souled Surya had done for me was for my benefit, I even grew angry with him.

While I was burning with the fierce energy of the goddess, the holy Surya said, 'Endure this burning for only a short while. It will soon cease and you will feel cool.' Indeed, soon my body was cool again.

Seeing me restored to ease, the Giver of light said to me, 'The whole of the Vedas with their Angas, together with the Upanishads, will appear within you through inner light, O Dvija! You will also know and abbreviate all of the Satapathas.

After that, your understanding will turn to the path of moksha. And you will attain to that end which both Samkhyas and yogins covet.' Having said these words to me, the divine Surya set beyond the Asta hills.

Hearing his parting words, and after he had gone from where I stood, I came home in joy and then remembered Devi Saraswati. As I thought of her, the auspicious Saraswati appeared instantly before my eyes, adorned with all the sacred vowels and the consonants; I first uttered the syllable Aum and then, according to the ordinance, offered the goddess the customary arghya, and dedicated another portion to Surya.

I discharged my duty and sat down, in devotion to both those deities. Thereupon, all of the Satapatha Brahmanas, with all their mysteries and with all their abstractions as also their angas, appeared of themselves before my inner eye, and I was filled with great joy.

I then taught these to a hundred good sishyas and thereby gave displeasure to my great Matulan, my maternal uncle Vaisampayana, with his disciples gathered round him. Radiant in the midst of my disciples, like the sun himself with his rays, I undertook to manage the yagna of your Mahatman father, O king of Mithila.

In that yagna a dispute arose between me and Vaisampayana as to who should be permitted to receive the dakshina that was paid for the recitation of the Vedas. In the very presence of Devala, I took half of that dakshina, the other half going to my uncle. Your sire and Sumantra and Paila and Jaimini and others all acquiesced in that arrangement.

I thus received from Surya Deva the fifty Yajuses. I then studied the Puranas with Romaharshana. Keeping before me those original mantras and the Devi Saraswati, helped by Surya's inspiration, I set myself to compile the excellent Satapatha Brahmanas, and succeeded in the task never before undertaken by anyone else.

I have taken that path which I wanted to take and I have also taught it to my sishyas. Indeed, I have imparted the whole of those Vedas with their angas and antas to them. As a result of my teachings, pure in mind and body, all those disciples have been filled with joy.

Having established for the benefit of others this gyana of fifty branches, which I had from Surya, I now meditate on the great goal of that final knowledge, the Brahman.

The Gandharva Viswavasu, well-conversant with the Vedanta scriptures, who wanted to know what is beneficial for Brahmanas in this knowledge, what truth occurs in it, and what its objective is, once questioned me.

He put altogether twenty-four questions to me relating to the Vedas. Finally, he asked me the twenty-fifth question relating to that branch of knowledge which is concerned with nyaya, the inferences of ratiocination.

Those questions are as follows: What is the universe and what is the not-universe? What is Aswa and what, again, is Aswa? What is Mitra? What is Varuna? What is gyana? What is the object of knowledge? What is unintelligent? What is intelligent? Who is Kah?

Who possesses the principle of change? Who does not possess it? What is he that devours the sun and what is the sun? What is vidya and what is avidya? What is immobile and what Mobile? What is without beginning, what is Akshara, indestructible, and what is Kshara, destructible?

The best of the Gandharvas asked me these excellent questions. After he, King Viswavasu, asked me these questions one after another, I answered them truly. At first, however, I told him to wait for a brief time, while I reflected on his queries! 'So be it,' the Gandharva said, and sat in silence.

Once again, in my mind, I thought of Goddess Saraswati. Then the replies to those questions arose naturally in my mind like butter from curds. Keeping in view the high science of inferential reasoning, I churned, with my mind, the Upanishads and the angas of the Vedas.

The fourth vigyana that deals with moksha, on which I have already discoursed to you, and which is based upon the twenty-fifth, the Jiva, I then expounded to him.

Having said all this, O Rajan, to King Viswavasu, I said to him, 'Listen now to the answers to the several questions that you have put to me. I now turn to the question, O Gandharva: What is the universe and what is the not-universe?

The universe is Avyakta, unmanifest, and the original Prakriti is endowed with the principles of birth and death, which are terrible to those who desire mukti. It possesses the three gunas of sattva, rajas and tamas, since it creates the tattvas, all of which are fraught with those attributes.

That which is the not-universe is Purusha divested of all gunas. By Aswa and Aswa are meant the female and the male, the former being Prakriti and the latter Purusha. Similarly, Mitra is Purusha, and Varuna is Prakriti. Gyana is Prakriti, while the object of knowledge is Purusha.

The unawakened Jivatman, and the knowing or intelligent are both the nirguna Purusha, for it is Purusha that becomes the Jiva when invested with ignorance. You have asked what Kah is, who is changeable and who is not.

I answer, Kah is Purusha. That which is changeable is Prakriti. He that is not is Purusha. Similarly, that which is called avidya, unknowing, is Prakriti; and that which is called vidya is Purusha.

You have asked me about the mobile and the immobile. That which is mobile is Prakriti, which undergoing change, constitutes the cause of creation and destruction. The Immobile is Purusha, for, without undergoing variations himself, he assists at creation and destruction.

According to a different system of philosophy, that which is Vedya is Prakriti; while that which is Avedya is Purusha. Both Prakriti and Purusha are said to be unintelligent, stable, indestructible, unborn, and eternal, according to the conclusions of philosophers conversant with the Adhyatma.

Prakriti, in the matter of creation, is indestructible, and is unborn;

hence Prakriti is not subject to decay or destruction. Purusha, again, is indestructible and unchangeable, for change it has none. The attributes of Prakriti may be destroyed, but not Prakriti herself. The learned, therefore, call Prakriti Akshara.

Prakriti also, by undergoing changes, operates as the cause of creation. The created outcomes appear and disappear, but not original Prakriti. For this reason also is Prakriti called indestructible. Thus have I told you of the conclusions of the fourth science, the turiya vigyana based on the principles of logical inference with mukti as its aim.

Having acquired by the science of Nyaya, inference, and by waiting upon gurus, the Riks, the Samans and the Yajuses, all the obligatory practices should be observed and all the Vedas studied with reverence, O Viswavasu! Foremost of Gandharvas, they who study the Vedas and all their angas, but who do not know the Paramatman from which all things take their birth and into which all things merge at the time of the Pralaya, and which is the one subject whose knowledge the Vedas seek to inculcate—indeed, they—who have no acquaintance with that which the Vedas seek to establish, study the Vedas to no purpose and bear the burden of such study in vain.

If a man wants butter and churns the milk of the female donkey, he does not find what he seeks but only encounters a substance as foul- smelling as ordure. In the same manner if, having studied the Vedas, one fails to grasp what is Prakriti and what is Purusha, one only demonstrates one's own foolishness and bears a useless burden in the form of Vedic lore.

With bhakti and dhyana, devotion and meditation, one should contemplate both Prakriti and Purusha, so that one may avoid repeated births and deaths. Reflection upon the fact of one's repeated births and deaths and avoiding the religion of rituals that produces at best only mortal results, one should take to the immortal religion of yoga.

Kasyapa, if one continuously reflects on the nature of the Jivatman and its connection with the Paramatman, one then succeeds in divesting oneself of all attributes and in beholding the Supreme Soul. Ignorant men regard the eternal and Avyakta Paramatman to be different from the Jiva, the twenty-fifth tattva.

Those who see both as truly one and the same are wise. Frightened by repeated births and deaths, the Samkhyas and yogins regard the Jivatman and the Paramatman to be identical.'

Viswavasu then said, 'Best of Brahmanas, you have said that the Jivatman is indestructible and indistinguishable from the Paramatman. This is difficult to grasp. Discourse on this topic to me once more.

I have heard discourses on this subject from Jaigishavya, Aista, Devala, the regenerate Parasara, the intelligent Varshaganya, Bhrigu, Panchasikha Kapila, Suka, Gautama, Arshtisena, the high-souled Garga, Narada, Asuri, the wise Pulastya, Sanatkumara, the great Sukra and my sire Kasyapa.

Subsequently I heard the discourses of Rudra and the Viswarupa Mahabuddhi, of several of the Devas, of the Pitris and the Daityas. I have gathered all that they say, for they generally speak on that eternal goal of all knowledge.

I desire, however, to hear what you, in all your wisdom, may say on those matters. You are the foremost of all, and a learned teacher of the shastras, and endowed with great intelligence. There is nothing that is unknown to you.

You are an ocean of the Srutis, as described in the world, of both the Devas and Pitris. The great Rishis who dwell in the world of Brahma say that Aditya himself, the eternal lord of all luminaries, is your guru in this knowledge.

Yajnavalkya, you have acquired the entire science of the Samkhyas, and in particular, the scriptures of the yogins. Without doubt, you are enlightened, and fully conversant with the mobile and immobile universe. I wish to hear you discourse on that knowledge, which may be likened to sweet ambrosial payasa.'

Yajnavalkya said, 'Best of Gandharvas, you are able to fathom every knowledge. Yet, since you ask me, hear me instruct you in that which I myself learned from my guru.

Prakriti, which is unintelligent, is apprehended by the Jiva. The Jiva, however, cannot be apprehended by Prakriti. As a result of the Jivatman being reflected in Prakriti, Prakriti is called Pradhana by Samkhyas and yogins who know the original Mahatattvas contained in the Srutis. Sinless one, the other, beholding, sees the twenty-fourth tattva, Prakriti, and the twenty-fifth, the Purusha; finally, not beholding, it beholds the twenty-sixth.

The twenty-fifth tattva thinks that there is nothing higher than itself. In reality, however, though seeing, it does not perceive the twenty-sixth tattva, which beholds it. Wise men should never accept the twenty-fourth, Prakriti, which is unintelligent, inert, as identifiable with the twenty-fifth, or the Purusha which has a real and independent existence.

The fish lives in water. It goes there impelled by its own nature. As the fish, though living in the water, is regarded as separate from it, the twenty-fifth tattva should be apprehended similarly: though it exists in a state of contact with the twenty-fourth, Prakriti, in its real nature, it is distinct from and independent of Prakriti.

When overwhelmed with the Consciousness of Ahamkara, and when unable to understand its identity with the twenty-sixth; in fact, in consequence of the illusion that fills it, of its co-existence with Prakriti, and of its own manner of thinking, the Jivatman always sinks down, but when freed from such Consciousness it rises upwards.

When the Jivatman succeeds in understanding that it is one, and Prakriti with which it resides is another, only then does it succeed in beholding the Paramatman and becomes one with the universe. Rajan, the Supreme is one, and the twenty-fifth, or the Jivatman is another. However, since the Supreme overlies the Jivatman, the wise regard both to be one and the same.

For these reasons, yogins and followers of the Samkhya, terrified by birth and death, blessed with the vision of the twenty-sixth tattva, pure in body and mind, and devoted to the Paramatman, do not recognise the Jivatman as Akshara, indestructible. When one beholds the Supreme Soul and merges with it, losing all consciousness of individuality, one then becomes omniscient, and possessed of omniscience one is freed from the obligation of rebirth.

I have thus spoken to you truly about Prakriti which is unintelligent, and the Jivatman which is intelligent, and the Paramatman which is omniscient, all according to the indications in the Srutis. That man who sees no difference between the knower or the known is both Kevala and Akevala, is the original cause of the universe, and is both Jivatman and the Paramatman.'

Viswavasu said, 'You have duly and adequately discoursed on that which is the origin of all the deities and which leads to mukti. You have spoken of what is true and excellent. May inexhaustible blessings always attend on you, and may your mind be ever united with intelligence!'

Yajnavalkya continued, 'Having said those words, the prince of the Gandharvas flew up towards heaven, shining in resplendent beauty. Before leaving me, he duly honoured me by circumambulating around my person in pradakshina, and I looked at him, highly pleased.

He taught the science he had obtained from me to those divinities that dwell in the regions of Brahma and other gods, to those that dwell on earth, to the dwellers of patala, and to those who have adopted the mukti-marga.

The Samkhyas are devoted to the practices of their system. The yogins are devoted to their practices. There are others too who desire to achieve moksha. To them this vigyana yields visible fruits, O lion among kings.

Mukti flows from gyana; without knowledge it can never be attained. Rajan, this is what the wise have said. Hence, one should strive to acquire true knowledge in all its depth and detail, and so succeed in freeing oneself from birth and death.

Acquiring knowledge from a Brahmana or a Kshatriya or Vaisya or even a Sudra of low birth, one must devotedly revere such gyana. Birth and death cannot assail one that has faith.

All orders of men are Brahmanas. All are sprung from Brahman. All men are Brahmavadis and utter Brahman. Helped by an understanding that is derived from and directed to Brahman, I inculcated this vigyana of Prakriti and Purusha in myself. Indeed, this whole universe is Brahman.

From the mouth of Brahma sprung the Brahmanas; from his arms, sprang the Kshatriyas; from his navel, the Vaisyas; and from his feet, the Sudras. All the varnas, having thus originated, should not be regarded as thieving from one another.

Impelled by ignorance, all men die and take birth once more, birth that is the cause of karma, deeds. Without knowledge, men of all varnas, dragged down by terrible avidya, fall into varied orders of being due to the tattvas that flow from Prakriti. For this reason, all must, by every means, seek to acquire knowledge.

I have told you that every person is entitled to strive for its attainment. One who possesses knowledge is a Brahmana. Others, Kshatriyas and Vaisyas and Sudras, also possess gyana. Hence, this science of mukti is always open to them all. This has been revealed by the wise.

I have answered all the questions you had asked me, and I have answered them all honestly. Discard all sorrow. Cross over the end of this quest. Your questions were excellent. Blessings be on you for ever!'"

Bhishma continues, 'Thus instructed by Yajnavalkya, the king of Mithila was filled with joy. The king honoured that best of sannyasis by circling around him in pradakshina. Given permission by the monarch, the sage left his court.

Having acquired the knowledge of mukti dharma, King Daivarati took his seat, and touching a million cows and vast quantities of gold and jewels, gave them away to numerous Brahmanas. Installing his son as the sovereign of the Videhas, the old king began to live according to the practices of the Yatis.

Meditating mainly on all ordinary duties and their derelictions as laid down in the shastras, the king began to study the entire science of the Samkhyas and the yogins. Regarding himself to be infinite, he began to reflect on only the Eternal and Independent One, the Brahman. He rejected all ordinary duties and their derelictions, punya and paapa, satya and asatya, janma and mrityu, and all other things pertaining to the tattvas of Prakriti.

Both the Samkhyas and yogins, in consonance with their sciences, regard this universe to be caused by to the action of the Vyakta, manifest, and the Avyakta, unmanifest. The learned say that Brahman is free from good and evil, is self-dependent, the Highest of the high, Eternal, and Pure.

Therefore, you too, O Rajan, become pure! The giver, the receiver of the gift, the gift itself, and that which is ordered to be given away, are all to be deemed as the unmanifest Atman. The Atman is the Atman's one possession. Who, therefore, can be a stranger to one?

Always think in this manner, never otherwise. He who does not know what Prakriti is with gunas and what is Purusha transcending them, only he, without knowledge, repairs to sacred waters and performs yagnas.

Not by the study of the Vedas, not by penances, nor by sacrifices, son of Kuru, can one attain to the condition of Brahman. Only when one succeeds in grasping the Supreme or Avyakta, does one come to be revered.

They who wait upon Mahat attain to the regions of Mahat. They who wait upon Chit, Consciousness, attain to the realm of Chetana. They who wait upon what is higher attain to places that are higher than these.

Those gyanis who succeed in apprehending eternal Brahman, who is higher than unmanifest Prakriti, succeed in obtaining that which transcends birth and death, which is free from attributes and qualities, and which is both existent and non-existent. I received this knowledge from Janaka, who had it from Yajnavalkya.

Gyana, knowledge, is the highest. Yagnas, sacrifices, cannot compare with it. With the help of gyana one succeeds in crossing samsara, the world's ocean so full of obstacles, suffering and danger. One can never cross that ocean with sacrifices. Men of knowledge say that one cannot prevail over birth and death, and other obstacles through yagnas, Rajan; indeed they declare that one cannot pass over samsara by ordinary exertion.

Men attain to heaven through yagnas, tapasya, vratas and other observances. But they again fall down into this world. Therefore, adore with reverence that which is Supreme, most pure, blessed, stainless, and sacred, and which transcends all states, being moksha itself.

By understanding Kshetra, and by performing the sacrifice that consists in the acquisition of knowledge, you will become truly wise. In an earlier age, Yajnavalkya did that good to King Janaka which can be derived from a study of the Upanishads. The eternal and immutable Paramatman was the subject on which the great Rishi discoursed to the king of Mithila. It enabled him to attain to that Brahman which is auspicious, and immortal, and which transcends every kind of sorrow.'

CANTO 320

"Yudhishtira says, 'Having acquired great power and great wealth, and having obtained a long life, how can one avoid death? By which of these means can one succeed in avoiding decay and death: tapasya, vratas, the diverse karmas laid down in the Vedas, or by knowledge of the Srutis, or the application of medicaments?'

Bhishma says, 'Listen to the old story of Panchasikha, who was a bhikshu in his practices, and Janaka. Once upon a time Janaka, the ruler of the Videhas, questioned the Maharishi Panchasikha, the foremost of all who knew the Vedas and whose doubts about the purpose and significance of all duties had been dispelled.

The king asked, "Through what conduct, O holy one, may one transcend decrepitude and death? Is it by tapasya, or by gyana? Or by religious deeds like yagnas and vratas, or by the study and knowledge of the shastras?"

Thus addressed by the ruler of the Videhas, the learned Panchasikha, knower of all things unseen, answered, "Decay and death cannot be prevented under any circumstances. Neither days nor nights, nor months, ever cease.

Only that man, who, though transient, adopts the eternal path of the religion of Nivritti, abstention from all actions, succeeds in evading birth and death. Destruction overtakes all creatures. All are ceaselessly borne along the infinite current of time.

Those that are borne along this infinite river infested by the two mighty crocodiles of decrepitude and death, without any rescue boat, sink down without anyone coming to their help. As they are swept along that current, men fail to find any friend for assistance and do not take an interest in any one else.

One meets with wives and other friends on one's way. A man encounters enjoyable companions but never for any length of time. Creatures, as they are borne along the river of time, become repeatedly attracted towards one another, and, like masses of clouds, blown by the wind, collide with a report of thunder.

Decay and death devour all creatures, like wolves. Indeed, they devour the strong and the weak, the short and the tall. In all transitory creatures, only the Soul exists eternally.

Why should he, then, rejoice when creatures are born or grieve when they die? Where do I come from? Who am I? Where shall I go? Whose am I? Before what do I rest? What shall I be? Why do you grieve and for what? Who else but you will behold swarga or patala? Thus, without discarding the shastras, we should offer dakshina and perform yagnas!'"

CANTO 321

"Yudhishtira says, 'Rajarishi of Kuruvamsa, who ever attained mukti, the annihilation of Buddhi, understanding, and the other faculties, without abandoning the domestic life, grihasta? Tell me this! How can the sthula and sukshma sariras, the gross and the subtle bodies, be cast off? Pitamaha, also tell me what the supreme excellence is.'

Bhishma says 'In this regard, the old tale is told of the discourse between Janaka and Sulabha. In days of yore, there was a king of Mithila by the name of Dharmadhyaja, of Janaka's vamsa. He was devoted to the practices of the religion of Vairagya, which is renunciation. He was deeply learned in the Vedas, with the scriptures on mukti, and with the shastras bearing on his own dharma as a king.

Subduing his senses, he ruled this earth. Hearing of his good conduct in the world, many wise men wanted to emulate him. In the same Satya yuga lived a woman called Sulabha who was a sannyasini; she practised the dharma of yoga and wandered over the whole world.

In the course of her wanderings, Sulabha heard from many Brahmana Dandis of different places that the ruler of Mithila was devoted to the dharma of mukti. Hearing this about Janaka and wishing to ascertain its veracity, Sulabha wanted to meet the king in person.

Using her powers of yoga, Sulabha abandoned her natural form and features, and assumed the most faultless figure and unrivalled beauty. In the twinkling of an eye and with the speed of the quickest arrow, the fair-browed devi of eyes like lotus-petals flew to the capital of the Videhas. Arriving at the city of Mithila, teeming with people, she adopted the guise of a mendicant and presented herself before the king.

Seeing her elegant and delicate form, the king was filled with wonder and asked who she was, whose she was, and where she came from. Welcoming her, he offered her an excellent seat, honoured her by giving her water to wash her feet, and gratified her with fine refreshments.

Refreshed and gratified with the hospitality offered to her, Sulabha urged the king, who was surrounded by his ministers and seated in the midst of learned scholars, to speak upon his adherence to the moksha dharma.

Doubtful of whether Janaka had succeeded in attaining to Mukti by following the religion of Nivritti, Sulabha, who had yoga-shakti, entered the mind of the king with her own mind. Wanting to know the truth, she blocked the rays issuing from the eyes of the king with the rays of light from her own eyes and bound Janaka with bonds of yoga.

That best of kings, who prided himself upon his own invincibility, foiled the intentions of Sulabha and indeed seized her will with his own. In his sukshma rupa, the king was without the royal chatra, parasol and sceptre. Sulabha, in hers, was without the tridanda, her mendicant's triple staff.

Both remained in the same sthula rupas, and so conversed with each other. Listen to that conversation as it transpired between Janaka and Sulabha.

Janaka said, "O sannyasini, to what course of conduct are you devoted? Whose are you? Where have you come from? After finishing your work here, where will you go? Only with questioning can one ascertain another's knowledge of the scriptures, their age or varna.

Since you have come to me, you must answer my questions. Know that I am truly free of all vanity for my raja chatra and raja danda, my royal parasol and sceptre. I wish to know you well. You truly deserve my respect.

Listen to me as I speak to you of mukti, for no one else can discourse to you on that subject. I will also tell you about the person from whom, in ancient times, I acquired this transcendent knowledge.

I am the beloved sishya of the high-souled and venerable Panchasikha, belonging to the pravarajya, the mendicant order of Parasara's vamsa. My doubts have been dispelled and I fully know the Samkhya and the yoga philosophies, and the Vidhis, the ordinances with respect to yagnas and other rites, which constitute the three well-known paths to moksha.

Wandering over the earth and pursuing the path pointed out in the shastras, the learned Panchasikha once lived joyfully in my palace for four months during the monsoons. That foremost of Samkhyas discoursed to me on the many means of attaining mukti, honestly and clearly, so that even I could easily comprehend them. He did not, however, command me to give up my kingdom.

Freed from attachments, and fixing my Soul on the supreme Brahman, I lived unmoved by companionship, practising in its entirety that threefold Pravritti which is laid down in the treatises on mukti. Renouncing all attachments is the highest means prescribed for emancipation.

It is from knowledge that Vairagya, the renunciation by which one is freed, is said to flow. The endeavour after yoga arises from gyana, and through that endeavour one attains to knowledge of the Atman. Through knowledge of the Atman one transcends joy and sorrow. This enables one to transcend death and achieve high success.

I have acquired that Chetana, the knowledge of the Atman, and accordingly, I have transcended all the pairs of opposites. Even in this life have I been freed from stupor and have risen above all attachments.

Just as soil, saturated with and softened by water, causes the sown seed to sprout, so do the actions of men cause rebirth. As a seed once fried cannot sprout, though it once could, has my heart been freed from desire; by the instruction of the holy Panchasikha of sannyasa, my mind no longer produces its fruit in the form of attachment to the objects of the senses.

I never experience love for my wife or hatred for my enemies. Indeed,

I keep aloof from both, clearly knowing the futility of attachment and anger. I regard both equally: him that smears my right hand with sandalwood-paste and him that wounds my left.

Having attained my true goal, I am content, and look equally upon a clod of earth, a piece of stone, and a nugget of gold. Though engaged in ruling a kingdom, I am free from attachments of every kind. In consequence of all this I am superior to all bearers of tridandas.

Some great men, who are conversant with the subject of mukti, say that it has three paths: gyana, yoga and karma, the way of yagnas and kriyas and other acts. Some regard gyana, having all worldly things for its objects, as the means to mukti. Some hold that the total renunciation of outer and inner actions is the means.

Another class of men who know the scriptures of emancipation say that gyana is the only means. Yatis, with subtle vision, hold that karmas, actions, are the means. The high-souled Panchasikha, discarding both the opinion about gyana and karma, knowledge and deeds, regards the third way, yoga, as the only means to mukti.

If men leading the grihasta life are endowed with yama and niyama, they become the equals of sannyasins. If, on the other hand, sannyasins are filled with desire and aversion, and attached to wives and honour, and vanity and affection, they become the equals of householders.

If one can attain mukti through knowledge, then emancipation may exist in tridandas, for nothing prevents the bearers of such staffs from acquiring the requisite gyana. Why then can emancipation not exist in the chatra and the danda as well, especially when there is equal reason in taking up the tridanda and the sceptre?

One becomes attached to all those objects and deeds which one needs for one's own self for particular reasons. If a man sees the faults of domestic life and discards it to adopt another mode fraught with great merit, he cannot, merely for such rejection and adoption, be regarded as one free from all attachments; for all that he has done is to attach himself to a new method after having freed himself from a previous one.

Sovereignty is fraught with the rewarding and the chastising of others.

The life of a mendicant is equally fraught with the same, for they too reward and chastise those they can. Since they are akin to kings in this respect, why would they alone attain mukti, and not kings?

Notwithstanding sovereignty, one is cleansed of all sins through of gyana alone, living the while in the Supreme Brahman. The wearing of brown cloths, shaving of the head, bearing the tridanda and the kamandalu, these are the outward signs of one's mode of life. These have no value in attaining mukti.

Notwithstanding the adoption of these symbols of a particular way of life, when knowledge alone is the cause of one's emancipation from sorrow, it would appear that the adoption of mere emblems is perfectly useless. Or, if you see the mitigation of sorrow in these symbols of sannyasa, why then should not the alleviation of sorrow be seen in the chatra and the danda that I have adopted?

Mukti does not exist in poverty; nor is bondage to be found in affluence. One attains to it through gyana, illumination, alone, whether one is indigent or wealthy.

For these reasons, know that I am living in a condition of freedom, though ostensibly engaged in the enjoyments of dharma, artha and kama, in the form of kingdom and wives, which, for most men, constitute bondage. I have severed the bonds of kingdom and prosperity, and the bondage to attachments, with the sword of renunciation, whetted on the stone of the scriptures on mukti.

As regards myself, I tell you that I have become liberated in this way. O sannyasini, I hold you in high esteem. But that should not prevent me from telling you that your conduct does not match the practices of the very mode of life that you have embraced!

You have great elegance and delicacy of form. You are shapely and beautiful. You are young. You have all these, and you have niyama, subjugation of the senses. I doubt it verily. By entering into me with the power of yoga, you have invaded my body to ascertain whether I am really emancipated or not.

Your action ill suits that mode of life whose emblems you bear. The tridanda is unfit for a yogin filled with desire. As regards yourself, you do not adhere to your staff. As regards those that are free, it is fitting that they protect themselves from falling.

Let me tell you about your transgression in consequence of your contact with me and having entered into my sthula sarira, this gross body, with the help of your understanding. Why have you entered my kingdom or my palace? At whose bidding have you entered into my heart?

You belong to the foremost of all the varnas, being, as you are, a Brahmana woman. As regards myself, however, I am a Kshatriya. There can be no union between us. Do not cause a varnasamkarsana, a mixing of castes.

You live by practising those dharmas that lead to mukti. I live in the grihasta mode of life. This deed of yours is thus another evil that you have done, for it produces an unnatural union of two opposite ways of life. I do not know whether you belong to my own gotra or not.

You, too, do not know who I am, and to what gotra I belong. If you are of my own gotra, by entering into my body you have created another evil—that of an unnatural union. If, again, your husband is alive and in a distant place, your union with me has produced the fourth sin of adultery, for you are not one with whom I may be lawfully united.

Do you perpetrate all these sins, driven by the motive of achieving a particular goal? Do you act from ignorance or from a perverted intelligence? If, again, because of your decadent nature, your behaviour has become thoroughly independent or unrestrained, I tell you that if you have any knowledge of the scriptures, you will understand that everything you have done has generated evil.

As a result of your actions, a third fault attaches to you, a fault that destroys peace of mind. By trying to display your superiority, you reveal the signs of an immoral woman.

Desirous of asserting victory as you are, it is not just me that you want to defeat, for it is clear that you wish to obtain a victory over my entire court consisting of these learned and superior Brahmanas; by casting your eyes in this manner towards all these meritorious Brahmanas, it is evident that you desire to humiliate them all and glorify yourself at their expense.

Bewildered by the pride and might of yoga born of your envy of my power, you have fused your understanding with mine and have mingled nectar with poison.

The union of man and woman, when each desires the other, is sweet as nectar. When, however, a woman desires a man who does not want her, the union of the two, instead of being a merit, becomes a flaw as noxious as poison.

Do not continue to touch me. Know that I am righteous. Conduct yourself according to your svadharma. Your search into whether I am or I am not emancipated is finished.

It is fitting for you not to conceal all your secret motives from me. It is not correct for you to disguise and hide from me what your purpose is: whether your action has been prompted by the desire of accomplishing your own objective or that of some other hostile king.

One should never appear fraudulently before a king; nor before a Brahmana; nor before one's wife when she is virtuous. Those who appear in deceitful guise before these three are soon ruined.

The power of kings lies in their sovereignty. The power of Brahmanas conversant with the Vedas is in the Vedas. Women wield high power because of their beauty, youth and blessedness. Possessing these strengths, all three are powerful.

He who wishes to accomplish his own goal should always approach these three with sincerity and honesty; insincerity and deceit fail to produce success in these three quarters. It is right for you to tell me your varna of birth, about your learning and conduct, and disposition and nature, and also why you have come here!"'

Bhishma continues, 'Though rebuked by the king in these harsh, offensive, and unseemly words, Sulabha was not at all abashed. After Janaka had spoken, the beautiful Sulabha replied in words more handsome than her person.

Sulabha said, "Rajan, speech should always be free of the nine verbal faults and the nine errors of judgement. While lucidly explaining the meaning of anything, speech should possess the eighteen well-known merits.

Ambiguity, ascertaining the merits and flaws of premises and conclusions, weighing the relative strength or weakness of those faults and merits, establishment of the conclusion, and the element of persuasiveness or otherwise that attaches to the conclusion arrived at: these five characteristics pertaining to the senses constitute the authoritativeness of what is said.

Listen now to the characteristics of all these requirements, as I expound them according to the combinations, beginning with ambiguity. As regards the comprehending of the subject, when knowledge rests on distinguishing the objects to be known being different from one another, and when the understanding rests upon many points that follow each other, the combination of words is said to be vitiated by ambiguity.

By ascertaining merits and flaws, the establishment, by elimination in premises and conclusions, adopting tentative meanings is called Samkhya. Krama or weighing the relative strength or weakness of the faults or merits, determined by the above process, consists in settling the appropriateness of the priority or sequence of the words used in a sentence. Those who are conversant with the interpretation of sentences or texts give this meaning to the word Krama.

Nigamana or Samapana, conclusion, means the final determination, after examining what has been said on the subjects of dharma, artha, kama and moksha, in respect of what it is that has specifically been stated in the text.

The sorrow born of attraction or revulsion increases to a great measure. The conduct, O Rajan, which one pursues to dispel the sorrow experienced is called Prayojanam.

Take my word for it, O king, that these characteristics of ambiguity and the others, numbering five in all, when occurring together, constitute a complete and intelligible sentence. What I say will be full of sense and meaning, judicious and free from ambiguity because each word will not symbolise many things.

They are logical, free from pleonasm or tautology, smooth, certain, free of bombast, sweet and agreeable, truthful, consistent with dharma, artha and kama, refined to be free from Prakriti, not elliptical or imperfect, gentle and easily grasped; they are characterised by correct order, not far-fetched in respect of sense, connected with one another as cause and effect, and each having a specific purpose.

I shall not tell you anything prompted by desire or wrath, fear or greed, abjectness or deceit or shame, compassion or pride. I will answer you because it is proper for me to respond to what you have asked.

When the speaker, the hearer and the words said, completely agree with one another in the course of speech, then the sense or meaning is revealed clearly. When, in the matter of what is said, the speaker shows disregard for the understanding of the hearer by uttering words whose meaning only he himself understands, then, however fine those words may be, they cannot be grasped by the hearer.

That speaker's words are faulty, again, if he abandons all regard for his own meaning and uses words that, though of excellent sound and sense, arouse only mistaken impressions in the mind of the listener.

That speaker, however, who uses words that are, while expressing his own meaning, intelligible to the hearer as well, truly deserves to be called a speaker. No other man deserves the name. It befits you, therefore, Rajan, to hear with concentrated attention my words that are laden with meaning and a wealth of significance.

You have asked me who I am, whose I am, and where I come from. O king, listen to me with an undivided mind as I answer your questions. As lac and wood, as grains of dust and drops of water, exist commingled when brought together, even so do the lives of all creatures.

Sabda, sparsa, rasa, rupa and gandha, these and the senses, though diverse in their essences, still exist in a state of commingling like lac and wood. It is well known that nobody asks any of these: who are you? Each of them also has no knowledge either of itself or of the others.

The eye cannot see itself. The ear cannot hear itself. The eye, again, cannot discharge the functions of any of the other senses, nor can any of the senses carry out the functions of any other sense save its own. Even if all of them combine together, they will fail to know their own selves, just as dust and water mingled together cannot know each other though existing in a state of union.

In order to discharge their respective functions, they await the contact with objects external to them. The eye, form and light, constitute the three requirements for seeing. The same is the case with respect to the working of the other senses and the ideas that result from them.

Again, between the functions of the senses, like vision and hearing, and the ideas which are their result, like form and sound, Manas, the mind, is an entity other than the senses and is regarded as having a function of its own. To arrive at certainty, one uses Manas to distinguish what is existent from what is non-existent in the matter of all ideas derived from the senses.

With the five senses of knowledge and five senses of action, Manas makes a total of eleven. The twelfth is the Buddhi, understanding. When doubt arises in respect of what is to be known, Buddhi comes forward and settles all doubts to help discernment.

After the twelfth, sattva is the thirteenth tattva. With its help creatures are distinguished as possessing more of it or less of it in their constitutions. After this, Chitta, Consciousness of self, is another tattva, the fourteenth. It helps one to understand the self as distinguished from what is not self.

Desire is the fifteenth principle. Unto it inheres the whole universe. The sixteenth principle is avidya. Unto it inhere the seventeenth and the eighteenth tattvas called Prakriti and Vyakti, which is maya and prakasa.

Joy and sorrow, decrepitude and death, acquisition and loss, the agreeable and the unpleasant—these constitute the nineteenth tattva and are called pairs of opposites. Beyond the nineteenth principle is another, Kaala, time, called the twentieth. Know that the births and death of all creatures are due to the action of this twentieth tattva.

These twenty exist together. Besides these, the Panchamahabhutas, the five great primal elements, and existence and non-existence, bring the total to twenty-seven. Beyond these are three others named Vidhi, Sukra and Bala, which make the tally reach thirty. These thirty tattvas occur in the body.

Some regard unmanifest Prakriti to be the source or cause of these thirty principles. This is the view of the atheistic Samkhya school. The Kanadas of gross vision regard the manifest or anus, atoms, to be their cause.

Whether the Avyakta, unmanifest, or the Vyakta, manifest, be their cause, or whether the two, the Supreme or Purusha and the Vyakta, be regarded as their cause, or whether the four together, the Supreme or Purusha and his maya, and the Jiva and avidya, ignorance, be the cause, they that are conversant with Adhyatma behold Prakriti to be the cause of all creatures.

That Prakriti, which is Avyakta, becomes manifest in the form of these tattvas. I, you, O king, and all others possessing a body are the result of that Prakriti so far as our bodies are concerned.

Insemination and other embryonic conditions are due to the mixture of the vital seed and eggs. In consequence of insemination the result which first appears is called Kalala. From Kalala arises Budbuda or the embryonic bubble.

From the stage called Budbuda springs what is called Pesi. From Pesi that stage arises in which the various limbs become manifest. From this last condition appear nails and hair.

Upon the end of the ninth month, king of Mithila, the creature takes its birth so that, its sex being known, it comes to be called a boy or girl. When the creature issues out of the womb, the form it presents is such that its nails and fingers seem to be of the colour of burnished copper.

The next stage is infancy, when the form that was seen at the time of birth changes. From infancy one reaches youth, and from youth, old age. As the creature advances from one stage into another, the form presented in the previous stage is altered.

The constituent elements of the body, which serve diverse functions, undergo change every moment in every creature. Those changes, however, are so minute that they cannot be observed. The birth of particles, and their death, in each successive condition, cannot be marked even as one cannot distinguish the changes in the flame of a burning lamp.

When such is the state of the bodies of all creatures—when that which is called the body is changing incessantly even like the swift movement of a horse of fine mettle—who then comes from where, or not, or whose is it or whose is it not, or from where does it not arise? What connection, in fact, exists between creatures and their own bodies?

As fire is generated from the contact of flint with iron, or from two sticks of wood rubbed against each other, even so are creatures generated from the combination of the thirty tattvas. Indeed, as you see your own body in your body, and your soul in your own soul, why is it that you do not see your own body and soul in the bodies and souls of others?

If it is true that you can identify yourself with others, why did you ask me who I am and whose? If it is true that you, O king, are free from the shackle of duality that says, 'this is mine and this other is not mine', then what use are such questions as 'who are you, whose are you and from where do you come?'

What indications of mukti can be said to be in a king who acts as others act towards enemies and allies and neutrals, and in victory and truce and war? What signs of mukti occur in him who does not know the true nature of the aggregate of three, dharma, artha and kama as manifested in seven ways in all deeds and who, on that account, is attached to that aggregate of three?

What indications of mukti exist in him who fails to cast an equal eye on the agreeable, on the weak, and the strong? You are unworthy, and your pretence of mukti should be put down by your advisors.

With so many faults, your efforts to attain emancipation is like the use of medicine by a patient who indulges in all kinds of forbidden foods and practices. Parantapa, reflecting upon spouses and other sources of attachment, one should find these in one's own soul. What else can be regarded as the indication of mukti?

Listen now to me as I speak fully of these and certain other minute sources of attachment pertaining to the four well-known actions of sleeping, pleasure, eating and dressing to which you are still bound though you profess have adopted mukti dharma.

That man who has to rule the whole world must, indeed, be an absolute king without a second. He is obliged to live in only a single palace. In that palace he has again only one sleeping chamber. In that chamber he has only one bed to lie on. Half that bed again he is obliged to give to his queen. This may serve as an example of how little a king's share is of all he is said to own.

This is the case with his objects of enjoyment, with the food he eats and with the garments he wears. He is thus attached to a very limited share of all things. Again, he is attached to the duties of rewarding and punishing.

The king is always dependent on others. He enjoys a very small share of all that he is supposed to own, and to that small share he is forced to be attached just as others are attached to their possessions.

In the matter of war and peace, the king is not independent. In the matter of women, of sport, and other kinds of enjoyment, the king's inclinations and choices are very constrained. In the matter of taking counsel and in the assembly of his councillors what independence can the king be said to have?

When he commands other men, he is said to be absolutely independent. But the very next moment, his autonomy is barred by the very men whom he has commanded.

If the king wishes to sleep, he cannot satisfy his desire, thwarted as he is by those who want to transact business with him. He must sleep when permitted, and while sleeping he is obliged to wake up to attend to those that have urgent business with him. 'Bathe, touch, drink, eat, pour libations on the fire, perform sacrifices, speak, listen'—these are the words which kings have to hear from others, and hearing them he becomes a slave to those that utter them.

Men come in groups to the king and ask him for gifts. As the guardian of the general treasury, however, he cannot make gifts to even the most deserving. If he makes these endowments, the treasury becomes exhausted. If he does not, he disappoints his solicitors who become hostile towards him. He is vexed and inimical feelings invade his mind.

If many wise and heroic and wealthy men live together, the king's mind becomes distrustful. Even when there is no reason to fear, the king becomes fearful of those that always wait upon him. These very men also find fault with him. Behold, in what ways the king's fears may arise from even them.

All men are kings in their own houses. All men are also householders in their own homes. Janaka, like kings, all men mete out rewards and punishments in their own homes. They, too, like kings, have sons and wives and themselves, treasuries and friends and stores. In these respects the king is not different from other men.

Like them, shouts of 'the kingdom is ruined', 'the city is consumed by fire', 'the best of elephants is dead', fill the king with anguish, and he yields to grief, not knowing that these impressions are all caused by ignorance and delusion.

The king is seldom free from mental suffering caused by desire, aversion and fear. He is also commonly afflicted by headaches and other similar maladies. Like others, he is troubled by the contradictory pairs of opposites like pleasure and pain. He is anxious about everything. Since the kingdom is full of enemies and impediments, the king, while he enjoys it, passes sleepless nights.

Sovereignty is thus blessed with an extremely small share of happiness, while it is imbued with great misery. It is as insubstantial and fleeting as burning flames fed by straw or bubbles seen on water.

Who would actually like to gain sovereignty, or having acquired it ever hope to win tranquillity? You regard this kingdom and this palace to be yours. You think that this army, this treasury and these advisors are yours. In reality, whose are they, and whose are they not?

Allies, ministers, the capital, the provinces, punishment, the treasury, and the king, these seven constitute the limbs of a kingdom and, depending upon one another, stand like pillars that together support one another and the kingdom. The merits of each are complemented by the merits of the others.

Which of them are superior to the rest? At certain times, some particular ones are regarded as more distinguished than the rest, when some important end is served through their agency. Superiority, for the time being, is said to belong to that which is most effective.

These seven limbs, along with the three others, form an aggregate of ten, support one another, and enjoy the kingdom like the king himself.

That king who is filled with great energy, and who is firmly attached to the Kshatriya dharma, should be satisfied with only a tenth part of the produce of his subject's field. Some kings are seen to be content with less than a tenth part of such produce. There is no one who owns the kingly office without someone else also owning it in the world; there is no kingdom without a king.

If there be no kingdom, there can be no righteousness, and if there be no dharma, from where can mukti arise? The most sacred and highest merit belongs to kings and kingdoms.

By ruling a kingdom well, a king earns the punya that attaches to the Aswamedha yagna with the whole earth given away as dakshina. But how many kings are there who rule wisely? Janaka, I can mention hundreds and thousands of faults like these that attach to kings and kingdoms. Then, again, when I have no real connection with even my body, how then can I be said to have any contact with the bodies of others?

You cannot charge me with having attempted to bring about varnasamkarsana, a mixing of castes. Have you not heard the mukti dharma explained in its entirety by Panchasikha, together with its means, its methods, its practices and its conclusion?

If you have prevailed over all your bonds and freed yourself from all attachments, may I ask you, O king, why do you still keep your connections with this royal chatra and these other symbols of sovereignty? I think you have not listened to the shastras, or that you have listened to them without any benefit, or, perhaps, you have listened to some other works passing for the shastras.

It seems that you have mere worldly knowledge, and that like an ordinary man of the world you are bound by the bonds of touch, wives, palaces and the like. If it be true that you have been emancipated from all bonds, what harm have I done you by entering your body with only my intellect?

With Yatis, among all varnas men, the custom is to live in uninhabited, deserted places. What harm then have I done, and to whom, by entering your understanding which is truly of real knowledge? I have not touched you, Rajan, with my hands, or arms, or feet, or thighs, or with any other part of my body.

You are born into a high race. You are modest. You have foresight. Whether the act has been good or bad, my entrance into your body has been a private one, concerning us two only. Was it not improper for you to publish that private act before your whole court?

These Brahmanas are all worthy of reverence. They are the foremost of gurus. Being their king, you are also entitled to their respect. Paying them reverence, you are deserving of receiving reverence from them.

Reflecting on all this, if you really know propriety with respect to speech, it was not right for you, before these foremost Brahmanas, to proclaim the fact of this intercourse between two persons of opposite sexes.

King of Mithila, I stay within you without touching you at all even as a drop of water stays on a lotus-leaf without wetting it. Despite the instructions of Panchasikha of the pravarajya, the mendicant order, your knowledge has become abstracted from the sensual objects to which it relates.

It is clear that while you have given up the grihasta way of life you have not yet attained mukti that is so difficult to achieve. You linger between the two, pretending that you have reached the goal of muktas.

The contact of one who is emancipated with another that is also free, or Purusha with Prakriti, cannot lead to an intermingling of the kind you dread. Only those who regard the Atman to be identical with the body, and who think that the varnas and asramas are really different from one another, err in supposing such an intermixing to be possible.

My body is different from yours. But my Atman is not different from your soul. When I am able to realise this, I have not the slightest doubt that my Buddhi is really not dwelling in yours, though I have entered into you by yoga.

A pot is carried in the hand. In the pot is milk. On the milk is a fly. Though the hand and pot, the pot and milk, and the milk and the fly, exist together, yet are they all distinct from each other. The pot does not share the nature of the milk. Nor does the milk have the nature of the fly. The condition of each is independent, and can never be altered by the condition of that other with which it may temporarily exist.

In this manner, varna and dharma, though they may exist together with and in one who is emancipated, do not really attach to him. How then can varnasamkarsana result from this union of ours?

Then, again, my varna is not superior to yours. I am not a Vaisya, nor a Sudra. I am, O king, of the same varna as you, born of a pure race. There was once a Rajarishi known as Pradhana. It is clear that you have heard of him. I am born in his vamsa, and my name is Sulabha.

Indra, accompanied by Drona and Satasringa and Chakradwara, and other great mountains, would attend the yagnas performed by my ancestors. Being born in such a vamsa, it was established that no fitting husband could be found for me. I was then instructed in the moksha dharma and now I wander over the earth alone, practising sannyasa.

I do not practise any hypocrisy in the matter of the life of renunciation. I am not a thief that appropriates what belongs to others. I do not confuse the practices of the different varnas. I am firm in the practices of that mode of life to which I properly belong. I am firm and resolute in my vows.

I never utter any word without reflecting on its propriety. Rajan, I did not come to you without careful deliberation. Having heard that your understanding has been purified by the kukti dharma, I came here to derive some benefit from it. Indeed, I came to ask you about emancipation.

I do not say this to glorify myself and humiliate my opponents. But I say it, impelled by sincerity alone. What I say is, he that is emancipated never indulges in that intellectual battle which is implied by a dialectical disputation for the sake of victory. He, on the other hand, is really liberated who devotes himself to Brahman, that sole seat of peace.

As a person of the mendicant order resides for only one night in an empty house, leaving the next morning, I too, shall remain for this one night in your body, which is like an empty chamber, destitute of knowledge.

You have honoured me with both speech and other offers that are due from a host to a guest. Having slept this one night in your body, O ruler of Mithila, which is as it were my own chamber now, I shall depart tomorrow."

Bhishma continues, 'Hearing these words full of reason and excellent sense, King Janaka failed to give any answer.'

CANTO 322

"Yudhishtira says, 'How was Suka, the son of Vyasa, in ancient days, won over to renunciation? I want to hear you narrate the story. My curiosity in this matter is irrepressible. You of the Kuru vamsa, it is fitting for you to instruct me about the conclusions in respect of the unmanifest, the cause, the manifest, the effects, and of the truth, and about Brahman that is in them, but unattached to them, as also of the acts of the Swayambhu Narayana, as you know them.'

Bhishma says, 'Beholding his son Suka living fearlessly as ordinary men do in practices that are considered harmless by them, Vyasa taught him all the Vedas and then discoursed to him one day in these words:

Vyasa said, "O son, becoming a master of the senses, do you suppress extreme cold and heat, hunger and thirst, and the wind also, and having subdued them, as yogins do, do you practise dharma? Do you duly observe truth and sincerity, and freedom from wrath and malice, and self-restraint and tapasya, and the duties of benevolence and compassion?

Do you pursue the truth, firmly devoted to righteousness, abandoning all sort of insincerity and deceit? Do you sustain yourself on vighasa, what remains of food after feeding the Devas and Atithis?

Your body is as transitory as the bubbles on the surface of water. The Jivatman sits unattached in it as a bird on a tree. The companionship of all agreeable objects is extremely short-lived. Why then, O son, do you sleep in such forgetfulness?

Your enemies are attentive and alert and ever ready to spring on you, always waiting for their chance. Why are you so foolish as to not know this?

As the days pass, one after another, your life is always being reduced. Indeed when your life is being incessantly shortened, why do you not hurry to learn the means of saving yourself?

Only they that are lacking in faith in the existence of the next life set their hearts on things of this world that only have the effect of increasing flesh and blood. They are totally unmindful of all that is concerned with the next world. Those men that are bewildered by erroneous understandings display a hatred for dharma.

The man who follows misguided persons who have adopted devious and sinful paths is equally afflicted by the ways of sin. Mahatmans, however, who are content, devoted to the scriptures, and possessed of immense power, pursue the path of righteousness.

Do you wait upon them with reverence and seek their instruction. Do you act according to the teachings of those wise men whose eyes are set upon dharma. With your understanding cleansed by such lessons and rendered superior, do you then restrain your heart which is ever ready to deviate from the right course.

They whose Buddhi is always concerned with the present, who fearlessly regard the future as something remote; they who do not observe any restrictions in the matter of food are really foolish men who fail to understand that this world is only a temporary field of trial.

Repairing to the flight of steps of dharma, climb those steps one after another. At present you are like a worm that weaves its cocoon around itself and so depriving itself of all means of escape.

Do you keep to your left, without any scruple, the atheist who transgresses all restraints, and courts destruction, who stands like a house beside a fierce and surging river, and who, to others, appears to stand like a bamboo with its tall head erect in pride.

Using the raft of yoga, cross the ocean of the world, this samsara, whose waters are constituted of your five senses. Its fierce monsters are moha, krodha and mrityu—desire, wrath and death; its vortex is janma, birth itself. With the raft of dharma, you must traverse the world affected by death and afflicted by decay, and upon which the thunder-bolts of days and nights fall incessantly.

Death seeks you at all moments, whether you are sitting or lying down; it is certain that you will be death's victim at any time. From where then will you find your rescue? Like the she-wolf taking a lamb, death snatches away one that is still engaged in earning wealth and still unsatiated in the indulgence of his pleasures.

When you are destined to enter into the dark, you hold up the blazing lamp of righteous understanding, whose flame has been kindled. Falling into various forms one after another in the world of men, a creature obtains the birth of a Brahmana with great difficulty. You have obtained that birth. Son, endeavour to maintain it properly.

A Brahmana has not been born for the gratification of desire. On the other hand, his body is intended to be subjected to mortification and penances in this world so that incomparable happiness may be his in the next. The status of Brahmanatva is acquired with the help of long, sustained and austere tapasya.

Having acquired that condition, one should never waste one's time in the indulgence of one's senses. Always engaged in penances and self-restraint, and desiring what is good for you, live and act in peace and serenity.

The life of every man is like a horse. The nature of that steed is Avyakta, unmanifest. The sixteen elements constitute its body. Its character is most subtle.

Kshanas, and trutis, and nimeshas are the hair on its body. The sandhyas, the twilights, constitute its shoulder joints. The light and the dark fortnights are its two eyes of equal power. Months are its other limbs.

That steed runs incessantly. If your eyes be not blind, see that charger race forward on its invisible course; set your heart on dharma, after hearing what your gurus have to say on the subject of the next world.

They that fall away from dharma and those who conduct themselves recklessly, who always display malice towards others and take to sin, are obliged to assume physical bodies in the regions of Yama and suffer diverse afflictions and torments.

That king who is devoted to dharma and who protects the good and punishes the evil, with discrimination, attains to those regions that belong to men of righteous deeds. Through diverse kinds of good karma, he attains to such faultless felicity which cannot be acquired by even thousands of births.

Furious dogs of frightful mien, crows with iron beaks, flocks of ravens and vultures and other dark birds, and blood-sucking worms torment the man who transgresses the commands of his parents and preceptors when he goes to hell after death. That sinful wretch who, because of his recklessness, violates the ten boundaries that have been fixed by Swayambhu himself is obliged to pass his time in great suffering in the wild wastelands in the dominions of the king of Pitris.

That greedy man, who is in love with falsehood, who always takes delight in deception and cheating, and who injures others by practising hypocrisy and deceit, has to go to a bottomless hell and suffer great anguish and tortures for his sins.

Such a man is forced to bathe in the broad Vaitarani river whose waters are boiling, to enter into a forest of trees whose leaves are as sharp as swords, and then to lie on a bed of battle-axes. He has thus to pass his days in dreadful hell in great agony.

You see only the regions of Brahma and other deities, but you are blind to that which is the highest—mukti! Alas, you are also blind to old age and decay that are followed by death.

Go along the path of mukti! Why do you delay? A frightful terror, destructive of your happiness, lies before you. Take swift steps to achieve liberation.

Soon after death you are sure to be taken before Yama. To obtain felicity in the next world, strive to attain to righteousness through the practice of difficult and austere vratas.

Regardless of the sufferings of others, the all-powerful Yama takes the lives of all, yours and your friends'. No one can resist him. Very soon the wind of Yama will blow and bear you into his presence. Very soon you will be taken to that dread presence all alone.

Do you achieve here what will be for your good there. Where now is that death-wind which will blow before you very soon? Are you mindful of it? Very soon, when that moment arrives, the points of the horizon will begin to spin before your eyes. Are you mindful of that?

O son, soon the Vedas will vanish from your sight as you are helplessly sucked into that terrifying presence. Set your heart, then, on that most excellent yoga of mukti. Seek to attain that sole treasure so that, after death, you will not have to grieve at the recollection of your former deeds, good and evil, all of which are characterised by error.

Decrepitude very soon weakens your body and robs you of your limbs, strength and beauty. Therefore, seek that unique treasure. Very soon the Destroyer, with disease for his sarathy, in order to take your life, will pierce and break your body with a mighty hand. Practise, then, austere penance.

Very soon those terrible wolves, which reside within your body, will attack you from every side. Endeavour, therefore, to achieve acts of righteousness. Very soon all alone, you will behold a thick darkness, and very soon you will see golden trees on the top of the mountain. Swiftly you must perform deeds of dharma.

Very soon your evil companions and enemies, your senses, dressed in the guise of friends, will swerve you from true vision. Do you, then, strive to achieve that which is of the highest good.

Earn that wealth which has no fear from either kings or thieves, and which one does not have to abandon even at death. Earned by one's own actions, that wealth has never to be shared with others. In the other world, each enjoys that which he has earned for himself.

O son, give that to others by which they may be able to live in the next world. Also set yourself to acquiring that wealth which is indestructible and eternal.

Do not think that you should first enjoy all kinds of pleasures and then turn your heart towards mukti, for before you are satiated with enjoyment you may be overtaken by death. In view of this, hasten to do acts of goodness.

Neither mother nor son, nor relatives, nor dear friends, even when implored honourably, accompany the man who dies. One has to go oneself, unaccompanied, to the regions of Yama.

Only those deeds, good and bad, that one did before dying, accompany the man into the other world. The gold and riches that one has earned by good and bad means do not benefit one when one's body meets with dissolution.

There is no better witness than the Atman, of all actions done or not done in life, of men that have gone to the other world. When the acting Chaitanya, the Jivatman, enters into the witness Chaitanya the destruction of the body takes place; this is seen by yoga-buddhi when yogins enter the firmament of their hearts.

Even here, Agni, Surya and Vayu, these three Devas, reside in the body. Beholding as they do all the deeds and practices of one's life, they become one's witnesses.

Days and nights, the former characterised by the virtue of revealing all things and the latter by concealing all things, run incessantly; touching all things they reduce their allotted periods of life.

Therefore, be observant of the duties of your own varna. The road in the other world, leading to the realms of Yama, is infested by many enemies in the form of iron-beaked birds and wolves, and by many repulsive and terrifying insects and worms.

Take care of your own actions, for only these will accompany you along that road. One does not share one's karma with others, but everyone enjoys or endures the fruits of his own actions.

As Apsaras and Maharishis attain to fruits of great felicity, in the same manner, men of righteous deeds, as the fruits of their respective righteous acts, obtain in the other world chariots of transcendent radiance that move everywhere at the will of the riders. Men of taintless deeds, cleansed souls and pure birth obtain the fruits, in the next world, which correspond with their own righteous acts in this life.

By walking along the high road marked by the duties of grihasta, men acquire happy ends and attain to the region of Prajapati or Brihaspati, or of him of a hundred yagnas. I can give you thousands and thousands of instructions. Know, however, that dharma, the mighty cleanser, keeps all foolish persons in the dark.

You have passed twenty-four years. You are now full twenty-five years of age. Your years are passing away. Do you begin to lay your store of righteousness. The Destroyer that dwells within error and heedlessness will very soon deprive your senses of their powers. Relying on your body alone, swiftly perform your duties before that consummation comes.

When it is your duty to go along that road on which you alone shall be in front and you alone behind, what need then do you have of either your body or your wife and children?

When men have to go by themselves, without companions, to the land of Yama, it is clear that in view of such a terrifying situation, you should seek to acquire that one unique treasure—dharma or yogasamadhi. The puissant Yama, regardless of the afflictions of others, snatches away and uproots the friends and relatives of one's vamsa. There is no one that can thwart him.

Seek to gather a stock of righteousness. Son, I impart to you these lessons that are all in accord with the shastras I follow. Observe them by acting according to their truth.

He who supports his body by following the duties laid down for his varna, and who gives dakshina to earn whatever fruits may attach to such deeds, is freed from the consequences born of ignorance and delusion. The knowledge which a man of righteous deeds acquires from Vedic practices leads to omniscience.

That omniscience is identical with moksha dharma, the vigyana of the highest object of human acquisition. Instruction in this, imparted to the grateful, is beneficial for it leads to the attainment of emancipation.

The pleasure that one takes in living amidst the dwellings of men is truly a shackle that binds fast. Breaking that shackle, men of righteous deeds repair to regions of great felicity. Evil men, however, fail to break that bond.

Since you have to die, what use have you of wealth, or of relatives, or with children? Employ yourself in searching for your soul which is hidden in a cave. Where have all your grandsires gone?

Do today that which you would keep for tomorrow. Do that in the morning which you would defer for the afternoon. Death does not wait for anyone, to see whether he has or has not accomplished his tasks. Following the body after one's death to the cremation ground, one's relatives and kinsmen and friends return quickly after throwing it on the funeral pyre.

Without hesitation avoid those who are sceptics, who are without compassion, and who are attached to evil ways; endeavour to seek, without listlessness or apathy, that which is for your highest good. When, therefore, the world is afflicted by death, do you wholeheartedly achieve dharma, aided all the while by unswerving patience.

That man who is conversant with the means of attaining mukti and who discharges his svadharma, certainly attains to great felicity in the other world. There is no destruction for you who never stray from the path of dharma and do not recognise death in the attainment of a different body.

He who increases his store of righteousness is truly wise. He who, on the other hand, falls away from dharma is said to be a fool. One who is engaged in doing good deeds attains swarga and other rewards as the fruits of those deeds; but he who is given to evil ways has to sink into naraka.

Having acquired the human condition, so difficult to attain, which is the stepping-stone to heaven, one should fix one's soul on the Brahman so that one may not once more fall away. One whose understanding, directed towards the path to swarga, does not stray from it, is regarded by the wise as a man of dharma, and when he dies his friends should indeed grieve.

The man whose understanding is not restless and is directed to Brahman, and who has attained swarga, is freed from naraka, a great terror. They who are born in the asramas of sannyasis and die there, do not earn much punya by abstaining from enjoyments and the indulgence of desire even for their entire lives.

However, he who possessing objects of pleasure casts them off and engages himself in tapasya succeeds in acquiring everything. I regard the fruits of the penances of such a man to be much higher.

There have been, and will be, hundreds and thousands of mothers and fathers, sons and wives in this world. Who, however, were they and whose are we? I am quite alone. I have no one whom I may call mine. Nor do I belong to anyone else. I do not see that person whose I am, nor do I see him whom I may call mine. They have nothing to do with you. You have nothing to do with them.

All creatures are born according to their karma, their acts of past lives. You, too, will go hence and be born into a new varna determined by your own deeds. In this world we see that the friends and followers of only those that are rich show devotion to the rich. The friends and followers of the poor fall away during their very lifetime.

Man commits countless heinous sins for the sake of his wife and children. From those evil deeds he derives much distress both now and in the next world. The wise man beholds the world of life destroyed by the actions of every living being.

Therefore, O son, act according to all the instructions I have given you!

The man of true vision, seeing this world to be only a field of karma, action, should, from desire of felicity in the next world, do good deeds. Time exerts his irresistible power, and cooks all creatures in his own cauldron with his ladle made of months and seasons, using the sun for his fire, and days and nights for his fuel; these days and nights are the witnesses of the fruits of every creature's karma.

Of what use is that wealth which is not given away and which is not enjoyed? For what purpose is that strength which is not employed in resisting or subjugating one's enemies? For what purpose is that knowledge of the scriptures which does not compel one to righteous deeds? And for what purpose is that atman which does not subdue the senses and abstain from evil?"'

Bhishma continues, 'Having heard these most beneficial words spoken by the island-born Vyasa, Suka leaves his father and goes forth to seek a guru who could teach him the moksha dharma.'"

CANTO 323

"Yudhishtira says, 'Pitamaha, if there is any value in dakshina, yagnas, and in tapasya well-performed, and in obedience rendered to gurus and other revered elders, speak to me of them.'

Bhishma says, 'An understanding, associated with evil, causes the mind to fall into sin. In this state one taints one's actions, and then falls into great misery.

Those who sin have to be born into the most indigent circumstances. They move from famine to famine, from pain to pain, and from fear to fear. They are deader than those who are dead.

Those who are possessed of bhakti, self-restrained and devoted to dharma, are prosperous, and go forth from joy to joy, from heaven to heaven, from bliss to bliss. Unbelievers have to pass, with groping hands, through realms infested by beasts of prey and elephants, and pathless tracts teeming with snakes and robbers and other terrors. What more need be said of these?

On the other hand, those who revere the Devas and Atithis, are generous, considerate to the virtuous, and offer dakshina in yagnas, walk on the path of felicity that belongs to men of cleansed and subdued souls. Those who are unrighteous will not be counted among men even as grains without kernel are not counted as grain, and as cockroaches are not counted among birds.

One's deeds follow one even when one runs fast. As the doer lays himself down, so also do his actions lie with him. Indeed, one's sins sit when the doer sits, and run when he runs. The sins act when the doer acts, and, in fact follow him like his very shadow. The doer's karma, by whatever means and under whatever circumstances, endures, and is sure to be enjoyed or endured with respect of its fruits by the doer in his next life.

From every side time always drags along all creatures, duly observing the laws of the distance to which they are flung, which is in keeping with their actions. As flowers and fruits, without being urged, never fail to blossom and appear at their proper time, even so one's past deeds make their appearance at their time.

Honour and dishonour, gain and loss, destruction and growth, are seen to set in. No one can resist them. None endure, for disappearance follows appearance.

The sorrows one suffers is the result of one's karma. The happiness one enjoys flows from one's karma. From the time when one lies within a mother's womb one begins to enjoy and suffer one's deeds of a past life. The consequences of good and evil deeds of one's childhood, youth, or old age are experienced in one's next life at the same ages.

As the calf recognises its mother among thousands of her kind, one's past exploits, without doubt, seek one out in one's next life, unerringly, although one may live among thousands of one's kind. As a piece of dirty cloth is whitened by being washed in water, in the same manner, cleansed by continuous exposure to the fire of fasts and penances, the righteous at last attain to unending bliss.

You of high intelligence, the desires and purposes of those whose sins have been washed away by sustained and well-performed tapasya are crowned with fruition. The path of the righteous cannot be discerned even as that of birds in the sky or that of fishes in water.

There is no need to speak ill of others, or to talk about the fall of others. On the other hand, one should always do what is pleasing, agreeable, and beneficial to one's own self.'"

CANTO 324

"Yudhishtira says, 'Tell me, O Pitamaha, how Mahatman Suka of austere penances was born as the son of Vyasa, and how did he succeed in attaining the highest goal? Which woman bore the son of Vyasa, rich in tapodhana? We do not know who Suka's mother was, nor do we know anything of the birth of that high-souled sannyasi. How was it that, when he was a mere boy, his mind became entirely drawn to the knowledge of the subtle Brahman?

Indeed, in this world, there is no other in whom such predilections have been marked at so early an age. I want to hear all this in detail. I am never satiated by your excellent and amrita-like words. Pitamaha, tell me, in their proper order, of Suka's greatness and knowledge, and of his union with the Paramatman!'

Bhishma says, 'The Rishis did not make punya depend upon life span, or decay, or wealth, or friends. They said that he who studied the Vedas was great. What you wish to know is rooted in tapasya.

Son of Pandu, that tapa rises from the subjugation of the senses. Without doubt, one errs in giving the reins of one's life to one's senses. It is only by restraining them that one finds true success.

The merit that attaches to a thousand Aswamedha yagnas or a hundred Vajapeyas is not even a sixteenth of the punya that arises from yoga. I will now tell you about the circumstances of Suka's birth, the fruits of his tapasya, and what he achieved by his deeds, subjects that cannot be grasped by those of uncleansed souls.

Once upon a time on Meru's peak, Mahadeva, adorned with karnikara flowers, sported with his terrible ganas. The daughter of Himavat-king of the mountains, Devi Parvati, was also there. Near that peak, the island-born Vyasa practised extraordinary austerities.

O best of the Kurus, using yoga he withdrew himself into his own Atman, engaged in dharana, and performed many penances to have a son. He addressed Mahadeva with a prayer "O puissant one, let me have a son who will have the power of Agni and Bhumi, Jala, Vayu and Akasa." Engaged in the most austere tapasya, the Rishi begged Siva, who cannot be supplicated by men of impure souls, using not words but his yoga-shakti.

The mighty Vyasa remained there for a hundred years, surviving on air alone, engaged in adoring Mahadeva of multifarious form, the lord of Uma. There stood all the Devarishis and Rajarishis and the Lokapalas and the Sadhyas along with the Vasus, and the Adityas, the Rudras, and Surya and Chandramas, and the Maruts, and the oceans, and the rivers and the Aswins, the Devas, the Gandharvas, and Narada and Parvata and the Gandharva Viswavasu, and the Siddhas, and the Apsaras.

There sat Mahadeva, also known as Rudra, decked with an excellent garland of karnikara flowers, blazing with effulgence like the moon with his rays. In those delightful, divine forests, peopled with Devas and heavenly Rishis, Maharishi Vyasa remained, engaged in high yoga dhyana, in order to obtain a son. His strength did not diminish, nor did he feel any pain.

The three worlds gazed at this penance in amazement. While the Rishi, of immeasurable energy, sat in yoga, his matted locks, in consequence of his tejas, were seen to burn like flames of fire. I heard this from the illustrious Markandeya. He would always narrate to me the exploits of the Devas. It is on account of that tejas that the matted jata of the Mahatman Krishna-Dwaipayana to this day seem to be of the colour of fire.

Gratified with the Rishi's tapasya and his fervent bhakti, Mahadeva resolved to grant him his wish. The three-eyed one smiled with pleasure, and said to him, "O island-born one, you will get a son as you wish! Possessed of greatness, he shall be as pure as Agni, as Vayu, as Bhumi, as Jala and as Akasa! He will possess the Consciousness of his being Brahman; his understanding and soul shall be devoted to Brahman, and he shall completely depend upon Brahman even so that he will be merged and one with Brahman!'"

CANTO 325

"Bhishma says, 'Having obtained this great boon from Mahadeva, one day the son of Satyavati was rubbing sticks to make a fire. While thus engaged, the illustrious Rishi saw the Apsara Ghritachi, who, because of her tejas, was of arresting beauty. Yudhishtira, seeing her in that forest Vyasa was overcome with desire.

Seeing the Rishi's heart aflame with by desire, Ghritachi transformed herself into a she-parrot and flew to that place. Although Vyasa now saw the Apsara in another form, his desire did not subside but spread over every part of his body.

Summoning all his patience, the Muni tried to suppress his desire; despite all his effort, however, Vyasa could not control his agitated mind. With fate moving him, inexorably, the Rishi's heart was smitten by Ghritachi's beautiful form.

To repress his lust, he earnestly continued with the task of making a fire, yet he helplessly ejaculated and his seed fell onto the ground. That best of Dvijas, however, continued to rub the sticks without feeling any misgivings for what had happened. From the seed that fell, a son was born to him, called Suka. It is because of these circumstances attending his birth that he was named Suka, after the parrot. Indeed, for the form his mother took, he himself often assumed a great parrot's head!

Thus, from the two arani sticks his father used for kindling a fire, was born that greatest of Rishi, and the highest of yogins. As in a yagna a blazing fire sheds its radiance all around when libations of ghee are poured upon it, so did Suka take his birth, radiating effulgence because of his own tejas.

Son of Kuru, assuming the excellent form and complexion of his father, Suka, of pure soul, shone like a smokeless fire. The greatest of rivers, the Ganga in her embodied form, came to the breast of Meru and bathed Suka after his birth with her sacred waters.

An ascetic's staff and a dark deer-skin fell from the sky for Mahatman Suka. The Gandharvas sang, the diverse tribes of Apsaras danced, and divine booming drums sounded. The Gandharva Viswavasu, and Tumburu and Varada, and others called Haha, and Huhu, eulogised the birth of Suka.

There arrived the Lokapalas with Sakra at their head, as also the other Devas and the Devarishis. Vayu rained showers of divine flowers upon the place. The entire universe, mobile and immobile, was infused with surging joy.

Accompanied by the Devi, and moved by love, Mahadeva of great refulgence came there, and soon after the birth of the Muni's son himself invested him with the sacred thread. Sakra lovingly bestowed upon him a celestial kamandalu of great beauty, and divine raiment.

Hamsas and satapatras and kraunchas in their thousands, and many sukas and chasas, O Bhaarata, wheeled over his head. Blessed with great splendour and intelligence, Suka, having obtained his birth from the two fire-sticks, continued to live there, engaged the while in the attentive observance of many vratas and upavasas.

As soon as Suka was born, the Vedas with all their mysteries and all their antas, came to dwell in him, even as they did in Vyasa. For all that, remembering the universal practice, Suka selected Brihaspati, who knew all the Vedas together with their angas, as his guru.

Having studied all the Vedas together with all their mysteries and abstractions, as also all the itihasas and the *Artha Shastra*, the Mahamuni Suka returned home, after paying his guru dakshina. Adopting the vow of a Brahmacharin, he then began practising the most severe tapasya, focusing all his being in dhyana.

In even his childhood, he came to be revered by the Devas and Rishis for his knowledge and penances. The mind of the great Muni, Rajan, took no pleasure in the three asramas of life, including the grihasta; his heart was set on just the mukti dharma.'"

CANTO 326

"Bhishma says, 'Thinking of mukti, Suka humbly approached his father and desiring to achieve his highest good, he saluted his great guru and said, "You are well versed in the mukti dharma. O illustrious one, discourse to me upon it, so that my mind may achieve the supreme peace."

Hearing his son's words, the Maharishi said to him, "Son, you must study the mukti dharma and all the various duties of life."

At his father's command, Suka, that foremost of men of dharma, mastered all the treatises on yoga, and also the Samkhya vigyana of Kapila. When Vyasa saw his son to be possessed with the knowledge of the Vedas, infused with the tejas of Brahman, and fully conversant with the mukti dharma, he said to him, "Go to Janaka, the ruler of Mithila. He will show you the way to your mukti."

Suka went forth to Mithila to ask its king about the truth of dharma and the refuge of emancipation. Before he set out, his sire further told him, "Go there by that path which ordinary men take. Do not use your yoga shakti which lets you fly through the skies."

Being humble by nature, Suka was not at all surprised by this. He was further told to go there with simplicity and not from any desire for pleasure: "Along your way do not seek friends and wives, since they are the causes of attachment to the world.

Although we preside over his yagnas, do not regard yourself superior to Janaka while you stay with him. Obey him and live under his direction. He alone will dispel all your doubts.

The king of Mithila is well versed in all dharma and fully knows the mukti shastras. He is one at whose yagnas I officiate. Without any hesitation, do what says."

Thus instructed, the righteous-souled Suka went to Mithila on foot although he was able to traverse through the skies over the whole earth with her seas. Passing over many hills and mountains, many rivers and lakes, and countless forests abounding with beasts of prey and other feral animals, he crossed the two Varshas of Meru and Hari successively and next the Varsha of Himavat, and came at last to the Varsha known by the name of Bharata.

Having seen many kingdoms inhabited by Chins and Huns, Mahamuni Suka at last reached Aryavarta. Obeying his father's commands and bearing them constantly in his mind, he gradually passed along his way over the earth like a bird passing through the air. Going through many delightful towns and thronging cities, he saw diverse kinds of wealth but waited not to observe them.

On his way he crossed many delightful gardens and many sacred waters. Soon he reached the realm of the Videhas that was protected by the virtuous Mahatman Janaka. There he saw many populous villages, and many kinds of food and drink and habitations of cowherds swelling with men and many herds of kine.

He saw many fields abounding with rice, barley and other grain, and many lakes inhabited by swans and cranes and adorned with beautiful lotuses. Passing through the Videha country with its prosperous subjects, he arrived at the wonderful gardens of Mithila rich with many species of trees.

Full of elephants and horses and chariots, and men and women, he passed by them without pausing to observe any of them closely. Bearing the thought, and ceaselessly dwelling upon it—the desire to master the mukti dharma—Suka of the cheerful soul who took his joy in only dhyana thus reached Mithila at last.

At the gate, he sent word through the dwarapalakas. Calm, devoted to dhyana and yoga, he entered the city, after having obtained permission. Walking down the main highway full of fine, rich men, he reached the king's palace and entered it without hesitation.

The guards forbade him with rough words. Without any anger, Suka stopped and waited. Neither the sun nor the long distance he had walked had fatigued him in the least. Neither hunger nor thirst, nor the exertion he had made, had weakened him. The heat of the sun had not seared him, or pained him even slightly.

Among those guards there was one who felt compassion for him, to see him stand there himself like the brilliant midday Surya. Worshipping him with due form and revering him properly, with folded hands he led him to the first chamber of the palace.

Seated there alone, Suka began to meditate on mukti. Possessed of serene splendour he looked with an equal eye upon both a shady spot and one exposed to the sun's rays. Soon, Janaka's minister came up to him with folded hands and led him to the second chamber of the palace.

That chamber led to a spacious garden which formed a part of the inner apartments of the palace. It looked like a second Chaitraratha. Beautiful pools of water he saw here and there, at regular intervals. Lustrous trees, all in bloom, graced the garden.

Women of transcendent beauty were in attendance. The minister led Suka from the second chamber to that enchanted place. Ordering those damsels to give the Muni a seat, the minister left him there.

Those exquisite women were young, of beautiful forms and faces, and shapely hips; they were clad in fine red raiment, decked with ornaments of burnished gold. They were skilled in pleasing conversation and maddening revelry, and thorough mistresses of the arts of singing and dancing.

Always smiling, they were equal to the very Apsaras in beauty. Accomplished in all the ways of dalliance, consummate in reading the thoughts of men upon whom they waited, fifty young women, of high varna and of easy virtue, surrounded Suka the ascetic.

Giving him padya, water to wash his feet, and worshipping him respectfully with the usual offerings or arghya, they gratified him with excellent foodstuffs suitable to the season. After he had eaten, one after another, they singly led him through the grounds, showing him every thing of beauty and interest, O Bhaarata. So knowing of the thoughts of all men, sporting and laughing and singing, they entertained that auspicious Muni of noble soul.

The pure-souled ascetic born from the two aranis, dutiful, having perfect control over all his senses, and a thorough master of his wrath, was neither pleased nor annoyed at all this. Then those foremost of beautiful women gave him an excellent asana to sit upon.

Washing his feet and his limbs, Suka said his sandhya vandana, his evening prayers, sat on that fine seat, and began to think of the object for which he had come there. In the first part of the night, he devoted himself to yoga. The puissant ascetic passed the middle portion of the night in sleep. Waking from his slumber, he went through the necessary rites of cleansing his body, and though surrounded by those beautiful women, he once again dedicated himself to yoga.

It was in this way, O Bhaarata, that the son of the island-born Vyasa passed the second half of that day and the whole of that night in the palace of King Janaka.'"

CANTO 327

"Bhishma says, 'The next morning, King Janaka, accompanied by his minister and his whole household, and with his priest going before him, came to Suka. Bringing with him costly asanas and diverse kinds of jewels and riches, and bearing the ingredients of the arghya on his own head, the monarch approached the son of his revered guru.

The king took that beautiful and costly asana, decked with jewels and overlaid with gold, from his priest, and, with his own hands, presented it with great reverence to Suka. After the son of the island-born Krishna had sat upon it, Janaka worshipped him according to prescribed kriyas.

He first offered him padya to wash his feet, and then gave him the arghya and kine as dakshina. The Muni accepted that worship offered with due kriyas and mantras. That Dvijottama accepted the worship and the cows the king offered and saluted the monarch.

Possessed of great tejas, he asked after Janaka's wellbeing and prosperity. Suka also included in his enquiry the wellbeing of the king's followers and ministers. With Suka's permission, Janaka sat down with all his party.

Of high birth and blessed with a high soul, the king of Mithila, with folded hands, sat down on the bare ground and in turn enquired after the wellbeing and unabated prosperity of Vyasa's son. Janaka then asked his guest about the purpose of his visit.

Suka said, "Be you blessed; my father said to me that his Yajamana, the ruler of the Videhas, known the world over by the name of Janaka, is well-versed in the mukti dharma. He commanded me to come to him promptly, if I ever wanted to dispel any doubts in the matter of the dharma of either Pravritti or Nivritti.

He gave me to understand that the king of Mithila would dispel all my doubts. I have, therefore, come here, at the command of my sire, for the purpose of learning from you. It is fitting for you, O foremost of all righteous ones, to instruct me!

What is the svadharma of a Brahmana, and what is the essence of mukti dharma? How is moksha to be obtained? Can it be acquired through the way of gyana or by tapasya?"

Janaka said, "Hear what the duties are for a Brahmana from the time of his birth. After his upanayana, investiture with the sacred thread, he should devote his attention to the study of the Vedas. By practising tapasya and dutifully serving his guru and observing the dharma of Brahmacharya, O puissant one, he should pay off the debt he owes to the Devas and the Pitris, and cast off all malice. Having studied the Vedas closely, subjugated his senses, and paying his guru dakshina, he should, with his guru's permission return home.

Returning home, he should adopt the grihasta way of life by marrying a woman and confining himself to her, and by freeing himself from every kind of evil, and establishing his grihapatya, his domestic fire. In this asrama, he should procreate sons and grandsons.

After that, he should retire into the forest, and continue to worship the same fires and receive guests with cordial hospitality. Living righteously in the forest, he should at last establish his fire in his Atman, and freed from all the pairs of opposites, and casting off all attachments from the soul, he should spend his days in sannyasa, otherwise known as the asrama of Brahman."

Suka said, "If one attains to such an understanding, purified by study of the scriptures and of the true conception of all things, and if the heart frees itself permanently from the effects of all pairs of contradictions, is it still necessary for one to adopt the three asramas of brahmacharya, grihasta and vanaprastha in succession? This is what I ask you. It is proper for you to tell me. O ruler of men, tell me this according to the true import of the Vedas!"

Janaka said, "Without a mind cleansed by study of the shastras and without that true conception of all things which is known by the name of vigyana, the attainment of moksha is impossible. That purified understanding, again, it is said, is unattainable without one's connection to a guru.

The guru is the helmsman, and gyana is the boat; both help one to cross samsara, the ocean of the world. After having acquired that boat, one is crowned with success; and having crossed the ocean, one may abandon both.

To prevent the destruction of all the worlds and to prevent the destruction of the karma upon which the worlds depend, the wise practised the dharma of the four asramas as the sages did in ancient days. By gradually abandoning karma, good and bad, agreeably to this order of asramas, over the course of many births, one attains mukti.

That man who, through penances performed during the course of many births, obtains a pure mind and understanding and soul is able to attain mukti in the very first stage of brahmacharya itself in a fresh birth. With a cleansed understanding, he attains mukti; with this knowledge in respect of all visible things, what further desire remains to be satisfied by observing the three other asramas?

One should always discard faults born of the gunas of rajas and tamas. Adhering to the path of sattva, one should know the self by the self. Beholding one's self in all creatures and all creatures in one's self, one should live without attachment like fish who live in water without being drenched by it.

He who succeeds in transcending all pairs of opposites and resisting their influence, succeeds in casting off every attachment, and attains to infinite bliss in the next world, going there like a bird soaring into the sky. In this connection, there is an ancient story narrated by King Yayati and remembered by all who are conversant with the shastras bearing on mukti.

The radiance of the Paramatman exists only in one's Atman, nowhere else. It is found equally in all creatures. One can see it oneself if one's heart is devoted to yoga. When a man lives in such a way that another does not fear his very sight, and when he is not himself frightened at the sight of others; when a man ceases to cherish, desire and hate, he is then said to attain to Brahman.

When a man does not sin against any creature in thought, word and deed, he then attains Brahman. By restraining the mind and the Atman, by discarding malice that darkens the mind, and by abjuring desire and torpor, one is said to reach Brahman.

When he equally respects all objects that he perceives with all his senses, and also all living creatures, and transcends all pairs of opposites, a man is then said to attain Brahman. When he casts an equal eye upon praise and censure, gold and iron, happiness and misery, heat and cold, good and evil, the agreeable and the disagreeable, life and death, he is then said to attain to Brahman.

On observing the practices of the mendicant orders, one should subdue one's senses and withdraw the mind even like a tortoise withdraws its outstretched limbs. A house cloaked in darkness can be seen with the help of a lamp; in the same manner can the Atman be kindled with the lamp of Buddhi, the understanding.

O Mahabuddhi, I see that all this knowledge already dwells in you. Whatever else should be known by one wishing to learn about the mukti dharma, you already know. O Devarishi, I am convinced that through the grace of your guru and his teachings, you have already transcended all the objects of the senses.

O Mahamuni, through your father's blessings, I have attained to omniscience, and hence know you well. Your knowledge is vaster than what you think you own. Your perceptions resulting from intuition are much greater than what you think you own. Your powers are mightier than what you are aware of.

Whether as a consequence of your tender age, or of the doubts you have been unable to dispel, or of the fear that is due to not having attained mukti, you are not conscious of that knowledge founded in intuition although it has arisen in your mind. After your doubts have been dispelled by those like me, you succeed in loosening the knots that bind your heart and then, by a righteous exertion, attain and become conscious of that gyana.

You have already acquired gyana. Your mind is calm and steady. You are free from greed and covetousness. For all that, O Brahmana, without effort you will not attain the Brahman, which is the highest acquisition.

You see no distinction between happiness and sorrow. You are not covetous. You have no longing for dance and song. You have no attachments. You have no attachment to friends. You have no fear of things that inspire fear. O blessed one, I see that you cast an equal eye upon a lump of gold and a clod of earth.

We, I and others possessed of wisdom, see you well set on the highest and indestructible path of tranquillity. You are true to the dharma which allows the Brahmana to obtain that fruit which should be his, which is identical with the essence of mukti. What else do you want to ask me?"'

CANTO 328

"Bhishma says, 'Having heard these words of King Janaka, Suka of cleansed soul and settled conclusions began to stay in his Soul with his Soul, having of course seen the self with his self. Having achieved his objective, he became happy and serene, and without questioning Janaka further, he flew northwards to the mountains of Himavat with the speed of the wind.

These mountains abounded with diverse tribes of Apsaras and echoed with exalted sounds. Teeming with thousands of Kinnaras and Bhringarajas, it was adorned, besides, with many Madgus and Khanjaritas, and many Jivajivakas of varied colours.

And there were many peacocks also of wonderful hues, uttering their shrill cries. Many flocks of swans, and many flights of joyful kokilas too, adorned the place. Garuda, the prince of birds, dwelt constantly on that peak.

The four Lokapalas, the Devas and diverse classes of Rishis always came there from the desire to do good to the world. It was there that the high-souled Vishnu had undergone the severest austerities to have a son.

It was there that the divine Senapati Kumara, in his younger days, disregarded the three worlds with all its inhabitants, hurled his spear and pierced the earth with it. As he hurled it, Skanda challenged the universe, crying, "If there is anyone mightier than me, or who holds Brahmanas dearer, or who can compare with me in devotion to the

Brahmanas and the Vedas, or has tejas like mine, let him draw up this spear or at least shake it!"

Hearing this challenge, the three lokas become anxious, and all creatures asked one another, "Who will draw out this lance?" Vishnu saw that all the Devas and Asuras and Rakshasas were distraught. He reflected upon what best could be done. Unable to bear that challenge of the spear, he cast his eyes on Skanda, the son of Agni.

With his left hand, Vishnu seized that blazing spear and began to shake it. Shaken by the awesome power of Vishnu, the whole earth with her mountains, forests, and seas, shuddered along with the spear. Although Vishnu was fully able to pull it out, he contented himself with shaking it. In this, the puissant Narayana kept the honour of Skanda intact.

Having shaken it himself, the divine Vishnu addressed Prahlada, saying, "Behold the might of Kumara. None else in the universe can move this lance!"

Unable to bear this, Prahlada resolved to pull out the spear. He seized it, but was unable to Hiranyakasipu plunged down onto the earth.

Taking himself to the northern side of those grand mountains, Mahadeva, the bull his emblem, had performed the austerest tapasya. The asrama where Siva had undergone those austerities is encircled on all sides with a blazing fire.

Only men of pure souls can approach that mountain known by the name of Aditya. There was a fiery girdle all around it, of the width of ten yojanas, and it cannot be approached by Yakshas and Rakshasas and Danavas.

The illustrious and tejas-filled Agni lived there and was engaged in removing all obstacles from the side of Mahadeva of fathomless wisdom who remained there for a thousand celestial years, all the while standing on one foot. Dwelling on the side of Himavat, Mahadeva Mahavrata scorched the Devas in their heavens with his fiery tapasya.

At the foot of those mountains, in a quiet and secluded place, Parasara's son, Mahamuni Vyasa, taught the Vedas to his sishyas. Those disciples were the highly blessed Sumantra, Vaisampayana, Jaimini of great wisdom, and Tapodhana Paila. Suka went forth to that delightful asrama where his father, the great Muni Vyasa, lived with his sishyas.

Seated here, Vyasa watched his son advance like a radiant fire scattering flames, resembling the sun himself. As Suka approached, he appeared not to touch the trees or the rocks of the mountain. Completely dissociated from all objects of the senses, engaged in yoga, the Mahatman Rishi came swiftly, even like an arrow loosed from a bow.

Born from the aranis, Suka drew near his sire and touched his feet. With due reverence he then approached his father's disciples. Joyfully, he narrated all the particulars of his conversation with King Janaka.

Vyasa, the son of Parasara, after the arrival of his great son, continued to dwell on Himavat engaged in teaching his disciples and his son. One day he was seated at his ease, and his sishyas, all proficient in the Vedas, with subdued senses, and with tranquil souls, sat around him. All of them had thoroughly mastered the Vedas with their angas. All were observant of penances. With folded hands they addressed their guru with the following words:

"Through your grace, we have been blessed with great tejas. Our fame also has spread. There is one boon that we humbly beg you to grant us."

Hearing these words, the regenerate Rishi answered them, saying, "Sons, tell me what is the boon you wish me to grant you?"

Hearing this reply from their preceptor, the disciples were filled with joy. Once more bowing their heads low before their guru and joining their hands, Rajan, in one voice all of them spoke these excellent words:

"If our guru is pleased with us, then, O best of sages, we are sure to be crowned with success! We all ask you, Maharishi, to grant us a boon. Be you graceful to us. Let no sixth sishya, besides us five, become famed. We are four. Our guru's son is the fifth. Let the Vedas shine forth in only us five. This is the boon that we seek."

Hearing them, Vyasa, the son of Parasara, of great intelligence, deeply learned in the meaning of the Vedas, having a righteous soul, and always engaged in thoughts that confer benefits on a man in the next world, spoke these virtuous words to his sishyas:

"The Vedas should always be given unto him who is a Brahmana, or unto him who desires to listen to Vedic teachings, and by him who eagerly wishes to dwell in the world of Brahma. Go forth and multiply. Let the Vedas spread through your exertions.

The Vedas should never be imparted to one who has not formally become a disciple. Nor should they be given to one who does not observe pure vratas. Nor should they be bestowed on one of impure soul.

These are the attributes of those who can be accepted as sishyas for the communication of Veda gyana. No knowledge should be imparted to one without a proper scrutiny of his character; just as pure gold is tested by heat, cutting and rubbing, so also should disciples be tested by their birth and accomplishments.

You should never set them tasks beyond their abilities, or tasks that are fraught with danger. One's knowledge is always commensurate with one's understanding and diligence. Let all sishyas overcome all obstacles, and let all of them meet with auspicious success.

You are competent to teach the shastras to persons of all the varnas. While teaching you must address a Brahmana, putting him first. These are the laws that govern the study of the Vedas; and this is regarded as a noble task.

The Vedas were created by the Self-born to praise the Devas. That man who, through the clouding of his mind, speaks ill of a Brahmana who knows the Vedas, is certain to face humiliation.

He who disobeys all the laws while seeking knowledge, and he who disregards dharma while imparting knowledge both fall from grace; instead of the devotion which should prevail between guru and sishya, such questioning and such instruction are certain to create distrust and suspicion.

I have now told you everything about the way in which the Vedas must be studied and taught. You must bear this instruction in mind while dealing with and teaching your sishyas.'"

CANTO 329

"Bhishma says, 'Hearing these words of their guru, Vyasa's tejasvin sishyas were filled with joy and embraced one another. Addressing one another, they said, "We will always remember what our illustrious teacher has said for our future good, and we shall do as he has said."

Having said this to one another with joyful hearts, the disciples of Vyasa, who were thorough masters of words, once more addressed him, "Mahamuni, if it pleases you, we wish to go down from this mountain into the world to undertake the task of dividing the Vedas!"

The mighty son of Parasara replied to them in words suffused with dharma and artha. "You may go to Bhumi or to Swargaloka, as you please. You should always be attentive, for the Vedas are such that they are always liable to be misunderstood."

Granted permission by their guru of truthful speech, the sishyas left him after circling around him in pradakshina and bowing their heads before him. Descending to the earth they performed the Agnishtoma and other yagnas; and they began to officiate at the sacrifices of Brahmanas and Kshatriyas and Vaisyas. Happily passing their days in the grihastasrama, they were revered by the Brahmanas. Famed and prosperous, they were employed in teaching the Veda and performing yagnas.

After his disciples had departed, Vyasa remained in his asrama with only his son in his company. The Rishi passed his days in anxious thoughtfulness and silence, sitting in a secluded corner of the hermitage. At that time Mahamuni Narada of great punya came there to see Vyasa, and spoke to him in mellifluous words.

Narada said, "O regenerate Rishi of Vasishta's vamsa, why have the Vedic mantras fallen silent? Why are you sitting quiet and alone, in meditation like one engrossed in some thought? Alas, shorn of Vedic echoes, this mountain has lost its beauty, like the moon shorn of splendour when assailed by Rahu or enveloped in a cloud.

Without the Vedas being heard, though inhabited by the Devarishis, the mountain no longer looks wondrous but resembles a village of Nishadas. The Rishis, the Devas and the Gandharvas, too, no longer shine forth as before, for they are without the Veda nadam!"

Hearing these words of Narada, the island-born Vyasa answered, "O Devarishi, you know all the declarations of the Vedas; I agree with all that you have said and it is right for you to say this to me. Omniscient one you have seen everything.

Your knowledge also embraces all things within its sphere. All that has ever occurred in the three worlds is known to you. O great Narada, command me. Tell me what I what should I do now. Separated from my sishyas, my mind has become despondent."

Narada said, "If the recitation of Vedas is suspended they are tainted. The Brahmanas are tainted by the non-observance of their vratas. The Balhika vamsa is the stain of the earth. Curiosity renders women impure. Recite the Vedas along with your most intelligent son, and drive out the terrors arising from Rakshasas with the echoes of their mantras.'"

Bhishma continues, 'Vyasa, the foremost of all who understand dharma and who are devoted to Vedic recitation, was filled with joy and said to Narada, "So be it." With his son Suka, he began to chant the Vedas in a loud sonorous voice, observing all the laws of orthoepy, correct pronunciation, and filling the three worlds with that sacred sound.

One day, as father and son, both conversant with all dharma, were engaged in chanting the Vedas, a violent wind arose that seemed to be driven by the storms that blow on the ocean's breast. Knowing that the hour was inauspicious, Vyasa immediately told Suka to stop chanting.

Suka was filled with curiosity. He asked his sire, "O Dvija, where does this wind come from? Tell me everything about what this wind is and means."

Vyasa heard Suka's question and was full of amazement at what had happened. He answered Suka telling him that such an omen indicated that the chanting of the Vedas should be stopped.

"You have attained spiritual vision. Your mind has of itself been cleansed of every impurity. You have been freed from the gunas of rajas and tamas. You now dwell in sattva. You now behold your Soul with your soul, even as one gazes at one's own reflection in a mirror. Establishing yourself in your own Atman, do you contemplate the Vedas.

The path of the Paramatman is called Devayana, the path of the gods. The path composed of tamas is called Pitriyana, the path of manes. These are the two paths in the next world. By one, men go to swarga. By the other, they go to naraka.

The winds blow over the earth's surface and in the sky. They blow in seven courses. Listen to me as I recount them one after another. The body is furnished with the senses which are controlled by the Sadhyas and many great beings of immeasurable power. These gave birth to an invincible son named Samana.

From Samana sprang a son called Udana. From Udana sprang Vyana, who gave rise to Apana; and lastly from Apana sprung the wind called Prana. That invincible scorcher of all enemies, Prana, remained childless.

I will now tell you about the different functions of those winds. Prana is the cause of the diverse functions of all living creatures, and because they live by it, it is called Prana, life.

The first wind is known by the name of Pravaha—Samana which blows along the first masses of clouds born of smoke and heat. Coursing through the sky, and coming into contact with the water contained in clouds, that wind reveals itself in effulgence among the flashes of lightning.

The second wind called Avaha blows deafeningly. This wind causes

Soma and the other luminaries to rise and appear. Within the body, which is a microcosm of the universe, that wind is called Udana by the wise.

The third wind, known as Udvaha, sucks up water from the four oceans, and conveys it to the clouds in the sky; and, having done this, offers them up to Indra, the god of rain.

The wind called Samvaha supports the clouds and divides them into many parts, turns them into vapour in order to pour down rain and once more makes them liquid; it is the roar of the thunderheads, which exist for the preservation and nurture of the world. The wind Samvaha bears the chariots of all celestial beings along the sky. The fourth in the enumeration, it is strong, with the power to destroy the very mountains.

The fifth wind is swift and forceful. It is dry and uproots and smashes down all trees. The clouds beside it are known by the name Balahaka. That wind causes diverse kinds of natural calamities, and roars deafeningly in the firmament. It is known by the name Vivaha.

The sixth wind bears the celestial waters through the skies and prevents them from falling down. That wind blows and supports the sacred waters of the Akasa Ganga, preventing them from falling down.

Obstructed by that wind from a distance, the sun, the source of a thousand rays, and which illumines the world, appears as a luminary of but one ray. Through the action of that wind, the moon, after waning, waxes again till he displays a full disc. Best of Rishis, that wind is known by the name Parivaha.

Stealing the life of all living creatures when the proper hour comes, its path is followed by Surya's son Yama; this wind is the source of that immortality attained by yogins of subtle vision who are always engaged in yoga dhyana.

This wind, Parivaha, in ancient times, helped the thousands of grandsons of Daksha Prajapati, by his ten sons, to attain to the ends of the universe. The touch of that wind Parivaha enables one to attain mukti by freeing oneself from the obligation to return to the world of samsara. No one can resist this foremost of all winds.

Marvellous are these winds, all sons of Diti. They can go everywhere and support all things, and they blow all around you without being attached to you at any time.

It is truly wonderful that this foremost of mountains should thus be suddenly shaken by this wind that now blows here. This wind is the breath of Vishnu's nostrils. When driven swiftly forward, it begins to blow with such great force that it agitates the whole universe.

When the wind begins to blow violently, persons who know the Vedas do not chant their mantras. The Vedas are a form of wind. If forcefully uttered at the wrong time, the outer wind is tortured."

Having said these words, and once the wind had ceased, the mighty son of Parasara bade his son to recommence his Vedic chanting. He then left that place to bathe in the waters of the celestial Ganga.'"

CANTO 330

"Bhishma says, 'After Vyasa had left the place, Narada, traversing the sky, came there and saw Suka studying the shastras. The Devarishi had come to ask Suka about the meaning of certain sections of the Vedas. Seeing the Devarishi Narada in his hermitage, Suka revered him by offering him the arghya according to Vedic rites.

Gratified with the honours bestowed upon him, Narada addressed Suka, saying, "Righteous one, tell me, how can I bring about what is for your highest good?"

Hearing Narada's words, Suka said to him, "Instruct me in that which may benefit me."

Narada said, "In ancient times, the illustrious Sanatkumara spoke these words to certain pure-souled Rishis who had approached him seeking the truth: 'There is no eye like that of gyana. There is no penance like sannyasa.

Abstaining from evil acts, steady practice of dharma, sadachara, good conduct, the correct observance of all religious duties, these constitute the highest good. Having obtained the condition of humanity, full of sorrow, he that becomes attached to it, is bewildered; such a man never succeeds in emancipating himself from grief.

A man's intellect becomes increasingly enmeshed in the net of stupor when he is attached to worldly things. Such a man becomes sorrowful, both in this world and the next.

One should, by every means in one's power, restrain both desire and wrath if one seeks to achieve what is for one's good. Desire and anger arise for only destroying one's wellbeing.

One should always protect one's tapasya from wrath, and one's prosperity from pride. One should always protect one's knowledge from honour and dishonour, and one's Atman from error.

Compassion is the highest virtue. Forgiveness is the highest power. The knowledge of the Atman is the highest knowledge. There is nothing higher than truth. It is always fitting to speak the truth. It is better again to speak what is beneficial than to speak what is true. I hold that to be truth which most benefits all creatures.

That man is said to be truly learned and wise who abandons every deed, who never indulges in hope, who is completely dissociated from all worldly surroundings, and who has renounced everything that pertains to the world.

He who, without attachment, enjoys all sensual desires with the help of restrained senses, who has a serene soul, who is never moved by joy of sorrow, who is engaged in yogadhyana, who lives in the company of the Devas controlling his senses, yet detached from them, and who, though having a body, never identifies himself with it, becomes emancipated and attains to the highest good.

O Muni, one who never sees others, never touches others, and never talks with others, soon achieves that highest good. One must not injure any creature. On the other hand, one must be friendly towards all. Having obtained the human condition, one should never behave inimically towards any being.

A complete disregard for all worldly things, perfect contentment, abandonment of all kinds of hope, and patience: these constitute the highest good of a man who has subdued his senses and acquired a knowledge of the self. Casting off all attachments, you must subjugate all your senses, and so attain felicity both here and in the next world.

They that are free from greed never have to suffer any sorrow. One should discard all covetousness from one's soul. By casting off greed, O amiable and blessed one, you will be able to free yourself from sorrow and pain.

One who wishes to conquer that which is unconquerable should live in tapasya, self-restraint, silence and a subjugation of the Atman. Such a man should live amidst attachments without being attached to them.

That Brahmana who lives in the midst of attachments without being attached to them and who always lives in seclusion, soon attains to the highest bliss. That man who lives in happiness by himself, surrounded by many creatures who delight in leading lives of sexual union, is one whose thirst has been slaked by knowledge. It is well known that he whose thirst has been slaked by knowledge never experiences grief.

One attains the status of the Devas through good karma and to the condition of Manavas through karma good and bad. By evil actions, one helplessly falls down among the lower animals. Always assailed by sorrow and decay and death, a living creature is being cooked in this world in the cauldron of time. Do you not know this?

You frequently regard that to be beneficial which is really harmful; that to be certain which is really uncertain; and that to be desirable and good which is undesirable and evil. Alas, why do you not awaken to a correct understanding of these?

Like a silkworm that ensconces itself in its own cocoon, you have wrapped yourself in a cocoon made of your own countless acts born of stupor and error. Alas, why do you not awaken to a clear awareness of your real state?

You have no need to attach yourself to worldly things. Attachment to worldly objects gives rise to evil. The silk-worm that weaves a cocoon round itself is finally destroyed by its own action. Those who become attached to sons and spouses and relatives meet with destruction in the end, even as wild elephants who sink into the mire of a lake are gradually weakened until they die.

Behold, all creatures that allow themselves to be enmeshed by love suffer great anguish just as fish do on land, dragged there by cruel nets. Relatives, sons, wives, the body itself, and all one's possessions stored with care, are insignificant and useless in the next world. Only one's good and evil karma follow one to the other world.

When it is certain that you will have to go helplessly to the other world, leaving behind all these things, why are you attached to such inconsequential and worthless objects, paying no attention to that which constitutes your real and lasting wealth?

The path you must travel is without any resting place. Along that way, there is no support one can use. The land through which it passes is unknown and undiscovered. It is cloaked in thick darkness.

Alas, how will you pass along that way without equipping yourself with the necessary means? When you go along that road, nobody will follow you. Only your deeds, good and bad, will follow when you leave this world for the next.

One seeks that foremost of goals by learning, actions, internal and external purity, and great knowledge. When that is attained, one is freed from rebirth.

The desire that one feels for living amidst human habitations is like a binding cord. The virtuous succeed in severing that bond and freeing themselves. Only the sinful do not succeed in breaking these ties.

Samsara, the ocean of life, is terrifying. Personal beauty of form, rupa, constitutes its banks. The mind is the speed of its current. Sparsa, touch, forms its island. Rasa, taste, constitutes its current. Gandha, scent, is its mire. Sabda, sound is its waters. That particular part of it which leads towards swarga is beset with great difficulties.

The body is the boat by which one must cross samsara. Forgiveness is the oar by which it is rowed. Truth is the ballast to steady that boat. The practice of dharma, righteousness, is the rope that must be attached to the mast to draw that boat along dangerous waters.

Dana is the wind that lifts the sails of that boat. It is with that swift boat that one must cross samsara. Shed both virtue and vice, truth and falsehood. Having cast off truth and falsehood, discard the means by which these are to be cast off.

By casting off all purpose, cast off virtue; by casting off all desire cast off sin also. Using the help of Buddhi, discard truth and falsehood; and, finally, by knowledge of the highest subject, the Paramatman, dispense with intelligence itself.

Cast off this body. It has bones for its pillars, sinews for its binding cords, flesh and blood for its outer plaster, and the skin for its outermost casing. It is full of urine and faeces and emits a stench.

Exposed to the assaults of decrepitude and sorrow, it is the seat of disease and is weakened by pain. With the attribute of rajas in predominance, it is neither permanent nor durable, serving only as the temporary abode for the creature it houses.

This entire universe of matter, and that which is called Mahat or Buddhi, are made up of the five Mahabhutas. That which is called Mahat is due to the action of the Paramatman.

The five senses, the three gunas of tamas, rajas and sattva, together with those which have been mentioned before, constitute a tale of seventeen. These seventeen, known as the unmanifest, with the manifest, that is the five objects of the five senses, rupa, rasa, sabda, sparsa and gandha, along with Chit and Buddhi, form the well-known account of the twenty-four principles.

When one possesses these twenty-four tattvas, one comes to be called Jiva or human. He who knows the aggregate of three, dharma, artha and kama, as also happiness and sorrow, life and death, truly, and in all their details, is said to know growth, decay and destruction.

The objects of knowledge should be known gradually, one after another. All objects that are grasped by the senses are called Vyakta, manifest. Those that transcend the senses and are known only by their indications are said to be Avyakta, unmanifest.

By restraining the senses, one wins great gratification, even like a thirsty and parched traveller at a torrent of rain. Having subdued the senses one beholds one's soul expand to embrace all objects within itself. Having its roots in gyana, the power of the man who beholds Narayana in his own self, who sees all creatures in all conditions in his own soul, is never lost.

He who uses knowledge to transcend all kinds of pain born of error and stupor is never touched by evil when he comes into contact with other creatures. Such a man, his understanding being fully displayed, never finds fault with the course of conduct that prevails in the world.

One conversant with mukti says that the Paramatman is without beginning and without end; that it takes birth as all creatures; that it resides as a witness in the Jivatman; that it is inactive, and without form. Only he who encounters pain as a consequence of his own misdeeds, slays many beings to ward off that pain.

As a result of such sacrifices, the actors have to attain rebirths and have necessarily to perform countless actions. Such a man, blinded by error, regards what is in fact a source of grief to be bliss and is always unhappy even like a sick man who eats food that is unfitting. Such a man is pressed and crushed by his actions like a substance that is churned and pounded.

Bound by his karma, he is reborn, the order of his life being determined by the nature of his acts. Suffering many kinds of torture, he travels in a repeated round of rebirths even like a wheel that turns ceaselessly. You, on the other hand, have cut through all your bonds.

You abstain from all karma! Omniscient and the master of all things, achieve success and be liberated from all existent objects. In earlier times, through control of their senses and the power of their tapasya, many have destroyed the bonds of karma and attained uninterrupted felicity.'"

"Bhishma says, 'Narada said, "By listening to the blessed shastras that bring about peace, dispel grief, and produce happiness, one attains a pure understanding, and having attained it obtains high felicity.

A thousand causes of sorrow, a hundred causes of fear, from day to day, afflict one that is bereft of Buddhi, but not one that is wise and learned. Listen, therefore to these ancient narratives as I recite them to you, in order to ease your sorrows. If one can conquer one's understanding, one is sure to attain happiness.

By associating with the undesirable and dissociating from what is agreeable, only foolish men are subject to mental anguish of every kind. One should not grieve over things past, thinking of their merits. He who thinks of the past with attachment can never emancipate himself.

One should always try to discover the faults in things one has become attached to. One must regard such things as fraught with much evil. By doing so, one can be freed from them.

The man who laments for what is past fails to acquire either wealth or fame or punya. That which no longer exists cannot be obtained. When such things pass away, they do not return, however keenly one may regret their passing.

Creatures sometimes acquire and sometimes lose worldly objects. No man in this world can mourn all that happens to him. Dead or lost, he who grieves for what is past, becomes unhappy. Instead of just one sorrow, he experiences two.

With the help of their intelligence, those men see clearly who do not weep when they behold the course of life and death in the world. They never have to shed tears at anything that takes place. When any such calamity, causing either physical or mental pain, which cannot be warded off by the best of efforts, occurs, one should stop reflecting on it with sorrowful regret.

Not to think about it, this is the medicine for sorrow. By thinking of it, one can never dispel it; on the other hand, by brooding on sorrow, one only increases it. Mental agony should be destroyed by wisdom; physical pain should be dispelled by medicines. This is the power of knowledge, gyana.

In such matters, one should not behave like men of little understanding. Youth, beauty, life, treasures, health and association with loved ones: all these are fleeting. One who is wise should never covet them.

One should not lament individually for a painful occurrence that concerns an entire community. Instead of indulging in grief, once stricken by it, one should seek to avert it and apply a remedy as soon as one sees the opportunity for doing so.

There is no doubt that in this life the measure of misery is far greater than that of joy. There is no doubt that all men show attachment for objects of the senses and that death is regarded as disagreeable.

The man who discards both joy and sorrow, is said to attain Brahman. When such a man leaves this world, sage men never grieve.

In spending wealth there is pain. In protecting it there is pain. In acquiring it there is pain. Hence, when one's riches are destroyed, one should not be sad.

Men of little understanding attain many levels of prosperity but fail to achieve contentment, and at last perish in misery. Men of wisdom, however, are always content. All are destined to end in dissolution.

All things that are high are fated to fall down and become low. Union is sure to end in disunion, and life is certain to end in death. Thirst is unquenchable. Contentment is the highest happiness. Hence, the wise regard contentment to be the most precious wealth.

One's allotted lifespan runs continually. It does not stop in its course for even a single moment. When one's body itself is not eternal, what other thing in this world can be considered so? Those who reflect on the nature of all creatures and conclude that it is beyond the mind's grasp, turn their attention to the highest path, and, when they advance on it, do not have to feel sorrow.

Like a tiger who seizes and flees with its prey, death seizes and makes off with the man who is engaged in unprofitable occupations and is unsatisfied with objects of desire and pleasure.

One should always seek to free oneself from sorrow. One should seek to dispel sorrow by acting joyfully, without indulging in grief, and having freed oneself from a particular sorrow, should act in such a manner as to ward off sadness by abstaining from all faults of conduct.

After enjoying sabda, sparsa, rupa, gandha and rasa, the rich and the poor alike find that these are hollow and futile. Before union with these, creatures are never subject to sorrow. One who is steadfast in one's original nature is never saddened when that union is ended.

One should control one's stomach and sexual appetite patiently. One should protect one's hands and feet with the help of the eye. One's eyes and ears and other senses should be protected by the mind. One's mind and speech should be governed by wisdom.

Casting off love and affection for those who are known and those unknown, one should conduct oneself with humility. Such a man is said to possess wisdom, and such a one surely finds bliss.

He who is pleased with his own Atman, devoted to yoga, who depends upon nothing beyond the self, who is without greed, and who conducts himself without depending on anything but his self, succeeds in attaining felicity.'"

CANTO 332

"**B**hishma says, 'Narada said, "When the vicissitudes of happiness and sorrow appear or disappear, these transitions cannot be avoided by either wisdom, policy or effort. Without allowing oneself to fall away from one's true nature, one should strive to protect one's own self.

He who takes such care and exertion, never perishes. Regarding the self greatly, one should always seek to rescue oneself from disease, decay, and death.

Mental and physical diseases afflict the body, like keen-pointed shafts shot from the bow by a mighty archer. The body of a man tormented by thirst, tortured by agony, perfectly helpless, and who wants to prolong his life, is dragged towards destruction.

Days and nights course ceaselessly, bearing away on their current the lives of all men. Like gushing rivers, these flow eternally without ever turning back.

The unending succession of the light and dark fortnights wastes away all mortals without ceasing for even a moment. Rising and setting, day after day, the sun, who is himself undecaying, continually stirs the joys and sorrows of all men in the cooking pot of time. The nights pass, taking with them all the unexpected good and bad that overtake man, that depend on karma and fate.

If the fruits of man's actions were not dependent on external circumstances, he would obtain everything he desires. Even men who are clever, intelligent, of restrained senses, if they do not act, they never succeed in earning any fruits.

Others, lacking in intelligence, without talents or accomplishments of any kind, and who are truly the lowest of men, even when they do not long for success, are seen to be crowned with the fruits of all their desires.

He who is always ready to injure all creatures, and who is engaged in deceiving all the world, is seen to bathe in happiness. One who sits idly obtains great prosperity, while another, exerting himself earnestly, is seen to miss desirable fruits that are almost within his reach.

Would you ascribe this to be one of the faults of man? The vital seed, originating in one's nature, with mere looking, passes from one to another. When placed in the womb, it sometimes produces an embryo and sometimes fails. When sexual union fails, it resembles a mango tree that puts forth a great many flowers without, however, producing a single fruit.

Often, one who desires progeny and who strives vigorously to achieve their objective by worshipping many Devas, fails to procreate. Another, fearing the birth of a child as one fears a poisonous snake, finds a long-lived son born unto him, seeming to be his own self come back to the stages through which he has himself passed.

Despondent men who ardently long for offspring, and at last beget children born after ten long months, after countless yagnas to many Devas and undergoing severe austerities, find them to be veritable wretches of their race. Others are blessed by progeny, obtained with the same blessed karmas and kriyas, who instantly inherit wealth and grain and other sources of enjoyment earned and stored by their sires.

In an act of sexual union between two persons of opposite sexes, the embryo is born in the womb, like a calamity afflicting the mother. Very soon after the suspension of the vital breaths, other physical forms possess that embodied creature whose gross body has been destroyed but whose deeds have all been performed with that gross body made of flesh and blood.

Upon the dissolution of the body, another body, just as destructible as the one that is destroyed, is ready for the burnt creature to migrate into even as one boat transfers its passengers into another. As a result of sexual union, a drop of the vital seed, which is inanimate, is placed in the womb.

I ask you, through whose or what care is the embryo kept alive? That part of the body into which the food that is eaten goes and where it is digested, is the place where the embryo resides, but it is not digested there. The fertilised egg does not reside in that part of the body where the food eaten is digested. It is in the womb, enveloped in urine and faeces, one's sojourn is regulated by nature.

In the matter of where it lives and from where it escapes, the born creature is not a free agent. He is perfectly helpless in these. Some foetuses fall from the womb prematurely, as yet undeveloped. Some come out alive and continue to live. As regards some, after being quickened with life, they are destroyed while still in the womb in consequence of some other bodies being ready for them because of their past karma.

A man inserts the semen in an act of sexual union, and obtains from it a son or daughter. The offspring thus gained, when the time comes, performs a similar act. When a man's allotted life span draws to a close, the five primal elements of his body attain to the seventh and the ninth stages and then cease to be. The man himself does not change.

Without doubt, when afflicted by diseases, as small animals assailed by hunters, men lose their powers of standing and moving. Even if such men want to spend vast wealth, the best efforts of physicians cannot alleviate their pain. This occurs even when skilled and knowledgeable doctors, equipped with excellent medicines, are themselves afflicted by disease like hunted animals.

Even if men drink many astringents and all kinds of medicated ghee, they are broken by age and disease like trees by mighty tuskers. When animals and birds and beasts of prey and poor men are ailing, who treats them with medicines? Indeed, they are not even regarded as being ill. Like larger animals attacking smaller ones, sicknesses afflict even fierce kings with inexorable prowess and ferocity. All men, unable to even utter cries of pain, and overwhelmed by grief, are seen to be borne away along the powerful current into which they have been flung. Embodied creatures, even when seeking to vanquish nature, are unable to conquer it, despite using wealth, sovereign power, or the most austere penances.

If all attempts men make were crowned with success, then they would never be subject to decay, would never experience anything disagreeable, and would be crowned with success in all their desires.

All wish to attain ultimate superiority of position. To gratify this, they strive to their utmost. The result, however, does not fulfil their desires. Even men that are perfectly attentive and honest, brave and powerful, are seen to look up to men intoxicated with the arrogance of wealth and wine.

There are those whose calamities disappear before even these are marked or noticed by them. There are others who have no riches and yet are free from all miseries. A great disparity may be observed with respect to the fruits of karma. Some are seen to bear chariots on their shoulders, while some are seen to ride them.

All men desire wealth and prosperity. Only a few have chariots and elephants and horses in their processions. Some do not have a single spouse when their first-wedded ones are dead; while others have hundreds to call their own.

Misery and happiness exist side by side. Men have either one or the other. Behold, this is a subject of wonder. Do not be bewildered at such a sight.

Cast off both dharma and adharma. Cast off also truth and falsehood. Having discarded both, then cast off that which helps you to cast them off! O best of Rishis, I have now told you about that which brings great unhappiness. With these instructions, the Devas, once all human beings, succeeded in leaving the earth and became the inhabitants of swarga."

Hearing these words of Narada, the wise and serene Suka reflected upon the teachings he received, but could not arrive at any certainty of conclusion. He understood that one suffers great misery because of children and spouses, and that one has to take great pains to acquire scientific and Vedic knowledge.

He, therefore, asked himself, "What is that situation which is eternal and which is free from misery of every kind but in which there are great riches?" Reflecting for a moment upon the path ordained for him, Suka, who was well acquainted with the beginning and the end of all duties, resolved to attain to the highest end that is fraught with the greatest felicity.

He questioned himself, saying, "How shall I break free from all attachments, and become perfectly free and attain that excellent goal? How, indeed, shall I reach that from which there is no return to samsara, the ocean of diverse kinds of birth?

I desire that condition of existence from which there is no return. Casting off all kinds of attachments, with the help of the mind, I will attain that goal after reflection and arriving at certainty. I shall reach that realm in which my Atman will be at peace, and I will be able to dwell for eternity without being subject to decay or change.

It is, however, certain that this end cannot be attained without yoga. He who reaches the state of perfect knowledge and enlightenment does not experience attachments through base deeds.

I shall, therefore, have recourse to yoga, and casting off this body which is my present home, I will transform myself into wind and enter the sun, that mass of effulgence. When the Jivatman enters the sun's radiance, he no longer suffers like Soma who, with the gods, upon the exhaustion of merit, falls down on the earth and having once more acquired sufficient merit returns to heaven.

The moon is always seen to wane and then wax. Seeing this waning and waxing that continue repeatedly, I do not wish for a form of existence in which there are such changes. The sun heats up all the world with his fiery rays. His disc never diminishes. Remaining unchanged, he saps the energy from all things. Hence, I desire to immerse myself into the blazing sun. Having discarded my body in the solar realms, I shall live there, invincible, my inner soul freed from all fear. With the great Rishis I shall enter the unbearable energy of the sun.

I declare unto all creatures, to these trees, these elephants, these mountains, the earth herself, the cardinal points of the horizon, the sky, the Devas, the Danavas, the Gandharvas, the Pisachas, the Uragas and the Rakshasas, that I shall enter into all creatures in the world. Let all the Devas along with the Rishis behold the prowess of my yoga today!"

With these words, Suka made his intentions clear to the illustrious Narada. Obtaining his permission, Suka then went to his father's dwelling. Arriving in the presence of the Mahamuni, the high-souled and island-born Krishna, Suka circled round him and enquired after his wellbeing.

Hearing of Suka's intention, the Maharishi was greatly pleased. Addressing him, Vyasa said, "O son, beloved son, do stay a while here so that I may look upon you and gratify my eyes."

Suka, however, did not heed that request. Freed from attachment and all doubt, he began to think only of mukti, and focused himself on the journey ahead. He left his father and walked to the majestic breast of Kailasa inhabited by thousands of enlightened ascetics.'"

CANTO 333

"Bhishma says, 'Having ascended the peak of the mountain, O Bhaarata, the son of Vyasa sat down upon an even grassless place and retired from the dwellings of other creatures. In accordance with the shastras and the laws laid down, the ascetic, conversant with the sequence of the successive processes of yoga, held his soul first in one place and then in another, starting with his feet and proceeding upwards through all the limbs.

Soon after the sun rose, Suka sat humbly, with his face turned eastwards, in a yogic posture, hands and feet drawn in. Where he sat, prepared for yoga, there were no flocks of birds, no sound, and no sight that was repulsive or terrifying. He beheld his own Atman freed from all attachments. Beholding that highest of all things, he laughed joyfully.

He readied himself for yoga to attain to emancipation. Becoming a great master of yoga, he transcended the element of space. He then circled around Narada, the Devarishi, in pradakshina and told him about his intentions to address himself to the highest yoga.

Suka said, "I have succeeded in beholding the path of mukti, and I have addressed myself to it. O you, blessed with the wealth of tapasya. Splendid one, through your grace, I will attain to the highest goal!"'

Bhishma says, 'Having received the permission of Narada, Suka the son of the island-born Vyasa saluted the divine Rishi and once more set himself to yoga and entered Akasa. He ascended from Kailasa and soared into the sky.

Identifying himself with Vayu, the blessed Suka of unchanging ends flew across the sky. All creatures watched him as he traversed the skies shining with the radiance of Garuda at the speed of the wind or thought itself.

Filled with the splendour of fire and the sun, Suka regarded the three worlds in their entirety as one homogenous Brahman, and travelled along that long path. Indeed, all creatures mobile and immobile cast their eyes upon him as he advanced with concentrated attention, and a tranquil, fearless soul. In accordance with the laws and their powers, all worshipped him with reverence.

The inhabitants of swarga rained showers of celestial flowers over him. On seeing him, all the tribes of Apsaras and Gandharvas were filled with wonder. The enlightened Rishis were equally amazed. And they asked themselves, "Who is this one that has attained to success by his tapasya? With his gaze withdrawn from his own body but turned upwards, he fills us all with joy with his glances!"

Of righteous soul and celebrated throughout the three worlds, Suka walked in silence, his face turned towards the east and his gaze directed towards the sun. As he went, he seemed to fill the entire sky with an all-pervading sound.

As they watched him approach, all the Apsaras were filled with awe and amazement. Led by Panchachuda and others, they looked at Suka with eyes wide with wonder. And they asked one another, "What deity is this one that has attained to such a high end? Without doubt, he comes here, freed from all attachments from all desires!"

Suka then went to the Malaya Mountains where Urvasi and Purvachitti dwelt. Both of them were awestruck as they beheld his tejas.

And they said, "How wondrous is the fixed attention to yoga of a Brahmana youth who was accustomed to the recitation and study of the Vedas. Soon, like the moon, he will traverse the whole sky.

He acquired this superior understanding through dutiful service and humble ministrations to his father. Of austere penances, he is firmly attached to his sire, and is much loved by him in return. Alas, why has he been dismissed by his inattentive father to tread a path from which there is no return?"

Hearing these words of Urvasi, and noting their significance, Suka, that foremost of all persons conversant with dharma, looked around him, and once again perceived the sky, all the earth with her mountains and forests, and her lakes and rivers. All the Devas and Devis folded their hands, paid reverence to the son of the island-born Rishi, and gazed upon him with wonder and respect.

That foremost of all righteous men, Suka, addressed them with these words, "If my sire should follow me and repeatedly call after me by my name, do all of you together give him my answer. Moved by the affection that you all bear for me, fulfil my request!"

Hearing Suka's words, all the points of the horizon, all the forests, all the seas, all the rivers, and all the mountains, answered him from every side, saying, "We accept your command, O regenerate one! It shall be as you say. Thus do we answer the words spoken by the Rishi!'"

CANTO 334

"Bhishma says, 'Having spoken to all in this way, Suka, the twice-born Rishi of austere penances, cast off the four kinds of faults. Casting off also the eight kinds of tamas, he dismissed the five kinds of rajas. Radiant with intelligence, he discarded even the sattva guna. All this was marvellous.

He then dwelt in that eternal place devoid of attributes, freed from every indication—that is, in Brahman, blazing like a smokeless fire. Meteors began to shoot out in every direction. The points of the horizon seemed to be ablaze. The earth trembled. All those phenomena were awesome to behold.

The trees began to shed their branches and the mountains their peaks. Loud claps of thunder were heard that seemed to rive the Himavat Mountains. The sun seemed at that moment to be shorn of splendour. Fire refused to blaze forth.

The lakes and rivers and seas were all agitated. Vasava poured torrents of fragrant rain. A pure breeze, bearing the scent of unearthly perfumes, began to blow.

As he coursed through the sky, Suka saw the two beautiful peaks of Himavat and Meru. These were close to each other. One of them was made of gold and appeared yellow; the other was white, being made of silver. O Bhaarata, both were a hundred yojanas in height and in breadth. As he journeyed towards the north, Suka saw those two magnificent peaks.

He dashed fearlessly against the two crests that appeared joined to each other. Unable to bear the force, they were rent in two. That sight was breathtaking.

Suka pierced through those peaks; they were unable to stop his onward course. Watching, the inhabitants of swarga cried out loud. The Gandharvas and the Rishis, and others who dwelt in those mountains were divided in two as Suka passed through.

A deafening echo was heard everywhere at that moment, and exclamations of "Uttamam! Excellent!" He was adored by the Gandharvas and the Rishis, by hosts of Yakshas and Rakshasas, and all tribes of the Vidyadharas.

Rajan, the whole sky was strewn with celestial flowers showered from heaven at the very moment when Suka breached that impenetrable barrier! From a height, the righteous-souled Suka saw the beautiful and divine Mandakini flowing below through a region adorned by many flowering groves and forests. Delightful Apsaras played in these waters. Seeing Suka who was bodiless those naked sprites felt shame.

Learning that Suka had undertaken his great journey, Vyasa, filled with love, followed him along the same path. Meanwhile, Suka, who moved through the sky higher than the region of the wind, displayed his prowess of yoga and united himself with Brahman.

In a flash, adopting the subtle path of high yoga, Vyasa of austere penances, reached the spot from where Suka began his journey. Travelling the same way, Vyasa saw the peaks Suka had cloven in two as he passed through them.

When they encountered Vyasa, the Rishis began to describe to him his son's achievements. Vyasa, however, began to lament, loudly calling his son's name, causing the three worlds to resound with his cries.

Meanwhile, the righteous-souled Suka, who had entered the very elements, had become their soul and acquired omnipresence, answered his father with a resounding *Bhoh*. At this, the entire universe of mobile and immobile creatures echoed Suka's reply by crying *Bhoh*.

From that time to this, as if to answer Suka, whenever sounds are

uttered in mountain-caves or on mountainsides, the echo comes back—
Bhoh!

By casting off all the attributes of sound, and disappearing with his
yoga-shakti, Suka attained to the highest condition. Seeing that glory and
power of his son of immeasurable energy, Vyasa sat down and sorrowfully
began to think of him.

Seeing him seated there, the Apsaras, who sported on the banks
of the divine Mandakini, became restless, embarrassed and despondent.
To hide their nakedness, some of them plunged into the stream, some
entered the forests nearby, and some quickly gathered up their clothes.
None of them had, however, betrayed any such signs of agitation at the
sight of his son Suka.

Seeing these movements, the Rishi understood that his son had been
liberated from all attachments, but that he, Vyasa himself, was not free
from them. He was filled with both joy and shame. As Vyasa sat there,
Siva, armed with Pinaka, surrounded by many Devas and Gandharvas,
and adored by all the Maharishis, came to that place.

Consoling the island-born Rishi who was burning with grief because
of his son, Mahadeva said to him. "You once prayed to me for a son with
the energy of Agni, Jala, Vayu and Akasa. Generated by your tapasyas
that very kind of son was born to you.

By my grace, he was pure and full of Brahmatejas. He has attained
to the highest end, one that cannot be won by anyone who has not
completely subdued his senses; nor can it be acquired by any of the
Devas even. Why then, O Rishi, do you grieve for that son?

As long as the mountains exist, as long as the ocean lasts, so long
will your son's fame endure undiminished. With my blessings, Maharishi,
you will, in this world, perceive a shadowy form resembling your son,
moving ever at your side, never deserting you even for a moment!"

Thus favoured by the illustrious Rudra himself, Vyasa saw the shadow
of his son by his side. He returned from that place, now filled with joy.

I have now told you, Bharatarishabha, everything regarding the birth
and life of Suka. Devarishi Narada and the great Vyasa repeatedly told

all this to me in ancient days when asked about it. One who serenely listens to this sacred history dealing with the subject of mukti is certain to attain to that highest end.'"

CANTO 335

"Yudhishtira says, 'If a man be a grihasta or a brahmacharin, a vanaprastha or a sannyasi, and if he desires to achieve success, what deity should he adore? How can he with certainty attain swarga and mukti?

According to what laws should he perform the homa in honour of the Devas and the Pitris? What is the realm to which one goes when one is emancipated? What is the essence of mukti? What should one do so that, having attained swarga, one will not fall from there?

Who is the Deity of the deities? And who is the Pitri of the Pitris? Who is he that is superior to him? Who is the Deva of the Devas? Tell me all this, Pitamaha!'

Bhishma says, 'Conversant with the art of questioning, O Anagha, you have asked me a question that that touches a deep mystery. Even if one were to strive for a hundred years, one would be unable to answer it using reason and the science of argumentation. Rajan, your question cannot be answered without the grace of Narayana, or of the highest gyana. Parantapa, though your subject is one of profound mystery, I shall yet expound it to you.

Let me narrate to you the ancient itihasa of the discourse between Narada and the Rishi Narayana. I heard it from my father that, in the Krita yuga, during the epoch of the Swayambhu Manu, the eternal Narayana, the Paramatman of the universe, took birth as the son of dharma in a quadruple form, as Nara, Narayana, Hari and the self-created Krishna.

Amongst them all, Narayana and Nara underwent the severest austerities by repairing to the Himalayan retreat of Badari, riding on their golden chariots. Each of these were furnished with eight wheels, constituted of the five primal elements, and were beautiful indeed.

Those original lords of the world, who had been born as the sons of Dharma, became emaciated because of the tapasya they had undergone. On account of those austerities and their tejas, the very Devas could not look at them.

Only that deity whom they propitiated could behold them. Devoted to them, and compelled by an ardent desire to see them, Narada descended onto Gandhamadana from a peak of the lofty mountains of Meru, and wandered over all the world.

At last he swiftly repaired to Badari's asrama. Driven by curiosity he entered it at the hour that Nara and Narayana performed their daily kriyas.

He said to himself, "This is truly the retreat of that Being in whom are established all the worlds including the Devas, the Asuras, the Gandharvas, the Kinnaras and the Nagas!

There was only one form of this great Being before. That single rupa took birth in four forms for the expansion of the race sired by Dharma. How wonderful it is that dharma has thus been honoured by these four great Devas—Nara, Narayana, Hari and Krishna!

Krishna and Hari lived here in earlier times. Nara and Narayana now dwell here, engaged in tapasya to increase their punya. These two are the highest refuge of the universe.

What is the nature of their daily rites? They are the procreators of all living things, and the illustrious Lords of all beings. Filled with high intelligence, which Deva do these two worship? Who are those Pitris whom these two Pitris of all beings adore?"

Reflecting on this, filled with devotion towards Narayana, Narada suddenly appeared before the two Devas. After they had finished worshipping their Devas and Rishis, they looked at the Devarishi who had arrived at their asrama. The latter was honoured with those eternal ceremonies that are ordained in the shastras.

Watching that extraordinary conduct of the two primordial Devas in themselves worshipping other Devas and Pitris, Rishi Narada took his seat there, pleased with the homage he had received. With a cheerful soul he gazed at Narayana, and bowing to Mahadeva he said:

"In the Vedas and the Puranas, in the angas and the subsidiary angas you are praised and revered; you are unborn and eternal. You are the Creator. You are the Mother of the universe. You are the embodiment of immortality and the foremost of all things.

The past and the future, indeed, the entire universe is founded in you! Men in all the four asramas of life ceaselessly propitiate you who have many forms.

You are the father and the mother and the eternal guru of the universe. Who is that Deva or that Pitri for whom you are performing yagnas today?"

The holy one replied, "This is one subject about which nothing should be said. It is an ancient mystery. But your devotion to me is great. Hence, O Dvija, I will openly discourse to you about it.

That which is minute, which is inconceivable, unmanifest, immobile, durable, without any connection with the senses and the objects of the senses, that which is dissociated from the five elements—that is called the Soul that dwells in all existent creatures. That is known by the name Kshetrajna.

It transcends the three gunas of sattva, rajas and tamas, and is regarded as Purusha in the shastras. From him has come the unmanifest that possesses the three attributes of sattva, rajas and tamas.

Though really Avyakta, unmanifest, she is the indestructible Prakriti and dwells in all manifest forms. Know that she is the source from which we two have sprung. That all-pervading Soul, which is made up of all existent and non-existent things, is adored by us.

Even he is what we worship in all the rites that we perform in honour of the Devas and the Pitris. There is no higher Deva or Pitri than he. O regenerate one, He should be known as our Atman. It is him that we worship.

He has propagated the path of dharma followed by men. It is his law that we should duly perform all the necessary kriyas for the Devas and the Pitris.

Brahma, Sthanu, Manu, Daksha, Bhrigu, Dharma, Yama, Marichi, Angiras, Atri, Pulastya, Pulaha, Kratu, Vasishta, Paramesthi, Vivaswat, Soma, he that has been called Kardama, Krodha, Avak, and Krita: these twenty-one Prajapatis were the firstborn.

All of them obeyed the eternal law of Narayana. Those most evolved of all men observed every rite ordained to honour the Devas and the Pitris, in detail, and achieved what they sought.

The divinities of heaven bow to that Supreme Deity and through his grace they attain to those fruits he ordains for them. This is the established conclusion of the shastras: those men are liberated who, freed from these seventeen attributes—the five senses of knowledge, the five senses of action, the five vital breaths, and Manas and Buddhi—have cast off all karma and are divested of the fifteen elements which constitute the sthula sarira, the gross body.

That which the emancipated attain to as their ultimate end is called Kshetrajna. In the shastras he is regarded both possessing and also free from all the gunas. He can be grasped by knowledge alone.

We two have sprung from him. Knowing him in that way, we adore that eternal Soul of all things. The Vedas and all the asramas of life, despite their differences of opinion, are all devoted to him.

Quick to be moved to grace, he grants them noble and blessed aims. In this world, those who are filled with his spirit, and are fully and absolutely devoted to him, attain to higher ends, for they succeed in entering and becoming merged in him.

Narada, I have now revealed to you this exalted mystery, as I am moved by the love I bear for you because of your devotion to me. Indeed, it is on account of this devotion that you have succeeded in listening to my discourse!'"

"Bhishma says, 'Thus addressed by Narayana, foremost of all beings, Narada, foremost of men, spoke again to Narayana for the good of the world.

Narada said, "O Swayambhu, let that objective be achieved for which you have taken birth in four forms in the house of Dharma! I will now repair to Sweta dwipa, the White Island, to gaze upon your true nature.

I always worship my elders. I have never divulged the secrets of others and I have studied the Vedas carefully. I have undergone austere tapasya. I have never lied. As ordained in the shastras, I have always protected the four varnas.

I have always behaved in the same manner towards friends and enemies. Wholly and steadfastly devoted to him, I ceaselessly adore the Paramatman, that first among Devas. Having cleansed my soul by these meritorious deeds, why will I not succeed in seeing that Infinite Lord of the universe?"

Hearing these words of Paramesthi's son, Narayana, protector of the shastras, gave him leave to go. Before dismissing him, he worshipped the Devarishi with those rites and rituals laid down in the scriptures. Narada also offered due adoration to the Rishi Narayana. After this worship had been mutually given and received, Narada left that place.

Blessed with high yogic powers, Narada soared into the sky and reached the peak of the mountains of Meru. Going to a secluded place there, the Maharishi rested for a while.

He then gazed towards the north-west and saw a magnificent sight there. Towards the north, in the ocean of milk, there is a great island named Sweta dwipa, the White Island. The learned say that its distance from the mountains of Meru is more than thirty-two thousand yojanas.

The inhabitants of that realm have no senses. They live without eating any kind of food. Their eyes do not blink. They always exude wonderful fragrances perfumes. Their complexions are white. They are unblemished by any trace of sin. They scorch the eyes of those sinners that look at them.

Their bones and bodies are as hard as the vajra. They regard honour and dishonour equally. They appear to be divine. All of them bear auspicious marks and have great strength.

Their heads appear like parasols. Their voices are deep like the roar of thunderclouds. Each of them has four Mushkas. The soles of their feet are marked by hundreds of lines.

They have sixty large white teeth and eight smaller ones. They have many tongues. With those tongues they seem to lick the very sun, which faces every direction. Indeed, they seem capable of devouring that deity from whom the entire universe has emerged, the Vedas, the Devas and the serene Munis.'

Yudhishtira says, 'O Pitamaha, you have said that those beings have no senses, that they do not eat anything, that their eyes do not blink, and that they always exude fragrant aromas.

I ask you, how were they born? What is the nature of their superior goal? Bharatarishabha, are the signs of those emancipated men the same as those by which all the inhabitants of the White Island are distinguished?

Dispel my doubts. I feel deeply curious. You are the repository of all histories and discourses. As for us, we depend entirely on you; we look to you for knowledge and instruction.'

Bhishma continues, 'Rajan, this story, which I heard from my father, is long. I will tell it to you. Indeed, it is regarded as the essence of all other narratives.

In ancient times, there lived a king on earth by the name of Uparichara. He was known to be the friend of Indra of the Devas. He was devoted to Narayana, who is also known as Hari.

He was observant of all the duties laid down in the shastras. Devoted to his father, he was always obedient and ready for any worthy action. He became the sovereign of the world on account of a boon he received from Narayana.

Following the ancient sattvata ritual established by Surya himself, King Uparichara worshipped Narayana, the Devadeva, and when this worship was over he adored the Pitris of the universe. After worshipping the Pitris, he worshipped the Brahmanas. He then divided the offerings among those who were dependent on him. With what remained after serving them, the king satisfied his own hunger.

Devoted to truth, Uparichara abstained from injuring any creature. With his whole soul, the king was devoted to Janardana, who is without beginning, middle and end, who is the Creator of the universe, and who does not decay or die.

Seeing Parantapa's devotion to him, Narayana shared his throne and palace with him. The king regarded his kingdom and wealth and spouses and animals as gifts from Narayana. He in turn offered up all his possessions to that great God.

Adopting the Sattvata ritual, King Uparichara would perform all his yagnas and ceremonies, both optional and obligatory, with the fullest concentration. In his palace, many great Brahmanas, well conversant with the Pancharatra ritual, would eat before all others the food offered to Narayana.

That Parantapa ruled his kingdom righteously; no untruth ever passed his lips and no wicked thought ever entered his mind. He never committed even the slightest sin.

The seven celebrated Saptarishis—Marichi, Atri, Angiras, Pulastya, Pulaha, Kratu and Vasishta of great tejas, who came to be known as the Chitra-sikhandins—uniting together on Meru, proclaimed an excellent treatise on the duties consistent with the four Vedas.

That discourse was uttered by seven mouths, and represent the best compendium of human duties and observances. Known by the name of Chitra-sikhandins, those seven Rishis constitute the seven Pravriti elements of Mahat, Ahamkara, and the rest, and Swayambhu Manu, who is the eighth in the enumeration, is the original Prakriti.

These eight uphold the universe, and it was these eight that promulgated this treatise. With their senses and minds under perfect control, and ever devoted to yoga, these eight Munis, with concentrated souls, know fully the past, the present and the future, and are devoted to the religion of truth.

Reflecting in their minds, that this is good, this is Brahman, this is valuable, those Rishis created the worlds, and the science of morality and duty that governs those worlds. In that treatise the authors discoursed on dharma, artha, kama and mukti.

In it they also laid down the various restrictions and limitations intended for Bhumi and also for swarga. They composed that discourse after having worshipped, along with many other Rishis, the puissant and illustrious Narayana, called also Hari, with tapasya for a thousand celestial years.

Gratified with their penances and worship, Narayana commanded Saraswati, the goddess of learning and speech, to enter into the bodies of those Rishis. For the good of the worlds, the Devi did as she was told. As a result of her entering into the Rishis, rich in penances, they were able to compose those most excellent treatises marked by the harmony of words, good sense and strong reasoning.

Having composed that treatise sanctified by Pranava, the syllable AUM, the Rishis first recited it to Narayana, who was delighted. The foremost of all Beings then addressed those Rishis in a divine voice and said, "These hundred thousand verses that you have composed are excellent. This treatise of a hundred thousand verses you have composed is exceptional.

The dharma and kriyas of all the worlds will flow from this your work! In complete accordance with the four Vedas, the Yajuses, the

Samans, and the Atharvans of Angiras, this treatise will be an authority with respect to both Pravritti and Nivritti in all the worlds.

In accordance with the shastras I have created Brahman from the attribute of grace, Rudra from my wrath, and yourselves, O Brahmanas, as representing the Pravriti-elements, of Mahat, Ahamkara, and the rest; Surya and Chandramas, Vayu and Prithvi, Jala and Agni, all the stars and planets and constellations, all creatures, and utterers of Brahma, the Vedas, all live and act in their respective spheres and all are respected as authorities.

This treatise you have composed shall be regarded by all men as a work of the highest authority. This is my command.

Guided by this treatise, Swayambhu Manu himself will declare to the world its course of duties and observances. When Usanas and Brihaspati arise, they also will promulgate their respective treatises on dharma, guided by and quoting from this your treatise.

After the promulgation of this treatise by Manu and of that by Usanas, and also by Brihaspati, this science composed by you will be acquired by King Vasu, also known as Uparichara. Indeed, O Dvijottamas, that king will acquire knowledge of this your work from Brihaspati.

That king, filled with all good thoughts, will become devoted to me. Guided by this treatise, he will perform all his karmas and kriyas. Verily, this treatise composed by you will be the best of all treatises on dharma. This excellent treatise, rich in wondrous mysteries, is fraught with instructions to acquire both material and spiritual punya.

As a result of this treatise, you will be the progenitor of a vast race. King Uparichara also will become great and prosperous. Upon his death, however, this eternal work will disappear from the world."

Having said these words to all those Rishis, the invisible Narayana left them and went to an unknown place. Then those sires of the world, those Rishis that bestowed their thoughts on the ends pursued by the world, duly promulgated that treatise which is the eternal origin of all kriya and karma.

Subsequently, when Brihaspati was born in Angiras's race in the

Krita yuga, those seven Rishis gave him the task of promulgating their treatise which was consistent with the Upanishads and the Vedangas. These upholders of the universe and the first promulgators of duties and religious observances went forth to their chosen place, having resolved to devote themselves to tapasya.'"

CANTO 337

"Bhishma says, 'With the end of the great kalpa, when the divine Purohita Brihaspati was born in the race of Angiras, all the Devas were delighted. The words Brihat, Brahma and Mahat all mean the same. Brihaspati was so called because he possessed all these qualities. King Uparichara, otherwise called Vasu, became a disciple of Brihaspati and soon became the foremost of his sishyas.

At the feet of his acharya, he then began to study the science composed by the seven Rishis known as Chitra-sikhandins. With his soul purified by tapasya and other rituals, he ruled the earth like Indra ruling swarga.

The illustrious king performed an Aswamedha yagna in which his guru Brihaspati became the Hota. The sons of Prajapati themselves, Ekata Dwita, and Trita, became the Sadasyas in that yagna.

There were others also who became Sadasyas at that sacrifice: Dhanusha, Raivya, Arvavasu, Parvavasu, the Rishi Medhatithi, the great Rishi Tandya, the blessed Rishi Santi otherwise called Vedasiras, Maharishi Kapila, who was the father of Salihotra, the first kalpa, Tittiri the elder brother of Vaisampayana, Kanwa and Devahotra, in all sixteen.

Rajan, all the required samagrahis were gathered for that great yagna. No animals were slaughtered. The king had so ordained it. He was full of compassion. Pure and tolerant of mind, he had discarded all desires, and knew all the rituals and ceremonies. The produce of the forests were used in that yagna.

Hari, the god of devas, was gratified with the king on account of that yagna. Hidden from everyone else, Narayana showed himself to his bhakta. Accepting his share, by imbibing its scent, he himself took up the Purodasa.

Unseen by anyone, Narayana took the offerings. Brihaspati was angered by this. Seizing the ladle he hurled it violently at the sky, and shed tears in wrath.

Addressing King Uparichara, he said, "Here, I place this as Narayana's share of the sacrificial offerings. Without doubt, he shall take it before my eyes.'"

Yudhishtira says, 'At the great sacrifice of Uparichara, all the Devas appeared openly to take their share of the arghya and were seen by all. Why is it that only Hari acted otherwise by taking his share without being seen?'

Bhishma continues, 'When Brihaspati was enraged, the great King Vasu and all his Sadasyas sought to pacify the Maharishi. Calmly they addressed Brihaspati, saying, "It befits you not to give way to anger.

In this Krita you, your wrath should not characterise anyone. The great God, for whom you set aside the share of the sacrificial offerings, is himself free from anger. O Brihaspati, he cannot be seen either by us or by you! Only he can behold him to whom He extends his grace."

Then the Rishis Ekata, Dwita and Trita, who knew the science of morality and duties compiled by the seven sages, addressed that assembly and began the following narration.

"We are the sons of Brahma, begotten by a command of his will, not in the ordinary way. Once upon a time we went to the north in order to obtain that which is for our highest good. Having undergone tapasya for thousands of years and acquired great punya, we again stood on only one foot like fixed stakes of wood.

The land where we performed tapasya lies to the north of the mountains of Meru and on the shores of the ocean of milk. Our goal was to behold the divine Narayana in his own form.

Upon the completion of our penances and after we had performed the final ablutions, we heard a divine voice, at once deep as that of the clouds and exceedingly sweet, filling our hearts with rapture.

The voice said, 'You Brahmanas have performed these penances with cheerful souls. Devoted to Narayana, you seek to know how you may succeed in beholding that God of great puissance!

On the northern shores of the ocean of milk there is a magnificent island called Sweta dwipa, White Island. The complexions of the men that inhabit that island are as white as the rays of the moon and they are devoted to Narayana.

Worshippers of that foremost of all Beings, they are devoted to him with all their souls. They all enter that eternal and illustrious deity of a thousand rays.

They are without any senses. They do not live on any kind of food. Their eyes do not blink. Their bodies are fragrant. Indeed, the inhabitants of the White Island worship only one God. Rishis, go there, for there I have revealed myself!'

Hearing these divine words, all of us went forth to the island described to us. Eagerly desiring to behold him, our hearts full of him, at last we arrived at that great island called Sweta dwipa.

There, we could see nothing. Indeed, our vision was blinded by the lustre of the Devadeva and so we could not see him. At this, the idea, due to the grace of the great God himself, arose in our minds—that one that had not undergone sufficient penances could not swiftly behold Narayana.

Under the influence of this idea, we once more set ourselves to the practice of rigorous tapasya, suited to the time and place, for a hundred years. Upon the completion of our vratas, we saw many men of auspicious features.

All of them were white like the moon with every mark of auspiciousness. Their hands were always joined in prayer. The faces of some were turned towards the north and of some towards the east. They were engaged in silently meditating upon the Brahman.

The japa performed by those Mahatmans was a silent, mental one with an audible recitation of any mantras. As a result of their minds and hearts being entirely focused upon him, Hari was gratified.

Maharishi, the effulgence emitted by each of those men resembled the splendours that Surya assumes at the time of the Mahapralaya, the dissolution of the universe. Indeed, we thought that that island was the home of all light. All the inhabitants were equal in energy. There was no superiority or inferiority among them.

Suddenly, we saw a light burning with the concentrated effulgence of a thousand suns. Together, the inhabitants ran joyously towards that light, with hands joined in reverence, uttering the one word Namas, we bow to you.

We then heard a booming sound made by them in unison. It seemed that those men were engaged in offering up a sacrifice to the great God.

We ourselves suddenly lost our senses by his unbearable tejas. Deprived of sight and strength and all our senses, we could not see or feel anything. We only heard a thundering voice in which those gathered there spoke as one.

They said, 'Victory to you, O you of eyes like lotus-petals! Salutations to thee, O Creator of the universe! Salutations to you, Hrishikesa, foremost of Beings, you who are the First-born!'

This is what we heard, uttered distinctly and in agreement with the laws of pronunciation. A pure and redolent breeze blew, bearing perfumes of divine flowers, and of certain herbs and plants germane to the occasion.

Those men, suffused with great devotion, with hearts full of reverence, conversant with the ordinances laid down in the Pancharatra, were worshipping Narayana with thought, words and action. Without doubt, Hari appeared in that place from where the sound they made arose.

Bewildered by his illusion, we could not see him. After the breeze had subsided and the yagna ended, our hearts were troubled with anxiety, O foremost of Angira's vamsa.

As we stood among those thousands of men, all of purest descent, no one honoured us with a glance or nod. Those ascetics, joyful and pious, all practising the Brahmatva, did not show any kind of feeling for us.

We were exceedingly weary. Our tapasya had emaciated us. At that moment, a divine Being spoke to us from the sky, saying, 'These white men, who are without their outer senses, have the capacity to behold Narayana.

Only those Dvijottamas whom these white men honour with their glances become competent to gaze upon the great God. Munis, go now to the place from where you have come.

That great deity cannot be perceived by one that is devoid of bhakti. Incapable of being seen because of his dazzling radiance, that illustrious deity can be beheld only by men who, in the course of long ages, succeed in devoting themselves only and absolutely to him.

You have a great duty to perform. After the passing of this, the Krita yuga, when the Treta yuga comes in the course of the Vivaswat cycle, a great disaster will engulf the worlds. O Munis, you will then have to join with the Devas to dispel that calamity.'

Having heard these wonderful words that were sweet as amrita, we soon returned to the place we desired, through the power of that great Deity. When we, with the help of even such austere tapasya and arghya, have failed to catch a glimpse of him, how can you expect to see him so easily?

Narayana is the Great Being, he is the Creator of the universe. He is adorned in sacrifices with offerings of ghee and other special food accompanied by the chanting of Vedic mantras. He has no beginning and no end. He is Avyakta. Both the Devas and the Danavas worship him."

Encouraged by these words spoken by Ekata and commended by his companions, Dwita and Trita, and entreated by the other Sadasyas, the high-minded Brihaspati brought that sacrifice to completion after duly offering the accustomed adorations to the Devas. King Uparichara also completed his mahayagna and began to rule his subjects righteously.

At last, casting off his body, he ascended into swarga. After some time, through the curse of the Brahmanas, he fell from those blissful realms and sank deep into the bowels of the earth.

O tiger among monarchs, King Vasu was always devoted to the true dharma. Although sunk deep in the bowels of the earth, his devotion to virtue did not abate. Ever devoted to Narayana, and ever reciting sacred mantras to him, he once more ascended to heaven through Narayana's grace.

Rising from the bowels of the earth, because of attaining that highest end, King Vasu went to a place even higher than Brahmaloka, dominion of Brahma himself.'"

CANTO 338

"Yudhishtira says, 'Despite being wholly devoted to Narayana, why did the great King Vasu fall from swarga and why did he have to sink below the surface of Bhumi?'

Bhishma says, 'O Bhaarata, in this regard listen to the old narrative of a discourse between the Rishis and the Devas. Long ago, the Devas addressed many foremost of Brahmanas and told them that yagnas should be performed by offering up Ajas as dakshina. Aja should be understood as the goat and no other animal.

The Rishis said, "The Vedic Sruti declares that in sacrifices the offerings should consist of seeds of vegetables. Seeds are called ajas. It befits you not to kill goats. The slaughter of animals is not prescribed in the dharma of the virtuous. This, again, is the Krita yuga. How can animals be killed in this age of righteousness?"'

Bhishma continues, 'While this discourse was underway between the Rishis and the Devas, King Vasu came that way. Abounding in prosperity, the king moved through the sky accompanied by his soldiers, chariots and animals.

Beholding the king arriving there, the Brahmanas said to the Devas, "This one will remove our doubts. He performs sacrifices. He is liberal in making gifts. He always seeks the good of all creatures. How could the great Vasu speak otherwise?"

Having thus spoken to each other, the Devas and the Rishis

approached King Vasu and asked him, "Rajan, with what should one conduct yagnas? Should one sacrifice with the goat or with herbs and plants? Dispel our doubts. We regard you as our judge in this matter."

Thus addressed, Vasu humbly joined his hands and said to them, "Tell me truly, O supreme Brahmanas, what in your opinion is entertained by you in this matter?"

The Rishis said, "In our understanding, yagnas should be performed with grain. The Devas, however, maintain that sacrifices should be done using animals. You be our judge and tell us which of view is correct.'"

Bhishma continues, 'Learning the position of the Devas on this matter, Vasu, moved by a partiality for them, said that yagnas should be performed with animals. All the Rishis, blazing with the splendour of the sun, were enraged at this choice.

To Vasu, who was seated on his chariot and who had wrongly taken up for the Devas, they said, "Since you have mistakenly taken the side of the Devas, you will fall from heaven. From this day on, you will lose the power of journeying through the sky. Through our curse you will sink deep below the surface of the earth."

After the Rishis had spoken, King Uparichara immediately plunged down into an abyss. But at the command of Narayana, Vasu retained his memory. To his good fortune, pained at the curse pronounced on him by the Brahmanas, the Devas began to think how that curse might be neutralised.

They said, "This high-souled king has been cursed for our sake. We, the inhabitants of heaven, must unite for his good in return for what he has done for us." Having swiftly reflected and decided thus, the Devas went to where King Uparichara was.

Arriving in his presence, they said to him, "You are devoted to Narayana, the great God of the Brahmanas. He, the ruler of both the Devas and the Asuras, is pleased with you and will save you from the curse. It is proper, however, that the high-souled Brahmanas should be honoured. Rajan, their penances must necessarily fructify. Indeed, you have already plunged from the sky to the earth. We desire, however, to favour you in one respect. O Anagha, as long as you live in this abyss, you will receive food and sustenance through our boon.

Those streaks of ghee which Brahmanas pour in yagnas with concentrated minds, accompanied by sacred mantras, and known as Vasudhara, shall be yours, throughout blessings. Indeed, neither weakness nor distress will touch you.

While dwelling in this hollow, neither hunger nor thirst will afflict you for you will drink those streams of ghrita called Vasudhara. Your energy will continue undiminished. As a consequence, the boon that we grant you, Narayana will be pleased with you, and he will bear you to the realm of Brahma!"

Having granted these boons to the king, the Devas and all those Tapodhana Rishis returned to their respective abodes. Then Vasu began to adore the Creator of the universe and to silently recite the sacred mantras that had come forth from Narayana's mouth in ancient days.

Parantapa, though dwelling in a pit of the earth, the king still worshipped Hari, the Lord of all the gods, in the five celebrated yagnas that are performed five times every day. As a result of these adorations, Narayana was pleased with him who had controlled his senses, and had shown himself to be entirely devoted to him, by relying upon him as his sole refuge.

The illustrious Vishnu, that giver of boons, addressed that foremost of birds, Garuda of great speed, who waited upon him as his servant. "O excellent and most blest Garuda, listen to what I say. There lives a great king by the name of Vasu who is of righteous soul and rigid vows. Through the wrath of the Brahmanas, he has fallen into an abyss of the earth.

The Brahmanas have been sufficiently honoured, since their curse has fructified. Go now to that king. At my command, Garuda, go to King Uparichara who now dwells in the depths of patala and can no more course through the sky. Go, Garuda, and swiftly raise him up."

Hearing Vishnu's words, Garuda spread his wings and going like the wind, entered the pit in which King Vasu was. He lifted up the king in his beak, soared into the sky and there he released Vasu. At that moment, King Uparichara once more acquired his divine form and re-entered the realm of Brahma.

Son of Kunti, in this manner did that great king first plunge down into the depths of the earth through the curse of the Brahmanas for a fault of speech, and once more ascend to swarga at the command of Vishnu.

Uparichara devoutly worshipped only the puissant Lord Hari, that foremost of all Beings. It was for this reverence that the king was freed from the curse of the Brahmanas and regained the felicitous regions of Brahmaloka.'

Bhishma continues, 'I have now told you everything regarding the origin of the spiritual sons of Brahma. Listen to me with undivided attention, for I will now narrate to you how Devarishi Narada went to the White Island in ancient times.'"

CANTO 339

"**B**hishma says, 'Arriving at Sweta dwipa, the illustrious Rishi saw those same white men possessed of lunar splendour of whom I have already spoken to you. Worshipped by them, the Rishi venerated them in return by bowing his head and revering them in his mind.

Wishing to behold Narayana, he began to live there, engaged in the silent recitation of sacred mantras, and observing the most difficult vratas. With dhyana, the regenerate Rishi, arms upraised, stood in yoga, and recited this mantra to the Lord of the universe, he, who is both saguna, the essence of attributes, and nirguna, without all attributes.

Narada said,[1] "Salutations to you, O God of gods, you who are free from all deeds! You are he who is nirguna, who is the Anudarshin of all the worlds, who is called Kshetrajna, who is the foremost of all Beings, who is infinite, who is called Purusha, who is the great Purusha, who is the foremost of all Purushas, who is the soul of the three attributes, who is called the Foremost, who is amrita, nectar, who is called Immortal, who is called Anantasesha, who is Akasa, space,

You are he who is without beginning, who is both Vyakta, manifest, and Avyakta, unmanifest, as existing and not-existent things, who is said to have his home in Satya, who is the foremost among the Devas;

---

[1]This is the Vishnu Sahasranama stotra.

Narayana, who is the giver of wealth, the fruits of one's actions, who is identified with Daksha and other Lords of the creation, who is the Aswattha and other mighty trees, who is the four-headed Brahma, who is the Lord of all created Beings, who is the Lord of speech.

You are he who is the Lord of the universe, Indra, who is the all-pervading Atman, who is the sun, who is prana, the breath, who is the Lord of the waters, Varuna, who is the Emperor or the king, who can be identified with the Lokapalas of the several points of the horizon, who is the refuge of the universe at the time of the final dissolution.

You are he who is concealed, who is the giver of the Vedas unto Brahma, who is associated with the sacrifices and Vedic studies achieved by Brahmanas with the help of their bodies, who is linked with the four principal orders of the Devas, who is every one of those orders, who shines radiantly with great effulgence, unto whom is offered the seven largest arghya along with the Gayatri and other mantras.

You are he who is Yama, who is Chitragupta and the other attendants of Yama, who is the wife of Yama, who is the Tushita order of the Devas, who is that other order called Mahatushita, the universal grinder, death, who is desire, and all diseases that have been created to ensure death.

You are he who is health and freedom from disease, who is subject to desire and passions, who is free from the influence of desire and passions, who is infinite as exhibited in species and forms, who is he that is chastised, who is he that is the chastiser,

You are he who is all the minor sacrifices of Agnihotra and others, who is all the principal sacrifices, those like Brahma, who is all the Ritvijas, who is the origin of all Vedic yagnas, who is fire, the very heart of all sacrifices, the mantras uttered in them, who is he who is revered in yagnas, who takes those shares of the arghya offered to him, who is the embodiment of the five sacrifices.

You are he who is the maker of the five divisions of time, day, night, month, season and year, who cannot be understood except by those shastras called Pancharatra, who fears nothing, who is unvanquished, who is only the mind, without a form, who is known only by name, who is the Lord of Brahma himself, who has completed all the vows and rituals told of in the Vedas.

You are he who is the Hamsa, bearer of the staff, who is the Paramahamsa without the staff, who is the foremost of all yagnas, who is Samkhya yoga, who is the embodiment of the Samkhya philosophy, who dwells in all Jivas, who lives in every heart, who resides in every sense, who floats on the ocean, who lives in the Vedas, who lies on the lotus as the egg from which the universe has sprung, who is the Lord of the universe, and whose forces spread far and wide to protect his devotees.

You take birth as all creatures. You are the origin of the universe. Your mouth is fire. You are that fire which courses through the waters of the ocean, gushing out from a horse's head. You are the sanctified ghee that is poured into the sacrificial fire. You are the charioteer, the fire and heat that charges the body and causes it to live and grow.

You are Vashat. You are the syllable AUM. You are Tapasya. You are Manas. You are Chandramas. You purify the sacrificial ghrita. You are Surya. You are the Dikgajas that are stationed at the four cardinal points of the horizon. You illuminate the cardinal points. You also brighten the subsidiary points. You are the Hayagriva and the Badava mukha.

You are the first three mantras of the Rig Veda. You are the protector of the varnas—Brahmanas, Kshatriyas, Vaisyas and Sudras. You are the five fires beginning with Garhapatya. You are he who has three times lit Nachi, the sacrificial fire.

You are the refuge of the six angas of the Vedas. You are the foremost of those Brahmanas that are employed to recite the Samans in yagnas and kriyas. You are Pragjyotisha, and you are he who sings the first Saman.

You keep the Vedic vratas and those observed by singers of the Samans. You are the embodiment of the Upanishad known as the Atharvasiras. You are he who is the subject of the five foremost scriptures, those that pertain to the worship of Surya, of Sakti, of Ganesa, of Siva and of Vishnu.

You are called the guru who subsists on only the froth of water. You are a Balakhilya. You are the embodiment of him who is steadfast in yoga. You are the epitome of the correct judgement of logic.

You are the beginning of the yugas, you the middle of the yugas and you are their end. You are Indra, Akhandala. You are the Rishis Prachina-garbha and Kausika. You are Purusthuta, You are Puruhuta, You are the Creator of the universe.

The universe has your form. Your movements are infinite. Your bodies are infinite; you are without end, without beginning and without middle. Your centre is unmanifest. Your end is unmanifest.

Your abode is in your vratas. You live in the ocean. Your home lies in fame, in penances, in self-restraint, in wealth, in knowledge, in grand achievements, and in everything belonging to the universe.

You are Vasudeva. You grant every wish. You are Hanuman who bore Rama on his shoulders. You are the mighty Aswamedha yagna. You receive your share of arghya in great sacrifices.

You bestow boons, joy and wealth. You are devoted to Hari. You are the subduer of the senses. You are vrata and kriya. You are mortifications, you are harsh mortifications, and you are the most relentless of mortifications.

You are he who observes vows and religious rites. You are free from all errors. You are a Brahmacharin. You were born in the womb of Prishni. From you have emerged all Vedic rites and karmas. You are unborn.

You pervade all things. Your eyes are on all things. You cannot be grasped by the senses. You are not subject to decay. You possess infinite power. Your body is inconceivably vast.

You are holy, beyond the ken of logic or argument. You are unknowable. You are the foremost of causes. You are the Creator of all creatures and you are their destroyer. You hold immense powers of maya. You are called Chitra-sikhandin.

You are the giver of boons. You take your share of the sacrificial offerings. You have acquired the punya of all yagnas. You are he who has been freed from all doubts. You are omnipresent. You have the form of a Brahmana. You are devoted to the Brahmanas.

The universe is your form. Your body is immeasurable. You are the greatest friend. You are kind to all your devotees. You are Brahmanyadeva, the great deity of the Brahmanas.

I am your devoted sishya. I seek to behold you. Salutations to you who are mukti.'"

CANTO 340

"**B**hishma says, 'Thus worshipped with names unknown to others, the Divine Narayana, having the universe for his form, revealed himself to the ascetic Narada.

His form, though purer than the moon, differed from the moon in some ways. He somewhat resembled a blazing fire in hue. The puissant Lord was somewhat of the form of Vishti.

He resembled in some respects the feathers of the parrot, and in some a mass of pure crystal. He appeared like a hill of antimony and also like a mass of pure gold.

His colour somewhat resembled the first formed coral, and was somewhat white. In some respects that complexion shone with the colour of gold and in some that of lapis lazuli. To some extent it radiated the blue of lapis lazuli and in some that of sapphire. In some respects it resembled the hue of the peacock's neck, and in some that of a string of pearls.

Bearing these diverse hues on his person, Narayana appeared before Narada. He had a thousand eyes and was splendid to behold. He had a hundred heads and a hundred feet. He had a thousand bellies and a thousand arms.

He was still inconceivable to the mind. With one of his mouths he uttered the syllable AUM and then the Gayatri following Pranava. With the mind under complete control, the great deity, called by the names of Hari and Narayana, by his other countless mouths, chanted many mantras from the Aranyaka of the four Vedas.

The Lord of all the Devas, he who is adorned in sacrifices, held a kamandalu in his hands, some awesome and sparkling jewels, a pair of sandals, and a bundle of kusa grass, a deer-skin, a staff and a small blazing fire.

With blissful soul, that foremost of Brahmans, Narada, bowed before Narayana and revered him. And he, the foremost of all the Devas, spoke the following words to Narada who bowed low in worship.

Narayana said, "The great Rishis Ekata, Dwita and Trita came to this realm to behold me. However, their wish remained unfulfilled. Nor can anyone have a vision of me other than those who are devoted to me with their whole being.

As for you, you are truly the foremost of all men who love and worship me with all their souls. These are my forms, the best ones that I assume. These were born, O Dvija, in the house of Dharma. Worship them always, and perform those kriyas that are laid down in the Vedas regarding that worship.

O Brahmana, ask of me the boons you desire. I am gratified with you today, and I appear to you now in my universal form free from decay and death."

Narada said, "Since, Holy One, I have succeeded in seeing you today, I consider that I have instantly gained the fruits of all my penances, of my self-restraint, and of all my vratas and punya karmas.

This, indeed, is the highest boon you have granted me for you have revealed yourself to me today. Eternal Lord, holiest one, the universe is your eye. You are Narasimha. Your form is identifiable with everything. Narayana, you are mighty and infinite."'

Bhishma continues, 'Having thus shown himself unto Narada, the son of Paramesthi, Narayana said to that Rishi, "Narada, go hence, do not delay! My devotees with moonlike complexions are without any senses and do not live on any food. They are, again, all emancipated. With minds wholly fixed on me, men should think only of me.

Such worshippers will never face any obstacles. These men are all crowned with ascetic success and are highly blessed. In ancient times, they deeply revered me. They have been freed from rajas and tamas. Without doubt, they are proficient to merge into my self.

He is that One who cannot be seen with the eye, touched with the sense of touch, smelt with the sense of scent, and who is beyond the sense of taste, who is untouched by sattva, rajas and tamas, who pervades all things and is the one witness of the universe, and who is described as the Soul of the entire universe.

He is that which is not annihilated upon the destruction of the bodies of all created things, who is unborn and unchangeable and eternal, who is freed from all attributes, who is indivisible and undivided; He who transcends the twenty-four tattvas, is regarded as the twenty-fifth.

He who is called by the name of Purusha, who is inactive, and who can only be grasped by true gyana, he into whom the foremost of the regenerate enter and attain mukti. He who is the eternal Paramatman is known by the name of Vasudeva.

Behold, O Narada, the greatness and puissance of Narayana. He is never touched by dharma and adharma, good and evil deeds.

Sattva, rajas and tamas are said to be the three original gunas. These dwell and act in the bodies of all creatures. The Jivatman, called Kshetrajna, enjoys and sanctions the action of these gunas. He, however, transcends them and they cannot touch him.

Freed from these attributes, he supports them and gets pleasure from them. Having created them himself, the Jivatman is above them all. Devarishi, when the hour of universal dissolution arrives, Bhumi, which is the refuge of the universe, disappears into Jala, Jala disappears into Agni, Agni into Vayu, Vayu disappears into Akasa, and Akasa into Manas.

Manas is a wondrous creature, and it disappears into Avyakta Prakriti. Unmanifest Prakriti disappears into inert Purusha. There is nothing higher than Purusha, which is eternal. There is nothing among mobile and immobile things in the universe that is immutable, other than Vasudeva, the eternal Purusha. Imbued with great power, Vasudeva is the Atman of all creatures.

Earth, wind, space, water and light are the Panchamahabhutas of great power. Merging together they form the body. Having subtle potency and invisible to all eyes, Vasudeva then enters the body, the combination of the five primal elements. This is called his birth, and taking birth.

He causes the body to move about and act. Without a combination of the five Mahabhutas, no body can be created. Without the entry of the Jiva into the body, the mind dwelling within it cannot cause it to move and act. He that enters the body is powerful and is called Jiva.

He is known also by other names, Sesha and Samkarshana. He that arises from that Samkarshana, by his own actions, Sanatkumara, and in whom all creatures merge at the end of the yuga, is the mind of all creatures, and is called by the name Pradyumna.

From Pradyumna arises he who is the Creator, and who is both cause and effect. It is from this that the mobile and immobile universe originates. This one is called Aniruddha. He is otherwise called Isana, and he is manifest in all deeds.

That illustrious one, Vasudeva, who is called Kshetrajna, and who is without gunas, should be known as the puissant Samkarshana, when he takes birth as the Jiva. From Samkarshana arises Pradyumna who is called 'He that is born as Manas.' From Pradyumna is he who is Aniruddha. He is Chit, Consciousness, he is Iswara, Supreme Lord.

It is from me, that the entire mobile and immobile universe springs. It is from me, Narada, that the indestructible and destructible, the existent and the non-existent, flow. They that are devoted to me enter into me and become free.

I am known as Purusha. Without karma, I am the twenty-fifth tattva. Transcending attributes, I am complete and indivisible. I am above all pairs of contradictions and free from all attachments. Narada, this you will not understand.

You see me as having a body. If I so wish I can dissolve this form in a moment. I am the Paramatman and the Jagadguru, the preceptor of the universe. What you see is only maya, an illusion. I appear to be endowed with the attributes of all created things. You are not consummate enough to know me.

I have now revealed my fourfold form to you. I am, Narada, the doer, I am cause, and I am effect. I am the sum of all living creatures. All beings have their refuge in me. Do not think that you have seen the Kshetrajna.

I pervade all things. I am the Jivatman of all creatures. However, when their bodies are destroyed, I am not annihilated. Those blessed ascetics who become wholly devoted to me are liberated from the rajas and tamas gunas, and succeed in uniting with me.

He who is called Hiranyagarbha, Brahma who is the beginning of the world, who has four faces, who cannot be understood through Nirukta, who is an eternal deity, attends to my work. Rudra, born of my wrath, springs from my forehead.

Behold, the eleven Rudras protrude on the right side of my body. The twelve Adityas are on the left. Behold, the eight Vasus, those best of Devas, are in my front, and look, the Aswini Kumaras, Nasatya and Dasra, the two divine physicians, are at my back.

Behold all the Prajapatis and the Saptarishis also in my body. Behold the Vedas, and all the countless yagnas, the amrita and all the medicinal plants and herbs, the tapasyas, and all the diverse vratas and kriyas. Behold the eight attributes of puissance, particularly those of sovereignty, all dwelling together in my body in their united and embodied forms.

Behold also Sree and Lakshmi, and Kirti, and Bhumi Devi with her mountainous undulations, and Saraswati, the mother of the Vedas, dwelling in me. Behold Dhruva, that foremost of luminaries ranging the skies, as also all the oceans and lakes and rivers dwelling in me. Behold the four most excellent Pitris in their embodied forms, and the three gunas, sattva, rajas and tamas, dwelling formlessly within me.

The actions performed to honour the Pitris are superior in punya to those done in honour of the Devas. I am the Pitri of both the Devas and the Pitris, and have existed before even them. Becoming the Badava mukha, I course through the western and the northern oceans, drinking sacrificial libations duly poured with mantras and arghya offered with devotion.

In ancient times, I created Brahma who adored me in sacrifices. Gratified with him, I granted him many excellent boons. I said to him that in the beginning of the kalpa he would be born to me as my son, and the sovereignty of all the worlds would be vested in him, and that diverse names would be bestowed on diverse objects that mark the creation of Ahamkara.

I also told him that none would ever violate the limits and boundaries he would assign for all creatures to observe and, further, that he would grant boons to those who asked him through yagnas and fitting deeds. I further assured him that he would be revered by all the Devas and Asuras, all the Rishis and Pitris, and the diverse beings of creation.

I also explained that I would always manifest myself to accomplish the ends of the Devas and that I would suffer myself to be commanded by him even as a son by his father. Gratified with Brahma, I granted these and other agreeable boons to him and once more embraced the course dictated by Nivritti.

The highest Nivritti is identical with the annihilation of all dharma and karma. By adopting Nivritti one should conduct oneself in complete felicity. Learned gurus, with firm convictions deduced from the truths of the Samkhya philosophy, have spoken of me as Kapila full of gyana, dwelling within the effulgence of Surya, and concentrated in yoga.

In the Chchandas, I have been repeatedly addressed as Hiranyagarbha. In the yoga shastras, I have been spoken of as one who delights in yoga. I am eternal. Assuming a form that is manifest, I dwell now in swarga.

At the end of a thousand yugas I shall once more withdraw the universe into myself. Having withdrawn all beings, mobile and immobile into myself, I shall exist all alone with only gyana for my companion. After the passing of time I will once again create the universe, with the help of that knowledge.

My fourth form creates the indestructible Sesha. That Sesha is called by the name of Samkarshana. Samkarshana creates Pradyumna. From

Pradyumna I am born as Aniruddha. Repeatedly, I create myself. From Aniruddha springs Brahma, from Aniruddha's navel. From Brahma are born all creatures.

Know that creation springs forth in this way repeatedly at the beginning of every kalpa. Creation and destruction succeed each other even as do sunrise and sunset. As time, infused with immeasurable energy, forcefully brings back the sun after his disappearance, in the same way I will assume the form of Varaha, the boar, and bring back the earth from her submergence, with her girdle of oceans, to her rightful place, for the benefit of all creatures.

I will then kill the proud powerful son of Diti, Hiranyaksha. For the good of the Devas, I will assume the form of Narasimha and slay Hiranyakasipu, the other son of Diti, who is a great destroyer of sacrifices.

Unto Virochana, the son of Prahlada, will be born a mighty son named Bali. That great Asura will be indestructible by the Devas, Asuras and Rakshasas. He will wrest sovereignty from Sakra.

After overthrowing the Lord of Sachi, when that Asura usurps the sovereignty of the three worlds, I will be born in Aditi's womb, by Kasyapa, as the twelfth Aditya. I will seize overlordship of the three worlds, restore it to Indra, and reinstate the Devas to their rightful places. As for Bali, that foremost of Danavas, who cannot be slain by all the Devas, I will thrust him down into patala.

In the Treta yuga, I will be born as Rama in the Bhrigu vamsa and annihilate the arrogant Kshatriyas, who boast of their strength and possessions. Towards the close of Treta and the beginning of Dwapara, I shall be born as Rama, the son of Dasaratha, in the Ikshvaku vamsa, in the royal house of the sun.

In that yuga the two sons of Prajapati, the Rishis Ekata and Dwita, harmed by their brother Trita, must be born as vanaras, losing their beautiful human forms.

Those vanaras that are born in the Ekata and Dwita vamsa, will be suffused with strength and tejas, equalling Sakra himself in prowess. They will become my allies for accomplishing the work of the Devas. I shall then slay the awesome ruler of the Rakshasas, that wretch of Pulastya's vamsa, the ferocious Ravana, along with his progeny and his followers.

Towards the close of the Dwapara and beginning of the Kali yuga, I will reappear in the world, taking birth in the city of Mathura for the purpose of slaying Kamsa. There, after destroying countless Danavas who incense the Devas, I will live in Kusasthali in Dwaraka.

While dwelling in that city I will slay the Asura Naraka, the son of Bhumi, who will assail Aditi and other Danavas, Muru and Pitha. Slaying also the king of Pragjyotisha, I will transplant his delightful city filled with diverse kinds of wealth into Dwaraka.

I will then subjugate Maheswara and Mahasena, who will become fond of the Danava Bana, their devotee, and protect him and exert themselves vigorously for him. Next defeating Bana, the son of the Danava Bali, with a thousand arms, I will obliterate all the inhabitants of the airborne Danava city called Saubha.

I will next, O foremost of Brahmanas, cause the death of Kalayavana, a mighty Danava endowed with the energy of Gargya. A proud Asura will appear as a king in Girivraja, his name Jarasandha, and he will oppose all the other kings of the world. His death will be compassed by me through another guided by my intelligence.

I will next annihilate Sisupala at the sacrifice of Dharmaraja Yudhishtira, a yagna to which all the kings of the world will bring tribute. In some of these feats, only Arjuna, the son of Vasava, will be my equal. I will establish Yudhishtira with all his brothers in his ancestral kingdom.

The people will call Arjuna and me Nara-Narayana, when we put forth our might and consume an untold number of Kshatriyas, for the good of the world. Having lightened the burden of the earth according to our wishes, I will absorb all the principal sattvas, and Dwaraka, my beloved city, into my own self, recollecting my all-embracing knowledge.

In this way I will accomplish many marvellous feats and finally attain those blessed realms of felicity created by me and honoured by all Brahmanas. Appearing in the forms of Hamsa, a swan; Matsya, a fish; Kurma, a tortoise; Narasimha, a man-lion; and Vamana, a dwarf, I will then incarnate myself as Rama of Bhrigu's race, then as Rama, the son of Dasaratha, then as Krishna the son of the Sattvata vamsa, and finally as Kalki the Destroyer.

When the auditions in the Vedas disappeared from the world, I brought them back. The Vedas with their auditions were recreated by me in the Krita yuga. They have again vanished or may only be partially heard scattered in the Puranas.

Many of my finest appearances in the world have become events of the past. Having achieved the good of the worlds in those forms in which I appeared, they have merged into my own Prakriti. Brahma himself has not seen this form of mine, which you, O Narada, have seen today because of your absolute devotion to me. I have now told you everything, you who are so totally devoted to me; I have disclosed my past and future incarnations to you, together with all their mysteries.'"

Bhishma continues, 'The holy and illustrious deity, of universal and immutable form, having said these words unto Narada, disappeared instantly. Narada, having obtained the high favour that he had sought, went swiftly to the hermitage called Badari, to have a vision of Nara and Narayana.

This great Upanishad, perfectly consistent with the four Vedas, in harmony with Samkhya yoga, named the Pancharatra scriptures, and recited by Narayana himself, was repeated by Narada in the presence of many in the abode of his father, Brahma, in exactly the same way in which Narayana, when he had revealed himself to him, had recited it, and which he had himself heard.'

Yudhishtira says, 'Was not Brahma, the Creator of all things, acquainted with this wonderful narrative of the glory and wisdom of Narayana that he had to hear it first from the mouth of Narada? Is the illustrious Pitamaha of all the worlds in any way different from or inferior to the great Narayana? How then is it that he was unfamiliar with the puissance of Narayana of immeasurable energy?'

Bhishma continues, 'Hundreds and thousands of Mahakalpas, hundreds and thousands of creations and dissolutions have come and gone in the past. In the beginning of every cycle of creation, Brahma, puissant Creator of all things, is remembered by Narayana.

Rajan, Brahma knows well that Narayana, that foremost of all Devas, is superior to him. He knows that Narayana is the Paramatman, that he is the Supreme Lord, that he is the Creator of Brahma himself.

This ancient story, perfectly consistent with the Vedas, was recited by Narada to that conclave of Rishis crowned with ascetic success. Surya Deva, having heard that account from those blessed Rishis, repeated it to the sixty-six thousand Rishis that follow in his train.

And Surya, who gives light to all worlds, repeated that narrative to those pure Beings who have been created by Brahma to always journey alongside him. The high-souled Rishis that follow in Surya's train, repeated that excellent tale unto the Devas assembled on the breast of Meru.

The best of Rishis, the regenerate Asita, having heard this from the Devas, repeated it to the Pitris. I heard it from my sire Shantanu who recited it to me. Myself having heard it from my father, I have repeated it to you, O Bhaarata.

Devas and Munis, who have heard this venerable Purana all adore the Supreme Soul. This narrative, belonging to the Rishis and thus handed down from one to another, should not be passed on by you to anyone who is not a devotee of Vasudeva. This one is really the essence of the hundreds of other narratives that you have heard from me.

In ancient times the Devas and the Asuras united to churn the ocean and to bring forth the amrita. In the same way, the Brahmanas united and churned all the scriptures and raised this narrative which resembles the nectar of immortality. He who frequently reads this narrative, and he who listens to it, with concentration and devotion, in a secluded place, succeeds in becoming an inhabitant possessing a lunar complexion of the vast island known as Sweta dwipa, the White Island.

Without doubt, such a man enters into Narayana of a thousand rays. By listening to this narrative from the beginning, a sick man is freed from his illness. The man who simply desires to read or listen to this narrative obtains the fruition of all his wishes. By reading or listening to it, the bhakta attains to the highest end that is kept for devout worshippers.

You, too, must always adore and worship that foremost of all Beings. He is the father and the mother of all creatures, and he is an object of reverence for the entire universe. Mahabaho Yudhishtira, let the illustrious and Eternal God of the Brahmanas, Janardana of high intelligence, be pleased with you!'"

Vaisampayana continued, "Having listened to the best of narratives, O Janamejaya, Dharmaraja Yudhishtira and all his brothers became devoted to Narayana. And from that day on, all of them began to practise silently meditating upon Narayana, and uttered these words to adore him, 'Victory to that holy and illustrious Being.'

Rishi Vyasa, best of gurus, devoted to tapasya, recited the word 'Narayana', that sublime mantra which is worthy of being recited in silence. Coursing through the sky to the ocean of milk which is always the abode of nectar, and worshipping the great God there, he came back to his own hermitage.

Bhishma continues, 'I have now repeated to you the tale that was told by Narada to the assembly of Rishis in the abode of Brahma. That narrative has descended from one person to another from the most ancient times. I heard it from my sire who told it to me.'"

In the Naimisa vana, among the Rishi Saunaka's sages, the Suta Romaharshana continued, 'I have now told you all that Vaisampayana narrated to Janamejaya. Having listened to Vaisampayana's narration, King Janamejaya discharged all his duties according to the rules laid down in the shastras.

You have all undergone severe tapasya and observed many high and excellent vratas. Living in this sacred forest of Naimisa, you are conversant with the Vedas. Foremost of regenerate ones, you all have come to this great yagna of Saunaka.

Adore and worship that Eternal and Supreme Lord of the universe in yagnas, properly pouring offerings of ghee into the fire, reciting mantras, and dedicating them to Narayana. As for myself, I heard this excellent account that has descended from generation to generation from my father who narrated it to me in earlier times.'

CANTO 341

Saunaka said, 'How is Narayana, fully conversant with the Vedas and their branches, at once the doer and the enjoyer of sacrifices? Ever forgiving, he has adopted the religion of Nivritti, abstention. He himself has established the duties of Nivritti.

Why then has he made many Devas take shares in yagnas, which, of course, are all due to the disposition of Pravritti? Why has he created some with a contrary disposition, for they follow the rules of Nivritti?

O Suta, dispel our doubt. This doubt seems to be eternal and intertwined with a great mystery. You have heard all discourses on Narayana, discourses that are consistent with the shastras.'

Sauti said, 'Excellent Saunaka, I shall recite to you what Vaisampayana, the disciple of the intelligent Vyasa, said when questioned on these very subjects by King Janamejaya. Having heard the discourse on the glory of Narayana who is the Soul of all embodied creatures, wise Janamejaya asked Vaisampayana these very questions.

Janamejaya said, "The whole world of Beings, with Brahma, the Devas, the Asuras and humans, is one that is deeply attached to actions which produce prosperity. You have said that mukti is the highest felicity marked by the end of existence.

Those who are without both paapa and punya succeed in becoming liberated when they enter the great God of a thousand rays. Brahmana, it appears that this mukti dharma is exceedingly difficult to practise.

Turning away from it, all the Devas now take pleasure in the pouring of ghee on sacrificial fires along with the chanting of mantras, and offering other customary havis.

Brahma, Rudra, the puissant Sakra the slayer of Bala, Surya, Chandramas, Vayu, Agni, Varuna, the living Akasa, the universe as conscious agent, and the other inhabitants of swarga, all seem to be ignorant of the way to make an end to conscious existence, which can be had through Atmagyana, self-realisation.

This is perhaps why they have not be taken themselves to the path that is certain, indestructible, and immutable. Hence perhaps, turning away from that path, they have adopted the religion of Pravritti which leads to conscious existence measured by time. This, indeed, is one great flaw in those attached to karma, for all their gains are terminable.

This doubt, regenerate one, is planted in my heart like a dagger. Remove it by narrating some old discourses on this subject. I am profoundly curious to listen to you.

Why do the Devas take their respective shares of havis offered to them with the help of mantras in yagnas of diverse kinds? Why are the Swargavasis revered in sacrifices? And, O Dvijottama, to whom do they, who take their shares of offerings in sacrifices performed in their honour, themselves make offerings when they perform mahayagnas?"

Vaisampayana said, "Rajan, the question you have asked me relates to another deep mystery. One who has not undergone tapasya and is not familiar with the Puranas, cannot answer it. I will answer you, however, by narrating what my guru Vyasa, the island-born Krishna, the Maharishi who divided the original Veda, said to us when we once questioned him.

Sumanta, Jaimini and Paila of firm vows, Suka and I were Vyasa's sishyas. Numbering five in all, endowed with self-restraint and purity of rituals, we had completely subdued wrath and controlled our senses. Our guru used to teach us the four Vedas, and the Mahabharata as the fifth.

Once while we were engaged in studying the Vedas on Mount Meru, inhabited by the Siddhas and Charanas, this very doubt, as expressed by you today, arose in our minds. We questioned Vyasa about it. I heard his reply.

I will now narrate that answer to you, O Bhaarata. Hearing these words addressed to him by his disciples, that dispeller of all kinds of darkness represented by avidya, the blessed Vyasa, the son of Parasara, said, 'I have undergone most severe, the austerest of tapasya. I am fully aware of the past, the present and the future.

On account of my tapasya and self-restraint, as I lived on the shores of the ocean of milk, Narayana was gratified with me. His pleasure granted me my desire for this Trikalagyana, perfect knowledge of the past, the present and the future. Listen now to me as I address this great doubt that has disturbed your minds.

With the eye of knowledge, I have seen all that has happened since the beginning of the kalpa. He whom both the Samkhyas and yogis call by the name of Paramatman comes to be regarded as Mahapurusha as a consequence of his own actions.

From him springs forth the unmanifest, Avyakta, whom the learned call Pradhana. From the unmanifest rises the manifest, Vyakta, for the creation of all the words. He is called Aniruddha. That Aniruddha is known among all creatures by the name of Mahat Atman.

It is that Aniruddha who, becoming manifest, created the Pitamaha Brahma. Aniruddha is known by another name, Ahamkara, endowed with every kind of energy. Bhumi, Vayu, Akasa, Jala and Agni are the five Mahabhutas that have sprung from Ahamkara. Having created these five Mahabhutas, he then created their attributes.

Combining the Mahabhutas, he created diverse embodied beings. Listen to me as I recount them to you. Marichi, Angiras, Atri, Pulastya, Pulaha, Kratu, Vasishta and the Swayambhu Manu, these should be known as the eight Prakritis. Upon these rest all the worlds.

Then, for the fulfilment of all creatures, Brahma created the Vedas with all their angas, as also the yagnas with their constituent limbs. From these eight Prakritis have sprung all this vast universe.

Then emerged Rudra from the principle of wrath, and he created ten others like him. These eleven Rudras are called Vikara Purushas. The Rudras, the eight Prakritis, and the several Devarishis, having being born, approached Brahma with the objective of upholding the universe and its workings.

Addressing the grandsire, they said, 'Holy One, we have been created by you. Pitamaha, tell us about our respective spheres of influence and authority. What particular jurisdictions have been created by you for supervising the various affairs of creation?

What kind of consciousness should each of us have, and which of these areas should we take charge of? Also endow each of us the measure of power that we are to have to discharge our duties.'

Thus addressed by them, Brahma replied unto them in the following way: 'You deities have done well in speaking to me of this matter. Blessed be you all! I was thinking of this very matter that has engaged your attention. How should the three worlds be upheld and kept stable? How should your powers and mine be employed towards that end?

Let all of us leave this place and repair to that unmanifest and foremost of Beings, who is the witness of the world, to seek his protection. He will inform us what is for our good.'

Those Devas and Rishis, with Brahma, went to the northern shores of the ocean of milk, wishing to do good to the three worlds.

Arriving there, they began to practise those austere tapasyas advocated by Brahma in the Vedas, those penances known by the name of Mahaniyama. They stood there with minds fixed, unmoving as wooden posts, with eyes and hands raised up above their heads.

For a thousand celestial years they engaged in rigorous tapasya. At the end of that period they heard these sweet words in harmony with the Vedas and their angas.

'I welcome you Devas and Rishis, blessed with the wealth of asceticism, with Brahma in your company, and to you I say that I know what is in your hearts. Your thoughts are indeed for the good of the three worlds.

I will increase your energy and strength with Pravritti, the propensity for action. You have devoutly worshipped me with tapasya. Foremost of Beings, enjoy now the fruits of your austerities.

This Brahma is the Lord of all the worlds. Endued with puissance, he is Prajapati of all creatures. You too are the best of the Devas. With dhyana, perform yagnas for my glory.

In these sacrifices always give me a portion of the sacrificial offerings. I will then assign to each of you your respective jurisdictions and ordain what will be for your good!'"

Vaisampayana continued, "Vyasa said, 'Hearing these words of the God of gods, all those Devas, Maharishis and Brahma were filled with such delight that the hair on their bodies stood on end. They immediately made arrangements for a yagna in honour of Vishnu according to the niyamas laid down in the Vedas.

In that sacrifice, Brahma himself dedicated a portion of the offerings to Vishnu. The Devas and Devarishis also dedicated similar portions each unto him. These portions, offered with great reverence, were in accordance with the rules established for the Krita yuga, both in measure and excellence.

In that yagna, the Devas and the Rishis and Brahma worshipped Vishnu Narayana as one with the complexion of the sun, as the foremost of Beings, situated beyond the reach of tamas, vast and infinite, pervading all things, the Supreme Lord of all, the giver of boons. Thus adored by them, invisible and formless, bodiless, He addressed those assembled divinities, saying to them:

"The offerings dedicated by you in this sacrifice have all reached me. I am gratified with all of you. I shall bestow rewards on you that will however be fraught with destinations from which there will be return.

Devas, because of my grace and compassion for you this shall be your distinctive feature from this day onwards. Performing sacrifices in every yuga, with large gifts, you will enjoy the fruits born of Pravritti. Men who perform yagnas according to the rules of the Vedas will give unto all of you shares of their havis.

In such yagnas, according to the Veda-sutras I compel a man to receive a share similar to that which he has himself offered in that sacrifice. You have been created to look after those affairs within your respective domains; uphold the worlds according to the measures of your power, which depend on the shares you receive in those sacrifices.

Indeed, drawing strength from those rites and rituals prevailing in the several worlds, arising from the fruits of Pravritti, and continue to uphold the affairs of those worlds. Strengthened by the yagnas that will be performed by men, you will strengthen me.

This is what I intend for you all. It is for this purpose that I have created the Vedas and sacrifices and plants and herbs. Duly revered by humans on earth, the Devas will be gratified. Foremost of deities, till the end of this kalpa I have ordained your creation, making your constitution depend upon the consequence of Pravritti dharma. Now, with regard to your respective spheres of influence, engage yourselves in seeking the good of the three worlds.

Marichi, Angiras, Atri, Pulastya, Pulaha, Kratu and Vasishta, these seven Rishis have been created by a fiat of the will, Manas. They will become the foremost of those conversant with the Vedas. In fact, they will become the teachers of the Vedas. They will be wedded to Pravritti dharma, for they are intended to devote themselves to procreation.

I reveal to you this eternal path of creatures engaged in kriyas and karmas. The puissant Lord who is charged with the creation of all the worlds is Aniruddha; Sana, Sanatsujata, Sanaka, Sanandana, Sanatkumara, Kapila and Sanatana, these seven Rishis are known as the spiritual sons of Brahma.

Their knowledge comes to them of itself, not dependent on study or exertion. These seven are wedded to Nivritti dharma. They are the foremost of all yogis. They possess deep knowledge of the Samkhya philosophy.

They teach the dharma of the shastras, and it is they who introduce the duties of Nivritti and cause them to arise in the worlds. From unmanifest Prakriti has flowed Consciousness and the three great gunas of sattva, rajas, and tamas. Transcending Prakriti is he called Kshetrajna.

I myself am that Kshetrajna.

The path of those wedded to karma emerging out of Ahamkara is fraught with return. That path does not reach the place from where there is no return. Different creatures have been created with different ends. Some are intended for the path of Pravritti and some for that of Nivritti. One enjoys the reward of the particular path he follows.

This Brahma is the master of all the worlds. With his power he creates the universe. He is your mother and father, and he is your grandfather. At my command, he will be the giver of boons unto all creatures.

His son Rudra, who has sprung from his brow at his command, will uphold all created beings. Go to your respective realms and, according to the laws, seek the good of the worlds. Let all the karma based on the shastras flow in all the worlds. Do not delay.

Most excellent divinities, ordain the deeds of all creatures and their goals. Determine also the limits of the periods for which all creatures are to live. This present yuga that has begun is the foremost of all, and should be known by the name of Krita.

In this yuga, living creatures should not be killed in the yagnas that may be performed. It should be as I command and not otherwise. In this age, righteousness, dharma, will flourish in its fullness.

After this age will come the Treta yuga. In that yuga, the Vedas will lose one quarter of themselves. Only three of them will exist. In the sacrifices performed in that epoch, animals, after dedication with sacred mantras, will be killed. Dharma, too, will lose one quarter; only three quarters of righteousness will flourish.

At the end of the Treta will come Dwapara, the mixed yuga. In that age, dharma will lose two quarters and only two quarters will thrive.

Upon the end of Dwapara, Kali yuga, under the influence of the Tisya constellation. Righteousness will lose full three quarters. Only a quarter thereof will exist in all places."

When Narayana spoke these words, the Devas and the Devarishis said to him, "If only a fourth part of dharma is to exist in that yuga in every place, tell us where shall we then go and what shall we do?"

The blessed and Holy One said, "In that yuga, you should repair to such places where the Vedas and yagnas, tapasya and satya and self-restraint, accompanied by duties filled with compassion for all creatures, still continue to flourish. Evil will never be able to touch you at all!"'

Vyasa continued, 'Thus commanded by the great God, the Devas with all the Rishis bowed their heads and went away to their destinations. After the Rishis and Devas had left, Brahma remained there, desirous of beholding the great deity in the form of Aniruddha.

The foremost of Devas then manifested himself to Brahma, having assumed a form that had a gigantic equine head. Bearing a kamandalu and the tridanda, he manifested himself before Brahma, reciting the while the Vedas with all their angas.

Beholding him in that form crowned with a badava mukha, a horse's head, Brahma, the creator of all the worlds, moved by the desire of doing good to his Creation, worshipped him with bowed head and folded hands. The great Deity embraced Brahma and then said:

"O Brahma, duly think of the paths of karma that creatures are to follow. You are the great ordainer of all created beings. You are the lord of the universe. Placing this burden on you I will soon be free from anxiety.

When it becomes difficult for you to achieve the purposes of the Devas I will appear in incarnate forms according to my Atmagyana." Having said these words that grand form with the horse's head disappeared in a flash. Having received his command, Brahma too, went swiftly to his own realm.

It is for this that Vishnu, Padmanabha with the lotus in his navel, accepted the first share offered in sacrifices and because of this he came to be called the eternal upholder of all yagnas. He himself adopted Nivritti dharma, the goal of those seeking everlasting felicity.

At the same time, he established Pravritti dharma for others, in order to furnish variety to the universe. He is the beginning, he is the middle, and he is the end of all created Beings.

He is their Creator and he is their one object of meditation. He is the actor and he is the act. Having withdrawn the universe into himself at the end of the yuga, he falls asleep, and awakening at the beginning of another yuga, he once again creates the universe.

Bow unto that illustrious one of high soul and who transcends the three gunas, who is un-born, whose form is the universe, and who is the abode or refuge of all the inhabitants of swarga. Bow unto him who is the Supreme Lord of all creatures, who is the Lord of the Adityas, and of the Vasus as well.

Bow unto him who is the Lord of the Aswins, and the Lord of the Maruts, who is the Lord of all the sacrifices ordained in the Vedas, and the Lord of the Vedangas. Bow unto him who always resides in the ocean, and who is called Hari, and whose hair is like the blades of the munja grass.

Bow unto him who is peace and serenity, and who imparts mukti dharma to all. Bow to him who is the Lord of penances, of all kinds of energy, and of fame, who is ever the Lord of speech and the Lord of all the rivers.

Bow unto him who is called Kapardin, Rudra, who is the Great Boar, and who possesses great intelligence, who is the sun, and who took the form with the horse's head; he Lord who is always displayed in a four-fold form. Bow unto him who is unrevealed, who is capable of being grasped through gyana alone, and who is both Akshara and Kshara.

The Supreme Deity, who is immutable, pervades all things. He is the Supreme Lord who can be only known with the eye of knowledge. It was with gyana that I perceived him in ancient times.

Sishyas, I have told you all that you asked me; now act according to what I have said and serve the Supreme Lord called Hari. Sing his praises in Vedic mantras; adore and worship him with all due rites!'"

Vaisampayana continued, "It was thus that Vyasa, the arranger of the Vedas, discoursed to us, when we questioned him. His son, the righteous Suka, and us, all his sishyas, listened avidly to him as he addressed us. We and our gurus then adored the great deity with verses, Riks extracted from the four Vedas.

I have now told you all that you asked me. Rajan, thus did our island-born preceptor instruct us.

He who has surrendered to Narayana and listens, with dhyana, to this discourse or reads or recites it to others, is filled with intelligence and health, beauty and strength. If ill, he is freed from that illness; if bound, he is freed from his bonds.

The man who desires receives the fruits of all his desires, and also attains to a long life. By doing this, a Brahmana becomes conversant with all the Vedas, and a Kshatriya is crowned with success. Following this a Vaisya makes vast profits, and a Sudra attains great felicity.

A sonless man obtains a son. A woman finds a desirable husband. A woman that has conceived gives birth to a son. A barren woman conceives and attains to the wealth of sons and grandsons.

He who recites this discourse on the way succeeds in passing joyfully along this path without any obstacles. If one reads or recites this story, he attains whatever objects he cherishes.

Hearing these assured and true words of the Maharishi, embodying the gunas of that high-souled one, listening to this narrative of the great assembly of Rishis and other inhabitants of swarga, men devoted to the Supreme Deity find great bliss."

CANTO 342

Janamejaya said, "Holy one, tell me the significance of those diverse names uttered by Maharishi Vyasa and his disciples to praise Madhusudana, the slayer of Madhu. I am keen to hear those names of Hari, that Supreme Lord of all creatures. By listening to those names, I shall be purified and cleansed like the bright autumn moon."

Vaisampayana said, "Listen, Rajan, to the significance of those names, diverse because of the many attributes and actions of Hari, as the puissant Hari himself explained them to Arjuna. That Parantapa once asked Krishna about the importance and meaning of some of the names by which he was adored.

Arjuna said, 'Krishna, Supreme ordainer of the past and the future, Creator of all Beings, immutable One, Refuge of all the worlds, Lord of the universe, dispeller of the fears of all men, from you I desire to know in detail the significance of all your names which have been enumerated by the great Rishis in the Vedas and the Puranas because of your awesome and diverse deeds. None other than you, Kesava, is competent to explain this.'

Krishna said, 'Arjuna, in the Rig Veda, in the Yajur Veda, in the Atharvans and the Samans, in the Puranas and the Upanishads, as also in the treatises on jyotisha, astrology, in the Samkhya and yoga shastras, and in the treatises on Ayurveda, the science of life, many are the names that have been mentioned by the great Rishis.

Some of those names are derived from my attributes and some of them relate to my deeds. Listen with concentration of the import of each of those names with reference to my exploits. I will recite them to you.

It is said that in ancient times you were half my body. Salutations to him of great glory, who is the Paramatman of all embodied creatures. Salutations to Narayana, unto him who is the universe, unto him that transcends the three primal gunas of sattva, rajas and tamas, unto him that is the Soul of those attributes.

From his grace has arisen Brahma and from his wrath Rudra. He is the source from which all mobile and immobile creatures emerge. Sattva is made up of eighteen qualities.

That attribute is Supreme Nature; her soul consists of Akasa and Bhumi and she upholds the universe with her creative forces. That Prakriti is identical with the fruit of all karma, in the form of the diverse realms of felicity which creatures attain through their actions.

She is also the pure Chit. She is immortal, and invincible, and is called the Soul of the universe. From her flows all the modifications of both creation and destruction. She is identical with my nature. Without sex, she or he is the tapasya that men undergo.

He is both the yagna performed and the sacrificer that performs it. He is the ancient and the infinite Purusha. He is otherwise called Aniruddha and is the source of the creation and the destruction of the universe.

When Brahma's night ended, through the grace of that Being of immeasurable energy, a lotus appeared, O you of eyes like lotus-petals. Within that lotus Brahma was born, springing from Aniruddha's grace.

Towards the evening of Brahma's day, Aniruddha was filled with anger, and from this there sprang from his forehead a son called Rudra with the power of destroying everything at the hour of Pralaya. Brahma and Rudra are the foremost of all the Devas, having sprung respectively from the auspiciousness and the wrath of Aniruddha.

Acting according to Aniruddha's command, these two Devas create and destroy. Although capable of granting boons to all creatures, in the matter of creation and destruction, they are mere instruments in the hands of Aniruddha. It is Aniruddha that does everything, making Brahma and Rudra the visible driving forces in the universe.

Rudra is otherwise called Kapardin. He sometimes has matted locks of hair; at other times he reveals a shorn head. He favours living in samsanas, cremation grounds, which are indeed his home.

He is an observer of the austerest vratas. He is a yogin of great power and energy. He is the destroyer of Daksha's sacrifice and of Bhaga's eyes.

Son of Pandu, it should be understood that Rudra always has Narayana for his Atman. If Maheswara is worshipped, then the puissant Narayana is also worshipped. I am the soul of all the worlds, of all the universe. Rudra, again, is my Soul.

It is for this that I always venerate him. If I do not adore the auspicious and boon-giving Isana nobody would then adore me. The laws I establish are followed by all the worlds. These must always be revered and for this reason I do adore them.

He who knows Rudra knows me, and he who knows me knows Rudra. He who follows Rudra follows me, Rudra is Narayana. Both are one; and the one is displayed in two different forms. Rudra and Narayana, forming one person, pervade all visible things and cause them to act.

Son of Pandu, no one other than Rudra can grant me a boon. Having realised this, in olden times, I revered Rudra to obtain the boon of a son. In adoring Rudra thus I adored my own self. Vishnu never bows his head to any god other than his own self. It is for this reason that I adore Rudra, for Rudra is my own self.

All the Devas, including Brahma and Indra, and the Maharishis worship Narayana, that foremost of deities, also known by the name of Hari. Vishnu is the foremost of all Beings past, present or future, and as such should always be adored and revered.

Bow to Vishnu. Bow your head unto him who protects everyone. Arjuna, bow to that great boon-giving God, that foremost of deities, who consumes the offerings made to him in yagnas.

I have heard that there are four kinds of worshippers: those who are eager for a religious life, those who are seekers, those who strive to understand what they learn, and those who are wise. Among them all, they who devote themselves to realising the self and do not adore any other deity, are the best. I am the end they seek, and though engaged in karma, they never seek its fruits.

The three other categories of my worshippers are those that desire the fruits of their actions. They attain to realms of great felicity, but once they have exhausted their punya they must fall from those realms. Those amongst my devotees who are fully awakened, and know that all happiness is transitory, other than what is attained by those who become united with me, obtain what is most invaluable.

Those enlightened ones may be engaged in adoring Brahma or Siva or the other Devas in heaven but they succeed at last in realising me. I have now told you about my diverse devotees.

Arjuna, you and I are known as Nara and Narayana. Both of us have assumed human bodies only for the purpose of lightening the burden of the earth. I am fully aware of my self.

I know who I am and from where I come. I know Nivritti dharma, and all that is responsible for the prosperity of all creatures. I am eternal and the sole refuge of all men. The waters have been called by the name Naara, for they sprang from him called Nara. And since the waters, in former times, were my refuge, I am, therefore, referred to as Narayana.

Assuming the form of the sun, I envelop the universe with my rays. And because I am home to all creatures, I am called by the name of Vasudeva. I am the end of all creatures and their beginning, Bhaarata.

I pervade the entire firmament and the earth, and my splendour transcends every other splendour. I am he whom all creatures wish to attain to at the hour of death. And because I pervade all the universe, I have been called the name Vishnu. Desiring mukti through subduing their senses, people seek to me, I who am swarga and Bhumi and the sky between the two. For this I am called Damodara.

The word prishni includes food, water, the Vedas and amrita. These four are always in my belly. Hence am I called Prishnigarbha. The Rishis once said that when the Rishi Trita was thrown into a well by Ekata and

Dwiti, the distressed Trita invoked me, saying, "O Prishnigarbha, rescue the fallen Trita!" Having thus implored me, Trita, the spiritual son of Brahma, was indeed rescued from the fathomless well.

The rays that emanate from the sun who gives heat to the world, from the blazing fire, and from the moon, constitute my hair. Hence do learned Brahmanas call me by the name of Kesava.

The Mahatman Utathya having impregnated his wife disappeared from her side through an illusion of the gods. The younger brother Brihaspati then appeared before her. To him who had approached Utathya's wife with the desire of sexual union, the child in her womb, whose body had already been formed of the five primal elements, said, "Giver of boons, I have already entered into this womb. It befits you not to assail my mother."

Hearing these words of the unborn child, Brihaspati was angered and cursed him, "Since you obstruct me so when I have come to you from desire of the pleasures of union, I curse you to be born blind!"

Through this curse the child of Utathya was born blind, and blind he remained for a long time. It was for this reason that that Rishi came to be known by the name of Dirghatamas, or long darkness.

He, however, acquired the four Vedas with their angas and subsidiary angas. After that he frequently invoked me by this secret name of mine. Indeed, according to the established rules, he repeatedly called upon me by the name Kesava.

Through the punya he acquired by uttering this name repeatedly, he was cured of his blindness and came to be called Gotama. Arjuna, this name of mine gives boons to them who that utter it, among all the Devas and the Devarishis.

Agni and Soma combine and fuse into one substance. It is for this reason that the entire universe of mobile and immobile creatures is said to be pervaded by them.

In the Puranas, Agni and Soma are spoken of as complementary to one another. They have Agni for their mouth. As their natures lead to their mingling, they balance each other and uphold the universe.'"

"Arjuna said, 'How did Agni and Soma come to be so similar in their original natures? This doubt has arisen in my mind. Dispel it, slayer of Madhu.'

Krishna said, 'I shall narrate to you an ancient story of events originating from my own energy. Listen carefully.

When four thousand yugas according to divine measure pass, the dissolution of the universe comes. The Vyakta, manifest, disappears into the Avyakta, unmanifest. All creatures, mobile and immobile, are destroyed. Agni, Bhumi and Vayu disappear. Tamas, darkness, spreads over the universe which becomes one infinite expanse of water.

When that vast expanse of water, Ekarnava, exists like Brahman without another, it is neither day nor night. Neither all nor nothing nor aught exists; neither the manifest nor the unmanifest. Then only undifferentiated Brahman exists.

When this is the condition of the universe, the foremost of Beings emerges from tamas—the eternal and immutable Hari who is the combination of all the attributes, including omnipotence, of Narayana, who is indestructible and eternal, without senses, inconceivable and unborn, who is truth's self fraught with compassion, who exists like the rays of the Chintamani jewel.

He is One that causes diverse kinds of desires to flow in many directions, who is devoid of hostility, and decay, death and destruction, who is formless and all-pervading, and who is endowed with the principle of universal creation and of eternity without beginning, middle or end.

There is a basis for this assertion. The Sruti declares: Day was not. Night was not. All was not. Nothing was not. In the beginning there was only tamas in the form of the universe, and she is the night of Narayana of universal form. This is the meaning of the word tamas.

That Purusha called Hari, thus born of tamas and having Brahman for his sire, gave birth to Brahma. Wishing to create creatures, Brahma caused Agni and Soma to spring from his own eyes.

After this, men were created in their proper order as Brahmanas and Kshatriyas. He who began life as Soma was none other than Brahma; and they who were born as Brahmanas were in reality all Soma. Those who started into being as Kshatriyas were none other than Agni.

The Brahmanas gained greater energy than the Kshatriyas. If you ask why, the answer is that this superiority of the Brahmanas to the Kshatriyas is manifest through the whole world. It happened thus.

With regards to men, the Brahmanas represent the oldest creation. None higher than them were created before. He who offers food into the mouth of a Brahmana pours libations into a blazing fire to gratify the Devas.

I say that having ordained things in this manner, Brahma then created all creatures. Having established all created beings in their respective places, he upholds the three worlds.

There is a similar declaration in the mantras of the Srutis: Agni, you are the Hotri in yagnas and the benefactor of the universe. You support the Devas, all men and all the worlds. There is no other authority for this purpose.

Agni, you are the Hotri of the universe and of sacrifices. You are the one through which the Devas and men do good to the universe. Agni is truly the Hotri and the performer of sacrifices.

Agni is again the Brahma of the yagna. No libations can be poured into the sacrificial fire without uttering mantras; there can be no tapasyas without someone to perform them; the Devas, Rishis and Manavas are worshipped by these offerings accompanied by mantras. Hence, O Agni, you have been regarded as the Hotri in sacrifices.

You are, again, all the other mantras that are have been associated with the Homa rites. It is the ordained duty of the Brahmanas to preside over yagnas.

The other two twice-born varnas, the Kshatriyas and Vaisyas, do not have the same duty. Brahmanas, like Agni, uphold sacrifices. The yagnas performed by them strengthen the Devas. Thus maintained they fructify the earth thereby supporting all living creatures.

But the result that may be achieved by the best of yagnas may as well be accomplished through the mouth of the Brahmanas. That learned man who offers food into the mouth of a Brahmana is said to pour libations into the sacred fire to gratify the Devas. In this way the Brahmanas have come to be regarded as Agni.

Those who are wise adore Agni. Agni is, again, Vishnu. Entering all creatures, he upholds their life-breaths.

In this regard there is a verse sung by Sanatkumara. Brahma, in creating the universe, first created the Brahmanas. The Brahmanas become immortal and ascend into swarga by studying the Vedas. Their Buddhi, kriyas and karmas, tapasyas, speech and faith, sustain both the earth and heaven like ropes of strings holding up nectarine milk.

There is no dharma higher than truth. There is no one more worthy of reverence than the mother. There is none more efficient than the Brahmana for conferring felicity both in this life and the next.

In places where Brahmanas are unsupported by gifts of land, the inhabitants become dejected. There, oxen do not carry the people or draw the plough, nor are they borne by carts or chariots. There milk kept in jars is never churned to yield butter.

On the other hand, the people become destitute and take to stealing instead of being able to enjoy the blessings of peace.

In the Vedas, the Puranas and other authoritative texts, it is said that Brahmanas, who are the souls of all creatures, who are the creators of all things, and who can be identified with all existing beings, sprang from the mouth of Narayana. It is said that the Brahmanas originated when he subdued his speech as a penance; the other varnas arose from the Brahmanas.

The Brahmanas are honoured above the Devas and Asuras, since they were created by me in my ineffable form as Brahma. As I have created the Devas and the Asuras and the Maharishis so have I placed the Brahmanas in their respective stations and have at times to punish them.

On account of his licentious assault on Ahalya, Indra was cursed by her husband Gautama, and had a green beard. Through that curse Indra also lost his testicles, which were later replaced by the testicles of a ram out of the compassion of the other Devas.

At the yagna of King Sarjati, when Maharishi Chyavana wanted to make the Aswins share in the Soma rasa, Indra objected. When Chyavana insisted, Indra wanted to hurl his thunderbolt at the sage. The Rishi paralysed Indra's arms.

Incensed at the destruction of his sacrifice by Rudra, Daksha once more began to practise severe tapasya and, attaining to high puissance, caused a third eye to appear on Rudra's forehead for the destruction of Tripurasura.

When Rudra tried to destroy this city of the Asuras, Sukra Usanas, the acharya of the Asuras, was provoked to tear a matted lock from his own head and cast it at Rudra. From that matted lock of Usanas sprang many serpents. Those serpents bit Rudra turning his throat blue.

In the ancient times of Swayambhuva Manu, it is said that Narayana seized Rudra by the throat, turning it blue. When the ocean was churned to raise up the amrita, Brihaspati of Angira's vamsa sat on its shores to perform the Puruscharana rite. When he took up a little water for the initial achamana, the water appeared murky.

Brihaspati was enraged and cursed the ocean, saying, "Since you continue to be so filthy despite my having come to you to touch you, since you have not become clear and transparent, from this day on you will be defiled with fish, sharks, tortoises and other aquatic creatures." From that time, the waters of the ocean have been infested with diverse kinds of sea creatures and monsters.

Viswarupa, the son of Tvashtri, once was the Hotri priest of the Devas. On his mother's side he was related to the Asuras, his mother being the daughter of a Danava. While publicly offering the Devas their shares of sacrificial offerings, he privately offered havis to the Asuras.

The Asuras, led by Hiranyakasipu, then went to their sister, the mother of Viswarupa, and obtained a boon from her, saying, "Viswarupa by Tvashtri, otherwise called Trisiras, is now the priest of the Devas. While he gives them their shares of sacrificial offerings publicly, he gives us our shares secretly. Thus the Devas are strengthened and we are weakened. Sister, prevail upon him to take up our cause."

The mother of Viswarupa went to her son who was dwelling in the Nandana forests of Indra and said to him, "How is it, son, that you advance the cause of your enemies and weaken that of your maternal uncles? It is not fitting for you to act in this manner."

Thus entreated by his mother, Viswarupa reflected on her words, paid his respects to her, and went over to the side of Hiranyakasipu. Upon his arrival, King Hiranyakasipu dismissed his old Hotri, Vasishta, the son of Brahma, and appointed Trisiras to that office.

Incensed, Vasishta cursed Hiranyakasipu, "Since you have dismissed me and appointed another as your Hotri, your yagna will not be completed, and some Being the like of whom has not existed before will destroy you!" As a result of this curse, Hiranyakasipu was slain by Vishnu in the form of a manticore, the Narasimha.

Viswarupa, having gone over to the side of his maternal relations, employed himself in severe tapasyas to elevate them. In order to distract him from his vows, Indra sent many beautiful Apsaras to him. Seeing these divine nymphs of transcendent beauty, Viswarupa's heart was agitated. Soon he became exceedingly attached to them.

Recognising this, one day these Apsaras said to him, "We will not stay here any longer. We will return to the place from where we came." The son of Tvashtri said to them, "Where will you go? Stay with me. I shall be good to you."

Hearing him say this, the Apsaras rejoined, "We are divine Apsaras. In the past we chose the illustrious and boon-giving Indra of great puissance."

Viswarupa then said to them. "This very day I will make all the Devas with Indra at their head cease to exist."

Saying this, Trisiras began to inwardly recite certain powerful sacred mantras. By virtue of those mantras he began to grow in tejas. With one of his mouths he began to drink all the Soma that Brahmanas poured on their sacred fires in their yagnas. With a second mouth he began to eat all food offered in those sacrifices. With his third mouth he began to consume the energy of all the Devas with Indra at their head.

Seeing him swelling with power and energy in every part of his body strengthened by the Soma he swallowed, all the Devas led by Indra flew to Pitamaha Brahma. Arriving in his presence, they said to him, "All the Soma that is offered in the yagnas performed everywhere is being drunk by Viswarupa. We no longer receive our due shares. The Asuras are being empowered while we are being weakened. Ordain what is for our good."

The Pitamaha replied, "The Maharishi Dadichi of Bhrigu's vamsa is even now engaged in performing severe austerities. Go to him and ask him for a boon. Do so that he may cast off his body. With his bones let a new weapon, the vajra, an adamantine thunderbolt, be created."

Thus instructed, the Devas set off for where the holy Dadichi was engaged in his tapasya. The Devas addressed the sage, saying, "Holy one, we hope that your austerities are being performed without hindrances."

Dadhichi said, "Welcome to all of you. Tell me what I may do for you. I will certainly do what you ask."

They said to him, "Cast off your body for the good of all the worlds."

The sage Dadhichi, who was a great yogin who regarded joy and sorrow equally, calmly focused his Atmashakti using his yoga and cast off his body.

When his soul left its temporary home, Dhatri took his bones and created an irresistible weapon, the vajra. Made with the bones of a Brahmana, it was indestructible, inexorable and pervaded by the energy of

Vishnu; using that weapon, Indra struck Viswarupa, the son of Tvashtri.

Having slain the son of Tvashtri, Indra severed his head from the body. The energy still dwelling in the lifeless body of Viswarupa, when it was kneaded, gave birth to a mighty Asura by the name of Vritra. Vritra became Indra's enemy, but Indra killed him also with the vajra and with deceit.

With this doubling of the sin of Brahmahatya, Indra was overcome with a great fear and he had to forsake the sovereignty of swarga. He entered a cool lotus stalk that grew in the Manasa Lake. Using the yoga siddhi of anima, he became minute and entered the fibres of that lotus-stalk.

When the Lord of the three worlds, the husband of Sachi, had thus vanished through the fear of the consequences of the sin of killing a Brahmana, the universe became lordless. The gunas, rajas and tamas, assailed the Devas. The mantras uttered by the great Rishis lost all efficacy. Rakshasas appeared everywhere. The Vedas were about to disappear.

Without a king, the inhabitants of all the worlds lost their strength and Rakshasas and other evil beings began to attack them. Then the Devas and the Rishis united and crowned Nahusha, the son of Ayusha, king of the three worlds.

Nahusha had on his forehead full five hundred luminaries of blazing effulgence, which had the power to destroy every fell creature of energy. Thus endowed he continued to rule heaven. The three worlds were restored to balance. Their inhabitants once more became happy and cheerful.

Nahusha then said, "Everything that Indra used to enjoy is mine. Only his wife Sachi is not." Saying this, he went to Sachi and said to her, "Blessed Devi, I have become the Lord of the Devas. You too, accept me."

Sachi replied, "You are, by your very nature, wedded to righteous behaviour. You also belong to the vamsa of Soma. It is not right for you to importune another's wife."

Nahusha said, "I now hold Indra's position and wield his power. I deserve to enjoy his dominions and all his precious possessions. Hence there can be no sin in my desiring to enjoy you. You were Indra's and should, therefore, now be mine."

Sachi said to him, "I am observing a vrata that has not yet been completed. After performing the final ablutions I will come to you, in a few days." Extracting this promise from Sachi, Nahusha left.

Sachi, indignant and grief-stricken, anxious to find her husband, and fearing Nahusha, she went to Brihaspati. Brihaspati instantly understood her agitation. Through the power of yoga, he understood that she was determined to restore her husband to his rightful place.

Brihaspati said to her, "With your tapasya and punya as a result of your vow, pray to the boon-giving Goddess Upasruti. Invoked by you, she will appear and show you where Indra dwells."

Sachi, observing her strict vrata, with the help of appropriate mantras, invoked the Devi. The goddess appeared before her and said, "I am here at your bidding. What is your wish?"

Bowing before her, Sachi said, "O Devi, show me where my husband is. You are truth. You are Rita."

Thus addressed, the Devi Upasruti took her to the Manasa Lake. Arriving there, she pointed out to Sachi her Lord Indra dwelling within the fibres of a lotus-stalk. Seeing his wife looking pale and emaciated, Indra was alarmed.

And the Lord of heaven said to himself, "Alas, great is my sorrow. I have fallen from the position that is mine. My wife, afflicted with grief on my account, seeks my lost self and comes to me."

Reflecting in this train, Indra said to Sachi, "In what condition are you now? What is your situation?" She answered him, "Nahusha called me to make me his wife. I obtained a week's brief respite from him, which has already elapsed."

Indra said to her, "Go and say to Nahusha that he should come to you on a chariot never used before—one yoked to some great Rishis; arriving in that manner he should marry you. Indra has many kinds of beautiful and wondrous chariots. All these have borne you. Nahusha should come on one such that Indra himself does not possess."

Thus advised by her husband, Sachi left that place with a hopeful heart. Indra once more entered the fibres of the lotus-stalk.

Seeing Indra's queen return to swarga, Nahusha said to her, "The time you had fixed to become mine has passed." Sachi repeated to him what Indra had directed her to say. Harnessing a number of great Rishis to his chariot, Nahusha set out from his palace for where Sachi lived.

Agastya, born in a jar, of the vital seed of Mitra and Varuna, saw those Maharishis being insulted by Nahusha in that way. Nahusha kicked him with his foot.

Agastya said, "Wretch, you have acted vilely and you will plunge down to the earth. You will be transformed into a snake and will continue to live in that form as long as the earth and her mountains exist."

As soon as these words were uttered by the great Rishi, Nahusha fell out of his chariot. The three worlds once more lost a master. The Devas and the Rishis united and went to Vishnu and appealed to him to restore Indra.

Approaching him, they said, "Holy one, it is right for you to rescue Indra who is blighted by the sin of killing a Brahmana."

Vishnu replied, "Let Sakra perform an Aswamedha yagna in my honour and he will be restored to his former position and glory."

The Devas and the Rishis began to search for Indra; not finding him, they went to Sachi and said to her, "O blessed one, go to Indra and bring him here."

Sachi went once more to the Manasa Lake. Indra rose from the waters and came to Brihaspati.

Devaguru Brihaspati made arrangements for a great Aswamedha, substituting a black deer for a regal back steed fit in every way to be offered up in sacrifice. Brihaspati had Indra, the Lord of the Maruts, ride on that horse he saved from slaughter, stole away, and led him to his own palace for Indra to perform his Aswamedha yagna. The king of swarga was then adored with mantras by all the Devas and the Rishis.

He continued to rule in swarga, cleansed of his sin; that paapa of Brahmahatya, the killing of the Brahmana Asura Vritra, was divided into four parts and ordained to dwell in woman, fire, trees and cows. It was thus that Indra, strengthened by the energy of a Brahmana, succeeded in slaying his enemy, and when, as the result of that act of his, he was overpowered by sin, it was the energy of another Brahmana that rescued him. In this manner Indra once again regained his place as the ruler of heaven.'

Krishna continued, 'Once, in olden times, while the great Rishi Bharadwaja was saying his prayers beside the celestial Ganga, one of the three feet of Vishnu, in his three-footed form, came to that place. Seeing that strange sight, Bharadwaja splashed Vishnu with a handful of water, upon which Vishnu's breast received a mark called the srivatsa.

Cursed by Rishi Bhrigu, Agni was obliged to become a devourer of all things.

Once upon a time, Aditi, the mother of the deities, cooked some food for her sons. She thought that, eating that food and being strengthened by it, the Devas would succeed in slaying the Asuras. After the food had been cooked, Budha, the presiding deity of the planet known by that name, having completed the observance of an austere vow, came before Aditi and asked her for dana.

Aditi did not offer him the food she had cooked, thinking that no one should eat it before her sons, the Devas, did. Enraged at her refusing him alms, Budha, who was Brahma's self through his vrata, cursed her, saying that she would have a pain in her womb when Vivaswat, in his second birth in her womb, was born in the form of an egg.

Aditi reminded Vivaswat at the time of his birth of Budha's curse, and it is for this reason that Vivaswat, who is adored in sraddhas, on emerging from Aditi's womb came to be called by the name of Martanda.

Prajapati Daksha became the father of sixty daughters. Of them, he gave thirteen to Kasyapa, ten to Dharma, ten to Manu and twenty-seven to Soma. Though all the twenty-seven, called Nakshatras, bestowed upon Soma were equal in beauty and accomplishments, Soma became most attached to just one, Rohini.

His other wives became jealous and left him; they went to their father and told him of Soma's conduct. "Father, although all of us are equally beautiful, Soma is attached only to our sister Rohini."

Angered by this treatment of his daughters, Prajapati Daksha cursed Soma, declaring that his son-in-law would be beset with phthisis and that disease would dwell in him. Through Daksha's curse, phthisis assailed the mighty Soma and entered into his body. Suffering, Soma came to Daksha.

Daksha said to him, "I have cursed you because of your unequal treatment of your wives. You are being weakened by this disease. There is a sacred body of water called Hiranyasara in the western ocean. Go and bathe there."

Reaching Hiranyasaras, Soma bathed in its holy waters. Performing his ablutions he washed away his sin. And because those waters were illumined, abhasita, by Soma, from that day they were called Prabhasa.

As a result, however, of Daksha's ancient curse, to this day Soma begins to wane from the night of the full moon until his total disappearance on the night of the new moon when he once more he begins to wax until the night of the full moon.

From that time on the bright moon was blemished, for since then the body of Soma has shown some dark spots, and has been tarnished by these. In fact, the splendid disc of the moon has, from then on revealed the mark of a hare.

Once upon a time, a Rishi called Sthulasiras was engaged in severe austerities on the northern breast of the mountains of Meru. While engaged in those tapasyas a pure breeze, suffused with many fragrant perfumes, began to blow and fan his body.

Scorched as he was by his rigorous tapasya, and living as he did only upon air, he was gratified by that delightful air which wafted around him. While he enjoyed this cool breeze that fanned him, the trees around him became envious and burst into a display of flowers to win his heart. Annoyed at this display, because it was prompted by jealousy, the Rishi cursed the trees, "Henceforth, you will not be able to flower in all seasons."

Once Narayana took birth as the Maharishi Badavamukha for the benefit of the world. While practising severe austerities upon the breast of Meru, he summoned the ocean into his presence. The ocean ignored his call. Infuriated at this, the Rishi, with the heat of his body, caused the waters of the ocean to become as salty as human sweat.

The sage said, "From now your waters will be undrinkable. Only when the equine-head eddying within you drinks from you, will they again become as sweet as honey. On account of this curse, the waters of the ocean remain salty to this day and are drunk by no one other than the Badavamukha.

Uma, the daughter of Himavat, was desired by Siva. After Himavat had promised her hand in marriage to Mahadeva, Maharishi Bhrigu approached Himavat, and said, "Give your daughter to me in marriage."

Himavat replied, "Siva is the bridegroom I have chosen for my daughter." Angered by this reply, Bhrigu said, "Since you refuse my proposal for your daughter's hand and insult me, you will lose your wealth of jewels and precious stones." And to this day the mountains of Himavat are without any jewels.

Such is the glory of the Brahmanas. It is through their favour that the Kshatriyas are able to possess the undecaying and eternal Bhumi Devi as their wife and enjoy her. The power of the Brahmanas is also made up of Agni and Soma. The universe is upheld by their united power.

It is said that Surya and Chandramas are the eyes of Narayana. The rays of Surya are my eyes. The sun and the moon respectively warm and rejuvenate the universe. And for this reason they have come to be regarded as the joy, the harsha, of the worlds.

Arjuna, it is because these actions of Agni and Soma that uphold the universe that I have come to be called Hrishikesa. Indeed, I am the boon-giving Isana, the Creator of the universe.

Through the punya of the mantras with which libations of ghee are poured into the sacred fire, I receive and imbibe the principal share of the sacrificial havis. My colour too is that of the most excellent of jewels called Harita. For these reasons I am known as Hari. I am the highest abode of all creatures and am known by knowers of the shastras to be identical with truth or amrita. For this reason I am called Ritadhama, the abode of truth, by learned Brahmanas.

When the Earth was submerged in the waters and disappeared from view, I retrieved her and raised her from the depths of the ocean. For this reason the Devas adore me by the name of Govinda. Sipivishta is another name of mine. Sipi means one without hair on his body. He who pervades all things in the form of Sipi is known by the name of Sipivishta.

The Rishi Yaksha in many a sacrifice invoked me by the name Sipivishta. It is for this that I bear this secret name. The Yaksha of great intelligence, having worshipped by the name Sipivishta, succeeded in restoring the Niruktas who had disappeared from the surface of the earth and sunk into the patalas.

I was never born. I never take birth. Nor shall I ever be born. I am the Kshetrajna of all creatures. Hence am I called by the name of Aja, unborn, birthless.

I have never spoken anything dishonourable or dissolute. The divine Saraswati who is truth's self, who is the daughter of Brahma and is otherwise known as Rita, represents my speech and always dwells in my tongue. The existent and the non-existent are united by me in my Atman.

The Rishis in Pushkara, the abode of Brahma, called me by the name of truth. I have never swerved from the attribute of sattva; know that this guna has flowed from me. Arjuna, even in this birth, my ancient sattva guna has not left me, so that in this life, establishing myself in sattva, I perform my karmas without wishing for their fruit.

Free of all sins through sattva, which is my nature, I can be perceived only by the knowledge that arises from the pursuit of sattva. I am counted among those who are devoted to this guna. For these reasons I am known as sattvata.

I plough the earth, taking the form of a large ploughshare of black iron. And because my complexion is black, I am called Krishna.

I have united Bhumi with Jala, Akasa with Manas, and Vayu with

Agni. Therefore I am called Vaikuntha. The highest state for a living being to attain is the cessation of separate conscious existence by union with Supreme Brahman. And since I have never swerved from that state I am Achyuta.

The earth and the sky are known to extend in all directions. And because I uphold them both, I called Adhokshaja. Those who know the Vedas and engage in interpreting their words adore me in yagnas by invoking me by this name. In elder days, while practising severe tapasyas, Maharishis said, "No one in the universe other than Narayana can be called by the name of Adhokshaja.

Sustaining the lives of all creatures in the universe, ghrita, ghee, constitutes my effulgence. It is for this reason that Brahmanas learned in the Vedas call me Ghritarchis.

There are three well-known constituent elements of the body. They have their origin in karma, and are called vata, pitha and kapham, or wind, bile and phlegm. The body is a union of these three. All living creatures are upheld by them, and when they abate, living creatures are also weakened. It is for this that those who know the shastra on Ayurveda call me Tridhatu.

Dharma is known among all creatures by the name of Vrisha. Hence I am called Vrisha in the Vedic text, Nighantuka. The word Kapi signifies the foremost of boars, and dharma means Vrisha. It is for this reason that that lord of all creatures, Kasyapa, the father of both the Devas and the Asuras, called me Vrishakapi.

The Devas and the Asuras have never been able to ascertain my beginning, my middle or my end. For this reason that I am praised as Anadi, Amadhya and Ananta. I am the Supreme Lord imbued with absolute puissance, and I am the eternal witness of the universe, for I witness its successive creations and destructions.

I always listen to words that are pious, pure and holy, Dhananjaya, and never speak anything that is sinful. Hence I am called Suchisravas.

Assuming the form of a boar with a single tusk, I raised the submerged earth from the bottom of the sea. For this reason am I named Ekasringa.

In this form of a mighty boar I had three humps on my back. On account of this peculiarity I have come to be called by the name Trikakud.

Those conversant with the Samkhya expounded by Kapila call the Paramatman Virincha. That Virincha is otherwise called Prajapati or Brahma. Verily I am identical with Virincha, since I breathe life into all living creatures, for I am the Creator of the universe.

The teachers of the Samkhya philosophy have clear knowledge of all subjects, and they call me the eternal Kapila dwelling in the sun with only gyana as my companion. On earth I am identified with him who has been revered in the Vedic mantras as the effulgent Hiranyagarbha who is worshipped by yogins.

I am regarded as the embodied form of the Rig Veda, which has twenty-one thousand verses. Men that know the Vedas also call me the embodiment of the Samans of a thousand branches. Learned Brahmanas who are my faithful devotees sing my praises in the Aranyakas.

In the Adhyaryus I am sung of as the Yajur Veda of six and fifty, and eight and seven, and thirty branches. Brahmanas conversant with the Atharvans regard me as identical with the Atharvans consisting of five kalpas and all the krityas.

Arjuna, know that all the angas of the Vedas and all their verses, and all the vowels in those verses, and all the rules in respect of their pronunciation, are my work. I am he who emerges at the beginning of creation from the ocean of milk at the earnest invocation of Brahma and all the Devas, and he who grants boons to all the Devas.

I am he who is the repository of the science of pronunciation contained in the angas of the Vedas. It was through my grace that, following the path indicated by Vamadeva, the Maharishi Panchala obtained from that eternal Being the techniques for reading the Vedas with respect to the division of syllables and words.

Born into the Babhravya vamsa, and having achieved great ascetic victory and obtained a boon from Narayana, Galava compiled the rules regarding the division of syllables and words for reading the Vedas. He also compiled the rules about the required emphasis and accent in reciting them, and shone as the first scholar who became knowledgeable in these two subjects.

Favoured by me, Kundrika and King Brahmadatta, thinking of the sorrow that attends birth and death, attained to that prosperity which is achieved by those devoted to yoga in the course of seven births. In ancient times, I was born as the son of Dharma, and in consequence of this birth I was celebrated as Dharmaja.

I took birth in two forms—Nara and Narayana. Riding on the vahana that helps in the performance of scriptural and other duties, I practised, in those two forms, undying austerities on the breast of Gandhamadana.

At that time Daksha performed his great yagna of Daksha. However, he refused to give a share of the havis to Rudra. Urged by the sage Dadichi, Rudra destroyed that sacrifice. He cast an arrow of blazing flames that consumed all the preparations for Daksha's yagna, and then coursed forcefully towards us, Nara and Narayana at Badari's asrama. That brutal barb fell squarely upon the chest of Narayana. Assailed by its energy the hair on Narayana's head became green. As a result of this change in the colour of my hair I came to be called Munjakesa.

Narayana blew off this arrow, its energy spent, and it returned to Siva. Enraged and fired by the power of his tapasya, Siva charged towards the Rishis Nara and Narayana. Narayana seized the advancing Rudra by his throat. Held by Narayana, the Lord of the universe, Rudra's neck changed colour and became dark. From that time Rudra came to be called Sitikantha.

Meanwhile, Nara pulled up a blade of grass and suffused it with mantras to kill Rudra. The blade of grass was transformed into a mighty battle-axe. Nara cast the axe at Rudra but it shattered into pieces. Because of that weapon being smashed, I received the name Khandaparasu.'

Arjuna said, 'Krishna, in that battle which could destroy the three worlds, who was victorious? Tell me this!'

Krishna said, 'When Rudra and Narayana were engaged in battle, all the universe trembled with anxious. Agni ceased to accept libations of even the purest ghee offered with Vedic mantras in yagnas. The Vedas no longer shone inward light in the minds of the Rishis of cleansed souls.

Rajas and tamas possessed the Devas. The earth shook. The vault of the sky appeared to be rent in two. All the stars were deprived of their brilliance. Brahma himself fell from his throne.

The ocean became dry. The Himavat Mountains were riven. When such terrible omens appeared everywhere, Brahma surrounded by all the Devas and the Devarishis, rushed to the raging battleground.

Brahma, who can be grasped only with the help of the Niruktas, joined his hands and said to Siva, "Bestow good upon the three worlds. Discard your weapons, Lord of the universe, and benefit all the Akhanda.

That which is unmanifest, indestructible, immutable, supreme, the origin of the universe, uniform, and the supreme actor, that which transcends all pairs of opposites, and is inactive, choosing to be manifested, has assumed this one blessed form, though it appears as two. This Nara and Narayana, the manifest forms of Supreme Brahman, have taken birth in the vamsa of Dharma.

The foremost of all deities, these two observe the highest vratas and severest tapasyas. Through some reason best known to him, I myself have sprung from his grace. Eternal as you are, for you have existed ever since all the past creations, you too, have sprung from his wrath.

Along with me, the Devas and all the Maharishis revere this form of Brahma, and let peace prevail in all the worlds without any delay."

Thus addressed by Brahma, Rudra instantly cast off the fire of his anger, and began to worship Narayana. Indeed, he placed surrendered himself to Narayana. And Narayana, with his anger and senses subdued, was gratified and reconciled with Rudra.

Adored by the Rishis, by Brahma and by all the Devas, the Lord of the universe, also known as Hari, then addressed the illustrious Isana, "He that knows you, knows me. He that follows you, follows me. There is no difference between you and me. Never think otherwise.

The mark that your spear made on my chest will from this day assume the form of a beautiful whorl; and the mark of my hand on your neck will also assume a beautiful shape and for this you shall from this day be called Sreekantha."

Krishna continued, 'Having mutually made marks on each other's bodies, the two Rishis Nara and Narayana were reconciled with Rudra; dismissing the Devas, they once more set themselves to the practice of penances with tranquil souls.

Son of Pritha, I have now told you how, in that ancient battle between Rudra and Narayana, the latter triumphed. I have also told you the many secret names of Narayana and the significance of one of those names which the Rishis bestowed upon him.

Arjuna, assuming diverse forms I roam the earth, the realm of Brahma himself and Golaka, that other high and eternal realm of felicity. Protected by me in the maha yuddha, you have won a great victory.

That Being whom you saw lurking in your chariot, during your battles, is none other than Rudra Kapardin. Otherwise known by the name Kaala, he should be known as one that has sprung from my wrath. Those enemies whom you have killed were all, in the first instance, slain by him.

Bow your head before that powerful God of gods, that Lord of Uma. With concentrated soul, bow unto that illustrious Lord of the universe, that indestructible deity, otherwise called by the name of Hara.

As I have told you, he is none other than one who has manifested from my anger. Arjuna, you have, before this, heard of his puissance and energy!'"

CANTO 344

Saunaka said, 'O Sauti, how excellent is this story that you have narrated. Verily, these ascetics, having heard it, have all been amazed. It is said that a discourse on Narayana is rewarded with more punya than pilgrimages to all the sacred asramas and ablutions performed in all the holy tirthas on earth. Having listened to your divine discourse on Narayana, which can cleanse one of every sin, all of us have certainly been blessed.

Adored in all the worlds, even the Rishis and the Devas, even Brahma, cannot easily behold that most celebrated of all gods. That Narada was able to obtain a glimpse of Narayana, otherwise called Hari, was because his of the special grace of that divine and powerful Lord.

Why then did Devarishi Narada, having succeeded in seeing the Supreme Lord of the universe, dwelling in the form of Aniruddha, go swiftly to Badarikasrama on the breast of Himavat to behold Nara and Narayana? O Sauti, tell us the reason for this.'

Sauti said, 'During his snake-sacrifice, Janamejaya, the royal son of Parikshita, availing himself of an interval in the sacrificial rites, when all the learned Brahmanas were resting, addressed the grandfather of his grandfather, the island-born Krishna, otherwise called Vyasa, that ocean of Vedic lore, that foremost of ascetics endued with power, with these words. Janamejaya said, "What did Devarishi Narada do next when he returned from the White Island, reflecting, as he came, on the words spoken to him by Narayana? Arriving at Badarikasrama upon the breast of the Himavat Mountains, and seeing the two Rishis Nara and Narayana engaged in stern tapasya, how long did Narada dwell there and on what subjects did they speak?

This discourse on Narayana, that is really an ocean of knowledge, has been culled by you by churning that vast histories of a hundred thousand verses, the Mahabharata. As butter is raised from curds, sandalwood from the mountains of Malaya, the Aranyakas from the Vedas, and amrita from medicinal plants, in the same manner, O Tapodhana, you have raised this ambrosial discourse that has Narayana for its subject from diverse itihasas and Puranas existing in the world.

Narayana is the Supreme Lord. Illustrious and formidable, he is the soul of all creatures. Indeed, Dvijottama, the energy of Narayana is irresistible. At the end of the kalpa, all the Devas led by Brahma, all the Rishis with the Gandharvas, and all things living and non-living enter into Narayana.

There is nothing holier on earth or in heaven, and nothing higher, than Narayana. A pilgrimage to all the sacred asramas on earth, and ablutions performed in all the holy waters, will not yield as much punya as a discourse on Narayana. Having listened from the beginning to this discourse on Hari, the Lord of the universe, which destroys all sins, we feel that we have been completely purified and sanctified.

It was not my ancestor Arjuna who was the real victor in the great battle on Kurukshetra; it should be remembered that Krishna was his ally. There is nothing unattainable in the three worlds for a man who has Vishnu himself for his ally. My forebears were extremely fortunate and worthy, for they had Krishna safeguarding their temporal and spiritual prosperity.

Adored by all the worlds, the holy Narayana can be seen only through tapasya. They, however, succeeded in seeing him, Narayana, adorned with the beautiful srivatsa on his chest. More fortunate than my ancestors was the Devarishi Narada, the son of Paramesthi. I am thankful that Mahatejasvin Narada, who transcends all destruction, went to Sweta dwipa, and that he had succeeded in seeing Hari.

It is clear he saw the Supreme Lord as a result only of the grace of that immortal Being. Fortunate was Narada to behold Narayana as existing in the form of Aniruddha.

Having seen Narayana in that form, why did Narada hasten once more to the asrama of Badari to behold Nara and Narayana? What was the reason for this? After his return from the White Island and on his arrival at Badari, where he met with the two Rishis? How long did Narada continue to live there, and what conversations did he have with them? What did those two Mahatman Rishis say to him? It is fitting that you tell me!"

Vaisampayana said, "Salutations unto the holy Vyasa of immeasurable energy. Through his grace I will relate this story of Narayana.

Arriving at the White Island, Narada beheld the immutable Hari. Leaving that place he hurried to the mountains of Meru, bearing in his mind the momentous words spoken by the Paramatman Narayana. Arriving at Meru he was struck at the thought of what he had achieved. And he said to himself, 'How wonderful it is! The journey I undertook was a long one. Having journeyed so far, I have returned safely.'

From the Meru mountains he moved towards Gandhamadana. Coursing through the skies he descended upon the vast retreat of Badari. There he beheld those ancient deities Nara and Narayana, engaged in tapasya while observing high vratas, and devoted to the worship of their own selves.

Both those revered beings bore the beautiful whorls called srivatsa on their chests, and both had matted jata on their heads. And because of their dazzling radiance with which they illumined the world they seemed to surpass even the energy of the sun. Their hands bore the mark of the swan's foot. The soles of their feet bore the sign of the discus.

Their chests were broad; their arms reached down to their knees. Each of them had four mushkas. Each had sixty teeth and four arms. Their voices were deep like rolling thunder.

Their faces were striking, their foreheads broad, their brows fair, their cheeks well-formed, and their noses aquiline. The heads of those two deities were big and round like parasols unfurled. All these features gave them a magnificent appearance.

Seeing them, Narada was filled with joy. He saluted them with reverence and was saluted by them in return. They received the Devarishi, welcomed him and enquired after his wellbeing.

Seeing them, Narada began to reflect, 'These two foremost of Rishis seem to be very alike in appearance to those I have seen in Sweta dwipa.' Thoughtfully, he circled around them in pradakshina and then sat down to rest on the seat made of kusa grass offered to him.

After this, those two famed Rishis, who were the abode of tapasya and tejas, of tranquil hearts and self-restraint, went through their morning rituals. With subdued senses, they worshipped Narada with arghya and water to wash his feet. Having finished their morning kriyas, necessary for receiving their guest, they sat down on two seats made of wooden planks.

When those two Rishis sat, that place began to glow with an unusual beauty even as the sacrificial altar does with the beauty of sacred fires when libations of ghee are poured upon them. Seeing Narada refreshed from fatigue, seated at his ease and gratified with the hospitality he had received, Nara and Narayana spoke to him.

Nara and Narayana said, 'In Sweta dwipa have you seen the Paramatman, who is eternal and divine, and who is the source from which we have sprung?'

Narada said, 'I have seen that beautiful Being who is immutable and who has the universe for his form. In him dwell all the worlds, and all the Devas with the Rishis. Even now I behold him in you two. Those marks and indications that characterise Hari of unrevealed form, characterise you that now have forms revealed to the senses.

Indeed, I see both of you by his side. Sent by the Paramatman, I have come here today. In energy and fame and beauty, who else in the three worlds can equal him than you both that have been born into the dharma vamsa? He has related to me the entire course of Kshetrajna dharma.

He has also instructed me in all his future incarnations in this world.

The inhabitants of the White Island, whom I have seen, are without the five senses that ordinary men possess. All of them are of awakened souls, endowed with true gyana. They are entirely devoted to the foremost of Beings, the Supreme Lord of the universe.

They are always engaged in worshipping that great deity, and he always sports with them. The Holy and Supreme Soul loves those that are devoted to him. He also cares for such Dvijas. Compassionate to his bhaktas, he dallies with them.

Enjoyer of the universe, pervading everything, Madhava is ever loving towards his worshippers. He is the actor; he is the Cause; and he is the Effect. He is omnipotent and magnificent.

He is the Cause from which all beings originate. He is the embodiment of all the rules of the shastras. He is the embodiment of all the tattvas. He is renowned. Uniting himself with tapasya, he radiates a splendour that is said to represent an energy that is higher than what is found in Sweta dwipa. Of the Soul cleansed by tapasya, he has ordained peace and tranquillity in the three worlds.

With such an auspicious intellect, he is observes a very superior vrata which is the very embodiment of holiness. The sun does not warm and the moon does not shine in his realm where he lives engaged in austere penance. There the Wind does not blow.

Having built a vedi measuring eight fingers' breadth there, the Creator of the universe is engaged in rigorous tapasya, standing on one foot, with arms raised and with his face turned towards the east, reciting the Vedas with their angas.

All libations of ghee or meat poured on the sacrificial fire according to the decrees of Brahma, by the Rishis, by Pasupati himself, by the rest of the principal Devas, by the Daityas, the Danavas and the Rakshasas, all reach the feet of that Great Divinity. Whatever karmas and kriyas are performed by those souls who are entirely devoted to him, are all received by him on his head.

No one is dearer to him in the three worlds than those who are awakened and enlightened. Dearer even is one completely devoted to him. Sent by him who is the Paramatman, I have come here at his command.

Henceforth, I shall dwell with you two, devoted to Narayana in the form of Aniruddha.'"

Vaisampayana said, "Nara and Narayana said, 'You are deserving of the highest praise, and have been highly favoured, since you have seen the puissant Narayana himself in the form of Aniruddha. No one else, not even Brahma who was born from the primal lotus, has been able to behold him. That foremost of Purushas is of unmanifest origin and cannot be seen.

What we say to you is the truth, O Narada. There exists no one in the universe that is dearer to him than one that adores him with devotion. It is for this that he revealed himself to you.

No one can repair to that realm where the Paramatman is engaged in tapasya other than us. The splendour of the place adorned by him resembles the effulgence of a thousand suns gathered together.

From him who is the origin of the creator of the universe springs the attribute of forgiveness which attaches to the earth. It is from that illustrious Being who seeks the welfare of all beings, that the rasa of taste has arisen. That rasa attaches to the waters which are liquid.

It is from him that Agni, having the attribute of form or sight, has arisen. It attaches itself to the sun which then is able to shine and radiate heat. It is from that illustrious and foremost of Beings that touch also has arisen. It is attached to Vayu, which enables it to move about in the world producing the sensation of touch.

It is from that Lord of the entire universe that sound has arisen. It attaches to Akasa, which allows it to exist uncovered and unconfined. It is from him that Manas, Mind, which pervades all Beings, has arisen. It attaches to Chandramas, and so Chandramas has the quality of revealing all things. In the Vedas, where Narayana, that partaker of the libations and other offerings, resides, with gyana alone for his companion, has been called Sat, the generative cause of all things.

The path of those who are stainless and free from both virtue and sin, is fraught with auspiciousness and felicity. Aditya, who is the dispeller of the darkness of all the worlds, is said to be the doorway through which the emancipated must pass. Entering Aditya, the bodies of such men are consumed by his fire. They then become invisible and cannot be seen by anyone at any time.

Reduced into invisible atoms, they pass into the form of Aniruddha, Narayana in manifested form, who dwells in the heart of the realm of Aditya. Losing all physical attributes and being transformed into pure mind, they then enter into Pradyumna. Passing out of Pradyumna, those that are conversant with Samkhya yoga and those that are devoted to the Supreme Deity then enter Samkarsana otherwise called Jiva.

After this, divested of the three primal gunas of sattva, rajas and tamas, those foremost of regenerate beings quickly enter the Paramatman, also called Kshetrajna, and which itself transcends these three primal attributes. Know that Vasudeva is he when called Kshetrajna.

Surely you must know that Vasudeva is the abode or original refuge of all things in the universe. Only those whose minds are focused, who practise restraint and subdue their senses, and who are devoted to him, succeed in entering Vasudeva.

We two have taken birth in the house of Dharma. Living in this delightful and vast hermitage we undergo the austerest tapasya. We are thus engaged being moved by the desire to benefit those manifestations of the Supreme Deity, dear to all the Devas, which will occur in the three worlds to achieve diverse and unrivalled feats.

In accordance with such rare rules that apply to us two only, we observe all excellent and high vratas fraught with the most rigorous of penances. O Devarishi, with the power of our tapasya, we saw you when you were in the White Island.

Having met Narayana, you have made a particular resolution, which is known to us. In the three worlds consisting of mobile and immobile beings, there is nothing that is unknown to us. Maharishi, of the good or evil that will occur or has occurred or is occurring, that Devadeva has informed you.'"

Vaisampayana continued, "Having heard these words of Nara and Narayana, Narada joined his hands in reverence and became entirely devoted to Narayana. He spent his time in mentally reciting countless sacred mantras that are in praise of Narayana.

Worshipping him, and adoring those two ancient Rishis who were born in the dharma vamsa, Rishi Narada continued to dwell in Nara and Narayana's asrama of Badari on Himavat for a thousand years of the Devas.'"

CANTO 345

Vaisampayana said, "On one occasion, while dwelling with Nara and Narayana, Narada the son of Paramesthi, having duly completed the rites and rituals to honour the Devas, set himself to perform the kriyas in honour of the Pitris.

Seeing him thus prepared, the eldest son of Dharma, Nara, addressed him, saying, 'Which Devas and Pitris are you worshipping with these rites and rituals? O foremost of all wise men, tell me this, in accordance with the shastras. What is this that you are doing? What are the fruits you desire by performing these rites?'

Narada said, 'On an earlier occasion you said to me that rites and rituals in honour of the Devas should be done. You said that the kriyas in their honour constitute the highest sacrifice equal to the worship of the eternal Paramatman. Instructed by that teaching, I perform these rites in honour of the immutable Vishnu.

It is from that Supreme Deity that Brahma, the Pitamaha of all the worlds, arose in the ancient times. That Brahma, or Paramesthi, filled with ananda, caused my father Daksha to come into being. I was the son of Brahma, created before all others, by a command of his will, although later, through the curse of that Rishi, I had to be born as the son of Daksha

O righteous and illustrious one, I am performing these kriyas in honour of the Pitris for the sake of Narayana, and conforming to the rules that were laid down by him. Narayana is the father, mother and grandfather of all creatures. In all yagnas performed in honour of the Pitris, it is that Lord of the universe who is adored and worshipped.

On one occasion, the Devas taught their children the Srutis. Having lost this knowledge themselves they had to again acquire it from those very sons unto whom they had communicated it. In this manner, the sons, who had to thus convey the mantras to their sires, achieved the status of fathers, and the fathers, who received the mantras from their sons, attained the status of sons.

Without doubt, what the Devas did on that occasion is known to you two. Sons and fathers had thus to worship each other. Having first spread some blades of kusa grass on the ground, the Devas and the Pitris, their children, placed three pindas there and worshipped each other. I now wish to know why the Pitris in ancient days acquired the name of Pindas.'

Nara and Narayana said, 'In the past, the earth, with her belt of seas, disappeared. Govinda, assumed the form of a colossal boar and raised her with his mighty tusk. Having restored the earth to her former position, that foremost of Purushas, his body smeared with water and mud, set himself to do what was necessary for the world and its inhabitants.

When the sun reached the meridian, and it was the hour for saying the morning prayers, Vishnu suddenly shook off three lumps of mud from his tusk and set them upon the earth in the place where he had spread blades of the kusa grass. He dedicated those lumps of mud to his own self, according to the rules laid down in the shastras.

After shaking off those lumps from his tusks as Pindas, he sat facing the east and himself performed the rites of dedication with the oil of sesame seeds that arose from the heat of his own body. Impelled by the desire to establish rules of conduct for the inhabitants of the three worlds, Vishnu, Vrishakapi, said these words: "I am the Creator of the worlds. I have resolved to create the Pitris."

Saying this, he began to think of those worthy laws that should regulate the rituals to be performed in honour of the Pitris. While thus engaged, he saw that the Pindas had fallen towards the south.

He then said to himself, "These Pindas have fallen on the surface of the earth towards the south. Based on this, I declare that these should from now on be known by the name of Pitris. Let these three round lumps come to be regarded as Pitris in the world.

In this way I am creating the eternal Pitris. I am the father, the grandfather and the great-grandfather, and I should be regarded as dwelling in these three Pindas. There is no one that is higher than me. Who can I worship and adore? Who is my father in the universe? I myself am my grandfather. I am, indeed, the Pitamaha and the sire. I am the one cause of all the universe."

Learned Brahmana, having said these words, Vrishakapi offered those Pindas on the breast of the Varaha Mountains, with elaborate rituals. With these he worshipped his own self, and having finished the worship, vanished. Hence the Pitris came to be called by the name of Pinda.

In accordance with these words of Vrishakapi on that occasion, the Pitris receive the worship offered by all. They who perform yagnas in honour of and adore the Pitris, the Devas, gurus or other revered elder guests, cows, superior Brahmanas, Devi Bhumi, and their mothers, in thought, word and deed are said to adore and sacrifice to Vishnu himself.

Pervading the bodies of all existent creatures, the illustrious Lord is the Soul of all things. Detached from happiness or misery, he regards all equally. Narayana has been said to be the Soul of all things in the universe.'"

CANTO 346

'Vaisampayana said, "Having heard these words of Nara and Narayana, Narada was filled with bhakti for the Supreme Being. With his whole being he devoted himself to Narayana. Having lived a full thousand years in the retreat of Nara and Narayana, having beheld the immutable Hari, and heard the excellent discourse on the subject of Narayana, the Devarishi repaired to his own asrama on the breast of Himavat.

Those foremost of Munis, Nara and Narayana, however continued to dwell in the delightful Badarikasrama, engaged in the practice of the severest tapasyas. You are born into the Pandava vamsa. You are of immeasurable energy. Having heard this discourse on Narayana from the beginning, you have certainly been cleansed of all your sins and your soul has been sanctified.

He who hates instead of loving and worshipping Hari, his is neither this world nor the world hereafter. The ancestors of those who hate Narayana, the foremost of gods, plunge into naraka forever.

Vishnu is the soul of all beings. How, then, can Vishnu be hated, for in hating him one would hate one's own self. He who is our guru, the Rishi Vyasa, the son of Gandhavati, has himself recited this discourse on the glory of Narayana to us, that glory which is the highest. I heard it from him and have narrated it to you exactly as I heard it.

Rajan this dharma, with its mysteries and the summary of its details, was obtained by Narada from Narayana himself. Such are the particulars of this great sect. I have earlier explained this to you in the Hari-Gita, with a brief reference to its niyamas.

Know that the island-born Vyasa is Narayana on earth. Who other than he could compile such an itihasa as the Mahabharata? Who else than that puissant Rishi could discourse upon the diverse kinds of duties and religions for men to adopt and follow?

You have resolved upon performing a great sacrifice. Let your yagna continue as determined by you. Having listened to the many kinds of duties and paths, let your yagna proceed."'

Sauti continued, 'Having heard this great discourse, Janamejaya began all those kriyas established in the shastras for the completion of his mahayagna. Saunaka, I have duly narrated that great sermon on Narayana to you and all these Rishis who dwell in the Naimisa vana. Formerly Narada recited it to my guru in the hearing of many Rishis and the sons of Pandu, and in the presence of Krishna and Bhishma also.

Narayana is the Lord of all the foremost of Rishis, and of the three worlds. He is the upholder of this vast Bhumi herself. He is the vessel that holds the Srutis and of the attribute of humility.

He is the great receptacle of all those laws that must be adhered to in order to attain peace of mind, as also of all those with the name Yama. He is always accompanied by the foremost of Dvijas. Let that Great Deity be your refuge.

Hari always does what is agreeable and beneficial to the inhabitants of swarga. He is the slayer of Asuras who trouble the three worlds. He is the receptacle of tapasya. He has great renown.

Known as Madhu and Kaitabha, he is also the slayer of the Daityas. He ordains the goals of those who know and observe scriptural and other duties. He dispels the fears of all. He takes the best of the havis offered in sacrifices. He is your refuge and protection.

He is Saguna, blessed with gunas; he is Nirguna, free from gunas. He has a quadruple form. He shares the punya arising from the dedication of holy tanks and the observance of similar religious rites. Unvanquished and mighty, it is he that always proclaims the goal of the Atmans of righteous Rishis.

He is the witness of the worlds. He is unborn. He is the one ancient Purusha. With the radiance of the sun, he is the Supreme Lord and is the refuge of all. Do all of you bow your heads before him, since Narayana himself who sprang from the primordial waters bows before him.

He is the origin of the universe. He is that Being who is called amrita, deathless. He is minute. He is the refuge upon whom all things depend. He is the one Being to whom the attribute of immutability attaches. The Samkhyas and yogins, of restrained souls, uphold him to be their eternal knowledge.'

CANTO 347

Sauti said, 'Janamejaya said, "I have heard from you of the glory of the divine Paramatman. I have heard also of the birth of the Supreme Deity in the house of Dharma, in the forms of Nara and Narayana. I have also heard about the origin of the Pinda from the mighty Varaha, the form that Vishnu assumed to raise the submerged earth.

I have heard from you about the Devas and Rishis that were ordained for Pravritti dharma and of those that were ordained for Nivritti dharma. You have also discoursed to us on other subjects. You have spoken to us of that vast form, Hayagriva with the equine head, of Vishnu, that partaker of the libations and other offerings, the form that appeared in the great ocean towards the north-east.

That form was seen by Paramesthi, the illustrious Brahma. What were the exact features, and what was the tejas, the like of which had never been seen before, of that form which Hari, upholder of the universe, revealed on that occasion? What did Brahma do after having seen him, whose likeness had never been seen before, him of immeasurable energy, him with the equine head, and who was sacredness itself?

On this ancient subject, this question arises in our mind. Why did the Supreme Deity assume that form and display himself in it to Brahma? You have certainly sanctified us by speaking to us on these diverse sacred subjects!"'

Sauti said, 'I shall recite to you that itihasa which is perfectly consistent with the Vedas, and which Vaisampayana recited to the son of Parikshita on the occasion of the great snake-sacrifice. Having heard the account of this mighty form of Vishnu, with the horse's head, the royal son of Parikshita too, had the same doubt and put the same questions to Vaisampayana.

Janamejaya said, "Tell me for what reason did Hari appear in that mighty form with a horse-head, which Brahma saw on the shores of the great northern ocean?"

Vaisampayana said, "Rajan, all existing objects in this world are the result of a combination of the five primal elements, a combination caused by the intelligence of the Supreme Lord. The puissant and infinite Narayana is the Supreme Lord and Creator of the universe.

He is the inner Soul of all things, and the giver of boons. Without gunas, he also possesses them. Listen now to me as I tell you about the Pralaya and how all things are destroyed.

At first, Bhumi merges in Jala and then nothing is seen save one vast expanse of water on all sides – the Ekarnava. Jala then merges into Agni, and Agni into Vayu. Vayu merges into Akasa which in turn merges into Manas, mind. Manas merges into the Vyakta, the manifest, or Chitta, Consciousness. The Vyakta merges into the Avyakta, the unmanifest or Prakriti. Prakriti merges into Purusha, the Jivatman, and Purusha merges into the Paramatman, or Brahman.

Then tamas spreads over the face of the universe, and nothing can be seen. From that primal darkness arises Brahma endowed with the principle of creation. Tamas is primeval and immortal. Brahma arising from this darkness develops by his own power into the idea of the universe, and assumes the form of Purusha.

This Purusha is called Aniruddha. Without gender, it is otherwise called Pradhana, supreme or primary. Rajan, It is also known by the name of Vyakta, a combination of the triguna. He exists with only gyana for his companion.

That renowned Being is otherwise called by the name of Viswaksena or Hari. Yielding to yoga-nidra, he lays himself down on the waters of the ocean Ekarnava. He then thinks of the creation of the universe with its diverse phenomena and immeasurable attributes. While engaged in thinking of creation, he recollects his own lofty gunas.

From this springs the four-faced Brahma who represents the consciousness of Aniruddha. Brahma, otherwise called Hiranyagarbha, is the Pitamaha of all the worlds. With eyes like lotus-petals, he is born within the lotus that springs from the navel of Aniruddha.

Seated on that lotus, the illustrious eternal Brahma saw himself surrounded by water. Adopting the attribute of sattva, Brahma Paramesthi, then began to create the universe.

In the primeval lotus, radiant like the Sun, two drops of holy water had been cast by Narayana. He, Narayana, looked at those two drops of water.

One of those two drops, beautiful and bright in form looked like a drop of honey. At the command of Narayana, a Daitya of the name of Madhu, with the attribute of tamas, sprang from that drop. The other drop of water within the lotus was very hard. From it sprang the Daitya Kaitabha composed of the attribute of rajas.

As soon as they were born, imbued with tamas and rajas, the two mighty Daityas armed with maces began to roam within that vast primeval lotus. In it they beheld the effulgent Brahma, engaged in creating the four Vedas, each with the most delightful form.

Seeing the four Vedas, the powerful Asuras suddenly seized the Vedas before the very eyes of their Creator. With the Vedas, the two Danavas dived into the ocean and swam to its bottom. Seeing the Vedas forcibly taken from him, Brahma was grief-stricken and addressed the Supreme Lord Narayana in these words.

Brahma said, 'The Vedas are my great eyes. The Vedas are my great strength. The Vedas are my great refuge. The Vedas are my high Brahman. They have been taken from me by the two Danavas. Deprived of the Vedas, the worlds I have created are plunged in darkness.

Without the Vedas, how can I bring creation into existence? Alas, great is the grief I suffer because of the loss of the Vedas. My heart is wounded and has become the home of a great sorrow.

Who is there that will rescue me from this ocean of grief in which I am drowning? Who is there that will bring me the Vedas I have lost? Who is there that will take pity on me?'

While he spoke, Brahma decided to sing the praises of Hari in these words. He joined his hands in reverence, grasped the feet of his Progenitor, and sang this hymn in honour of Narayana.

Brahma said, 'I bow to you, O heart of Brahman. I bow to you that was born before me. You are the origin of the universe. You are the foremost of all abodes. You are the ocean of yoga with all its angas. You are the Creator of both the Vyakta and the Avyakta.

You walk the path of vast and immeasurable auspiciousness. You devour the universe. You are the Antaraloka, the Inner Soul, of all creatures. You have no origin. You are the refuge of the universe. You are Svayambhu; your origin is none other than yourself.

As for myself, I have sprung through your grace. I have been born from you. My first birth, which is regarded sacred by all regenerate persons, was from a fiat of your mind. My second birth was from your eyes. Through your grace, my third birth was from your speech.

My fourth birth was from your ears. My fifth birth was from your nose. O Lord, My sixth birth was, through you, from an egg. This is my seventh birth. It has occurred, O Lord, within this lotus, and it is meant to stimulate the intellect and desires of all creatures.

In each birth I am born as your son. Indeed, I take birth as your eldest son constituted of sattva, the purest of the three gunas. Your own nature is Supreme. You are born from yourself.

I have been created by you. The Vedas are my eyes. Hence, I transcend Time itself. Those Vedas, which care my eyes, have been taken from me and I have become blind. Awaken from your yoga-nidra. Give me back my eyes. I am dear to you as you are to me.'

Thus praised by Brahma, the illustrious Purusha, with face turned in every direction, shook off his slumber and resolved to recover the Vedas from the Daityas that had taken them. With his yoga-shakti, he assumed a second form. His body, with an excellent nose, became as luminous as the moon. He assumed an equine head of great effulgence, which was the abode of the Vedas.

The sky, with all its stars and constellations, became the crown of his head. His locks of hair were long and flowing, and had the splendour of the rays of the sun. The realms above and below became his two ears. The earth became his forehead. The two rivers Ganga and Saraswati became his two hips.

The two oceans became his two eyebrows. The sun and the moon became his two eyes. The twilight became his nose. The AUM became his memory and intelligence. Lightning became his tongue. The Soma-drinking Pitris became his teeth. Goloka and Brahmaloka became his upper and lower lips.

The terrible night that follows the Pralaya, transcending the three attributes, became his neck. Having assumed this form with the horse's head and having diverse things for its diverse limbs, the Lord of the universe disappeared in an instant, and plunged down into patala.

Having reached that realm, he set himself to high yoga. Adopting a voice regulated by the rules of the science called siksha, he began to recite the Vedic mantras aloud. His enunciation was distinct and melodious, and reverberated through the air. The sound of his voice filled patala from end to end. Suffused with the properties of all the elements, it produced great grace and merit.

The two Asuras determined to return to the Vedas quickly, flung them aside and ran towards the place from where those sweet sounds issued.

Meanwhile, the Supreme Lord with the horse's head, otherwise called Hari, picked up all four Vedas. Returning to Brahma, he gave him Vedas to him. Having restored the Vedas to Brahma, Narayana once more returned to his own nature.

Narayana returned to his form with the equine head in the north-eastern region of the great ocean. Having re-established Brahma who was the abode of the Vedas, he once more became the equine-headed form that he was. The two Danavas, Madhu and Kaitabha, did not find the source of the sounds and swiftly returned to that place. They looked around but did not find the Vedas. The Asuras rapidly rose from the nether region. Returning to the primeval lotus from which they had taken birth, they saw the puissant Being, the original Creator, dwelling in the form of Aniruddha of fair complexion and the splendour of the moon.

Of immeasurable prowess, he was under the influence of yoga-nidra, asleep, his body stretched on the waters and occupying a space as vast as itself. Glowing with great effulgence and the stainless sattva guna, the body of Vishnu lay on the hood of a resplendent snake that emitted flames of fire.

Beholding the Lord thus, the two Danavas roared with laughter. Imbued with the attributes of rajas and tamas, they said, 'This is that Being of white complexion. He now lies asleep. Without doubt, this one has brought the Vedas away from patala. Whose is he? Who is he? Why is he thus asleep on the hood of a snake?'

These words of the two Danavas awakened Hari from his yoga-slumber. Narayana, thus awakened, understood that the two Danavas intended to fight him. Seeing this, he also set his mind to gratify their desire.

A battle broke out between those two on one side and Narayana on the other. The Asuras Madhu and Kaitabha were embodiments of rajas and tamas. To please Brahma, Narayana killed them both. Thus he came to be called Madhusudana, the slayer of Madhu. Having destroyed the two Asuras and restored the Vedas to Brahma, Vishnu assuaged Brahma's grief.

With the help of Hari and the Vedas, Brahma created all the worlds with their mobile and immobile creatures. Granting the intelligence of creation to Brahma, Hari disappeared from there and returned to where he had come from.

It was thus that Narayana, having assumed the form with the horse-head, slew the two Danavas Madhu and Kaitabha. Once more he assumed the same form to cause Pravritti dharma to flow in the universe. Thus did the blessed Hari assume that grand form of Hayasiras. This is celebrated as the oldest and most powerful of all his forms. He who frequently listens or mentally recites the story of how Narayana assumed that form will never lose his Vedic knowledge.

Having adored this illustrious deity with rigorous tapasya, the Rishi Panchala, also known as Galava, acquired the knowledge of Krama by treading the path shown by Rudra. Rajan, I have now recited to you the ancient story of Hayasiras, consistent with the Vedas, about which you asked me.

Whatever forms the Supreme Deity desires to assume with a view to ordain the affairs of the universe, he assumes those forms within himself by exercising his own inherent powers. Narayana is the receptacle of the Vedas. He is the receptacle of tapasya as well. Hari is yoga.

He is the embodiment of the Samkhya yoga. He is that Parabrahman of which we hear. Truth has Narayana for its refuge. Rita has Narayana for its Atman. Nivritti, from which there is no return, has Narayana for its abode. The basis of Pravritti equally has Narayana for its soul.

The foremost of all the attributes that belong to the earth is smell. Scent has Narayana for its soul. The attributes of water are various kinds of tastes. These too have Narayana for their soul.

The foremost attribute of light is form. Form also has Narayana for its soul. Touch, which is the attribute of wind, also has Narayana for its soul. Sound, which is an attribute of space, has like the others Narayana for its soul. Mind also, which is the attribute of the unmanifest Prakriti, has Narayana for its soul.

Time which is computed by the movement of the celestial luminaries has similarly Narayana for its soul. The Devas of fame, of beauty and of wealth have him for their soul. Both the Samkhya philosophy and yoga have Narayana for their soul.

As Purusha, the Supreme Being is the cause of all this. He is the origin of everything, as Pradhana or Prakriti. He is Svabhava, the basis on which all things rest. Through his agency we witness the variety in the universe.

He is the various kinds of energy that act in the universe. In these five ways he is that all-controlling invisible influence of which men speak. Those who study the many areas of knowledge regard Hari to be identical with these five causes and as the final refuge of all things.

Narayana, endowed with the highest yoga-shakti is the only one topic of enquiry. The thoughts of the all the inhabitants of all the worlds, including Brahma and the high-souled Rishis, of those that are Samkhyas and yogins, of those that are Yatis, and of those that are conversant with the Atman are fully known to Kesava, but none of these can know what his thoughts are.

Whatever deeds are performed in honour of the Devas or the Pitris, whatever gifts are made, whatever penances are performed, have Vishnu established by his own laws for their refuge. He is named Vasudeva because he is the abode of all creatures. He is immutable. He is Supreme.

He is the foremost of Rishis. He is mighty. He transcends the three gunas. Just as time which runs seamlessly manifests itself in the form of succeeding seasons, even so, though nirguna, does he manifest himself.

Even they that are Mahatmans cannot understand what he does. Only those foremost of Rishis with knowledge of their Atmans succeed in beholding in their hearts that Purusha who transcends all gunas.'"

CANTO 348

Janamejaya said, "The illustrious Hari is gracious to those who are devoted to him with their entire beings. He accepts also all that is offered to him in accordance with the shastras.

Men who have burnt away their karma, those without paapa and punya, and those who have attained the knowledge handed down from guru to guru always attain that fourth and highest end, the essence of the Purushottama or Vasudeva. Devoted to Narayana with their whole souls, they attain that highest goal instantly.

Undoubtedly, bhakti dharma seems to be superior to that of gyana, and is very dear to Narayana. Those who adhere to it, without going through the three successive stages of Aniruddha, Pradyumna, and Samkarshana, at once attain to the immutable Hari.

In my view, the end that is attained by Brahmanas, who duly study the Vedas with the Upanishads according to the niyamas regulating such study, and by those that adopt the religion of Yatis, is inferior to that attained by persons devoted to Hari with all their heart."

Janamejaya said, "Who first promulgated this bhakti dharma? Was it some Deva or some Rishi that declared it? What are the practices of those that are said to be devoted with their entire souls? When did those practices begin? I have questions about these subjects. Dispel these doubts. Great is my interest in hearing you explain these to me."

Vaisampayana said, "When the eighteen aksauhinis of the Pandava and the Kaurava armies were drawn up ready for the battle and when Arjuna became despondent, Krishna himself explained what is and what is not the end attained by persons of different characters. I have earlier narrated his words to you.

The dharma taught by the Holy One between two teeming armies is difficult to understand. Men of uncleansed souls cannot grasp it at all. Rajan, having created this dharma in the ancient Krita yuga, in perfect consonance with the Samans, it is borne by the Supreme Lord Narayana himself.

Arjuna asked this very question of Narada in the midst of the Rishis and in the presence of Krishna and Bhishma. My guru, Vyasa, heard what Narada said. Receiving it from the Devarishis, Vyasa imparted it to me in exactly the same way in which he had obtained it from Narada.

I will now tell it to you in the same way as it was received from Narada. Listen to me.

In that kalpa when Brahma took his birth in the mind of Narayana and emerged from his mouth, Narayana himself performed his Daiva and Paitra rites in accordance with bhakti dharma. Those Rishis that subsist upon the froth of water then obtained it from Narayana.

From the froth-eating Rishis, this dharma was obtained by the Vaikanasa Rishis. From the Vaikanasas, Soma had it. Later, it disappeared from the universe.

After his second birth, when he sprang from the eyes of Narayana, Brahma received this bhakti dharma from Soma. Having received it thus, Brahma instructed Rudra in it.

In the Krita yuga of that ancient kalpa, Rudra, devoted to yoga, imparted it to all the Balakhilya Rishis. Through the illusion of Narayana, it once more vanished from the universe.

In the third birth of Brahma, which was from the speech of Narayana, this dharma once more arose from Narayana himself. Rishi Suparna obtained it from that foremost of beings. Suparna used to recite it three times during the day. Hence it came to be called Trisauparna.

This religion has been referred to in the Rigveda. Its duties are strenuous to practise. Vayu, who sustains the lives of all creatures, obtained this eternal dharma from Rishi Suparna.

Vayu transmitted it to those Rishis who live on the sacrificial offerings that remain after feeding guests and others. From those Rishis this dharma was obtained by the Great Ocean. It once more disappeared from the universe and merged into Narayana.

Listen now to what happened in the kalpa when, in his next birth, Brahma sprang from the ear of Narayana. When Hari resolved upon creation, he thought of a being who would have the power to create the universe. While thinking of this, a being sprang from his ears, one that was competent to create the universe. The Lord called him by the name Brahma.

Addressing Brahma, the Supreme Narayana said to him, 'Son, create all kinds of creatures from your mouth and feet. I will do what benefits you, for I shall empower you with both energy and strength needed to make you equal to this task. You will also receive from me the sattvata dharma. With it you will create the Krita yuga and duly establish it.'

Thus addressed, Brahma bowed his head before Hari, and received from him that foremost of all paths with all its mysteries and its details, together with the Aranyakas, which emanated from Narayana's mouth.

Narayana then instructed Brahma in that dharma and said to him, 'You are the creator of the duties that are to be observed in the respective yugas.' Having said this, Narayana disappeared and went to the place which is beyond the reach of tamas, where the Avyakta, unmanifest, resides and which is known to those whose deeds are without the desire for fruits.

After this, the boon-giving Brahma, the Pitamaha of the worlds, created the different worlds with their mobile and immobile creatures. The age that first commenced was perfectly auspicious and came to be called Krita. In that age, only the sattva dharma existed, pervading the entire universe. With that primeval religion of righteousness, Brahma, the Creator of all the worlds, worshipped the puissant Hari Narayana.

To spread that dharma for the welfare of the worlds, Brahma

instructed that Manu who is known by the name of Svarochisha in that dharma. Svarochisha Manu gave that knowledge to his own son Sankhapada.

Sankhapada communicated this knowledge to his own son Suvarnabha who was the ruler of the cardinal and subsidiary directions. When the Krita yuga ended, the Treta yuga began and the dharma once more disappeared from the world.

In a subsequent birth of Brahma, which was derived from the nose of Narayana, with eyes like lotus petals, the Lord himself recited this doctrine in the presence of Brahma. Then Sanatkumara, the son of Brahma, created from his thought, studied this doctrine.

From Sanatkumara, in the beginning of the Krita yuga, the Prajapati Virana learned the dharma. Having studied it, Virana taught it to the ascetic Raivya. Raivya, in his turn, imparted it to his pure and wise son Kushki, of high vratas, that righteous ruler of the cardinal and subsidiary points of the horizon. Again, this dharma, born of the mouth of Narayana, vanished from the world.

In the next birth of Brahma, when he emerged from an egg which sprang from Hari, this doctrine once more issued from the mouth of Narayana. It was received by Brahma who practised it duly in all its aspects. Brahma then transmitted it to those Rishis known as Barhishada.

From the Barhishadas it was obtained by a Brahmana known as Jyeshtya, learned in the Sama Veda. And because he was knowledgeable about the Samans, he is also known by the name of Jyeshtya-Samavrata Hari. It was obtained by a king of the name of Avikampana from this Brahmana. After this, the doctrine once more disappeared from the world.

At the beginning of this kalpa, in the seventh birth of Brahma from the lotus that sprang from the navel of Narayana, this dharma was re-established by Narayana himself, and given to the creator of all the worlds. Brahma gave it to Daksha, one of his sons Created by a thought of his mind.

Daksha, in his turn, imparted it to the eldest of all the sons of his daughters, Aditya, who was older than Savitri. From Aditya, Vivaswat obtained it. In the beginning of the Treta yuga, Vivaswat transmitted this knowledge to Manu. To protect and support all the worlds, Manu gave it to his son Ikshvaku.

Promulgated by Ikshvaku, the bhakti dharma spreads across the whole world. When Pralaya comes, it will once more return to Narayana and be merged in him. The religion which is practised by the Yatis, has been earlier narrated to you in the Hari Gita, with a summary of all its rules.

Along with its mysteries and details, Devarishi Narada got it from Narayana himself. This foremost of doctrines is primeval and eternal. Difficult to grasp and arduous to practise, it is always upheld by persons devoted to the sattva guna.

Hari becomes gratified by actions performed with a full knowledge of dharma without injury to any creature. Some adore Narayana with only a single form, that of Aniruddha. Some adore him as having two forms, that of Aniruddha and Pradyumna.

Some adore him as having three forms, Aniruddha, Pradyumna and Samkarshana. Others revere him as consisting of four forms, Aniruddha, Pradyumna, Samkarshana, and Vasudeva.

Hari is himself the Kshetrajna. He is whole, without parts. He is the Jiva in all creatures, transcending the five Mahabhutas. He is Manas, the mind that directs and controls the five senses. Having the highest intelligence, He is the ordainer of the universe, and its Creator.

He is both active and inactive. He is both cause and the effect. He is the one immutable Purusha, who sports as he likes. Thus have I recited to you the dharma of those who worship without desire, one that cannot be understood by those of uncleansed souls; this knowledge I acquired through the grace of my guru.

Men who are devoted to Narayana with their whole souls are rare. If the world had been full of such men with universal compassion, having Atmagyana, always engaged in doing good to others, then the Krita yuga would have set in. All men would have set themselves to deeds without desire of fruit.

In this way, my preceptor, that foremost of regenerate ones, knower of all duties, Krishna-Dwaipayana Vyasa, discoursed to Dharmaraja Yudhishtira on this bhakti dharma, in the presence of many Rishis and in the hearing of Krishna and Bhishma. He himself had received it from Tapodhana Narada.

Those who worship Narayana with all their souls and are without desire, succeed in attaining to the realm identical with Brahma, pure in complexion, possessing the effulgence of the moon and immutable."

Janamejaya said, "I see that those Dvijas whose souls have been awakened practise diverse kinds of dharmas. Why is it that other Brahmanas, instead of practising these, observe other kinds of vratas and kriyas?"

Vaisampayana said, "Bhaarata, three kinds of dispositions have been created for all embodied creatures, that which relates to the attribute of sattva, that which relates to the attribute of rajas, and lastly that which relates to the attribute of tamas.

One who is devoted to the sattva guna will certainly attain mukti. This guna allows one to understand him who knows Brahman.

Mukti is entirely dependent upon Narayana. Hence those who strive for emancipation are considered to be endowed with this sattva guna. By thinking of Purushottama, the man who revers Narayana acquires great wisdom.

Those who are wise and have taken up the practices of Yatis and mukti dharma, and have quenched their longing, always find that Hari favours them with the fruits of their desire.

That mortal man subject to birth and death upon whom Hari looks kindly should be known as one endowed with the sattva guna and devoted to mukti. The dharma of one devoted to Narayana is regarded as similar or equal in merit to the system of the Samkhyas. By adopting that doctrine one attains to the highest end, moksha which has Narayana for its soul.

That person upon whom Narayana looks with compassion succeeds in becoming awakened. No one, Rajan, can become enlightened through his own wishes. That nature which partakes of both rajas and tamas is said to be mixed.

Hari is not benevolent towards one with such a mixed nature, with Pravritti dharma, who is subject to birth and death. Only Brahma, the Pitamaha of the worlds, looks kindly upon such a man because his mind is overwhelmed by the two inferior attributes of rajas and tamas.

Without doubt, the Devas and the Rishis are devoted to the sattva guna. But they do not have that attribute in its subtle form and hence are of a mutable nature."

Janamejaya said, "How can one that is fraught with the principle of change succeed in attaining to that Purushottama? Tell me this, which, no doubt, is known to you. Discourse to me also of Pravritti."

Vaisampayana said, "That which is the twenty-fifth tattva in the Samkhya system, when it becomes able to abstain entirely from karma, succeeds in attaining to the subtle Purushottama, which is invested with the sattva guna, and which is filled with the Spirit symbolised by the letters A, U and M. The Samkhya system, the Aranyaka Veda, and the Pancharatra shastras are all one and the same and form parts of one whole. This is the dharma of those devoted to Narayana with their whole souls, that which has Narayana for its essence.

As waves of the ocean, rising from the ocean, rush away from it only to return to it in the end, even so diverse kinds of knowledge, springing from Narayana, return to Narayana in the end. I have thus explained to you, son of the Kuru vamsa, what the sattva dharma is. If you are able, then practise it fittingly.

Thus did Narada explain to my guru Vyasa the eternal and immutable course, called Ekanta, followed by the white- as also by the yellow-robed Yatis. Vyasa, in turn, imparted this to the wise and just Yudhishtira.

I, too, received it from Vyasa and have passed it on to you. For these reasons this dharma is difficult to practise. Hearing it, others are as bewildered as you have been. It is Krishna who is the protector of the universe and its beguiler. It is he who is the destroyer and the cause."

CANTO 349

Janamejaya said, "The Samkhya yoga, the Pancharatra shastras and the Aranyaka-Vedas, all these different systems of gyana or dharma are prevalent in the world. Do they all teach the same course of duties, or are these different from one another? I ask you to instruct me on Pravritti in the proper order."

Vaisampayana said, "I bow to that great Rishi who dispels darkness, whom Satyavati bore to Parasara in the midst of an island, who possesses vast knowledge and who is endowed with a great and liberal soul.

The learned say that he is the origin of Brahma; that he is the sixth form of Narayana; that he is the foremost of Rishis; that he has the might of yoga; that as the only son of his parents he is an incarnate amsa of Narayana; and that, born under extraordinary circumstances on an island, he is the inexhaustible receptacle of the Vedas.

In the Krita yuga, Narayana of great tejas created him as his son. The Mahatman Vyasa is unborn and ancient, and the limitless vessel that contains the Vedas."

Janamejaya said, "Best of the regenerate, you earlier told me that the Rishi Vasishta had a son by the name Saktri and that Saktri had a son named Parasara, and that Parasara had a son named the Krishna Dwaipayana or Vyasa. Now you tell me that Vyasa is the son of Narayana. I ask you, was it in some former birth that Vyasa was born from Narayana? Tell me of that birth of Vyasa from Narayana."

Vaisampayana said, "Wanting to understand the meaning of the Srutis, my guru, that ocean of tapasya devoted to observing all scriptural duties and the acquisition of knowledge, lived for a while in a particular realm of the Himavat Mountains. Because of the great effort of composing the Mahabharata, he was worn out by his penances. At that time, Sumanta and Jaimini, and Paila, and myself the fourth, and Suka his own son, attended on him. All of us waited dutifully upon him, engaged in doing all that was necessary to dispel his exhaustion.

Surrounded by his five sishyas, Vyasa shone in beauty on the breast of the Himavat Mountains like Mahadeva in the midst of his ghostly ganas. One day, with great reverence, we approached our guru who, having divided and summarised the Vedas with all their angas, and also the meanings of all the verses in the Mahabharata, and having subdued his senses, was at that time immersed in thought.

Availing ourselves of an interval in the conversation, we asked him to expound to us the meanings of the Vedas and the verses in the Mahabharata, and also to narrate to us the events of his own birth from Narayana. Knowing as he was of all subjects of enquiry, he first spoke to us on the interpretations of the Srutis and the Mahabharata, and then began to tell us the following incidents.

Vyasa said, 'Listen, my sishyas, to this most excellent narrative, to this best of histories, which tells of the birth of a Rishi. Pertaining to the Krita yuga, I have learnt of it through my tapasya. On the occasion of the seventh creation, that which was due to the primeval lotus, Narayana, endowed with the austerest penances, transcending both good and evil, and possessing unrivalled splendour, at first created Brahma from his navel.

After Brahma was born, Narayana said to him, "You have sprung from my navel. You possess the powers of creation so set yourself to the task of creating diverse kinds of creatures, rational and irrational."

Thus addressed by his Creator, Brahma felt troubled by the magnitude of this charge and was reluctant to do as he was commanded.

Bowing his head before Hari, the Lord of the universe, Brahma said to him, "I bow to you, O Lord of the Devas, but what powers do I have to create diverse creatures? I have no wisdom. Knowing this, direct me to do what is possible."

Thus addressed by Brahma, Narayana vanished instantly from Brahma's sight. The Supreme Lord then began to meditate. The goddess of intelligence appeared before Narayana. Himself transcending all Yoga, Narayana, by dint of yoga, appealed to the goddess of intelligence.

The immutable Hari, said to the Devi who was endowed with the goodness and power of yoga, "To accomplish the task of creating all the worlds you must enter into Brahma." And she entered Brahma.

When Hari saw that Brahma had been united with intelligence, he once more addressed him, saying "Now create diverse kinds of creatures." Brahma reverently accepted the command of his creator.

Narayana then disappeared from Brahma's presence, and in a moment repaired to his own place, known by the name of Divya, light or effulgence. Returning to his own nature of being unmanifest, he remained in that state of oneness.

After the task of creation by Brahma, another thought arose in Narayana's mind. He reflected, "Brahma, otherwise called Paramesthi, has created all these creatures, Daityas and Danavas, Gandharvas and Rakshasas. The fragile earth has become burdened with the weight of these creatures.

Many among the Daityas and Danavas and Rakshasas will become mighty. With tapasya, they will at times succeed in acquiring many powerful boons. They will swell with pride and strength because of those boons, and will oppress and afflict the most powerful Devas and Rishis.

Thus, from time to time, it is fitting for me to lighten the burden of the earth by assuming diverse forms for each occasion. I will achieve this task by destroying the evil and upholding the righteous. In this manner, protected by me, the earth, the embodiment of truth, will succeed in bearing her load of creatures.

Assuming the form of a mighty snake I will have to uphold the earth in empty space. Thus, she will be able to support all creation, mobile and immobile. In the different ages, I will incarnate on Bhumi in different forms to rescue her from danger."

Having reflected in this way, Madhusudana created diverse forms in his mind in which to appear from time to time. And he thought, "Assuming the forms of Varaha, of Narasimha, of Vamana, and of men, I shall defeat and destroy all the enemies of the Devas." After this, Narayana once more uttered the syllable *Bhoh*, making the air resound with it. From this syllable, Saraswati, arose a Rishi named Saraswat. This son, born of the speech of Narayana, also came to be called Apantaratamas. Powerful and all-knowing of the past, the present and the future, he was firm in the observance of vratas and truthful in speech.

Narayana, the original Creator of the Devas, possessing an immutable nature, said to the Rishi Saraswat, "You must devote your attention to the dissemination of the Vedas. O Rishi, accomplish what I command."

Obeying this command of the Supreme Lord from whose speech he had sprung into existence, Rishi Apantaratamas organised and distributed the Vedas in the Kalpa named after Swayambhuva Manu. Hari became gratified with the Rishi and his well-performed penances, his vows and observances, and his subduing of his senses and passions.

Narayana said, "In each Manvantara, you will disseminate the Vedas, and as a result you will be immutable and unsurpassable.

When the Kali yuga sets in, certain princes of Bharata's vamsa, called the Kauravas, will be born from you. They will be celebrated over the earth as high-souled princes ruling over powerful kingdoms. However, dissensions will break out among them ending in their destruction at one another's hands.

Dvijottama, in that age also, you will spread the Vedas to the diverse varnas. Indeed, in that dark age, your complexion, too, will darken. You will cause various kinds of dharma and gyana to surge.

Although steeped in austere penances, you will never be able to free yourself from desire and attachment to the world. Your son, however, through the grace of Madhava, will be freed from every attachment and be united with the Paramatman. It shall not be otherwise.

He whom learned Brahmanas call the mind-born son of the wise

Vasishta, an ocean of tapasya, whose splendour exceeds that of the sun himself, will be the progenitor of a vamsa into which Maharishi Parasara, filled with tejas and prowess, will be born. That foremost of men, that ocean of Vedas, that abode of penances, will be your father in the Kali yuga.

You will be born to an unmarried woman through her union with Rishi Parasara. You will have no doubts about the significance of things past, present and future. Imbued with penances and instructed by me, you will be able to see the events of thousands of ages past. You will also see thousands of yugas into the future.

In that birth, you will behold me on earth, I who am without birth and death, as Krishna of the Yadava vamsa, armed with the Sudarsana Chakra. All this will occur through the punya you will have acquired as a result of your ceaseless devotion to me. These words of mine shall come true.

You will be among the foremost of all the created. Great will be your fame. Surya's son Sani, Saturn, will be born as the great Manu in a future Kalpa. During that Manvantara, your punya will be superior to all the Manus of the several ages. This you will be through my grace.

Whatever exists in the world is the outcome of my exertion. The thoughts of others may not correspond with their actions. As for me, I always ordain what I think, without the slightest hindrance!'"

Vyasa continued, 'Having said these words to the Rishi Apantaratamas, the Supreme Lord dismissed him. Sishyas, I am he that was born as Apantaratamas through Narayana's command. Once more I have been born as Krishna-Dwaipayana of the Vasishta vamsa.

I have thus told you the circumstances of my former birth, which was due to the grace of Narayana in so much that I was a very part of Narayana himself. In ancient times, I undertook the severest of penances with the help of the highest abstraction of the mind.

Moved by my great love for you who revere me, I have told you everything you wished to know about me, from my first birth to the present one!'"

Vaisampayana continued, "As desired by you, Rajan, I have told you about the circumstances connected with the former birth of our revered guru, Vyasa of unstained mind. Now listen to more. There are many kinds of doctrines that go by the names of Samkhya, yoga, the Pancharatra, Vedas and Pasupati.

The creator of the Samkhya yoga is the great Rishi Kapila. The primeval Hiranyagarbha is the promulgator of the yoga system. The Rishi Apantaratamas, also called Prachina-garbha, is said to be the teacher of the Vedas.

The Pasupata doctrine was disseminated by the son of Brahma, the Lord of Uma, that master of all creatures, the always joyful Siva, otherwise known as Sreekantha. Narayana himself is the promulgator of the contents of the Pancharatra shastras.

In all these, it is seen that Narayana is the sole subject of exposition. According to these shastras and the knowledge they contain, Narayana is the only object of worship.

Those who are blinded by tamas, fail to understand that Narayana is the Paramatman who pervades the entire universe. Those wise men, the authors of the shastras, say that Narayana, who is a Rishi, is the one object of reverent worship in the universe. I say that there is no other being like him. The Supreme Deity, called Hari, lives in the hearts of those who, with the help of the scriptures and of inference, have succeeded in dispelling all doubts.

Madhava never dwells in the hearts of those who doubt and dispute everything using false dialectics. They who are conversant with the Pancharatra shastras, who are duly observant of prescribed duties, and who are devoted to Narayana with their very souls, succeed in entering into Narayana.

The Samkhya and the yoga systems are eternal. All the Vedas are eternal. All the Rishis have declared that this universe existing from ancient times is Narayana's self. You must know that all actions, whether good or bad, are laid down in the Vedas and all events in heaven and earth, between the sky and the waters, are caused by and flow from that ancient Rishi Narayana."

CANTO 350

Janamejaya said, "Regenerate one, are there many Purushas or is there only one? Who in the universe is the foremost of Purushas? What, again, is said to be the source of all things?"

Vaisampayana said, "In the speculations of the Samkhya and the yoga systems many Purushas have been spoken of. Those that follow these systems do not accept that there is but one Purusha in the universe. In the same manner in which the many Purushas are said to have one origin in the Supreme Purusha, it may be said that this entire universe is identical with that one Purusha of superior attributes.

I shall explain this now, after bowing to my guru Vyasa, who knows the Atman, who is observant of tapasya and self-restraint, and is worthy of reverence. Rajan, this speculation on Purusha occurs in all the Vedas. It is well known to be identical with Rita and Satya. Vyasa has reflected upon it.

Many Rishis, descended from Kapila, have contemplated about, and commented on what is called Adhyatma. Through the grace of Vyasa, I will expound to you what Vyasa has said on this subject of the Oneness of Purusha. There is an ancient story of the discourse between Brahma and the three-eyed Mahadeva on this matter.

In the midst of the ocean of milk, there is a lofty mountain of great golden radiance known as Vaijayanta. Going there alone, from his own abode of great splendour and felicity, Brahma would often spend his time contemplating the course of Adhyatma.

While the four-faced Brahma was seated there, his son Mahadeva, who had sprung from his forehead, encountered him in course of his wanderings through the universe. While coursing through the sky, Mahayogi Siva saw Brahma seated on that mountain and descended on its peak.

Joyfully he appeared before his Creator and worshipped his feet. Beholding Mahadeva prostrated at his feet, Brahma raised him up with his left hand. Having raised him up, Brahma, Lord of all creatures, on meeting his son after a long time, spoke to him.

Brahma said, 'Mahabaho, you are welcome. It is my good fortune to see you after such a long time. I hope, my son, that all is well and proper with your penances and Vedic studies and your japa. You always observe the most austere tapasya. So I ask you about their practice and wellbeing.'

Rudra said, 'Through your grace, all is well with my penances and Vedic studies. All is also well with the universe. I saw you long ago in your own dwelling of felicity and effulgence. I am come from there to this mountain that is now your abode.

I am curious about your withdrawal into such a solitary place from your usual realm of splendour. Great must the reason be, Pitamaha, for this.

Your own foremost abode is free from the pains of hunger and thirst, and inhabited by both Devas and Asuras, by Rishis of immeasurable radiance, as also by Gandharvas and Apsaras. Abandoning such a place of felicity, you live alone on this best of mountains. The reason for this must be grave.'

Brahma said, 'This foremost of mountains called Vaijayanta is always my dwelling. Here, with my mind concentrated in dhyana, I meditate on the one universal Purusha of infinite proportions.'

Rudra said, 'You are Swayambhu, self-born. Many are the Purushas that have been created by you. More yet are still being created by you. The Infinite Purusha, of whom you speak, is one and single. Who is that

Purusha, Brahma, on whom you meditate? I am greatly curious about this. I beg you, dispel my doubt.'

Brahma said, 'Son, many are those Purushas of whom you speak. The one Purusha, of whom I am thinking, is hidden and transcends all other Purushas. That one Purusha is the foundation of the many Purushas that exist in the universe; and since that one Purusha is the source of all the countless Purushas, the rest, if they succeed in divesting themselves of gunas, succeed in entering into that one Purusha who is all the universe, who is supreme, who is eternal, and who is himself without and above all attributes."

CANTO 351

"Brahma said, 'Listen now to the description of that Purusha. He is eternal and immutable. He is undecaying and immeasurable. He pervades all things.

That Purusha cannot be seen by you, or by me, or any other. Those who are filled with the understanding and the senses but lacking in self-restraint and tranquillity of soul cannot catch a glimpse him. The Supreme Purusha is said to be one that can be seen only with the help of gyana.

Though without a form, he dwells in every body. Though he lives in bodies, he is never touched by the actions of men. He is my Antaratma, my inner soul. He is your inner soul. He is the all-seeing witness dwelling within every embodied creature and marks their deeds. No one can totally grasp him at any time.

The universe is the crown of his head. The universe is his arms. The universe is his feet. The universe is his eyes. The universe is his nose. Alone he ranges freely through all kshetras without any restriction.

Kshetra is another name for body. And because he knows all kshetras, as also all good and bad deeds, therefore he, who is the soul of yoga, is named Kshetrajna. No one can perceive how he enters into embodied creatures and how he leaves them.

In accordance with the Samkhya shastra, with the help of yoga, duly observing its rules, I am engaged in meditating upon the origin of that

Purusha, but, alas, I cannot comprehend that cause. According to the measure of my knowledge, I will discourse to you upon that eternal Purusha and his Oneness and supreme greatness.

The learned speak of him as the singular Purusha. That one eternal Being deserves the name of Mahapurusha. Fire is an element, but it may be seen to blaze up in a thousand places under thousand different circumstances. The sun is one and single, but his rays spread over the universe. Penances are of diverse kinds, but they have one common origin from which they flow.

The wind is one, but it blows in many forms in the world. The great ocean is the one parent of all the waters in the world seen in different circumstances. Nirguna, that one Purusha, is the universe displayed in infinite forms and ways. Flowing from him, the infinite universe enters into him again at the time of the pralaya.

By casting off the consciousness of body and the senses, by casting off all acts good and bad, by casting off both truth and falsehood, one succeeds in ridding oneself of gunas. The person who realises that inconceivable Purusha and grasps his subtle existence in the four forms of Aniruddha, Pradyumna, Samkarshana and Vasudeva, and who, as a result of such understanding, attains perfect tranquillity of heart, succeeds in entering into and identifying himself with that one auspicious Purusha.

Some wise men speak of him as the Paramatman. Others regard him as the one Soul. A third class of learned men describe him just as the Atman. The truth is that he who is the Supreme Soul is always nirguna, without attributes. He is Narayana.

He is the universal soul, and he is the one Purusha. He is never affected by the fruits of actions even as the leaf of the lotus is never drenched by the water one may throw upon it.

The Karmatman, the soul of actions, is different. That soul is sometimes engaged in karma and when it succeeds in discarding karma, attains mukti or union with the Paramatman. The soul of karma has seventeen attributes.

Thus it is said that there are many kinds of Purushas in due order.

In reality, however, there is but one Purusha. He is the abode of all the laws that govern the universe. He is the highest subject of knowledge. He is at once the knower and the object to be known. He is at once the thinker and the object of thought. He is the one that eats and the food that is eaten.

He is the smeller and the scent that is smelled. He is at once he that touches and the object that is touched. He is the agent that sees and the object that is seen. He is the hearer and what is heard. He is the conceiver and that which is conceived. He possesses attributes and is also free from them; he is both saguna and nirguna.

What has earlier been called Pradhana, and is the mother of the Mahat tattva, is no other than the effulgence of the Paramatman because he is eternal, without destruction, without end, and ever changeless. He it is who creates the prime ordinance in respect of Dhatri himself.

Learned Brahmanas call him by the name Aniruddha. All karma, possessing excellent merits and fraught with blessings, flowing in the world from the Vedas, have been caused by him. All the Devas and all the Rishis, with tranquil souls, occupying their places on the vedi, honour him with the first share of their sacrificial offerings.

I, Brahma, the primeval master of all creatures, was born from him, and you have been born from me. From me have flowed the universe with all its mobile and immobile creatures, and all the Vedas, with their mysteries. Divided into four parts, Aniruddha, Pradyumna, Samkarshana and Vasudeva, he sports as he pleases. That illustrious and divine Lord is awakened by his own knowledge.

I have answered your questions, my son, according to the manner in which the matter is expounded in the doctrines of Samkhya and yoga.'"

CANTO 352

Sauti said, 'After Vaisampayana had explained to king Janamejaya the glory of Narayana, he began to discourse on another subject by narrating Yudhishtira's question and the answer that Bhishma, who lay on his bed of arrows, gave in the presence of all the Pandavas and the Rishis, and also of Krishna himself.

Vaisampayana said, "Yudhishtira says, 'Pitamaha, you have discoursed to us on the duties pertaining to mukti dharma. Now tell us about the foremost duties of men belonging to the various asramas.'

Bhishma says, 'The kartavyas or dharmas ordained for each asrama, if well performed, can lead to swarga and the high fruit of truth. Duties are like doors to yagnas, and none of their practices is futile. Bharatarishabha, one who adopts particular duties with dedication and reverence praises these to the exclusion of the rest.

This is the very subject which, in ancient times, was the focus of the conversation between Devarishi Narada and Indra. Narada, revered by all the world, is a siddha, one whose sadhana has been met with fulfilment. He wanders through all the worlds without hindrance, like the all-pervading wind itself.

Once upon a time he repaired to the abode of Indra. Duly honoured by the king of the Devas, he sat close to his host. Seeing him seated at his ease and free from fatigue, the Lord of Sachi addressed him, saying, "Maharishi, is there anything wonderful that you have beheld?

Crowned with ascetic success, you roam through the universe of mobile and immobile objects, witnessing all things. There is nothing in the universe that is unknown to you. Do tell me, therefore, of any wonderful occurrence that you may have felt, seen or heard of."

Thus questioned, Narada began to recite to Indra the vast history that follows. Listen to me as I narrate that story which unfolded. I shall recount it in the same manner in which the Devarishi did, and for the same purpose that he had in mind.'"

CANTO 353

"Bhishma says, 'In the town of Mahapadma, situated on the southern side of the Ganga, there lived a Brahmana of concentrated Soul. Born into the Atri vamsa, he was blessed with an amiable nature. With his doubts dispelled by faith and contemplation, he was well conversant with the path he was to follow.

Ever observant of his dharma, he had his anger under perfect control. Always content, he was a master of his senses. Devoted to tapasya and the study of the Vedas, he was respected by all good men.

He earned wealth by righteous means and his conduct in all things was true to his varnasrama and svadharma. The family to which he belonged was large and celebrated. He had many kinsmen and relatives, and many wives and spouses. His behaviour was always respectable and faultless.

Seeing that he had many children, the Brahmana undertook religious karmas on a large scale. His observances were in accordance with the customs of his own family.

The Brahmana reflected that three kinds of duties have been laid down for observances. Firstly, there were the duties ordained in the Vedas with regard to one's varna and asrama, namely that of a Brahmana observing the rules of grihasta.

Secondly, there were the duties prescribed in the scriptures, namely in the Dharmashastras. And, thirdly, there were those duties that famed and revered men in earlier times had followed though these were not to be found in the Vedas or the Dharmashastras.

Which of these duties should I follow? Which of them, if followed by me, are likely to lead to my benefit? Which, indeed, should be my refuge? Thoughts like these always troubled him. He could not resolve his doubts.

While troubled with such reflections, another great Brahmana came to his house as a guest. The grihasta duly honoured his atithi according to the niyamas of worship laid down in the shastras. When his guest appeared refreshed and was seated at ease, the Brahmana addressed him in the following words.

The Brahmana said, "Sinless one, I have become devoted to you because of your agreeable conversation. You have become my friend. Listen to me, for I want to ask something. After handing over the duties of a householder to my son, I wish to discharge the highest purushartha of man. What, O Dvija, should be my path?

Relying upon the Jivatman, I wish to live in the one Paramatman. Alas, bound to the ties of attachment, I do not have the will to actually set myself to accomplish that task. And since the best part of my life has passed away in the duties of a grihasta, I now want to devote the rest of my life to acquiring the means to meet the expenses of my future journey.

I desire to cross samsara, the illusory ocean of life. Where will I find the raft of dharma to realise my purpose? I hear that even the Devas must endure the fruits of their actions; beholding the rows of Yama's standards and flags floating over the heads of all creatures, my heart fails to derive pleasure from the diverse sensual objects with which it comes into contact.

I do not respect the dharma of the Yatis as they, too, depend upon alms for their sustenance. My revered guest, you who are endowed with intelligence and reason, set me on the right path of kartavya and karma!'"

Bhishma continues, 'The wise guest, hearing his host's righteous words, said these sweet words in a melodious voice.

The guest said, "I, too, am puzzled about this subject. The same thought occupies my mind and I am unable to arrive at any definite conclusions. Swarga has many doors.

There are some that commend mukti. Some praise the fruits attained by tapasya. Some take refuge in sannyasa way of life. Some follow grihastasrama.

Some rely upon the punya attained by an observance of Kshatriya dharma. Some rely upon the fruits of self-restraint. Some believe that the merits of dutiful obedience to gurus and elders are efficacious.

Some undertake to restrain their speech. Some have attained felicity by waiting dutifully upon their departed ancestors. Some have risen to swarga by practising compassion, and some by practising truth.

Some rush into battle and, after laying down their lives, attain heaven. Some attain it by practising the Unccha vrata. Some have devoted themselves to the study of the Vedas. These men, of intelligence and tranquil souls, having subdued their senses, attain swarga.

Others characterised by simplicity and truth have been slain by evil men. These have become honoured inhabitants of heaven. In this world, it is seen, that men attain swarga passing through a thousand doors of dharma, all standing wide open. My understanding has been troubled by your question, like a soft cloud by the wind."'"

CANTO 354

"Bhishma says, 'The guest continued, "For all that, Brahmana, I will duly instruct you. Listen to me as I recite what I have heard from my guru. In the Naimisa forest situated on the banks of the Gomati, where the wheel of dharma was set in motion during a former age of creation, there is a city named after the Nagas. There, in ancient times, the assembled Devas had performed a mahayagna. There Mandhatri, the foremost of earthly kings, defeated Indra, the king of the gods.

In that city lives a mighty Naga. He is known by the name of Padmanabha or Padma. Walking in the triple path of karma, gyana and bhakti, he gratifies all creatures in thought, word and deed. Reflecting upon all things with great attention, he protects the good and punishes the evildoer with the fourfold system of conciliation, provoking dissensions, giving gifts or bribes, and using force.

Go there and ask him all the questions you want. He will show you what is truly the highest dharma. That Naga is welcoming towards all guests.

He is wise and knows the shastras. He has all the desirable virtues not to be seen in any other. By nature he is always observant of those duties which are performed with or in water.

He is devoted to the study of the Vedas. He is marked by penances and self-restraint. He has great wealth. He performs yagnas and offers dakshina, abstains from inflicting injury and practises forgiveness. His conduct in all respects is exemplary. Truthful in speech and free from malice, his behaviour is righteous and his senses are under control. He eats only after feeding all his guests and attendants.

He is kind of speech. He has knowledge of what is beneficial, and what is simple and right and what is censurable. He takes stock of what he does and what he leaves undone. He never acts with hostility towards anyone. He is always engaged in doing what is beneficial to all creatures. He belongs to a family that is as pure as the water of a lake in the midst of the Ganges.""""

CANTO 355

"Bhishma continues, 'The host replied, "I hear your comforting words with as much gratification as a heavily burdened man feels when his load is taken from his head or shoulders. I am filled with the delight that a traveller who has made a long journey on foot feels when he at last lies down on a bed, that which a man feels when he finds a seat after having stood for a long time, or that which is felt by one who is thirsty when he finds cold water to drink.

On hearing your words, I am suffused with the pleasure felt by a hungry man when he finds tasty food set before him, or that which a guest feels when satisfying food is placed before him at the proper time, or that felt by an old man when he gets a long coveted son, or that which is experienced by one when meeting a dear friend or kinsman about whom one has been anxious.

Like one with upturned gaze I have heard what has fallen from your lips and am reflecting upon their significance. With your wise words you have truly instructed me. Yes, I shall do what you have commanded me to.

You may leave tomorrow at dawn, after passing the night happily with me and dispelling your fatigue by resting. Behold, the rays of the divine Surya have been dimmed and he is setting."'

"Bhishma continues, 'Hospitably waited upon by that Brahmana, the learned guest passed that night in the company of his host. Both talked cheerfully with each other on the subject of the sannyasa dharma. So engrossing was the nature of their conversation that the night passed swiftly.

When morning came, the guest was worshipped with due rites by the Brahmana whose heart was now set upon the accomplishment of what would be beneficial for him, according to the discourse of the guest. The righteous Brahmana, resolved to achieve his purpose, took leave of his kinsmen, and soon set out for the abode of that foremost of Nagas, with his mind steadily directed towards it.'"

CANTO 356

"Bhishma says, 'Passing through enchanted forests, lakes and sacred pools, the Brahmana at last arrived at the asrama of a certain sannyasi. On arriving there, he asked the ascetic, in fitting manner, about the Naga of whom he had heard from his guest, and instructed by him he continued on his journey. Focused upon his purpose, the Brahmana arrived at the dwelling of the Naga.

Entering, he announced himself, saying, "Ho! Who is within? I am a Brahmana, come here as a guest."

Hearing him, the virtuous wife of the Naga, of great beauty and devoted to the observance of every dharma, came out. Attentive to the duties of hospitality, she welcomed and revered her guest, and said, 'What can I do for you?'

The Brahmana said, 'I am sufficiently honoured by your gentle words. My weariness has also been dispelled. O blessed devi, I wish to see your husband. This is my goal and the one object of my desire. It is for this that I have come today to the abode of the Naga.'

The wife of the Naga said, 'Revered one, my husband has gone to draw Surya's chariot for a month. Learned Brahmana, he will be back in fifteen days, and will meet you then. I have now told you the reason of my husband's absence. What else can I do for you? Tell me.'

The Brahmana said, 'I have come here to see your husband. I will remain in the nearby forest and await his return. When he comes home, kindly tell him that I have arrived in this place driven by the fervent desire to meet him.

You should also inform me of his return. Devi, until then, I will dwell on the banks of the Gomati, waiting for his return and living upon frugal fare.'

Having said this repeatedly to the wife of the Naga that Brahmana went to the riverbank to live there until the Naga's return.'"

CANTO 357

"Bhishma continues, 'The Nagas of that city were distressed when they saw that Brahmana, devoted to tapasya, continued to live in the forest, entirely abstaining from food, as he waited for the return of the Naga lord. All the kinsmen and relatives of the great Naga, including his brother, children and wife, came together to the Brahmana.

Reaching the banks of the Gomati, they saw him seated in solitude, not eating but engaged in observing vratas and silently reciting certain mantras. Approaching, the Naga's kinsmen and family revered him, and then spoke to him words of simple sincerity.

"O Tapodhana, this is the sixth day since your arrival here but you have not said a word about your food. You are devoted to righteousness. You have come among us. We are here in attendance upon you. It is vital that we should fulfil our duties of hospitality towards you.

We are all kinsmen of our Naga lord whom you wish to see. Roots or fruits, leaves, or water, or rice or meat, you must partake of some food. By your living in this forest and completely abstaining from food, the entire community of Nagas, young and old, does suffer, since this your fast implies negligence on our part to discharge the duties of hospitality and we do not know the reason for it

None amongst us has been guilty of killing a Brahmana. None of us has ever lost a son immediately after birth. No one has been born in our vamsa that has eaten before serving the Devas or atithis or kinsmen coming to his house."

The Brahmana said, "I will break my fast for your entreaties. I will wait eight more days for the lord of the Nagas to return. If he does not come back with the passing of the eighth night, I will break this fast by eating. This vow of abstaining from all food that I am observing is on account of my high regard for the Naga lord.

You should not grieve for what I am doing. Return to your homes. This my vrata is on his account. You should not do anything to mar it."

Thus addressed, the assembled Nagas were dismissed by the Brahmana, and they returned to their homes.'"

CANTO 358

"Bhishma says, 'Upon the expiry of full fifteen days, the Naga Lord Padmanabha, having finished his task of drawing Surya's chariot and taking the sun god's leave, returned home. His wife washed his feet and dutifully discharged other tasks of a similar nature.

She then took her seat by his side. The Naga, refreshed and rested, addressed his wife, saying, "During my absence I trust that you have not been unmindful of worshipping the Devas and atithis in keeping with the instructions I gave you, and according to the laws laid down in the shastras.

I hope that during my absence, without yielding to your impure Buddhi, you have been firm in the observance of the duties of hospitality. I trust you have not transgressed the boundaries of karma and dharma."

The wife of the Naga said, "The duty of sishyas is to wait with reverence upon their guru doing his bidding; that of Brahmanas is to study and memorise the Vedas; that of servants is to obey the commands of their masters; that of the king is to protect his people by defending the good and punishing the evil.

It is said that Kshatriya dharma includes the protection of all creatures from wrong and oppression. The duty of the Sudra is to serve with humility persons of the three higher varnas, Brahmanas, Kshatriyas and Vaisyas.

The dharma of the householder, O my Lord of the Nagas, consists in doing good to all creatures. Frugality of fare and observance of vows in due order constitute punya for men of all classes, because of the connection that exists between the senses and the duties of religion.

Who am I? From where have I come? What are others to me and what am I to others? These are the thoughts to which the mind should ever be directed by him who leads a life which leads to mukti.

Chastity and obedience to the husband constitute the highest dharma of the wife. I have learnt this well through your teaching. I am fully conversant with my kartavya.

I have you, who are devoted to righteousness, for a husband; why then will I, swerving from the path of duty, walk on the path of disobedience and sin? During your absence from home, I have continued to worship the Devas. I have also, without the slightest negligence, attended to the duties of hospitality towards those who arrived as guests in your home.

Fifteen days ago a Brahmana has arrived here. He has not disclosed his purpose to me. He desires to speak with you. Dwelling on the banks of the Gomati he anxiously awaits your return. Of firm vows, that Brahmana sits there, engaged in chanting the Vedas.

Lord of the Nagas, I have given him my word that I will send you to him as soon as you return. Having heard what I have said, it is fitting for you to go to him. You who hear with your eyes, you must grant that Dvija whatever has brought him here!"'"

CANTO 359

"Bhishma continues, 'The Naga said, "O you of delightful smiles, what have you taken that Brahmana for? Is he really a human being or is he some god that has come here in the guise of a Brahmana? Who is there among humans that would want to see me and be fit to meet me?

Can a Manava who wishes to see me dare leave a command with you to send me to him? Among the Devas and Asuras and Devarishis, the Nagas are endowed with great tejas.

Nagas are swift and fragrant. They deserve to be revered for they can grant boons. Indeed, we too, are worthy of our followers. We cannot be seen by men."

The wife said, "Judging by his simplicity and openness I know that this Brahmana is not any Deva who lives on air. I also know that he reveres you with all his heart. His heart is set upon the accomplishment of some goal that depends on your help.

As the chataka waits eagerly for rain to quench its thirst, even so does that Brahmana keenly wait to meet you. Let no misfortune befall him on account of his failure to see you. No one born into an honourable family as you are can be considered worthy of honour if he neglects a guest arrived at his house.

Discard that anger that is so innate in you and go and meet the Brahmana. It befits you not to be consumed by sin through disappointing the Dvija. By refusing to wipe the tears of one who has come to him with hopes of succour, even a king incurs the sin of foeticide.

By abstaining from speech one attains wisdom. By giving generous dakshina one acquires great fame. By being truthful in speech, one acquires the gift of eloquence and is honoured in swarga. By giving away land one attains to that high end which is ordained for Rishis living in sannyasa.

By earning wealth through righteous means one attains many desirable rewards. By doing what is beneficial to oneself, one avoids going to naraka. That is what the wise say."

The Naga said, "I had no arrogance caused by conceit. However, because of my birth, my arrogance was once great but no more. Of wrath born of desire, I have none. It has all been destroyed by the fire of your profound instructions.

I do not consider any darkness to be more impenetrable than anger. As the Nagas have a surfeit of anger, they have become objects of reproach with all men. By succumbing to the influence of wrath, the ten-headed Ravana became the rival of Sakra, and for that reason was killed by Rama in battle.

Hearing that Rama of Bhrigu's vamsa had entered the inner rooms of their palace to take away their father's calf of the Homa cow, the sons of Kartavirya yielding to anger deeming it an insult to their royal house, and they met with destruction at the hands of Rama. Indeed, Kartavirya, who was like the thousand-eyed Indra himself, was slain in battle by Rama of Jamadagni's vamsa because he yielded to anger.

And so, my beloved wife, I have heeded your words and have curbed my fury, that enemy of tapasya that destroys all that is good. I am fortunate to have you for my wife, you who possess every virtue and have inexhaustible merits.

I will go at once to the Brahmana. I will address him in a respectful manner and he will leave only when his wishes have been fulfilled.""""

CANTO 360

"Bhishma says, 'Having said these words to his wife, the lord of the Nagas went to that place where the Brahmana sat awaiting him. As he went, the Naga thought of the Brahmana and wondered about what had brought him to the Naga city.

When he arrived in the Brahmana's presence, that righteous Naga addressed his guest in sweet words, "O Brahmana, do not be angry for I come to you in peace. What has brought you here? What is your purpose? Dvijottama, whom do you worship in this secluded place on the banks of the Gomati?"

The Brahmana said, "Know that my name is Dharmaranya, and that I have come here to see the Naga Padmanabha. I have some work with him. I have heard that he is not at home and so I sit here waiting for him to return.

Like a chataka waiting in expectation of the clouds, I am waiting for him whom I esteem highly. To dispel all evil from him and bring about what is beneficial to him, I am engaged in reciting the Vedas until he comes, and I am engaged in yoga and pass my time blissfully."

The Naga said, "Your behaviour is upright. You are pious and devoted to the good of all righteous persons. Blessed Brahmana, every praise is due to you.

You behold the Naga with a loving gaze. Learned Rishi, I am that Naga whom you seek. Command me as you wish, tell me what is agreeable to you and what I can do for you. Having heard from my wife that you are here, I have come to meet you.

You have come here, and you are certain to return with your desire fulfilled. Use me for any task with full confidence. We are all in your service on account of your punya, for you have disregarded your own good and have spent your time in seeking our welfare."

The Brahmana said, "Most blessed Naga, I have come here driven by the desire to see you. I am ignorant, and I have come here to ask you something. I wish to attain to the Paramatman, the Supreme Soul that is the end of the Jivatman. I am neither attached to nor detached from samsara.

You shine with the effulgence of your punya with a radiance that is as enchanting as the moon's. You who live on air alone, first answer this question of mine. Afterwards, I will reveal to you the object of my visit!"""

CANTO 361

"Bhishma continues, 'The Brahmana said, "You have been away to draw the single-wheeled chariot of Surya. Describe to me anything wonderful that you may have seen in those realms through which you journeyed."

The Naga said, "The divine Surya is the refuge of innumerable wonders. All the creatures that inhabit the three worlds have flowed from him. Countless Munis crowned with ascetic success, together with all the Devas, dwell in the rays of Surya like birds perching on the branches of trees.

What, again, can be more wonderful than this that the mighty Vayu, issuing from Surya, takes refuge in his rays and courses over the universe? What can be more wonderful than this that Surya, dividing Vayu into many parts to do good to all creatures, creates the rain that falls in the monsoon?

What can be more wonderful than this that the Paramatman, himself bathed in blazing effulgence, looks out upon the universe from within the solar orb? What can be more wonderful than this that Surya has a dark ray which transforms itself into clouds charged with rain and pours down that rain when the season comes?

What can be more wonderful than this that after absorbing water for eight months, he pours it down once again in the monsoon? The soul of the universe is said to dwell in certain rays of Surya. From him comes the seed of all things, and it is he that upholds the earth with all her mobile and immobile creatures.

Brahmana, what can be more wonderful than this that the foremost of Purushas, eternal, powerful and effulgent, and without beginning and without end, dwells in Surya? Listen to one more thing that I will now tell you. It is the most marvellous wonder. I have seen it in the clear sky, from having been close to Surya.

One day, at the hour of noon, while Surya was shining in all his glory and emanating heat we saw a Being come towards him, who seemed to shine with a brilliance equal to that of Surya himself. Causing all the worlds to blaze up with his glory and filling them with his energy, he came towards Surya, rending the sky, as it were, to make his path through it.

The rays of his body seemed to resemble the blazing radiance of libations of ghee poured into the sacrificial fire. His splendour did not allow anyone to look directly at him. His form was indescribable. Indeed, he did appear to us to be a second Surya.

As soon as he was near, Surya extended his two hands receiving him respectfully. To honour Surya in return, he also extended his right hand. Piercing through the sky, he entered into Surya's disc. Merging with Surya's energy, he seemed to be transformed into Surya's self.

When the two blinding energies thus united, we were so bewildered that we could not distinguish between them. We could not make out who was Surya we bore on his chariot, and who was the Being we had seen coming through the sky. Confused, we addressed Surya, saying, 'Illustrious One, who is this Being that has united himself with you and has been transformed into your second self?'"""

CANTO 362

"**B**hishma says, 'The Naga continued, "Surya said, 'This Being is not Agni, and he is not an Asura. Nor is he a Naga. He is a Brahmana who has attained swarga because he has succeeded in observing the Unccha vrata.

This person had lived only upon fruits and roots and the fallen leaves of trees. He sometimes subsisted upon water, and sometimes upon air alone, passing his days in dhyana. Siva Mahadeva was gratified by his constant recitation of the Samhitas.

He had tried to accomplish those deeds that lead to heaven and bliss. Through their punya he has now attained swarga. Without wealth and without any desire, he kept the Unccha vrata to sustain himself. This learned Brahmana had been devoted to the good of all creatures.

Neither Devas nor Gandharvas, neither Asuras nor Nagas can be regarded as superior to those creatures that are merged into Surya. Such was the most wondrous incident I saw on high. That Brahmana, who was crowned with success by the observance of the Unccha vrata, continues, even to this day, to circle the earth, remaining within the body of the incandescent Surya Deva!'"'"

CANTO 363

"**B**hishma continues, 'The Brahmana said, "Naga, this is indeed marvellous and I am gratified by listening to you. With your words, subtle in their meaning, you have shown me the way I must follow. I wish to leave now; remember me occasionally and enquire after me by sending your servant."

The Naga said, "You have not yet revealed to me the reason that brought you here. Where will you go? Tell me, Dvija, what I can do for you, and what is it that brought you here?

After you have accomplished your task, whatever it may be, revealed or hidden in speech, you may take my leave, and I will let you go cheerfully. You have conceived a friendship for me.

O Rishi, sitting under the shade of this tree, do not leave so soon after merely seeing me. Certainly, you have become dear to me and I to you. All the inhabitants of this city are yours. What objection could you have to passing some time in my home?"

The Brahmana said, "You are wise, Naga, and have acquired a knowledge of the Atman. It is true that the Devas are not superior to you in any respect. He that is you is also me, as he that is me is truly you. You, I and all other creatures will all have to enter into the Paramatman.

Doubt had seized my mind, king of Nagas, with regard to the best means to win punya. What you said has dispelled that doubt, for I have learnt the value of the Unccha vrata. I will now practise that most efficacious vow and attain to my goal.

I am certain of this now and I take your leave. Blessings be upon you. O Naga, my objective has been achieved."'

CANTO 364

"Bhishma says, 'Having saluted that foremost of Nagas, and having firmly resolved to follow the Unccha way of life, Dharmaranya went to Chyavana of Bhrigu's vamsa, to seek formal instruction and to be initiated in that lofty and recondite vrata. Chyavana performed the samskara rites of the Brahmana and formally initiated him into the Unccha way of life.

Rajan, the son of Bhrigu recited this history to King Janaka in his palace. King Janaka, in his turn, narrated it to Devarishi Narada. Finding himself in the palace of Indra one day, Narada instructed Indra in this itihasa upon being asked by him.

Indra, having obtained it from Narada, recited this blessed history to an assembly of all the foremost Brahmanas. When I encountered Rama of Bhrigu's vamsa on Kurukshetra, the celestial Vasus narrated it to me.

Since you asked me, I have recited this history that is sacred and filled with great merit. You asked me what constitutes the highest dharma, Rajan. This itihasa is my answer to your question.

A brave man he was that practised the Unccha vrata in this way, without expectation of any reward. Instructed by Padmanabha, the Naga king about his dharma, that Brahmana Dharmaranya began the practice of Yama and Niyama; he lived only on such food as was allowed by the Unccha vow, and went away to another forest.'"

PART I
Anusasana Parva

CANTO 1

A UM! HAVING BOWED down to Narayana, and Nara the most exalted of Purushas, and also the Devi Saraswati, I invoke the spirit of Jaya!

Vaisampayana said, "Yudhishtira says, 'Pitamaha, serenity is said to be subtle and of diverse forms. Despite listening to all your discourses, I have not achieved this tranquillity. You have spoken of many ways of stilling the mind, but how can actual peace of mind be had from mere knowledge of the various kinds of peace, when I myself am the means of realising this?

Seeing your body covered with arrows and festering with wounds, I cannot find any peace at the thought of the evil I have brought about. Great Kshatriya, seeing your body drenched in blood, like a mountain overrun with water from its springs, I suffer like a lotus in the rains.

What can be more agonising than this, that you, O Pitamaha, have been reduced to this plight because of me and my allies fighting our enemies on this Kurukshetra? Other princes also, with their sons and kinsmen, have been destroyed on my account. What can be more painful than this!

Pitamaha, tell us what is our destiny and that of the sons of Dhritarashtra, who, driven by fate and anger, have acted in this terrible manner? Master of men, I think Duryodhana fortunate that he does not see you like this. But I, who am the cause of your death as well as of that of our friends, am denied all peace of mind seeing you fallen on the bare earth in this wretched condition.

Evil Duryodhana, the most infamous of his vamsa, with all his forces and his brothers, has perished in battle, observing his Kshatriya dharma. That malevolent one does not see you lying on your cruel bed. And for this I regard death as being preferable to life. Virtuous Kshatriya, if only I along with my brothers had been killed by our enemies on Kurukshetra, I would not see you like this, fallen and pierced with arrows. Surely, we were born to become perpetrators of evil deeds. Pitamaha, if your wish me well, instruct me so that my sins may be washed away at least in the next world.'

Bhishma replies, 'Fortunate one, why do you consider your Soul, which is dependent on God and destiny and time, to be the cause of your actions? Its inaction is subtle and imperceptible to the senses. Listen, in this regard to the ancient story of the conversation between Mrityu and Gautami with Kaala and the hunter and the serpent.

There was once an old woman called Gautami who was patient and tranquil. One day she found her son lying dead having been bitten by a snake. An angry hunter, Arjunaka, bound the snake with a rope and brought it before Gautami.

He said to her, "This wretched serpent caused your son's death. Tell me quickly how I should killed it. Shall I throw it into the fire or hack it into pieces? This killer of a child does not deserve to live."

Gautami replied, "Arjunaka of little understanding, release this serpent. It does not deserve death at your hands. Who is so foolish as to ignore inevitable destiny and burden himself with such folly to sink into sin?

Those who are virtuous manage to cross samsara as a ship crosses the ocean. But those who make themselves heavy with sin sink to the bottom, like an arrow shot into the water.

By killing the serpent, my son will not be restored to life, and by letting it live, no harm will come to you. Who would go to the realm of Yama by killing this living creature?"

The hunter said, "I know you know the difference between right and wrong, and that the great suffer the pain of all creatures. But these your words are filled with instruction for only a serene person and not for one plunged into sorrow. Therefore, I must kill this snake.

Those who value peace of mind assign the cause of everything to the passage of Kaala, but practical men assuage their grief with revenge. Through constant delusion, men fear the loss of grace in the next world for acts like these. Allay your grief by allowing me to kill this serpent."

Gautami replied, "People like us are never afflicted by such misfortune. Good men are always intent on virtue. The death of the boy was predestined; I cannot approve of your killing this snake. Brahmanas do not harbour resentment, because resentment leads to pain. Good hunter, forgive this serpent and release him out of compassion."

The hunter replied, "Let us earn great and inexhaustible punya hereafter by killing this creature, even as a man acquires great merit, and also confers it on his victim sacrificed upon the vedi. Punya is acquired by killing an enemy: by killing this despicable creature, you will acquire true merit in the hereafter."

Gautami replied, "What good is there in tormenting and killing an enemy, and what good is won by not releasing an enemy in our power? You of benign countenance, why should we not forgive this serpent and try to earn punya by releasing it?"

The hunter replied, "Many creatures ought to be protected from the evil of this one, instead of this single creature being spared. Virtuous men abandon the vicious to their doom; therefore, kill this evil snake."

Gautami replied, "By killing this serpent my son will not be restored to life, nor do I see that any other end will be attained by its death. Hunter, release this living creature."

The hunter said, "By killing Vritra, Indra secured the best part of the havis, and by destroying a yagna Siva secured his share of sacrificial offerings. You must destroy this snake immediately without any misgivings!'"

Bhishma continues, 'Though repeatedly incited by the hunter to kill the snake, Gautami was not swayed to that sin. Bound with the rope, the serpent wriggled and groaned in pain but then, finding its composure spoke slowly in a human voice.

The serpent said, "O foolish Arjunaka, what fault is mine? I have no independent will of my own. Mrityu sent me for this task. Directed by him I bit this child, not out of any anger or choice on my part. If there be any sin in this, it is Mrityu's."

The hunter said, "If you have been led by another to do this evil deed, the sin is yours also for you are the instrument in the act. As in the making of an earthen vessel the potter's wheel and axle are regarded as causes, so are you the cause that has produced this effect. He that is guilty deserves death at my hands. Serpent, you are guilty. Indeed, you have yourself confessed to it!"

The serpent said, "As all these, the potter's wheel and rod are not independent causes, even so I am not an independent cause. Therefore, you should concede that this is no fault of mine. If you think otherwise, then these are to be considered as causes working in unison with one another.

Working with one other, a doubt arises regarding their relation as cause and effect. This being the case, it is no fault of mine, nor do I deserve death on this account, nor am I guilty of any sin. Or, if you think that even in such causation there is sin, the sin lies in the aggregate of causes."

The hunter said, "Even if you are neither the prime cause nor the agent in this matter, you are still the cause of this child's death. And so you do deserve death. If you think that when an evil deed is done, the doer is not implicated in it, then there can be no cause in this matter; but having done this, you certainly deserve to die. What else do you think?"

The serpent said, "Whether any cause exists or not, no effect is produced without an intermediate act. Therefore, causation being of no moment in either case, only my agency as the cause ought to be considered in its proper context. If you truly think me to be the cause, then the guilt of this act of killing a living being rests on the shoulders of another who incited me."

The hunter said, "Wretch, you do not deserve to live; why do you rant so much? You deserve death at my hands. You have done a terrible thing by killing this child."

The serpent said, "Hunter, as the Brahmanas presiding at a yagna do not acquire the merit of their actions by making offerings of ghee into the fire, so should I be viewed with regard to the outcome in this matter.'"

Bhishma continues, 'After this, Mrityu, who had sent the snake, himself appeared there and spoke to the creature.

Mrityu said, "Guided by Kaala, O serpent, I sent you to this task, but neither you nor I is the cause of this child's death. As the clouds are tossed in all directions by the wind, I, like the clouds, am influenced by Kaala. All deeds pertaining to sattva, rajas or tamas are goaded by Kaala, in all creatures.

All creatures, mobile and immobile, in heaven and on earth, are influenced by Kaala. The whole universe is imbued with this influence of time. All actions in this world and all abstentions, as also all their modifications, are provoked by Kaala.

Surya, Soma, Vishnu, Jala, Vayu, Agni, Varuna, Bhumi, Mitra and Parjanya, Aditi and the Vasus, rivers and oceans, all existent and non-existent objects, are created and destroyed by Kaala. Knowing this, why do you, O serpent, consider me to be guilty? If any fault attaches to me, then you, too, are to be blamed."

The serpent said, "Mrityu, I do not blame you, nor do I absolve you from all blame. I only insist that I am directed and influenced by you in my actions. If any blame attaches to Kaala, or it does not, is not for me to decide. We have no right to do so. Just as I want to absolve myself of this charge, so is it my duty to see that no blame attaches to Mrityu."

The serpent then said to Arjunaka, "You have listened to what Mrityu has said. Since I am innocent it is not right that you bind me with this rope and torment me." The hunter said, "I have listened to you and to Mrityu, but these words, serpent, do not absolve you from all blame. Mrityu and you are the causes of the child's death. I consider both of you to be the cause and you truly are that cause. Cursed be the evil and vengeful Mrityu that brings affliction to the innocent and the good. And you who are guilty of sinful deeds, I shall kill you too!"

Mrityu said, "We are both not free agents, but are dependent on Kaala, and ordained to do our appointed work. If you think carefully about this, you will not find fault with us."

The hunter said, "If both Mrityu and you are dependent on Kaala, I am curious to know how pleasure, arising from doing good, and anger, arising from doing evil, are caused."

Mrityu said, "Everything is done under the influence of Kaala. Kaala is the cause of all, and that for this reason we both, acting under Kaala's command, do our appointed work; hence we do not deserve to be censured by you in any way!'"

Bhishma continues, 'Then Kaala arrived at that place where the serpent and Mrityu and Arjunaka were disputing this point of dharma and spoke to them.

Kaala said, "Hunter, neither Mrityu nor this serpent nor I are guilty of the death of any creature. We are merely the immediate causes of the event. Arjunaka, the karma of this very child is the existing cause of our action. There is no other cause of this child's death. It was killed as a result of its own karma.

It has met with death as the result of its karma of the past. Its own karma has been the cause of its dying. We all are subject to the influence of our respective karma. Karma is a means to salvation even as sons are, and karma also is an indicator of virtue and vice in man. We incite one another even as acts provoke one another.

As men make what they wish from a lump of clay, even so do they achieve the results determined by karma. As light and shadow are related to each other, so are men related to karma through their own actions. Therefore, neither you nor I, neither Mrityu nor the serpent, nor this old Brahmana woman is the cause of this child's death. He himself is the cause."

When Kaala expounded the matter in this way, Gautami, convinced that men suffer according to their deeds, said to Arjunaka, "Neither

Kaala nor Mrityu, nor the serpent is the cause. This child met with death as the result of its own karma. That my son has died is also the consequence of my past actions. Let Kaala and Mrityu now leave this place, and Arjunaka, you must release this snake."'

Bhishma continues, 'Then Kaala and Mrityu and the serpent went back to their respective abodes, and Gautami and the hunter were pacified. Rajan, having heard this, put aside all grief, and find peace of mind.

Men attain swarga or naraka as the result of their own karma. This evil is neither your creation nor Duryodhana's. Know this that these lords of earth have all been slain in this war as a result of the actions of Kaala.'"

Vaisampayana said, "Having heard all this, Yudhishtira was appeased, and asks his next question."

CANTO 2

"Yudhishtira says, 'Wisest Pitamaha, you are learned in all the shastras, and I have listened to this mahakatha. I want now to hear some story full of religious instruction, and you must satisfy my craving. Tell me if any grihasta has ever succeeded in conquering Mrityu through the practice of dharma.'

Bhishma says, 'This ancient story is told to illustrate the subject of a grihasta's victory over Mrityu through the practice of virtue. Prajapati Manu had a son called Ikshvaku. Illustrious as Surya, a hundred sons were born to him.

His tenth son was named Dasaswa, and this virtuous prince of infallible prowess became the king of Mahismati. Dasaswa's son was a righteous ruler who was devoted to the practice of truth, devotion and benevolence. He was known as Madiraswa and ruled over the earth as her lord. He was devoted to the study of the Vedas and of the science of arms. Madiraswa's son was King Dyutimat who had great fortune and power, strength and energy. Dyutimat's son was the devout and pious king famed in all the worlds as Suvira. His soul was dedicated to dharma and he possessed wealth like another Indra.

Suvira, too, had a son who was invincible in battle; known by the name Sudurjaya, he was the best of all warriors. And Durjaya, too, possessed of a body like that of Indra, and had a son who radiated the splendour of Agni. He was the great King Duryodhana who was among the foremost of royal sages. Indra would send down timely and ample rain into the kingdom of this king who was brave and heroic as Vasava himself.

His cities and all his lands overflowed with wealth and jewels, and cows and grain. There was no miser in his kingdom nor any person afflicted by suffering or poverty. Nor was there in his kingdom any person who had a weak or sickly body.

Duryodhana was intelligent and skilled, eloquent in speech, without envy, a master of his passions, of a righteous soul, full of compassion, and humble. He performed sacrifices, and was self-restrained, devoted to Brahmanas and truth. He never humiliated others, was charitable, and learned in the Vedas and the Vedanta.

The celestial river Narmada, auspicious and sacred and of cool waters came embodied and courted him. She gave birth to a lotus-eyed daughter named Sudarsana. Yudhishtira, no woman had ever borne such a beautiful child as the daughter of Duryodhana.

Agni himself courted the exquisite princess Sudarsana, and coming as a Brahmana, sought her hand from the king. The king was unwilling to give his daughter in marriage to the Brahmana, who was poor and not of the same status as himself. Thereupon Agni disappeared from his mahayagna.

The sorrowful king said to the Brahmanas, "What sin have I or you, excellent Brahmanas, been guilty of that Agni should disappear from this yagna, as good done to sinful men vanishes from their estimation. Our sin must be great for Agni to thus disappear. Either the sin must be yours or mine. Do you fully examine the reason for this."

The Brahmanas silently concentrated their minds on seeking the protection of the god of fire. Agni, resplendent as the autumnal sun, appeared before them, enveloped in glorious radiance.

Agni said to the Brahmanas, "I seek the daughter of Duryodhana for myself."

Those Brahmanas were astounded, and the next day they told the king what Agni had said. The wise ruler was delighted and said, "Let it be so!"

The king asked the fire god for a boon, "You, O Agni, remain here with us always."

"Tathaastu," said the divine Agni to that Lord of the earth. For this reason, to this very day, Agni has always been present in the kingdom of Mahishmati and was seen by Sahadeva in course of his southern conquests.

King Duryodhana gave his daughter, dressed in new clothes and decked with jewels, to the Mahatman Deva, and Agni too, accepted, according to Vedic rites, the princess Sudarsana as his bride, even as he accepts libations of ghee at yagnas. Agni was well pleased with her appearance, her beauty, grace, character and nobility of birth, and was eager to beget offspring upon her.

And a son by Agni was soon born to her. Also named Sudarsana, he, too, was as handsome as the full moon, and even in his childhood he attained to a knowledge of the supreme and everlasting Brahman.

There was another king called Oghavat, who was the grandfather of Nriga. He had a daughter named Oghavati, and a son by the name of Ogharatha. King Oghavat gave his daughter Oghavati, with goddess-like beauty, to the learned Sudarsana for his wife. Sudarsana lived the life of a grihasta with her in Kurukshetra. He took a vow to conquer Mrityu even while leading the life of a householder.

Sudarsana said to Oghavati, "You never act contrary to the wishes of those that seek our hospitality. You should not have any misgivings about the means by which guests are to be welcomed, even if you have to offer your own person to an atithi. Beautiful one, this vrata must always be remembered, since there is no higher virtue for grihastas than hospitality accorded to guests.

If my words carry any authority with you, always bear this in mind without ever doubting it. Sinless and blessed one, if you have any faith in me, you must never disregard a guest whether I am at your side or far away!"

With hands folded and placed on her head, Oghavati replied, "I will do everything that you have commanded."

Mrityu, wanting to trick Sudarsana, began to watch him to discover his lapses. Once, when the son of Agni went out to collect firewood from the forest, a handsome Brahmana sought the hospitality of Oghavati saying, "O beautiful devi, if you have any you faith in the virtue of hospitality as laid down for householders, then I ask you to extend that hospitality to me today."

Oghavati welcomed him according to the rites prescribed in the Vedas. Having offered him a seat, and water to wash his feet, she asked, "What is your wish? What can I offer you?"

The Brahmana said to her, "I desire you. Give yourself to me without any hesitation in your mind. If the duties established for grihastas are acceptable to you, gratify me."

Though tempted by Oghavati with offers of other gifts, the Brahmana refused to accept any dakshina other than the offer of her own person. Seeing his resolve, and remembering her husband's instructions, although overcome with shame, she said to the Brahmana, "Let it be so."

Remembering the words of her husband who wished to attain the virtue of grihastas, she calmly approached the visiting Rishi. Meanwhile, having collected his firewood, the son of Agni returned home. The fierce and inexorable Mrityu was constantly by his side, as one attending upon a devoted friend.

Reaching his asrama, Sudarsana called out to Oghavati repeatedly, and receiving no answer, exclaimed, "Where have you gone?" Locked in the Brahmana's embrace, the chaste woman, devoted to her husband, did not reply. Indeed, that virtuous woman, regarding herself defiled, was overcome with shame and remained silent.

Sudarsana again exclaimed, "Where can my faithful wife be? Where has she gone? Nothing can be of greater importance to me than her. Why does my simple and dutiful wife not answer my call today with sweet smiles as she has always done?"

Then that Brahmana, who was within the hut, replied to Sudarsana, "Son of Pavaka, know that a Brahmana guest has arrived, and though tempted by your wife with many offers of welcome I desired only her person, and the beautiful woman is engaged in satisfying me. You are free to do whatever you think to be appropriate."

Mrityu, armed with his iron mace, pursued the Rishi at that moment, wanting to destroy him who would, he thought, deviate from his promise. Sudarsana was astonished, but discarding all jealousy and anger of gaze, word, deed or thought, said, "Enjoy yourself, Brahmana. It gives me great pleasure. A grihasta gains the highest punya by honouring a guest.

The wise say that there is no higher merit for a householder than what accrues to him from a guest departing from his house after having been duly honoured. My life, my wife, and my other worldly possessions are all dedicated for the use of my guests.

This is the vow I have taken. With this I will attain to the knowledge of the Atman. The five elements of fire, air, earth, water and sky, and the mind, the intellect and the soul, and time and space, and the ten organs of sense, all exist in the bodies of men, and always witness the good and evil deeds that men do.

I have uttered this truth today, and let the gods bless me for it, or destroy me if I have spoken falsely." At this, Bhaarata, a voice arose in all directions, in repeated echoes, crying: *This is true, this is not false.*

Then the Brahmana came out of the hut and, like the wind rising and encompassing both earth and sky, and making the three worlds echo with Veda nadam, called out to that virtuous man by name and praised him saying, "Sinless one, I am Dharma. All glory to you. I came here to test you, and I am pleased to know that you are virtuous.

You have subdued and conquered Mrityu, who always pursued you, seeking your lapses. No one in the three worlds has the ability to insult this chaste woman, devoted to her husband, even with looks, far less to touch her person. She has been protected from defilement by your virtue and by her own purity.

There can be nothing contrary to what this honourable woman will say. Imbued with austere tapasya, she will metamorphose into a mighty river for the salvation of the world. And you will attain to all the worlds in this your body, and, as truly as the vigyana of yoga is within her control, this blessed woman will follow you with only half of her earthly self, and with the other half she will be celebrated as the river Oghavati!

And along with her, you will attain all the worlds that are acquired through penances; and even in your gross body you will attain those eternal and everlasting worlds from which no one returns. You have conquered Mrityu, and attained to the highest of all felicities, and with your own power of mind, with the speed of thought, you have risen above the power of the five elements!

By thus cleaving to the duties of a grihasta, you have subdued your passions, desires and anger, and Oghavati by serving you has conquered affliction, desire, illusion, enmity and lassitude!"'

Bhishma continues, 'Riding a fine chariot drawn by a thousand white horses, the glorious Vasava then approached that Brahmana. Mrityu and Yama, all the worlds, all the elements, Buddhi, Manas, Kaala and Akasa, as also kama and krodha were all conquered. And so, bear this in mind that to a householder there is no higher divinity than the guest.

It is said by sages that the blessings of an honoured guest are more valuable than the merit of a hundred yagnas. Whenever a deserving guest seeks the hospitality of a householder and is not honoured by him, he takes away with him all the virtues of the grihasta and leaves behind his sins.

I have now told you this ancient story about Mrityu was defeated by a grihasta. This narration confers glory, fame and a long life upon those who listen to it. The man that seeks worldly prosperity should consider it useful for removing every evil.

Bhaarata, he who recites this story of the life of Sudarsana every day attains the realms of the blessed.'"

CANTO 3

"Yudhishtira says, 'Rajan, if Brahmanatva is so difficult to attain by Kshatriyas, Vaisyas and Sudras, how did the high-souled Viswamitra, though a Kshatriya by birth, become a Brahmarishi? I want to know this. I beg you, tell me all about it.

With his tapasya shakti, Viswamitra instantly annihilated the hundred sons of the Mahatman Vasishta. Under the influence of his rage, he created countless mighty Rakshasas who resembled the great destroyer Kaala himself.

He established the great and learned Kusika vamsa, numbering hundreds of regenerate sages praised by all Brahmanas. Sunashepa of austere penances, the son of Richika, was to be sacrificed as a yagnapasu in the Ambarisha mahayagna, but found deliverance through the grace of Viswamitra.

Having pleased the gods at a sacrifice, Harishchandra became a son of the wise Viswamitra. For not honouring their eldest brother Devarata, whom Viswamitra got as a son from the Devas, his other fifty brothers were cursed by their father, and all of them became Chandalas.

Trisanku, the son of Ikshvaku, also became a Chandala through the curse of Vasishta; when he was abandoned by his friends and remained suspended head down in the sky it was Viswamitra who sent him up into swarga. Kaushika, the sacred and most auspicious river of Viswamitra, was frequented by Devarishis, Devas and Rishis.

For disturbing his devotions, the famed Apsara Rambha was cursed and turned into a rock. In olden times, fearing Viswamitra, the glorious Vasishta bound himself with creepers and threw himself into a river, but he rose up released from his bonds. Because of this, that mighty and holy river became celebrated by the name Vipasa.

Viswamitra prayed to the glorious and puissant Indra who, gratified by him, released him from a curse. Remaining in the northern sky, he sheds his lustre from a position in the midst of the Saptarishi and Dhruva, the son of Uttanapada. These, among others, are his achievements.

Descendant of Kuru, as all these were performed by a Kshatriya, my curiosity has been roused. So do I ask you to explain this to me truly. Without casting off his body and taking on another, how could Viswamitra become a Brahmana?

Pitamaha, tell me about this just as you narrated to the story of Matanga. Matanga was born as a Chandala, and, despite all his tapasya, could not become a Brahmana; so how could this Kaushika become a Brahmarishi?'"

CANTO 4

"Bhishma says, 'Listen truly in detail as to how in olden times Viswamitra attained the status of a Brahmana Rishi.

In the Bharata vamsa there was a king named Ajamida, who performed many yagnas and was a virtuous man. His son was the great King Jahnu. Ganga was the daughter of this righteous Kshatriya. The famed and equally virtuous Sindhudwipa was the son of this prince.

From Sindhudwipa sprang the great Rajarishi Balakaswa. His son was named Vallabha and was like a second Dharma. His son was Kusika who had radiant glory like the thousand-eyed Indra. Kusika's son was the illustrious King Gadhi who, being childless and wanting to have a son, went into the forest.

Whilst living there, a daughter was born to him. She was called Satyavati, and in beauty she had no equal on earth. The illustrious son of Chyavana, celebrated by the name of Richika, of the Bhrigu vamsa, of austere penances, sought the hand of this woman to be his wife. Gadhi, thinking him to be poor, did not give her in marriage to Richika.

But when the latter, thus dismissed, was leaving, the king said to him, "If your give me a marriage dowry you will you have my daughter for your wife."

Richika said, "Rajan, what dowry can I offer you for the hand of your daughter? Tell me truly, without feeling any hesitation."

Gadhi said, "Descendant of Bhrigu, give me a thousand horses as swift as the wind, with the colour of moonlight, and each having one ear black."'

Bhishma said, 'That mighty son of Chyavana, who was the foremost of Bhrigu's race, entreated Varuna, the son of Aditi, who was the lord of all the waters, "Best of Devas, I pray to you to give me a thousand horses, all swift as the wind, with a complexion as luminous as the moon's, but each having one black ear." Varuna said to Richika, "Be it so. Wherever you are, the horses will appear before you."

As soon as Richika thought of them, there arose from the waters of the Ganga a thousand high-mettled horses, as lustrous as the moon. Not far from Kanyakubja, the sacred bank of Ganga is still famed among men as Aswatirtha because of the appearance of those horses at that place.

The delighted Richika, that best of sannyasis, gave those thousand excellent horses to Gadhi as the marriage offering. King Gadhi was filled with wonder and, fearing that he would be cursed, gave his daughter, decked with jewels, to that son of Bhrigu. And he accepted her hand in marriage according to the prescribed rites.

The princess, too, was pleased becoming the wife of that Brahmana. That foremost of Rishis was happy with her conduct and expressed a wish to grant her a boon. She related this to her mother.

The mother said to her unassuming daughter who stood before her, "My daughter, it is fitting for you to secure a favour for me also from your husband. That sage of austere tapasya has the power to grant me a boon: the birth of a son."

Returning to her husband, the princess told him what her mother had asked for. Richika said, "By my favour, blessed one, she will soon give birth to a virtuous son. From you, too, there will be born a mighty and glorious son who, full of dharma, shall perpetuate my vasma. Truly do I say this to you!

When you two shall bathe in your fertile season, she should embrace a pipal tree, and you should likewise embrace a ficus tree, and by doing so you will attain the object of your desire. Both she and you will partake of these two portions of charu, along with mantras, and then you will have your sons."

Satyavati was delighted and told her mother all that Richika had said and also about the two balls of charu. Then the mother said to her daughter Satyavati, "Daughter, as I deserve greater consideration from you than from your husband, you must do as I say.

You must give me the charu which your husband has given you and take the one that has was meant for me. O joyful and pure daughter, if you have any respect for me, let us exchange the trees designated for us.

Everyone desires to possess an excellent and stainless being for his own son. The glorious Richika, too, must have acted from a similar motive, as will be revealed later. For this reason, my heart inclines towards your charu, and your tree, and you too, must consider how to secure an exceptional brother for yourself."

The mother and the daughter Satyavati pursued this plan and both conceived their children, Yudhishtira. And that great Rishi was happy to find his wife pregnant, but he said to her, "Devi, you have not you done well in exchanging the charu as will soon become apparent. It is also clear that you have exchanged the trees.

Know that I infused your charu with Brahmatejas and Kshatriya energy in the charu of your mother. I intended that you would give birth to a Brahmana whose virtues would be famed throughout the three worlds, and that your mother would give birth to a redoubtable Kshatriya.

But now you have reversed the charu, and your mother will give birth to a splendid Brahmana and you will bring forth a fierce Kshatriya. You have not done well by acting out of love for your mother."

Hearing this, Satyavati was grief-stricken and fell to the ground like a beautiful creeper cut in two. When she regained her senses, she bowed her head before her lord and said, "Dvija, you who know Brahman, take pity on me, your wife, who pleads with you so that a Kshatriya son may not be born to me. Let my grandson be the one to be famous for his terrible achievements, but not my son. I beg you, do this for me."

"So be it," said Richika to his wife and she gave birth to a blessed son named Jamadagni. Her mother, the celebrated wife of Gadhi, gave birth to the Rishi Viswamitra, knower of Brahmatva.

The devout Viswamitra, though a Kshatriya, attained to the status of a Brahmarishi and became the founder of a vamsa of Brahmanas. His sons became high-souled progenitors of many races of Brahmanas who were devoted to austere penances, were learned in the Vedas, and founders of many clans.

The adorable Madhuchchanda and the mighty Devarata, Akshina, Sakunta, Babhru, Kaala patha, the celebrated Yajnavalkya, Sthula of strict vratas, Uluka, Mudgala, and the sage Saindhavayana, the illustrious Valgujangha and the great Rishi Galeva, Ruchi, the celebrated Vajra, as also Salankayana, Liladhya and Narada, the one known as Kurchamuka, and Bahuli, and Mushala were all sons of Viswamitra.

So also were Vakshogriva, Anghrika, Naikadrik, Silayupa, Sita, Suchi, Chakraka, Marrutantavya, Vataghna, Aswalayana, Syamayana, Gargya and Javali, as also Susruta, Karishi, Sangsrutya, Para Paurava and Tantu.

The Maharishi Kapila, Tarakayana, Upagahana, Asurayani, Margama, Hiranyksha, Janghari, Bhavravayani, and Suti, Vibhuti, Suta, Surakrit, Arani, Nachika, Champeya, Ujjayana, Navatantu, Vakanakha, Sayanya, Yati, Ambhoruha, Amatsyasin, Srishin, Gardhavi Urjjayoni, Rudapekahin, and the great Naradin—these Munis were all sons of Viswamitra and were proficient in the knowledge of Brahman.

Yudhishtira, the austere and devout Viswamitra, although a Kshatriya by birth, became a Brahmana because Richika had infused the charu meant for his wife with the tejas of the supreme Brahman. I have now told you the story of the birth of Viswamitra who was possessed of the energy of Surya, Chandramas and Agni.

Rajan, if you have doubts with regard to any other matter, do you tell me, so that I may remove them.'"

CANTO 5

"Yudhishtira says, 'You who know the truths of dharma, I wish to hear of the merits of compassion, and of the characteristics of devout men. Pitamaha, describe them to me.'

"Bhishma says, 'Listen to the ancient tale of Vasava and the high-minded Suka. In the kingdom of Kasi, a hunter went from his village on a hunt with poisoned arrows in search of antelope. In a vast forest, while in pursuit of the chase, he discovered a herd of antelope not far from him, and discharged his arrow at one of them.

The arrow missed the deer and pierced a mighty tree instead. Struck by that arrow tipped with virulent poison, the tree withered away instantaneously, shedding its leaves and fruits.

The tree died, but a parrot that lived in a hollow of its trunk all his life did not leave his nest out of love for the towering Lord of the forest. Motionless and without food, silent and grieving, that grateful and virtuous parrot also perished slowly after the tree.

Indra was amazed by that great and generous bird's extraordinary resolve and detachment. He thought, "How has this bird come to possess such extraordinary humane and generous emotions which are not found among the lower creatures? Yet, perhaps there is nothing wonderful about this, for all creatures appear to exhibit kind and generous feelings towards others."

Assuming the form of a Brahmana, Sakra descended onto the earth and came to the bird. "Suka, O parrot, Daksha's granddaughter Suki is blessed to bear you as her child. I ask you, why do you not leave this dead tree?"

Thus questioned, Suka bowed to him and replied, "Welcome to you, Indra. I have recognised you by the merit of my tapasya."

"Uttamam! Well done!" exclaimed Indra. He praised Suka in his mind, thinking how great was his gyana. Although Indra knew that the parrot was virtuous in character and noble in deed, still he pressed him about the reason for his love for the tree.

"This tree has withered; it is without leaves and fruits and is unfit to be the refuge of birds. Why do you cling to it? This forest is vast and in it are many other fine trees whose hollows are covered with leaves, and you can choose freely from them. Patient one, discern wisely and abandon this old tree that is dead and useless, shorn of all its leaves and no longer of any good to you."

Hearing this from Sakra, Suka heaved a deep sigh and replied sadly, "Consort of Sachi, and king of the Devas, the laws of the gods must always be obeyed. Listen to my reasoning on this matter.

Here, within this tree, I was born, and here in this tree I acquired all the good traits of my character, and here in this tree I was protected in my childhood from predators. Sinless one, why, in your kindness, do you seek to taint my principles in life?

I am compassionate, virtuous and steadfast in my conduct. Kindness is the great test of virtue amongst the good, and this same compassion is the source of everlasting felicity to the virtuous. All the Devas look to you to remove their doubts on dharma, and for this reason you have sovereignty over them.

It is not fitting for you to tell me to abandon this tree. When it was capable of good, it supported my life. How can I forsake it now?"

The virtuous destroyer of Paka was pleased with these words of the parrot and said to him, "I am gratified with your compassionate nature. Ask any boon of me."

The loyal parrot said, "Let this tree revive!" Knowing the great attachment of the noble parrot to that tree, Indra showered amrita on the tree. That tree was restored and attained its former grandeur through the tapasya of the parrot, who, by virtue of his compassion, found Indra's own companionship at the end of his life.

Thus, Lord of men, through friendship and association with the pious, men attain all the objects of their desire even as the tree did through its companionship with the parrot.'"

CANTO 6

"Yudhishtira says, 'Pitamaha, tell me which is more powerful, effort or fate.'

Bhishma says, 'Hear this ancient story of the conversation between Vasishta and Brahma. In ancient times, Vasishta asked Brahma what influenced a man's life more: the karma acquired in this life, or that acquired in previous lives, which is called fate. Brahma, who had sprung from the primeval lotus, answered him in these exquisite and well-reasoned words, full of meaning.

Brahma said, "Nothing comes into existence without seeds. Without seeds, fruits do not grow. From seeds spring other seeds. Hence fruits are known to be generated from seeds. As good or bad is the seed that the farmer sows in his field, so are the fruits that he reaps.

Just as the soil, unsown with seeds, becomes fruitless, so also karma is of no use without individual exertion. One's own actions are like the soil, and destiny, the sum of one's deeds in previous births, can be compared to the seed. The union of the soil and the seed produces the harvest. Every day in the world, we see that the doer reaps the fruit of his good and evil deeds; that happiness results from good deeds, and pain from evil ones; that actions always bear fruit; and that, if not done, there is no fruit. A man of good deeds acquires merit with good fortune, while a lazy man loses his lands, and reaps evil like the infusion of alkaline matter injected into a wound.

With devoted application, one acquires beauty, fortune, and wealth of many kinds. Everything can be secured through exertion, but nothing can be gained by a lazy man through destiny alone. Even so does one attain heaven, and all the objects of enjoyment, as also the fulfilment of one's heart's desires—by well-directed individual effort.

All the luminous stars and planets in the sky, all the Devas, the Nagas and the Rakshasas, as also the sun and the moon and the winds, have attained to their lofty positions by evolution from a human condition, by dint of their own deeds. Riches, friends, prosperity from generation to generation, as also the blessings of life, are difficult to attain without exertion.

The Brahmana attains prosperity through pure and virtuous living, the Kshatriya by prowess, the Vaisya with manly exertion, and the Sudra through service. Riches and other pleasures do not follow the miser, nor the weak, nor the idler. Nor are these ever attained by the man who is not active or manly or devoted to the performance of religious austerities.

Even he, the adorable Vishnu, who created the three worlds with the Daityas and all the Devas, even he is engaged in tapasya in the depths of the ocean. If one's karma bore no fruit all actions would become fruitless, and relying on destiny all men would become idlers. He who follows destiny alone, without pursuing the human modes of action, acts in vain, like the woman with an impotent husband.

In this world, the dread that accrues from doing good or evil deeds is not so great if destiny is unfavourable, as one's fear in the other world if one make no effort in this world. Man's powers, if properly exerted, only follow his destiny, but destiny alone cannot confer any good where exertion is wanting.

When we see that even in swarga the position of the Devas is unstable, how would they maintain their position or that of others without proper karma? The Devas do not always encourage the good deeds of others in this world, and they even thwart such actions fearing their own overthrow.

There is a constant rivalry between the Devas and the Rishis, and even if they must perform karma, it can never be asserted that there is no such thing as destiny, for it is the latter that initiates all karma. If destiny is the source of human action, how does karma originate? It does so through an accumulation of many virtues in the divine realms.

One's own self is one's friend and one's enemy too, as also the witness of one's punya and paapa. Good and evil manifest themselves through karma. Good and evil actions do not have adequate results. Dharma is the refuge of the Devas, and through dharma everything is attained. Destiny does not obstruct the man who has attained virtue and righteousness.

In olden times, falling from his high position in heaven, Yayati descended onto the earth but was again restored to the celestial realms by the good deeds of his virtuous grandsons. The royal sage Pururavas, the celebrated descendant of Ila, attained swarga through the intercession of Brahmanas.

Though exalted by the performance of the Aswamedha and other yagnas, Saudasa, the son of Kosala, became a man-eating Rakshasa through the curse of a great Rishi. Aswatthaman and Rama, though both warriors and sons of Munis, failed to attain swarga because of their own fell deeds in this world.

Though he performed a hundred yagnas like a second Vasava, Vasu was sent to naraka for uttering a single falsehood. Bound by his promise, Bali, the son of Virochana, was consigned to the patalas below the earth by the power of Vishnu.

Was not Janamejaya, who followed in the footsteps of Sakra, thwarted by the Devas for killing a Brahmana woman? Was not the Rishi Vaisampayana, who unwittingly killed a Brahmana, and was tainted by the slaying of a child, censured by the Devas?

In ancient times, the Rajarishi Nriga was transformed into a lizard. He had made great gifts of cows to the Brahmanas at his mahayagna, but to no avail.

The royal sage Dhundhumara was overtaken by age, decay and fatigue even while engaged in performing his sacrifices, and forgoing all their merits he fell asleep at Girivraja. The Pandavas, too, regained their lost kingdom, which had been seized by the powerful sons of Dhritarashtra, not through the intercession of the fates, but by recourse to their own valour.

Do the Munis of rigid vows, and devoted to the practice of austere tapasyas, denounce their curses with the help of any supernatural power or by the exercise of their own power attained by individual deeds? All the punya possessed by dissolute men, attained with difficulty in this world, they soon lose.

Destiny does not help the man steeped in spiritual ignorance and greed. When fanned by the wind, even as a small fire becomes a conflagration, so does destiny, when joined with individual exertion, increase in its potential. As the oil in the lamp reduces, its light is extinguished; so also is the influence of destiny lost if one's actions cease.

Having gained vast wealth, women, and all the enjoyments of this world, the man without action is not able to enjoy them long; but the high-souled man, who is ever diligent, is able to find treasures buried deep in the earth and watched over by spirits. The good man who is prodigious in giving religious charity and performing sacrifices is sought by the very Devas for his conduct, but the house of the miser, though abounding in wealth, is regarded by the Devas as a home of the dead.

The man who does not exert himself is never content in this world nor can destiny alter the course of a man that has gone wrong. So there is no authority inherent in destiny. As the sishya follows his own individual perception, so does destiny follow exertion. Destiny reveals itself in the matters in which one's own efforts are put forth.

Vasishta, having known their true significance with my yogic powers, I have thus described all the merits of individual exertion. By the influence of destiny, and by exerting individual effort, men attain swarga. The union of destiny and exertion is effective.""

CANTO 7

"Yudhishtira says, 'Bharatarishabha, I wish to know what the fruits are of good deeds. Do you enlighten me on this subject.'

Bhishma said, 'Yudhishtira, listen to what I tell you; it is the secret knowledge of the Rishis. Listen to me as I explain what desirable ends are attained by men after death.

Whatever actions are performed by particular beings, their fruits are reaped by the doers in similar bodies. The fruits of actions done with the mind are enjoyed in dreams, and those actions performed physically are enjoyed in the waking state.

In whatever states creatures perform good or evil deeds, they reap the fruits in similar states of succeeding lives. No action done with the five organs of the senses is ever lost. The five sense organs and the immortal soul, which is the sixth, remain eternal witnesses.

One should devote one's eye and one's heart in the service of the atithi; one should speak words that are agreeable; one should also follow and worship one's guest. This is called Panchadakshina yagna, the sacrifice with five gifts.

He who offers good food to unknown and weary travellers after a long journey, attains great punya. Those who use the sacrificial platform as their only bed in this birth, obtain commodious palaces and beds in subsequent births. Those who dress only in rags and barks of trees obtain luxurious clothes and ornaments in their next births.

The man who possesses tapasya and fixes his soul on yoga, gets chariots and horses as the fruit of his renunciation in this life. The king who lies down beside the sacrificial fire attains vigour and valour.

The man who renounces the enjoyment of all delicacies attains prosperity, and he who abstains from animal flesh, receives children and kine. He who sleeps with his head hanging down, or who lives in water, or who lives in seclusion practising brahmacharya, attains to all the desired ends.

He who offers refuge to a guest and welcomes him with water to wash his feet, as also with food and rest, attains to the merits of the Panchadakshina yagna. He who lies down on a warrior's bed on the battlefield in the posture of a warrior, goes to those eternal realms where all desires are fulfilled.

A man who makes charitable endowments finds riches. One secures obedience to one's command through the vow of silence, all the enjoyments of life with the practice of tapasya, long life by brahmacharya, and beauty, prosperity and freedom from disease by ahimsa, non-violence.

Sovereignty is theirs who subsist on fruit and roots. Swarga is attained by those that live only on the leaves of trees. A man is said to gain happiness by abstaining from food. By restricting one's diet to just herbs, one becomes wealthy. By living on grass one attains to the celestial realms.

By foregoing sexual union with one's wife, performing ablutions three times during the day and by inhaling only air for subsistence, one gains the merit of a sacrifice. Swarga is attained by the practice of truth, nobility of birth by yagnas.

The Brahmana of pure practices that subsists on water alone, performs the Agnihotra ceaselessly, and recites the Gayatri, obtains a kingdom. By giving up food or by regulating it, one attains swarga.

Rajan, by abstaining from all but the prescribed diet while engaged in sacrifices, and by making a pilgrimage for twelve years, one attains to a place better than the realms reserved for Kshatriyas. By reading all the Vedas, one is instantly liberated from misery, and by practising virtue in thought, one attains to swarga. That man who is able to renounce that intense yearning of the heart for pleasure and material enjoyments—a yearning that is difficult for foolish men to conquer, and which does not decrease with the abatement of bodily strength and that clings like a fatal disease to him—is assured bliss.

As the young calf is able to recognise its mother from among a thousand cows, so does the past karma of a man pursue him in all his transformations. As the flowers and fruits of a tree, without any visible influences, never miss their proper season, so does karma from a previous existence unerringly bring its fruit in proper time. With age, man's hair grows grey, his teeth become loose, and his eyes and ears become dim; but the one thing that does not weaken is his desire for pleasure.

Prajapati is pleased with those deeds that please one's father, the earth is pleased with those acts that please one's mother, and Brahma is adored with those that please one's acharya. Dharma is honoured by him who honours these three. Those who do not respect these three do not benefit from them, whatever they may do.'"

Vaisampayana said, "The princes of Kuru's vamsa are filled with wonder upon listening to this discourse of Bhishma. All of them are overwhelmed with joy. Like mantras that are recited only to have victory, or the performance of the Soma yagna without proper dakshina, or offerings poured on the fire without proper mantras are rendered useless and lead to evil consequences, even so sin and evil results flow from false speech.

O prince, I have thus narrated to you the doctrine of the fruition of good and evil acts, as told by the ancient Rishis. What else do you wish to hear?"

CANTO 8

Vaisampayana continued, "Yudhishtira says, 'Who are deserving of worship? Who are they unto whom one may bow? Who are they, Bhaarata, before whom you would bend your head? Who, again, are they whom you love? Tell me all this.

What does your mind dwell upon when you are overwhelmed by misery? Speak to me about what is beneficial in this world of humans, and also hereafter.'

Bhishma says, 'I revere those evolved men whose highest wealth is Brahman, whose swarga consists of the knowledge of the Atman, and whose tapasya is constituted by their diligent study of the Vedas. My heart yearns for those in whose vamsa both the young and the old diligently bear their ancestral burdens without being weighed down by them.

Skilled in several branches of knowledge, self-restrained and gentle in speech, conversant with the shastras, dutiful, possessing the knowledge of Brahman and righteous in conduct, Brahmanas discourse in auspicious conclaves like flocks of swans.

Yudhishtira, their words are auspicious, pleasing, excellent and finely pronounced; they speak with voices deep as thunderheads. Suffused with joy both earthly and spiritual, they speak such words in the courts of kings, where they are received with honour and served with reverence by those rulers of men. Indeed, my heart yearns for those who listen to the words spoken in such pure assemblies or royal sabhas by those endowed with gyana and all desirable gunas, and respected by others.

My heart longs for those who offer, with devotion, food that is clean, well cooked and wholesome to gratify Brahmanas. It is easy to fight in battle, but not so to make a gift without pride or vanity.

In this world, Yudhishtira, there are brave men and heroes by the hundreds. While counting them, he who is heroic in gifts must be regarded as superior. Even if I had been a common Brahmana, I would have regarded myself as great, not to speak of one born into a Brahmana family replete with righteousness of conduct, and devoted to penances and learning.

Son of Pandu, there is no one that is dearer to me than you are in this world, but those Brahmanas are dearer to me than even you. And since I love these Brahmanas more than you, it is through that truth that I hope to attain to all those realms of felicity in which my father Santanu dwells. Neither my sire, nor his sire, nor anyone else related to me by blood, is dearer to me than the Brahmanas.

I do not expect any reward, small or great, from my worship of the Brahmanas, for I revere them as Devas. Even though I am lying on a bed of arrows, because of what I have done for Brahmanas in thought, word and deed, I do not feel any pain.

People would refer to me as the one devoted to Brahmanas. This manner of address always pleased me most. To do good to Brahmanas is the most sacred of all sacred acts. Having walked with adoration behind Brahmanas, I behold many realms of grace waiting for me. Very soon shall I repair to those lustrous realms for ever.

In this world, Yudhishtira, the duties of women allude to and depend on their husbands. To a woman, the husband is the deity and he is the highest end after which she should strive. As the husband is to the wife, even so are the Brahmanas unto Kshatriyas. If there be a Kshatriya of full hundred years of age and a good Brahmana child of only ten years, the latter should be regarded as a father and the former as a son, for among the two the Brahmana is undeniably superior.

A woman in the absence of her husband takes his younger brother for her lord; even so Bhumi Devi, not having obtained the Brahmana, made the Kshatriya her master. Brahmanas must be protected like sons and worshipped like fathers or gurus. Indeed they must be adored even as people wait with reverence upon their homa fires.

The Brahmanas are filled with simplicity and virtue. They are devoted to truth. They are always engaged in the good of every creature. Yet when enraged they are like poisonous snakes. For these reasons, they must always be waited upon and served with reverence and humility.

Yudhishtira, always be wary of both tejas and tapasya. Both these must be avoided or kept at a distance. The effects of both are swift. However, tapasya is the more powerful, that is why tapodhana Brahmanas, if angered, can easily make ashes of the object of their wrath regardless of the tejas of that man.

Tejas and tapasya, each in the largest measure, are powerless if applied against a Brahmana who has conquered anger. If the two are set against each other, then both will be destroyed. However, if energy is applied against penances it is sure to be destroyed without leaving a trace; but tapasya applied against tejas cannot be completely annihilated.

As the herdsman, stick in hand, protects the herd, even so must the Kshatriya always protect the Vedas and the Brahmanas. Indeed, the Kshatriya should protect all righteous Brahmanas even as a father protects his sons. He must watch over the houses of the Brahmanas and ensure that they do not lack in their means of livelihood.'"

CANTO 9

"Yudhishtira says, 'Pitamaha, what happens to those men who, through inertia and torpor, do not make gifts to Brahmanas after having promised to make those offerings? You who are the most righteous of men, tell me what the laws are in this respect. Indeed, what is the end of those who do not give after having promised to give.'

Bhishma says, 'One who having promised does not give, be it little or much, has the mortification of seeing his hopes in all directions become fruitless like the hopes of a eunuch who wishes for children. Whatever good deeds such a man does between the day of his birth and that of his death, Bhaarata, whatever libations he pours on the sacrificial fire, whatever gifts he makes, and whatever penances he performs, all become fruitless.

They that know the shastras declare this to be their opinion, having arrived at it with the help of a studied understanding. These learned men are also of opinion that such a man may be redeemed by giving away a thousand pale horses with dark ears.

Listen to the old story of the conversation between a jackal and a monkey. Once, when both were humans, they were intimate friends. After they died, in their next birth one of them became a jackal and the other a monkey.

One day, seeing the jackal eating the carcass of an animal in a cremation ground, the monkey, remembering his own and his friend's past birth as men, said to him, "What terrible sin did you commit in your last birth that in this one you are obliged to feed upon the putrid carcass of an animal in the samsana?"

The jackal replied to the monkey, "Having promised to give gifts to a Brahmana I did not do so. It is for that sin that I have fallen into this wretched existence. It is for this reason that, when hungry, I am obliged to eat such repugnant food.'"

Bhishma continues, 'The jackal then said to the monkey, "What sin did you commit for which you have become a monkey?"

The monkey said, "In my past life I used to steal fruits belonging to Brahmanas. And so I have been born as a monkey. It is clear that one who has intelligence and learning must never take what belongs to Brahmanas. One must also avoid all disputes with Brahmanas. Having promised, one must necessarily give them the promised gift.'"

Bhishma continues, 'Rajan, I heard this from my guru while he discoursed upon the subject of Brahmanas. I heard this from that righteous man when he recited the old and sacred pronouncement on this subject. I heard this from Krishna also, while he was speaking of Brahmanas.

The property of a Brahmana should never be seized. They should always be left undisturbed. Poor, miserly, or young, they should never be disregarded. Brahmanas have always taught me this.

Having promised to make them a gift, the gift must be made. A superior Brahmana's expectations must always be fulfilled. It has been said that a Brahmana whose expectation has been raised is like a blazing fire. That man upon whom a Brahmana with raised expectations casts his angry eye is certain to be consumed even as a pile of dry grass is by a blazing fire.

When the Brahmana who is honoured by the king with gifts addresses the king in agreeable and loving words, that Brahmana becomes a source of great benefit to the king, for he continues to live in the kingdom like a physician, combating the many diseases of the body. Such a Brahmana, with his power and grace, is sure to sustain the sons and grandsons, animals and relatives, ministers and other officers, and the city and provinces of the king.

This great tejas of the Brahmana is like that of the radiance of Surya himself on Bhumi. Yudhishtira, if one wishes to attain an honourable and happy next birth, having promised a Brahmana a gift, one must not neglect to bestow that gift.

By making gifts to a Brahmana one is sure to attain to the highest heaven. The giving of gifts is the highest of human deeds. With the gifts one makes to a Brahmana, one supports the Devas and the Pitris. Hence one who is wise must always make gifts to Brahmanas. Lord of the Bharatas, the Brahmana is regarded as the highest entity unto whom gifts must be made. At no time should a Brahmana be received without being properly worshipped."

CANTO 10

"Yudhishtira says, 'Tell me whether any fault is incurred by one who, whether from interested or disinterested friendship imparts instruction to one who belongs to a low varna. Pitamaha, expound this to me in detail. The course of dharma is so subtle, and men are often bewildered in respect of that path.'

Bhishma says, 'I will narrate to you what I heard certain Rishis say in olden days. Instruction should not be imparted to one who belongs to a low or mean caste. It is said that the guru who instructs such a person incurs great blame.

Listen, Yudhishtira, to this ancient story of the evil consequences of instructing a low-born person fallen into distress. This event occurred in the asrama of those illumined sages who lived on the auspicious breast of Himavat.

There, on the breast of that prince of mountains, was a sacred asrama adorned with trees of diverse kinds. Covered with diverse species of creepers and plants, it was the home of many animals and birds. Inhabited by Siddhas and Charanas, it was delightful because of the trees that flowered in every season.

Many brahmacharins and vanaprasthas lived there. Many Brahmanas residing there were highly blessed and resembled Surya or Agni in energy and refulgence. Ascetics of many kinds lived there, observant of various restraints and vows, and others who had taken diksha and were frugal in fare and possessed pure souls.

Large numbers of Balakhilyas and many who had taken the sannyasa vrata also dwelt there. The asrama echoed with the chanting of the Vedas and other sacred mantras by its inhabitants.

Once upon a time, a Sudra who loved all creatures came to that asrama. On arriving, he was duly honoured by all the ascetics. The Sudra was delighted to see those sannyasis of great tejas, who resembled the Devas in purity and power, observing diverse kinds of vratas.

Beholding everything, he felt persuaded to devote himself to the practice of tapasya. Touching the feet of the Kulapati, he said to him, "With your blessings, I want to learn and practise the duties of dharma.

Discourse to me on those duties and with the rites of initiation induct me into a life of sannyasa. I am certainly inferior in varna, illustrious one, for I am a Sudra. I desire to wait upon and serve you here. I humbly seek your refuge; I beg you, oblige me."

The Kulapati said, "It is impossible that a Sudra should adopt the practices of sannyasis. If it pleases you, you may stay here, engaged in waiting upon and serving us. Have no doubt that by such service you will attain to many realms of high felicity.'"

Bhishma continue, 'Thus addressed by the sannyasi, the Sudra reflected and said, "What should I do now? Great is my reverence for dharma, which leads to punya. But I will do what will benefit me."

Going to a remote place, he made a hut from the branches and leaves of trees. He erected a sacrificial platform and, making a little space to sleep, and a vedi for the Devas, he began to lead a life regulated by demanding vratas and tapasya, while abstaining entirely from speech.

He began to perform ablutions three times a day, to observe other vratas of food and sleep, perform yagnas for the Devas, pour libations on the sacrificial fire, and worship the deities. Subduing all sensual desires, living abstemiously upon fruits and roots, controlling all his senses, every day he welcomed and honoured all who came to his hermitage, offering them roots and fruit that grew all around in abundance. In this way he lived in that asrama for a long time.

One day an ascetic came to that Sudra's asrama to meet him. The Sudra welcomed and worshipped the Rishi with the due rites, and gratified him. Possessing great tejas and a righteous soul that Rishi talked with his host on many pleasant subjects and told him from where he had come.

That Rishi came to the Sudra's asrama several times. On one of these occasions, the Sudra said to the Rishi, "I want to perform the rites that are ordained for the Pitris. You must instruct me in this matter."

"Very well," replied the Brahmana.

The Sudra purified himself by bathing and brought water for the Rishi to wash his feet; he also brought some kusa grass, and wild herbs and fruits, and a sacred seat called Vrishi. The Sudra, however, placed the Vrishi towards the south, with its head facing west.

On seeing this and knowing it to be against the laws, the Rishi said to the Sudra, "Set the Vrishi with its head turned towards the east and, having purified yourself, sit with your face facing the north." The Sudra did as the Rishi directed.

Possessed of great intelligence and righteousness, the Sudra received every instruction from the sage about the sraddha, as laid down in the shastras—regarding the manner of spreading the kusa grass, and placing the offerings, and the rites to be observed in the matter of the libations to be poured and the food to be offered. After the rituals in honour of the Pitris had been completed, dismissed by the Sudra, the Rishi returned to his own abode.

After passing a long time in the practice of such penances and vows, the Sudra ascetic died in the forest. As a result of the punya he acquired through those practices, in his next life the Sudra was born into the family of a great king, and in the course of time became endowed with great splendour.

The Rishi also, when the time came, died. In his next life, he was born into the family of a priest. It was in this way that those two were reborn, that Sudra who had lived a life of tapasya and that Rishi who had generously instructed the Sudra in the rites performed in honour of the Pitris: the one as a son of a royal vamsa and the other as the member of a Brahmana's family.

Both of them acquired great knowledge in the customary branches of study. The Brahmana became well versed in the Vedas as also in the Atharvans. The reborn Rishi attained excellence in the matters of all yagnas ordained in the Sutras, of that Vedanga which deals with religious rites and observances, astrology and astronomy. He also took great delight in the Samkhya philosophy.

When the king, his father, died, the reborn Sudra who had become a prince performed his last rites; and after he had purified himself by performing all the necessary ceremonies, his father's subjects enthroned him as their king. Soon after his being crowned, he appointed the reborn Rishi as his priest.

Indeed, having made the Brahmana his purohita, the king began to pass his days in great happiness. He ruled his kingdom righteously and protected and cherished all his subjects. Every day, however, when he received blessings from his priest and during the performance of religious and other sacred rites, the king smiled or laughed at him loudly. In this way, the Sudra who had been reborn as a king laughed at the very sight of his purohita on countless occasions.

Marking that the king always smiled or laughed whenever he looked at him, the Brahmana became angry. One day, he met the king alone and pleased the king with an agreeable discourse. Taking advantage of that moment, he said to the king, "Splendid one, I entreat you to grant me a single boon."

The king said, "I am ready to grant you a hundred boons, why do you speak of only one? With the love I bear you and the reverence in which I hold you, there is nothing that I cannot give you."

The priest said, "You are gratified by me; Rajan, I desire only one boon. Swear that you will tell me the truth and not any lie."

"Thus addressed by the priest, Yudhishtira, the king said to him, 'So be it. If what you ask me is known to me, I will certainly speak of it to you truthfully. If, on the other hand, the matter is unknown to me,

I will not say anything.'

The Brahmana said, "Every day, when you take my blessings, and again when I am engaged in the performance of religious rites on your behalf, and also during the homa and other kriyas of propitiation, why is it that you laugh when you see me? My mind shrinks with shame when you do that.

I have asked you to swear that you will answer me truthfully. It fitting that you will not lie to me. There must be some solemn reason for your behaviour. Your laughter cannot be without cause. I am curious to know what it is. Speak to me honestly."

The king said, "When you have spoken to me in this way, I am bound to enlighten you, even if it is a matter that should not be divulged in your hearing. I must tell you the truth. Listen to me with close attention, O Dvija. Listen to me as I disclose what happened to both of us in our last births. I remember that birth. Listen and I will tell you everything.

In my past life I was a Sudra engaged in the practice of severe tapasya. You were a Rishi of austere penances. Gratified with me, and wishing to do me good, you once gave me some instruction in the kriyas I performed in honour of my Pitris.

The instructions you gave me were in respect of the manner of spreading the Vrishi and the kusa blades and of offering libations and meat and other food to the manes. As a result of your transgression you have been born as a purohita, and I have been born as a king.

Behold the vicissitudes of Kaala. You have reaped this fruit because you instructed me in my previous birth. It is for this reason, O Brahmana, that I smile or laugh when I see you. I certainly do not do so to ridicule or disrespect you. You are my guru.

I am repentant for this change of circumstances; my heart seethes at the thought. I smile or laugh in remorse when I see you because I remember our former births. Your tapasya was lost because you taught me.

Relinquish your present position of purohita and endeavour to regain a superior birth. Exert yourself so that, in your next life, you may not obtain a birth inferior to your present one. Take as much wealth as you need, learned Brahmana, and purify your soul."

Dismissed by the king, the Brahmana made many gifts of wealth, land and villages to persons of his own varna. He observed many rigid and severe vratas as laid down by the foremost of sages. He travelled to many sacred tirthas and made many gifts to Brahmanas in those places.

Making gifts of cows to those of twice-born varnas, his soul was purified and he succeeded in attaining Atmagyana. Repairing to that very asrama where he had lived in his past birth, he practised severe tapasya. As the result of all this, that Brahmana succeeded in attaining to the highest, indeed to mukti. He was revered by all the sannyasis who lived in that asrama.

In this way, that Rishi fell into great distress; therefore, Brahmanas should never impart knowledge to Sudras. The Brahmana should avoid instructing the low-born, for it was because of his teaching the Sudra in the forest that the Brahmana came to grief.

Rajan, the Brahmana should never desire to obtain instruction from or instruct one that belongs to the lowest varna. Brahmanas and Kshatriyas and Vaisyas, the three varnas, are regarded as being twice-born. By giving instruction to these, a Brahmana does not incur any fault. Righteous men should never discourse on any subject before persons of the fourth varna.

The course of dharma is exceedingly subtle and cannot be grasped by men of impure minds. It is for this reason that sannyasis adopt the vow of silence, and being respected by all, they pass through diksha, initiation, without using words.

For fear of saying what is false or what may offend, ascetics often forego speech itself and take the mowna vrata. Even righteous and accomplished men, of honest and simple conduct, have been known to incur great fault because of unfittingly spoken words.

Instruction should never be given on any subject unthinkingly. If in consequence of teachings imparted, the one taught commit, any sin that sin attaches to the Brahmana who taught him. The wise man, who desires to earn punya, should always act with wisdom. Knowledge which is taught in exchange for money always pollutes the teacher.

Solicited by others, one should say only what is correct after reflecting upon it. One should teach in such a way that one may earn merit. I have thus told you everything on the subject of sacred instruction. Very often men suffer because of wrongly teaching knowledge. Hence it is proper that one should abstain from giving instruction to others.'

CANTO 11

"Yudhishtira says, 'Tell me, Pitamaha, in what kind of man or woman does the Devi Lakshmi of prosperity always dwell?'

"Bhishma says, 'Listen while I narrate to you what I have heard happened. Once upon a time, beholding the goddess of wealth radiant with beauty, blessed with the complexion of the lotus, the princess Rukmini, the mother of Pradyumna whose banner bore the makara emblem, was filled with curiosity and asked this question in the presence of Devaki's son Krishna.

"Who are those beings by whose side you remain and whom do you favour? Who are those whom you do not bless? You who are dear to Him that is the Lord of all creatures, tell me this truly, you that are equal to a Maharishi in penances and power."

Thus addressed by the beautiful princess and moved by grace, in the presence of Krishna who has Garuda on his banner, Lakshmi replied with pleasing words.

Sree said, "Blessed devi, I always dwell with him that is eloquent, active, attentive to his work, free from anger, given to the worship of the Devas, grateful, has his passions under complete control, and is high-minded.

I never remain with one who is inattentive to his work, is an unbeliever, who causes an intermingling of varnas through his lust, who is ungrateful, of impure practices, uses harsh and cruel words, who is a thief, malicious towards his gurus and other elders, those that have little energy, strength, life and honour, and that are troubled by everything trivial, and are always choleric.

I never live with these that think in one way and act in another. I also never remain with him who never desires anything for himself, who is so blinded as to be content with his lot without any effort, or with those that are contented with few possessions.

I dwell with those that observe the duties of their own varna, or those that are conversant with dharma, or those that are devoted to the service of the aged or those that have subdued their passions, those that have pure souls, those that observe the virtue of forgiveness, those that are capable and timely in action, or with such women as are forgiving and self-restrained.

I reside also with women that are devoted to truth and sincerity, and who worship the Devas. I do not dwell with women that do not attend to household duties, leaving furniture and provisions scattered everywhere in the house, and who always utter words contrary to the wishes of their husbands. I always avoid those women that are fond of the houses of other people and that have no modesty.

On the other hand, I reside with those women that are devoted to their husbands, that are blessed in conduct, and who are always well-dressed and decked in ornaments. I always dwell with those women that are truthful in speech, who are of handsome and pleasant features, and are blessed and accomplished.

I always avoid such women as are sinful and unclean or impure, who always lick the corners of their mouths, who have no patience or fortitude, and as are fond of disagreement and quarrelling, as are given to much sleep, and are slothful.

I always dwell in chariots and the animals that draw them, in young girls, in ornaments and good clothing, in sacrifices, in clouds charged with rain, in blooming lotuses, and in those stars that deck the autumn sky. I reside in elephants, in the cow shed, in fine asanas, and in lakes adorned with lotuses.

I live also in such rivers that murmur sweetly in their course, melodious with the music of cranes, with rows of diverse trees on their banks, where Brahmanas and Rishis dwell. I always dwell in those rivers that are deep with surging waters muddied by lions and elephants plunging into them to bathe or slake their thirst.

I reside in angry elephants, in bulls, in kings and good men. I always dwell in that house in which the inhabitant pours libation on the sacrificial fire and worships cows, Brahmanas and the Devas. I live in that house where offerings are made unto the deities at the auspicious times during the course of worship.

I always live in those Brahmanas who are devoted to the study of the Vedas, in Kshatriyas devoted to the observance of dharma, in Vaisyas devoted to cultivation, and the Sudras devoted to the service of the three higher varnas.

With a firm and steadfast heart, I reside in Narayana, in my embodied self. In him is dharma in its perfection and full measure, devotion to Brahmanas and the quality of enchantment.

Dear devi, I do not live in my embodied form in any of these places that I have mentioned, other than in Narayana. He in whom I reside in spirit, increases in dharma, kirti and artha and gains the objects of his desire.""'"

CANTO 12

"Yudhishtira says, 'Rajan, tell me truly which of the two, man or woman, derives the greater pleasure from an act of sexual union with each other. Pitamaha, dispel my doubts in this matter.'

Bhishma says, 'In this regard, I will tell you the ancient story of the discourse between Bhangaswana and Sakra.

In the olden days, there lived a king named Bhangaswana. He was righteous and was known as a Rajarishi. He was, however, childless, and performed a sacrifice to have children. The mighty ruler performed the Agnishtuta yagna.

This sacrifice, which worships only Agni Deva, is always abhorred by Indra. Yet it is the sacrifice that is performed by men when they seek to purify themselves of their sins in order to have children.

When Indra learned that the king desired to perform the Agnishtuta, from that moment he began to look for the weaknesses of that royal sage of tranquil soul, for if he did find any he could then punish the king who had shown him disrespect. Despite all his vigilance, Indra failed to find any flaw or weakness in the king.

One day, the king went on a hunting expedition. Indra saw this as an opportunity to baffle Bhangaswana. Riding alone on his horse, the king suddenly found himself confounded because Indra had stupefied his senses. Afflicted with hunger and thirst, the king's panic was so great that he could not even determine where he was. Parched with thirst, he began to wander aimlessly in a daze.

He then saw a crystalline lake shimmering with clear water. Alighting from his horse, he drank deeply and then led his horse to drink. When his mount's thirst was quenched, the king tied the steed to a tree and plunged into the lake to perform his ablutions.

To his amazement he found that he had been transformed by the waters into a woman. The king was overcome with shame. With his senses and mind agitated, he began to reflect deeply in this strain:

"Alas, how will I ride my horse now? How will I return to my capital? As a result of the Agnishtuta sacrifice I have got a hundred mighty sons, all children of my own loins. What shall I say to them? What shall I say to my wives, my relatives and well-wishers, and to the subjects of my city and my kingdom?

Rishis who know the truths of dharma say that mildness and softness and being prone to extreme agitation are the attributes of women, and that action, strength and energy are those of men. Alas, my manliness has disappeared. For what reason have I been overcome with femininity? Being so transformed, how will I mount my horse again?"

Thinking these sad thoughts, the king, though transformed into a woman, mounted his steed with some effort and returned to his capital. Seeing that extraordinary transformation, his sons and wives and servants, and his subjects were astounded.

That royal sage, that most eloquent men, said to them all, "I was on a hunt, accompanied by a large force. Driven by destiny, losing all knowledge of the points of the horizon, I entered a thick and terrible forest. In that forest, I was afflicted by a strange thirst and quite lost my senses. I then saw a beautiful lake abounding with birds of every description. Plunging into those waters to perform my ablutions, I was transformed into a woman!"

The king summoned his wives and counsellors, and all his sons by their names, and said to them, "My sons, enjoy this kingdom in happiness. As for myself, I shall go away into the forest."

Having said this to his children, the king Bhangaswana, now a woman, set off for the vana. There, she came upon an asrama inhabited by a sannyasi. By him the transformed king gave birth to a hundred sons. Taking these sons to the capital, to where her former children were, she said to the latter, "You are the sons of my loins while I was a man. These are my children brought forth by me as a woman. My sons, all of you must enjoy my kingdom together, like brothers born of the same parents."

At this command, all the brothers, united together, began to take delight in their kingdom jointly. Seeing those children enjoying the kingdom as brothers born of the same parents, Indra, filled with wrath, began to reflect, "By changing this royal sage into a woman, it appears that I have done him good instead of an injury."

Saying this, Indra assumed the form of a Brahmana and went to Bhangaswana's capital and, meeting all the princes, succeeded in disuniting them. He said to them, "Brothers never remain at peace even when they are born of the same father. The sons of Rishi Kasyapa—the Devas and the Asuras—fought against each other for the sovereignty of the three worlds.

As for you princes, you are the sons of Rajarishi Bhangaswana. These others are the sons of a sannyasi. The Devas and the Asuras are the progeny of a common sire, and yet they fought. How much more, therefore, will you fall out among yourselves? This kingdom, your paternal inheritance, is being enjoyed by these children of an ascetic."

Thus Indra succeeded in causing a rift between them, so that they fought and annihilated one another. Hearing this, Bhangaswana, who was living as an ascetic woman, burned with grief and poured forth her lamentations.

Indra, in the disguise of a Brahmana, came to where the sannyasini was living and on meeting her said, "O beautiful one, what sorrow burns you so that you lament so loudly?"

The woman said to him in a pitiful voice, "Two hundred sons of mine have been slain by Kaala. Learned Brahmana, I was once a king, and in that state I had a hundred sons. These I begot in my own likeness. Then, one day I went on a hunt. Suddenly dazed, as if someone had cast a spell on me, I wandered in a dense forest afire with thirst.

At last seeing a fine lake, I plunged into it. Emerging from the water, I found that I had become a woman. Returning to my capital I installed my sons in the sovereignty of my dominions and came into the forest. Now as a woman, I bore a hundred sons to my husband who is a high-souled ascetic. All of them were born in the sannyasi's asrama.

I took them to the capital. Through the influence of time, my sons fought each other and they all died. And afflicted by festiny, I am sorrowing.

Indra addressed her in these harsh words, "In the past, you injured me greatly by performing a yagna that I loathe. Indeed, though I was present, you did not invoke me with any honour. You of little understanding, I am Indra. It is me with whom you have crossed swords."

Beholding Indra revealed before him, the Rajarishi fell at his feet, touching them with his head, and said, "Be gratified with me, foremost of all Devas. I performed the yagna of which you speak from a desire to have sons and not from any wish to offend you. I beg you, forgive me."

Seeing the transformed monarch prostrate himself before him, Indra was gratified and, wanting to grant him a boon, asked, "Which of your sons do you wish to revive? Those that were brought forth by you as a woman, or those that you sired as a man?"

The ascetic woman folded her hands and said to Indra, "Vasava, let those sons of mine come to life that were borne by me as a woman."

Filled with wonder at this reply, Indra asked her, "Why do you feel less fondness for those children born to you as a man? Why is your love greater for the sons borne by you as a woman? I wish to hear the reason for this difference. Tell me everything."

Bhangaswana said, "The love experienced by a woman is much greater than that which is felt by a man. Hence it is, O Sakra, that I wish those sons to be revived that were borne by me as a woman.'"

Bhishma continued, 'Thus addressed, Indra was pleased and said to her, "Let all your sons come back to life. Ask for another boon, foremost of kings, whatever boon you like. Take from me whatever gender you choose, that of a woman or of a man."

The sannyasin said, 'Sakra, I want to remain a woman. I do not wish to be restored to manhood, Vasava."

Hearing this answer, Indra asked her, "Why is it, powerful one, that you seek to remain a woman?"

Bhangaswana replied, 'In acts of sexual union, the pleasure that women enjoy is always far greater than what is enjoyed by men. It is for this reason that I wish to remain a woman. Indra, truthfully do I say to you that I derive greater pleasure in my womanhood. I am content with this that I now have. You may leave me now, O Swargaraja."

Hearing these words, Indra said, "So be it", and bidding her farewell, returned to swarga. Yudhishtira, thus it is well known that a woman derives much greater pleasure than a man during sexual union.'"

CANTO 13

"Yudhishtira says, 'What should a man do in order to pass pleasantly through this and the next world? How should one conduct oneself? What practices must one adopt with this end in view?'

Bhishma says, 'One must avoid the three sins that are done with the body, the four that are done with speech, the three that are done with the mind, and the ten paths of sin.

The three physical sins to be avoided are killing, theft and the enjoyment of other men's wives. The four sins of speech, never to be indulged in or even thought of, are evil talk, harsh words, talking about other people's faults and lies.

Coveting the possessions of others, doing injury to others, and doubting the rules of the Vedas, are the three sins of the mind which should always be avoided. Hence, one must never do any evil at all with body word or mind. By doing good and evil deeds, one is sure to enjoy or endure their consequences. Nothing can be more certain than this.'"

CANTO 14

"Yudhishtira says, 'O Gangaputra, you have heard all the names of Maheswara, the Lord of the universe. Pitamaha, tell us all the names that are applied to him who is called Isa and Sambhu. Tell us all those names that are applied unto him who is called Babhru or vast, him that has the universe for his form, him that is the illustrious guru of all the Devas and the Asuras, who is called Swayambhu and who is the cause of the origin and dissolution of the universe. Describe to us the puissance of Mahadeva.'

Bhishma says, 'I am not competent to recite the virtues of Mahadeva. He pervades all things in the universe and yet is not seen anywhere. He is the Creator of the universal self and the Prajna, the knowing self, and he is their master. All the Devas, from Brahma down to the Pisachas, adore and worship him.

He transcends both Prakriti and Purusha. It is of him that Rishis, who know yoga and have a knowledge of the tattvas, think and reflect. He is indestructible and the Supreme Brahman. He is both existent and non-existent. Agitating both Prakriti and Purusha with his energy, He created Brahma.

Who is there that is competent to speak of the virtues of that God of gods that is endowed with supreme intelligence? Man is subject to conception in the mother's womb, to birth, decay and death. Being such, what man like me has the capacity to understand Bhava?

Only Narayana, that bearer of the discus and the mace, can comprehend Mahadeva. He is without deterioration. He is the foremost of all beings in attributes. He is Vishnu, because he pervades the universe. He is omnipotent.

Imbued with spiritual vision, he is possessed of supreme tejas. He sees all things with the eye of yoga. It is in consequence of the devotion of Krishna to Siva, whom he gratified through tapasya in Badarikasrama, that Krishna succeeded in permeating all the universe.

It is through Maheswara of divine vision that Krishna has obtained the attribute of universal charm, which is more delightful than all the wealth in the world. For a full thousand years he underwent the austerest penances and at last succeeded in gratifying the illustrious and boon-giving Siva, that master of all the mobile and the immobile universe.

In every new yuga, through such tapasya, Krishna has gratified Siva. In every yuga Mahadeva has been pleased with the devotion of Krishna. How wonderful is the puissance of the Mahatman Mahadeva, that original cause of the universe, who was seen by Hari, who himself transcends all decay, when he was engaged in tapasya to obtain a son in the asrama of Badari.

Bhaarata, I do not hold anyone superior to Mahadeva. Only Krishna is competent to expound the names of Siva fully and absolutely. This Mahabaho of Yadu's race alone can speak of the attributes of the illustrious Siva. Only he is able to discourse on the power, in its entirety, of the Supreme Deity.'"

Vaisampayana continued, "Having said this, Bhishma Pitamaha addresses Krishna and speaks on the subject of the greatness of Bhava.

Bhishma says, 'You are the master of all the Devas and the Asuras. You are famed and illustrious. You are Vishnu because you pervade the whole universe. It is fitting that you discourse on Siva of universal form about whom Yudhishtira has asked me.

In ancient times, the Rishi Tandin, sprung from Brahma, recited in Brahma's realm before Brahma himself, the thousand names of Mahadeva. Recite those names before this gathering so that these tapodhana Rishis, who observe high vratas, who possess self-restraint, Vyasa among them, may hear you. Discourse on the holiness of him who is immutable, who is always joyful, who is hotri, who is the universal Protector, who is Creator of the universe, and who is called Mundin and Kapardin.'

Krishna says, 'The Devas, including Indra and Brahma, and the Maharishis, cannot fathom the course of Mahadeva's actions. He is the end that all righteous people attain. The very Adityas who have keen sight, cannot gaze upon his abode. How then can a mere man comprehend him?

I will tell you some of the attributes of that illustrious slayer of Asuras, who is regarded as the Lord of all tapasya and vratas.'"

Vaisampayana continued, "And after purifying himself by touching water, Krishna began his discourse on the attributes of Siva.

Krishna says, 'Hear, you best of Brahmanas and you also Yudhishtira, and hear you too, Ganga's son, the names of the Kapardin. Listen to how I obtained a vision, so difficult to have, of that Great God, for the sake of Samba. In those days I saw him through the power of yoga.

Twelve years after wise Pradyumna, the son of Rukmini, killed the Asura Sambara, my wife Jambavati came to me and, seeing Pradyumna, Charudeshna and my other sons born to Rukmini, Jambavati, herself wanting a son, said to me, "Give me a heroic son, the foremost of mighty men, handsome in appearance, sinless in conduct, and like you in every way. And let there be no delay on your part in granting this wish of mine. There is nothing in the three worlds that is unattainable to you, O perpetuator of Yadu's vamsa; you can create other worlds by merely wishing it.

Observing a vow for twelve years and purifying yourself, you worshipped Siva and then begot upon Rukmini her sons Charudeshna and Sucharu and Charuvesa and Yasodhana and Charusravas and Charuyasas and Pradyumna and Samba. Grant to me a son like those powerful sons of Rukmini."

Thus addressed by the princess, I replied, "Give me leave to go away for some time. I will certainly obey your command!"

She said to me, "Go, and may you always be accompanied by success and prosperity. Let Brahma and Siva and Kasyapa, the great rivers, those Devas that preside over the mind, all plants, those chchandas that bear the libations poured in sacrifices, the Rishis, Bhumi, the oceans, the sacrificial dakshina, and those syllables that are uttered for completing the intonations of Samans, all protect you.

Yadava, let the Rikshas, the Pitris, the Navagrahas, the consorts of the Devas, the Apsaras, the Devis, the great kalpas, cows, Chandramas, Savitri, Agni, Savitri, the knowledge of the Vedas, the seasons, the year, the small and great divisions of time, the kshanas, the labas, the muhurtas, the nimeshas, and the yugas in succession, protect you, and keep you in happiness, wherever you may dwell. Let no danger overtake you on your way, and be not careless."

Thus blessed by her, I took her leave. I then went into the presence of my father, of my mother, of the king, and of Ahuka, and I told them what the sorrowing daughter of the Vidyadhara prince had said to me. Taking their leave as well, I went sadly to Gada and to Rama of vast might.

They said to me, "Let your tapasya increase without any obstacle." Having received their leave, I thought of Garuda. He came instantly to me and, at my bidding, bore me to Himavat. Arriving at Himavat, I let him go.

There on that foremost of mountains, I saw many wonderful sights. I saw a pleasant asrama in which to perform tapasya. That delightful asrama was presided over by the high-souled Upamanyu who was a descendant of Vyaghrapada. It is celebrated and revered by the Devas and the Gandharvas, and appeared to be mantled in Vedic beauty.

It was adorned with dhavas and kakubhas and kadambas and cocas, with kuruvakas and ketakas and jambus and patalas, with nyagrodhas and varunakas and vatsanabhas and bilwas, with saralas and kapitthas, and piyalas and salas, and palmyras, with badaris and kundas and punnagas, and asokas and amras and kovidaras and champakas and panasas, and other trees laden with flowers and fruit. That asrama was also decked with the straight stems of the sweet banana.

Truly, that hermitage was adorned with diverse trees laden with fruit that formed the food of many kinds of birds. Heaps of the ashes of sacrificial fires were scattered all around, adding to the beauty of the scene. It abounded with ruru deer, monkeys, tigers, lions and leopards, with deer of diverse species and peacocks, and with wild cats and snakes. Indeed, many bison and bears could also be seen there.

Pleasant breezes blew bearing the melodious voices of Apsaras. The murmur of mountain streams and springs, the sweet notes of winged choristers, the deep grunts of elephants, the delicious strains of kinnaras, and the auspicious voices of ascetics singing the Samans, and other kinds of music, rendered that asrama utterly charming.

The mind cannot imagine another asrama as delightful as the one I saw. There were large housings for the sacred fire, all covered with flowering creepers. It was adorned with the clear and sacred water of the river Ganga. The daughter of Jahnu always lived there.

Many sannyasis, the foremost of all righteous men, endowed with great souls, and who resembled Agni himself in tejas, were its ornaments. Some of those ascetics subsisted on air and some on water, some were devoted to japa, and some were engaged in purifying their souls by practising the virtues of compassion, while some among them were yogins devoted to yoga dhyana.

Some amongst them subsisted upon only smoke, and some on fire, and some on milk. Thus was that asrama adorned with many great and evolved men. And some there had taken the vow of eating and drinking like cows; they no longer used their hands. And some used only two pieces of stone to husk their grain, and some used only their teeth. And some existed by drinking only the rays of the moon, and some by drinking only froth. And some had vowed to live like deer.

There were some who lived on the fruits of the ficus tree, and others who survived on water. Some dressed themselves in rags and some in animal skins and some in barks of trees. Indeed, I saw diverse ascetics of the best orders observing these and other painful vratas. I then wished to enter that asrama.

That retreat was honoured and adored by the Devas and all high-souled beings, by Siva, and by all righteous creatures. It stood in all its beauty on the breast of Himavat, like the moon in the sky. The mongoose sported there with the snake, and the tiger with the deer, as friends, forgetting their natural enmity, and this was because of the blissful tejas of those sannyasis of blazing tapasya and for their proximity to those Mahatmans.

As soon as I entered that asrama, enchanting to all creatures, inhabited by many great Brahmanas, all knowers of the Vedas and their angas, and by many high-souled Rishis celebrated for their difficult vratas, I saw a mighty Rishi with matted locks on his head and dressed in rags, who seemed to blaze forth like fire with his tapasya and tejas. Waited upon by his disciples and of tranquil soul, that foremost of Brahmanas was young. His name was Upamanyu.

I bowed to him and he said, "You are welcome, you of eyes like lotus petals. Today, with your visit, we see that our penances have borne fruit. You are worthy of our adoration, yet you revere us. You are worthy of being seen, but you come to see me."

With folded hands, I asked him about the well-being of the animals and birds that lived in his asrama, about the progress of his spiritual advancement, and his disciples. The illustrious Upamanyu said to me sweetly, "Krishna, you will undoubtedly have a son like yourself. Gratify Isana, the Lord of all creatures, with stern tapasya.

That divine master sports here with his wife beside him. It was here that in ancient times the Devas with all the Rishis pleased him with their penances and celibacy, their truth and self-restraint, and had their wishes fulfilled. That illustrious God is the infinite vessel of all tejas and tapasya.

Projecting into existence and withdrawing once more unto himself all good and evil things, that inconceivable deity whom you seek lives here with his wife. The Danava Hiranyakashipu, whose strength was so great that he could shake the very mountains of Meru, succeeded in obtaining from Mahadeva the power of all the Devas and enjoyed it for ten millions of years.

Mandara, foremost among all Hiranyakashipu's sons, also has a boon from Siva and succeeded in fighting Indra for a million years. Vishnu's terrible Sudarsana Chakra and Indra's vajra, both, could not make the slightest impact upon the body of that great cause of universal affliction.

The discus that you bear was given to you by Mahadeva after he had slain a Daitya who was proud of his strength and once lived within the waters. Siva created that chakra, blazing with energy like Agni. Wonderful and irresistible, he gave it to you. Because of its blazing energy no one could look upon it other than Siva Pinakin himself.

Indeed, it was for this reason that Siva named it Sudarsana. From that time the name Sudarsana came to be used in all the worlds. Krishna, even that weapon failed to have the slightest effect on the body of Hiranyakashipu's son Mandara, who appeared like an evil planet in the three worlds. Having obtained a boon from Mahadeva, hundreds of chakras like yours and thunderbolts like those of Indra, could not inflict even a scratch on the body of that malignant planet.

Afflicted by the mighty Mandara, the Devas fought hard but in vain against him and his supporters, all of whom had received boons from Mahadeva. Pleased with another Danava named Vidyutprabha, Siva granted to him the sovereignty of the three worlds. That Danava remained the ruler of the three worlds for a hundred thousand years.

And Mahadeva said to him, 'You will become one of my ganas.' He further bestowed upon him the boon of a hundred million sons. The Lord of all creatures further gave the Danava the realm of Kusadwipa for his kingdom.

Another great Asura, Satamukha, was created by Brahma. For a hundred years he poured the flesh of his own body on the sacrificial fire as an offering to Siva. Gratified with such tapasya, Sankara said to him, 'What can I do for you?'

Satamukha replied, 'Let me have the power of creating new creatures. Give me also eternal power.'

Siva said to him, 'So be it.'

In earlier times, Swayambhu Brahma, concentrating his mind in yoga, performed a yagna for three hundred years, with the aim of having children. Mahadeva granted him a thousand sons with the attributes befitting the merits of the sacrifice.

Krishna, you doubtless know him who is praised by the Devas. The Rishi Yajnavalkya is exceptionally virtuous. By adoring Mahadeva he has acquired great fame. The great ascetic Vyasa, who is Parasara's son, with soul set on yoga, has gained great renown by adoring Sankara.

One day the Balakhilyas were disregarded by Indra. In anger, they worshipped Siva. That Lord of the universe, thus gratified by the Balakhilyas, said to them, 'By your tapasya, you will succeed in creating a bird that will rob Indra of the amrita.'

In the past, on account of the wrath of Mahadeva, all the waters of the world disappeared. The Devas worshipped him by performing the Saptakapala yagna, and through his grace caused other waters to flow. Truly, when he was pleased, water once more appeared in the world.

The wife of Atri, who knew the Vedas well, left him in anger and said, 'I shall no longer live in subjection to that sannyasi.' And she sought the protection of Siva. Through fear of her lord, Atri spent three hundred years without all food. And all this time she slept on wooden blocks to gratify Bhava.

Mahadeva appeared before her and smilingly said to her, 'You shall have a son. And you will get that son without needing a husband, but just through the grace of Rudra. That son, born in his father's vamsa, will be celebrated for his worth, and take a name after you.'

Devoted to Siva, the illustrious Vikarna also successfully gratified him with severe tapasya.

Sakalya, too, adored Bhava in a mental sacrifice that he performed for nine hundred years. Pleased with him the illustrious deity said to him, 'You will become a great Kavi. Your fame will be boundless in the three worlds. Your vamsa also will be infinite and will be adorned by many great Rishis that shall take birth in it. Your son will become the foremost of Brahmanas and will arrange the Sutras of your work.'

In the Krita yuga there was a celebrated Rishi of the name of Savarni.

Here, in this asrama, he underwent austere penance for six thousand years. Siva said to him, 'I am pleased with you, sinless one. Without being subject to decay or death, you will become a poet renowned through all the worlds.'

In ancient days, in Varanasi, Sakra, filled with bhakti, adored Mahadeva who is clothed by empty space and who is smeared with ashes. Having done so, Indra obtained the sovereignty of the Devas.

Once Narada, too, adored the great Bhava with a devoted heart. Gratified with him, Mahadeva, that guru of the divine guru, said, 'No one will be your equal in tejas and tapasya. You will always attend upon me with your singing and your vina.'

Krishna, hear also how I succeeded in obtaining a sight of that God of gods, that master of all creatures; hear also in detail for what purpose. With senses and mind subdued I invoked that Deva of supreme energy. I will tell you all that I succeeded in obtaining from Maheswara, that God of gods.

In the Krita yuga there was a famed Rishi named Vyaghrapada. He was celebrated for his knowledge and mastery over the Vedas and their angas. I was born as the son of that Rishi, and Dhaumya as my younger brother.

Once, accompanied by Dhaumya, I came upon the asrama of certain evolved Rishis. There I saw a cow that was being milked. I saw the milk and it resembled amrita itself in taste. I then came home, and impelled by childishness, I said to my mother, 'Give me some food prepared with milk.'

There was no milk in the house, and so my mother was saddened by my asking for it. My mother took a lump of cooked rice and boiled it in water. The water became white and my mother placed it before us saying that it was milk and told us to drink it.

Once before this I had drunk milk when my father took me to the house of some of our great kinsmen at the time of a yagna. A divine cow, who delights the Devas, was being milked. Drinking her milk that was like amrita in taste, I knew what the qualities of milk were. I knew at once what our mother had set before us as milk. Its taste gave me no pleasure at all. Again, I childishly said to my mother, 'This, O mother, is not any preparation of milk.'

Filled with sorrow at this, and embracing me lovingly and sniffing the top of my head, Madhava, she said to me, 'My child, where can ascetics of pure souls get food prepared with milk? We live in the forest and subsist upon bulbs and roots and fruits. Where will we, who live by the banks of rivers that are the resort of the Balakhilyas, we who have mountains and forests for our home, from where shall we get milk?

We live sometimes on air and sometimes on water. We dwell in the hearts of forests. We habitually abstain from all kinds of food that are eaten by those who live in villages and towns. We are accustomed to only such food as the wilderness provides. Child, there cannot be any milk in the wilderness where there are no offspring of Surabhi.

Dwelling on the banks of rivers or in caves or on mountainsides, or in tirthas and other wild places, we pass our time in the practice of tapasya and the chanting of sacred mantras, with Siva as our highest refuge. Without gratifying him of unfading glory, he who has three eyes, from where can one obtain food prepared with milk or grand robes and other objects of worldly enjoyment?

Devote yourself, dear son, to Sankara with your whole soul. Through his grace you are sure to receive all that will satisfy your desires.'

On hearing these words of my mother, I joined my hands in reverence and bowing to her, said, 'O mother, who this Mahadeva? In what manner can one gratify him? Where does that God dwell? How can he be seen? With what is he seen? What also is the form of Sarva? How may one succeed in gaining knowledge of him? If gratified, will he show himself to me?'

Govinda, after I had said these words to my mother, with tears in her eyes she lovingly sniffed my head. Gently patting my arms, she spoke to me with great humility.

She said, 'Mahadeva is very difficult to be known by those uncleansed souls. Impure men cannot bear him in their hearts, indeed they cannot comprehend him at all. They cannot retain him in their minds. They cannot grasp him, nor can they obtain a vision of him.

Men of wisdom aver that his forms are many. Many, again, are the places in which he dwells. Many are the forms of his grace. Who is there that can understand the deeds of Isa in all their aspects, or all the forms he has assumed in times gone by? Who can relate how he sports and how he is gratified?

Maheswara of universal form lives in the hearts of all creatures. While Munis discoursed on his auspicious and extraordinary deeds, I have heard from them how, impelled by compassion towards his bhaktas, he grants them a glimpse of himself. To honour the Brahmanas, the inhabitants of swarga recited to them the diverse forms that were taken by Mahadeva. You have asked me about these and I will recite them to you.'

My mother continued, 'Siva assumes the forms of Brahma and Vishnu and the king of the Devas, of the Rudras, the Adityas and the Aswins; and of those Devas that are called Viswadevas. He assumes the forms also of men and women, of Pretas and Pisachas, of Kiratas and Savaras, and of all marine animals. That illustrious God assumes the forms of also those Savaras that dwell in forests.

He assumes the forms of tortoises, fishes and conches. He it is that takes the forms of those corals used as ornaments by men. He assumes also the forms of Yakshas, Rakshasas and Nagas, of Daityas and Danavas. Indeed, he assumes the forms of all those creatures that live hidden in hollows.

He takes the forms of tigers and lions and deer, of wolves and bears and birds, of owls and of jackals as well. It is he that assumes the forms of swans and crows and peacocks, of chameleons and lizards and storks. He it is that assumes the forms of cranes and vultures and chakravakas. Truly, it is he that assumes the forms of chasas and of mountains.

It is Mahadeva that assumes the forms of cows and elephants and horses and camels and donkeys. He also takes the forms of goats and leopards, and diverse other animals. It is Siva who assumes the forms of a variety of birds of beautiful plumage. It is Mahadeva who assumes the forms of men with staffs and those with umbrellas and those with swords, among Brahmanas.

He sometimes becomes six-faced and sometimes multi-faced. He sometimes assumes forms having three eyes and forms having many heads. And he sometimes assumes forms having many millions of legs and forms having countless bellies and faces, and forms with many arms and sides. He sometimes appears surrounded by innumerable bhutas and pretas, spirits and ghosts.

He it is that assumes the forms of Rishis and Gandharvas, and of Siddhas and Charanas. His form is sometimes rendered white with the ashes he smears on it and is adorned with a half-moon on his forehead. Adored with diverse mantras uttered in diverse kinds of voice and worshipped with diverse mantras filled with encomiums, he, that is sometimes called Sarva, is the destroyer of all creatures in the universe, and it is upon him, again, that all creatures rest.

Mahadeva is the soul of all creatures. He pervades all things. He discourses on dharma and karmas. He dwells everywhere, in the hearts of all creatures in the universe. He knows the desires of each of his devotees. He becomes one with the object which one reveres. If it pleases you, do you seek his protection.

He sometimes rejoices, and sometimes yields to wrath, and at others utters a deafening humkara. At times, he sometimes arms himself with the chakra, at times with the trisula, at times with the gada, sometimes with the Pinaka, and sometimes with the khatvanga. He it is that assumes the form of Sesha who holds the world on his head.

He has snakes for his girdle, and his ears are adorned with earrings that are snakes. Snakes form also the sacred thread he wears. His upper garment is an elephant skin. He sometimes laughs and at others sings, and sometimes dances most wondrously and madly.

Surrounded by many spirits and ghosts, he plays on musical instruments. Diverse are these instruments, and sweet are their sounds. He roams across cremations grounds, yawns, cries, and makes others weep.

He assumes the guise of one who is mad, and also of one who is intoxicated, and he sometimes speaks words that are exceedingly sweet. He laughs fiercely, frightening all creatures with his dreadful eyes. He sleeps and remains awake and sometimes yawns as he pleases.

He recites sacred mantras and becomes the deity of those mantras. He performs tapasya and becomes the one who is adored by those penances. He makes gifts and receives those very gifts; at times he immerses himself in yoga and at times becomes the object of the yoga dhyana of others.

He may be seen on the vedi, the sacrificial platform, or in the stamba, the sacrificial stake; in the goshala or in the Agni. Again, he may not be seen there. He may be seen as a child or as an old man. He dallies with the daughters and the wives of the Rishis.

His hair is long and straight. He is perfectly naked, for he has the sky for his raiment. He has terrifying eyes. He is fair, he is dark; he is dark, he is pale; he is the colour of smoke, and he is red. He has big and fierce eyes. Akasa is his covering and it is he who covers all things.

Who is there that can comprehend the limits of Mahadeva who is formless, who is one and indivisible, who conjures up illusions, who is the cause of all creation and destruction in the universe, who assumes the form of Hiranyagarbha, and who is without beginning and without end, and who is without birth?

He lives in the heart of every creature. He is the prana, he is Manas, and he is the Jiva. He is the soul of yoga, and it is that which is called yoga. He is the yoga dhyana into which yogins enter. He is the Paramatman. Indeed Maheswara, the purity in essence, can be understood not by the senses but only through the Atman seizing his existence.

He plays on many musical instruments. He sings. He has a hundred thousand eyes, he has one mouth, he has two mouths, he has three mouths, and he has many mouths. Devote yourself to him, set your heart upon him, depend upon him, and accept him as your only refuge; you adore Mahadeva and then you will have the fruits of all your wishes.'

Hearing these words of my mother, from that day my devotion was focused solely on Mahadeva. I applied myself to the practice of the austerest penances to gratify him. For one thousand years I stood on my left toe.

After that I passed one thousand years subsisting only upon fruits. The next one thousand years I lived on the fallen leaves of trees. The next thousand years I passed subsisting upon water only. After that I passed seven hundred years on air alone.

In this way, I adored Siva for a full thousand years of the Devas. After this, the Master of the universe was gratified with me. Wanting to know whether I was solely devoted to him and him alone, he appeared before me in the form of Sakra surrounded by all the Devas.

As the celebrated Sakra, he had a thousand eyes and was armed with the vajra. And he rode on a pure white elephant with four tusks, with eyes red, ears folded, the temporal juice trickling down his cheeks, with trunk contracted, and terrifying to behold. Indeed, riding on such an elephant, the illustrious chief of the Devas seemed to blaze forth with splendour.

With a beautiful crown on his head and adorned with garlands round his neck and bracelets round his arms, he neared where I stood. A white chatra was held over his head. And he was waited upon by many Apsaras, and many Gandharvas sang his praise. Addressing me, he said, 'Dvijottama, I am pleased with you. Ask me for whatever boon you desire.'

These words of Sakra did not please me. Krishna, I answered him in these words: 'I do not desire any boon from you or any other god. I tell you truly that it is only from Mahadeva that I seek boons. That I say to you is nothing but the truth.

Only words which relate to Maheswara fill me with joy. At the command of Pasupati, I am ready to become a worm or a tree with many branches. If I do not receive the blessings of Mahadeva's boons, the very sovereignty of the three worlds would not be acceptable to me.

Let me be born among the very Chandalas but let me still be devoted to the feet of Siva. Without being devoted to him, I would not like to be born in the palace of Indra himself. If a man lacks devotion to him, that master of the Devas and the Asuras, he will suffer even if he can subsist upon only air and water for want of food.

No other discourses on dharma are needed by those who live every moment thinking of the feet of Mahadeva. When the Kali yuga comes, one must devote one's heart every moment to Mahadeva.

One that has drunk the amrita of devotion to Siva is freed from the fear of samsara. One that has not obtained the grace of Mahadeva can never succeed in devoting oneself to him for a single day, or for half a day, or for a muhurta, or even for a kshana or a lava. At the command of Mahadeva I would cheerfully become a worm or an insect, but I have no wish for even the sovereignty of the three worlds, if you, Sakra, were to bestow it upon me.

At his word I would become even a dog. In fact, that would be my highest wish. If not given by Maheswara, I would not have the sovereignty of the very Devas. I do not wish to have dominion over swarga. I do not wish to have the sovereignty of the celestials. I do not wish to have the realm of Brahma. Indeed, I do not even wish to have moksha, that cessation of individual existence and a complete identification with Brahman.

But I want to become the dasa of Hara. As long as that Lord of all creatures, with crown on his head and luminous body of the moon, does not become gratified with me, so long shall I endure all the afflictions, due to a hundred cycles of decay, death and birth that befall all embodied beings.

Who can obtain peace without gratifying Rudra, who is free from decay and death, who is imbued with the effulgence of the sun, the moon, or the fire, who is the root or original cause of everything real and unreal in the three worlds, and who exists as one indivisible entity? If I am reborn because of my faults, I will, in those new births, devote myself solely to Mahadeva.'

Indra said, 'What reason can you assign for the existence of a Supreme Being or for his being the cause of all causes?'

I, Upamanyu, said, 'I solicit boons from that great deity named

Siva who has been described as existent and non-existent, manifest and unmanifest, eternal and immutable, one and many. I solicit boons from Him who is without beginning and middle and end, who is knowledge and puissance, who is inconceivable and who is the Paramatman. I solicit boons from he from whom comes all power, who has not been created by anyone, who is immutable, and who, though himself not sprung from any seed, is the seed of all things in the universe.

I solicit boons from him who is blazing effulgence, beyond tamas, who is the essence of all tapasya, who transcends all our faculties that we may use to understand him, and by knowing whom we are liberated from sorrow. Purandara, I worship him who is conversant with the creation of all elements and the thought of all living beings, and who is the original cause of the existence or creation of all creatures, who is omnipresent, and who has the power to give everything.

I solicit boons from him who cannot be grasped by reason, who is the focus of the Samkhya and the yoga systems of philosophy, and who transcends all things, and whom all wise men worship and adore. I solicit boons from him who is the soul of Maghavat himself, who is said to be the God of the gods, and who is the master of all creatures.

I solicit boons from him who it is that first created Brahma, Creator of all the worlds, having filled space with his energy and brought the primeval egg into existence. Who else than that Supreme Lord could be the creator of Agni, Jala, Vayu, Bhumi, Akasa and Manas, and that which is called Mahat?

Sakra, tell me, who else than Siva could create Manas, Buddhi, Chitta or Ahamkara, the Tanmatras, and the indriyas? Who is there higher than Siva?

The wise say that Brahma is the Creator of this universe. Brahma, however, acquired his puissance and prosperity by worshipping and gratifying Mahadeva. Consisting of the three attributes of creation, preservation and destruction, that power, which dwells in that illustrious Being who is endowed with the quality of being One, who created Brahma, Vishnu and Rudra, was derived from Mahadeva. Tell me who is there that is superior to the Supreme Lord?

Considering the sovereignty and oppressive power of the Daityas and the Danavas, who else can unite the sons of Diti and confer upon them power and dominion? Know that the different points of the horizon, time, the sun, all fiery entities, the planets, wind, water, and the stars and constellations come from Mahadeva. Tell me who is higher than the Supreme Lord?

Who else is there, other than Mahadeva, in the matter of the creation of sacrifice and the destruction of Tripura? Who else other than Mahadeva, that Parantapa, has given regency to the principal Devas?

What need is there of clever and refined speech, when I behold you of a thousand eyes, best of the Devas, who are worshipped by Siddhas, Gandharvas and the other Devas and the Rishis? All this is due to the blessings of Mahadeva.'

Krishna, know that this all, consisting of animate and inanimate existences with swarga and other unseen entities, which occur in this world, and which has the all-pervading Lord for their soul, has flowed from Maheswara and has been created by him for the Jiva's enjoyment. In the worlds that are known as Bhur, Bhuvah, Svah, and Maha, in the midst of the mountains of lokaloka, in the islands, in the Mountains of Meru, in all things that yield happiness, and in the hearts of all creatures, there resides Mahadeva.

If the Devas and the Asuras could see any other more powerful than Siva, would both of them, especially the former when attacked by the latter, not have sought that other's protection? In all conflicts between the Devas, the Yakshas, the Uragas and the Rakshasas, which end in mutual destruction, it is Siva who assigns them their respective positions dependent upon their karma.

Tell me, who else is there than Maheswara to bestow boons upon, and then again punish Andhaka, Sukra, Dundubhi, many great Maharishis, Yakshas, Indra and Bala, and Rakshasas and the Nivatakavachas?

Was not the vital seed of Mahadeva, master of both the Devas and the Asuras, poured as a libation upon the fire? From that seed sprang a mountain of gold. Who else is there whose seed can be said to be of such power?

Who else in this world is praised for having only the very sky for his garments? Who else can be said to be a brahmacharin with his always vital seed drawn up? Who else is there that has half his body occupied by his Devi? Who else is there that has been able to subdue Kama, the god of desire?

Tell me, Indra, what other Being possesses that high realm of supreme felicity which is lauded by all the deities? Who else has the cremation ground for his playing field? Who else is there that is extolled for his dancing?

Whose puissance and worship remain immutable? Who else sports with bhutas and pretas? Tell me who else has companions who possess strength like his own and who are thus proud of that vigour and power?

Who else is there whose status is acclaimed as unchangeable and revered by the three worlds? Who else pours rain, gives heat, and blazes forth with tejas? From whom else do we derive our treasure of herbs and plants? Who else upholds all kinds of wealth? Who else sports as much as he pleases in the three worlds of mobile and immobile beings?

Indra, know Maheswara to be the original cause of everything. He is adored by yogins, by Rishis, by Gandharvas, and by Siddhas, with the help of gyana, of tapasya, and of the rites laid down in the shastras. He is adored by both the Devas and the Asuras using tapasya and karma, and the rituals laid down in the sacred scriptures.

The fruits of action can never touch him for he transcends them all. Being such, I call him the original cause of everything.

He is both sthula and sukshma, embodied and pure spirit. He is without equal. He cannot be conceived by the senses. He is both with and without attributes. He is the Lord of gunas, for he controls them. Such is Maheswara's standing.

He is the cause of the creation and preservation of the universe. He is the cause of the universe and the cause also of its destruction. He is the past, the present and the future. He is the sire of all things. Truly, he is the cause of everything.

He is that which is mutable; he is the unmanifest, he is vidya; he is avidya; he is every action, he is every omission; he is dharma and he is adharma. Him I call the cause of everything.

Indra, behold the features of both the genders in the image of Mahadeva, the Ardhanariswara. He is the cause of both creation and destruction, and unites in his body the characteristics of both male and female as the one cause of the creation of the universe. My mother told me that he is the cause of the universe and the one cause of everything.

There is no one that is higher than Isa. If it pleases you, surrender yourself to his kindness and protection. You know that the universe has sprung from the union of the sexes, as represented by Mahadeva. You know the universe to be the sum of what is endowed with attributes and what else is divested of attributes and has the seeds of Brahma and others for its immediate cause.

Brahma and Indra and Hutasana and Vishnu and all the other Devas, along with the Daityas and the Asuras, crowned with the fruition of a thousand desires, always say that there is none that is higher than Mahadeva. I am compelled to seek that God known to all the mobile and immobile universe, he who has been spoken of as the highest of all the gods, and who is auspiciousness itself, so that I may attain, without delay, mukti, that highest of all acquisitions.

What need is there to find any more evidence to prove what I believe? The supreme Mahadeva is the cause of all causes. We have never heard that the Devas worship the emblem of another god. Tell me, if you ever heard of any other whose sign has been or is being worshipped by all the deities?

He whose emblem is always worshipped by Brahma, by Vishnu, by you Indra, with all the other Devas, is the foremost of all deities. Brahma has for his sign the lotus, Vishnu has for his the discus, and Indra has the thunder-bolt. But the creatures of the world do not bear any of these.

On the other hand, all creatures bear the signs that mark Mahadeva and Uma. Hence, all creatures must be regarded as belonging to

Maheswara. All creatures of the female sex, have their origin in Uma's nature, and so bear the mark of femininity, the yoni that distinguishes her; all creatures that are male, having sprung from Siva, bear the masculine mark, the linga that distinguishes him.

Anyone who says that there is, in the three worlds with their mobile and immobile creatures, any other cause than the Supreme Lord, and that which is not marked with the mark of either Mahadeva or his consort should be regarded as wretched and should not be counted among the creatures of the universe. Every being with the mark of the male sex should be known to be of Isana, while every being with the mark of the female sex should be known to be of Uma. This universe of mobile and immobile creatures has either a male or female form.

It is from Mahadeva that I wish to obtain boons. Failing in this, I would prefer death itself. Slayer of Bala, go or remain as you wish. I wish to have boons or curses from Mahadeva. No other deity shall I ever accept, nor would I want my wishes to be granted by any other.'

Having said these words to Indra, I was overwhelmed with grief at the thought of Mahadeva not having been gratified with me despite my severe austerities. However, in an instant, I saw the celestial elephant before me transformed into a bull as white as a swan, or the jasmine flower, or a stalk of the lotus, or silver, or an ocean of milk.

Of a massive body, the tuft of its tail was black and the colour of its eyes was brown like honey. Its horns were hard as steel and had the colour of gold. With their sharp red points, the bull seemed to cleave the earth. The animal was adorned all over with ornaments made of the purest gold.

Its face and hooves and nose and ears were exceedingly beautiful and its loins well-formed. Its flanks were handsome and its neck was broad. Its whole form was utterly beautiful to behold. Its hump radiated great beauty and appeared to occupy the whole of its shoulder. And it looked like the peak of a mountain of snow or like a cliff of white clouds in the sky.

Upon the back of that animal I saw seated the illustrious Mahadeva along with Uma. He shone like the lord of stars, the moon while he is at his full. The fire born of his energy was brilliant like the lightning that flashes amidst clouds. It looked as if a thousand suns rose there, filling every side with dazzling splendour. The tejas of the Supreme Lord was like the Samvartaka fire which destroys all creatures at the end of the yuga.

Suffused with that tejas, the sky darkened and I could see nothing. I was filled with anxiety and wondered what it could mean. That dark energy did not pervade every side for long, through Siva's illusion, and soon the horizon cleared.

I then saw Maheswara seated on the back of his bull, of blessed and benign appearance and looking like a smokeless fire. And the Great God was accompanied by Parvati of unblemished features. Indeed, I beheld Nilakanta, blue-throated Sthanu, detached from everything, that wielder of all kinds of force, as having eighteen arms and adorned with all kinds of ornaments.

Clad in white raiment, he wore white garlands and had white liniments smeared upon his limbs. His matchless banner was white in colour. His sacred thread was also white. With powers equal to his own, he was surrounded by his ganas, who were singing or dancing or playing on various musical instruments.

A pale crescent moon formed his crown, and set on his brow it was like the moon that rises in the winter sky. He seemed ablaze with splendour, because of his three eyes that were like three suns. The garland of the purest white on his body shone like a festoon of lotuses, adorned with jewels.

I also saw Siva's weapons in their embodied forms bursting with every kind of energy. The deity held a vari-coloured bow whose colours were like those of the rainbow.

That bow, the famed Pinaka, is really a mighty snake. Indeed, that male snake of seven heads and immense body, of ample neck, of sharp fangs and virulent poison, was twined round with the rope that served as its bowstring.

And there was a shaft as splendid as the sun or the fire that appears at the end of the yuga. Indeed, that arrow was the mighty and unrivalled Pasupata, indescribable for its power, and striking fear into every creature.

Of vast proportions, it seemed to constantly shoot out tongues of fire. It has one foot, large teeth, a thousand heads and thousand bellies, a thousand arms, a thousand tongues and a thousand eyes. It seemed to continually emit fire.

Mahabaho, that weapon is superior to the Brahma, the Narayana, the Aindra, the Agneya, and the Varuna astras. It can make ashes of every other weapon in the universe. Using that astra Mahadeva had once, burnt down the Tripura, the triad cities of the Asuras in a flash. With that single arrow, Krishna, he, Siva, achieved that impossible feat with the greatest ease.

Shot by Mahadeva's arms, that astra can consume the entire universe with all its mobile and immobile creatures in the twinkling of an eye. Everyone in the universe, including even Brahma and Vishnu and the Devas, that weapon can slay. I saw that incomparable astra in the hand of Mahadeva.

There is another mysterious and powerful weapon which is equal, even superior to the Pasupata. I also saw that one. It is celebrated in all the worlds as the sum of the Sula-armed Mahadeva. Cast by him, it can rive the earth, dry up the waters of the ocean or indeed annihilate the universe.

In the past that Sula made ashes of Yuvanaswa's son, King Mandhatri, conqueror of the three worlds, ruler of a vast empire and endowed with prodigious energy, along with all his army. Mighty, and like Sakra himself in prowess was Mandhatri, but the Rakshasa Lavana killed him with the Sula which he received from Siva.

The Sula has such sharp prongs that they verge on being invisible. It can terrify all and make the hair of the mightiest stand on end. I saw that trident in Mahadeva's hand, and it seemed to roar with rage, having contracted its forehead into three furrows. It resembled, Krishna, a smokeless fire or the sun that rises at the end of the yuga. The handle of that Sula, was a mighty snake. It is indescribable. It looked like Yama himself armed with his noose with which he draws out souls from living creatures. I saw this astra in the hand of Mahadeva.

I beheld also another weapon, the battle-axe Khatvanga, which the gratified Siva once gave to Parasurama Bhargava and with which Rama exterminates all the Kshatriyas of the world. It was with this weapon that Rama destroyed the great Kartavirya in furious battle. It was with that weapon that Jamadagni's son was able to annihilate the Kshatriyas on twenty-one occasions.

Searingly sharp, that axe hung on Siva's shoulder, adorned with his snake. Indeed, it glowed on Mahadeva's body like the flame of a blazing fire. I saw many other divine weapons with Mahadeva. I have named only a few most important ones.

On the left side of the Great God was Brahma seated on a chariot drawn by swans swift as the mind. On the same side Vishnu could also be seen riding on Garuda, and bearing the sankha, chakra and gada.

Close to the Goddess Parvati was Skanda on his peacock, bearing his deadly arrow and bells, and looking like another Agni. In front of Mahadeva stood Nandi armed with his Sula and looking like a second formidable Siva.

The Munis led by Manu and Rishis led by Bhrigu, and the Devas with Indra at their head, all came there. All the tribes of bhutas and pretas, and the divine matrikas, stood surrounding Mahadeva and worshipping him.

The Devas were singing hymns in his praise. Brahma recited a Rathantara to praise Mahadeva. Narayana chanted the Jyeshta Saman to eulogise him and Indra did the same with the Sata-Rudriyam.

Brahma, Narayana and Sakra shone there like three sacrificial fires. In their midst the illustrious Siva blazed like Surya in the midst of his corona, emerged from behind dark clouds. I beheld many suns and moons in the sky. I then praised the illustrious Lord of everything, the supreme master of the universe.

Upamanyu continued,[2] "I said, 'Salutations to you, illustrious one, you that are the refuge of all things, you that are called Mahadeva! Salutations to you that assume the form of Sakra, that are Sakra, and that disguise yourself in the form and robes of Sakra.

Salutations to you that are armed with the thunderbolt, to you that are tawny, and you that are always armed with the Pinaka. Salutations to you that always bear the conch and the trisula.

Salutations to you that are clad in black, to you that have dark and matted hair, to you that possess a dark deer-skin for your upper garment, to you that preside over the eighth lunation of the dark fortnight. Salutations to you that are of white complexion, to you that are called auspicious, to you that are clad in white robes, to you that have limbs smeared with white ashes, to you that are ever engaged in pure deeds.

Salutations to you that are red in colour, to you that are clad in red vestments, to you that have a red banner with red pennants, to you that wear red garlands and use red unguents. Salutations to you that are brown in colour, to you that are clad in brown vestments, to you that have a brown banner with brown pennants, to you that wear brown garlands and use brown liniments.

Salutations to you that have the royal parasol over your head, to you that wear the best of crowns. Salutations unto you that are adorned with half a garland and half an armlet, to you that are decked with one ring for one year, to you that are endowed with the speed of the mind, to you that are filled with great refulgence. Salutations to you that are the foremost of deities, to you that are the foremost of ascetics, to you that are the foremost of divinities.

Salutations to you that wear half a wreath of lotuses, to you that cover your body with many lotuses. Salutations to you that have half your body smeared with sandalwood paste, to you that have half your body decked with garlands of flowers and smeared with fragrant oils.

Salutations to you that are of the complexion of the sun, you are

---

[2] This is Siva Sahasranama of the Mahabharata.

like Surya, to you whose face is like that of the sun, to you whose eyes are each like the sun. Salutations to you that are Soma, to you that are as gentle as the moon, to you that bear the lunar disc on your brow, to you that are of lustre like the moon, to you that are the foremost of all creatures, to you that are adorned with bright teeth.

Salutations to you that are of a dark complexion, to you that are of a fair complexion, to you that have a form half-tawny and half-white, to you that has a body half-male and half-female, to you that are both male and female. Salutations to you that have Nandi for your vahana, to you that ride on the most majestic of elephants, to you that are obtained with difficulty, to you that can easily access places inaccessible to others.

Salutations to you whose praises are sung by the Ganas, to you that are devoted to the Ganas, to you that follow the path of the Ganas, to you that are steadfast in your devotion to the Ganas.

Salutations to you that are white like the clouds, to you that glow like the evening clouds, to you that are indescribable, to you that are unique and incomparable.

Salutations to you that wears a beautiful red garland, to you that are dressed in red robes. Salutations to you that wears a jewelled crown, to you that are adorned with a crescent moon, to you that have eight flowers on your head.

Salutations to you that have a fiery mouth and burning eyes, to you that have eyes as lustrous as a thousand moons, to you that have the form of fire, to you that are handsome and enchanting, to you that are inconceivable and mysterious. Salutations to you that range through the firmament, to you that love and dwell in the pastures of cows, to you that walk on the earth, to you that are the earth, to you that are infinite, to you that are auspicious.

Salutations to you that are digambara, clothed only by the sky, to you that make a joyful home of every place in which you find yourself. Salutations to you that have the universe for your home, to you that have both knowledge and grace for your Soul.

Salutations to you that wears a crown, to you that wears a magnificent armlet, to you that has a snake for the garland round your neck, to you that wears many beautiful ornaments. Salutations to you that have Surya, Chandramas and Agni for your three eyes, to you that possess a thousand eyes, to you that are both male and female, to you that are without gender, to you that are a Samkhya, to you that are a yogin.

Salutations to you that are of the grace of those Devas who are worshipped in yagnas, to you that are the Atharvans, to you who alleviate all kinds of disease and pain, to you that dispel every sorrow. Salutations to you that roar like resounding thunder, to you that create illusions, to you that preside over the soil and over the seed that is sown in it, to you that are the Creator of everything.

Salutations to you that are the Lord of all the Devas, to you that are the master of the universe, to you that are swift like the wind, to you that are of the form of the wind. Salutations to you that wear a garland of gold, to you that sport on hills and mountains, to you that are adored by all the Asuras, to you that possess fierce speed and energy.

Salutations to you that tore out one of Brahma's heads, to you that slew Mahishasura, to you that assume three forms, to you that bear every form. Salutations to you that are the destroyer of the Tripura of the Asuras, to you that are the destroyer of Daksha's yagna, to you that are the destroyer of Kama's body, to you that wield the rod of destruction.

Salutations to you that are Skanda, to you that are Visakha, to you that are the staff of the Brahmana, to you that are Bhava, to you that are Sarva, to you that are of universal form. Salutations to you that are Isana, to you that are the destroyer of Bhaga, to you that are the slayer of Andhaka, to you that are the universe, to you that are possess maya, to you that are both conceivable and inconceivable.

You are the one goal of all creatures, you are the foremost, and you are the heart of everything. You are Brahma of all the Devas, you are the Nilardhita of the Rudras. You are the Atman of the creatures, you are he that is called Purusha by the Samkhyas, you are the Rishabha among all things sacred, you are that which is called auspicious by yogins and which, according to them, is indivisible.

Among those in the various asramas, you are the grihasta, you are the great Lord amongst the lords of the universe. You are Kubera among the Yakshas, and you are Vishnu among all sacrifices.

You are Meru among mountains, you are the moon among all luminaries of the firmament, you are Vasishta amongst Rishis, and you are Surya among the planets. You are the lion among all wild beasts, and among domestic animals you are the bull that is worshipped by all men.

Among the Adityas you are Vishnu, among the Vasus you are Pavaka, among birds you are Garuda, and among snakes you are Ananta. Among the Vedas you are the Saman, among the Yajuses you are the Sata-Rudriyam, among yogins you are Sanatkumara, and among Samkhyas you are Kapila.

Among the Maruts you are Sakra, among the Pitris you are Devarata, among all the realms created for living you are Brahmaloka, and among all the ends that creatures attain to, you are moksha. You are the ocean of milk among oceans, among all lofty mountains you are Himavat, among all the varnas you are the Brahmana, and among all learned Brahmanas you are he that has undergone and is observant of the Diksha.

You are the sun among all things in the world, you are the destroyer Kaala. You are whatever else possesses the superior tejas of eminence that exists in the universe. You are supremely powerful. This is my certain conclusion.

Salutations to you, you that are kind to all your devotees. Salutations to you, Lord of yogins. I bow to you, the original cause of the universe. Be you gratified with me, your worshipper dejected and powerless; Eternal Lord, you become the refuge of this weak and wretched one who adores you.

It is fitting for you to pardon all my sins, taking pity on me because I am your devoted worshipper. I was mystified by you, on account of the disguise in which you appeared before me. O Maheswara, I did not even give you the arghya or padya to wash your feet.'

Having sung the praises of Isana in this way, I offered him, with great devotion, water to wash his feet and the ingredients of the arghya, and then, with folded hands, I surrendered myself to him, being prepared to do whatever he commanded.

An auspicious shower of flowers fell upon my head, possessing divine fragrance and sprinkled with cool water-drops. The Gandharvas began to play on their drums. A perfumed breeze began to blow and fill me with delight.

Then Mahadeva accompanied by his wife, having been gratified with me, addressed the divinities gathered there, his words filling me with great joy, 'Behold, you Devas, the devotion of Upamanyu. It is steadfast and great, and entirely immutable, for it exists unalterably.'

Thus addressed by the great God armed with the Sula, the Devas bowed before him and said with reverence, 'Illustrious one, God of the gods, master of the universe, Lord of all, let this Dvijottama obtain from you the fruit of all his desires.'

Thus addressed by all the Devas including Brahma, Mahadeva, also called Isa and Sankara, said these words as if smiling upon me. Sankara said, 'Upamanyu, I am pleased with you. Foremost of Munis, learned Rishi, you are firmly devoted to me and have been well you tested by me. I have been delighted with you because of your bhakti. Today I will satisfy all your desires.'

Thus addressed by Mahadeva, so great was my emotion that I wept tears of joy and my hair stood on end. Kneeling down and bowing to him, with a voice choked with rapture, I said to him, 'Siva, I feel that until now I did not live and that only today have I been born, and that my birth has borne fruit today, since I am now in the presence of Him who is the master of both the Devas and the Asuras!

Who else is more praiseworthy than I, since my eyes behold him of immeasurable power, whom the very Devas cannot see without worship? The wise and the learned say that the highest of all subjects, which is eternal, which is distinguished from all else, which is unborn, which is gyana, which is indestructible, is identical with you; you that are the beginning of all, you that are immortal and unchanging, you that know the laws that govern all things, you that are the foremost of Purushas, you that are the highest of the high.

You are he that created from your right side Brahma, the Creator of all things. You are he that has created from your left side Vishnu to preserve that creation. You are that puissant Lord who created Rudra at the end of the yuga for the dissolution of that creation.

That Rudra, who sprang from you destroyed creation with all its moving and immobile beings, assuming the form of Kaala, of the cloud Samvartaka full of water which all the oceans cannot hold, and of the all-consuming fire. When the time for the dissolution of the universe arrives, that Rudra stands ready to swallow it.

You are that Mahadeva, who is the original Creator of the universe with all that it contains. You are he who, at the end of the kalpa, withdraws all things into yourself. You are he that permeates all things, are the soul of all things, for you are the Creator of the creator of all things.

You cannot be seen even by the Devas; you are he that encompasses all entities. If you are gratified with me and if you can grant me boons, let this be my one boon, Lord of all the gods—that my devotion to you may remain unwavering. Let me, through your grace, have knowledge of the present, the past and the future. Let me, with all my kinsmen and friends, always eat food mixed with milk. And you, O celebrated Lord, always be present in our asrama.'

Mahatejasvin Maheswara, that Jagadguru of all things, who is worshipped by all, spoke these words to me.

Siva said, 'Be you free from every sorrow and pain, and above decay and death. May you possess fame, be filled with great tejas, and let atma-gyana be yours. Through my blessings, you will always be sought after by the Rishis.

May your conduct ever be good and righteous, may every desirable attribute be yours, may you obtain universal knowledge, and may you be radiant and handsome. Let your youth be undiminished, and let your energy be like that of fire. Wherever you desire the presence of the Kshirasagara, ocean of milk, there that ocean will appear before you to be used by you and your friends for your food. May you and your friends always obtain food prepared with milk, and with amrita also mixed with it.

After the expiration of a kalpa you will have my companionship. Your family and kinsmen will be limitless. Your devotion to me will be eternal. And, best of Brahmanas, I shall always be present in your asrama. Live wherever you like, and without worry. Merely think of me, and I will grant you a vision of myself again.'

Having said these words, and granted me these boons, Isana, shining with the splendour of millions of suns, disappeared. Krishna, in this manner, with austere tapasya, I saw that God of gods. I also received what he said. Krishna, behold these Siddhas living here, and these Rishis and Vidyadharas and Yakshas and Gandharvas and Apsaras. Behold these trees and creepers and plants yielding all sorts of flowers and fruits. Behold them bearing the flowers of every season, with beautiful leaves, and spreading sweet fragrance all around.

Mahabaho, all these are endowed with a divine nature through the grace of that God of gods, that Supreme Lord, that Mahatman Mahadeva."'

Krishna continues, 'Hearing his words and seeing before my own eyes all that he narrated to me, I was filled with wonder. I then said to Mahamuni Upamanyu, "You are worthy of great praise, for whose hermitage, other than yours, enjoys the honour of the presence of Siva? Will the great Sankara also reveal himself to me and show me kindness?"

Upamanyu said, "Without doubt, you will soon obtain a vision of Mahadeva, even as I succeeded in beholding him. I see with my spiritual eyes that you will behold Mahadeva in the sixth month from now. Foremost of the Yadavas, Maheswara and his consort will grant you twenty-four boons. I tell you this truly.

Through Siva's grace, the past, the present and the future are known to me. The great Hara has favoured thousands of Rishis. Why will he not show you his favour?

The meeting of the gods is always praiseworthy, more so with you, with one devoted to Brahmanas, with one that is full of compassion and faith. I will give you some mantras. Chant them repeatedly. With this you are certain to gain a vision of Sankara."'

The blessed Krishna continues, 'I said to him, "Mahamuni, through your grace, I shall behold the Lord of the Devas, that destroyer of the whole host of Diti's sons."'

Bhaarata, eight days passed there as but an hour, all of us being immersed in talk about Mahadeva. On the eighth day, I underwent the diksha according to the due rites at the hands of that Brahmana and received the danda from his hands. I underwent the prescribed shaving of my head. I took up some kusa blades in my hand. I wore rags for clothes. I rubbed my body with ghee. I tied a cord woven of munja grass around my waist.

For one month I lived on fruits. The second month I subsisted upon water. I passed the third, fourth and the fifth months by living on air alone. I stood all the while, foregoing sleep, supporting myself on one foot and with my arms also raised over my head.

Then I saw a blinding radiance in the sky like that of a thousand suns combined. At its heart I saw a cloud like a mass of blue hills, adorned with rows of cranes, embellished with many magnificent rainbows, with flashes of fiery lightning and thunder.

Within that cloud was the luminous Mahadeva, accompanied by Uma. The great God seemed to shine with his penances, energy, beauty, effulgence, and also his wife beside him. The puissant Maheswara and Uma shone in the midst of that cloud. He looked like the sun among a bank of clouds, with the moon by his side.

Son of Kunti, the hair on my body stood on end, and my eyes were wide with wonder upon beholding Siva, the refuge of all the Devas and the dispeller of all their sorrows. Mahadeva wore a crown on his head. He was armed with his Sula. His loins covered in tiger-skin, his hair was matted and he carried the staff of the ascetic in one of his hands. He was armed with his Pinaka and the trisula.

His teeth were sharp. His upper arm was decked with an incomparable bracelet. His sacred thread was a snake. He wore a garland of many colours on his chest, a mala reached down to his toes. I saw him like a radiant moon on a winter evening.

Surrounded by diverse clans of spirits and ghosts, he was like a sun difficult to gaze at. Eleven hundred Rudras stood around him of restrained soul and pure deeds, who was seated upon Nandin. All of them were singing his praises. The Adityas, the Vasus, the Sadhyas, the Viswadevas and the twin Aswins praised that Lord of the universe with the mantras from the shastras. The puissant Indra and his brother Upendra, the two sons of Aditi, and Pitamaha Brahma, all recited the Rathantara Saman before him.

Countless masters of yoga, all the greatest Rishis with their sons, all the Devarishis, the Devi Bhumi, the sky, the constellations, the planets, the months, the fortnights, the seasons, night, the years, the kshanas, the muhurtas, the nimeshas, the yugas one after another, all the divine vigyanas and angas of knowledge, and all beings conversant with truth, were seen bowing down before that Supreme Guru, that great Father, that giver of yoga.

Yudhishtira, I saw Sanatkumara, the Vedas, the itihasas, Marichi, Angiras, Atri, Pulastya, Pulaha, Kratu, the seven Manus, Soma, the Atharvans, and Brihaspati, Bhrigu, Daksha, Kasyapa, Vasishta, Kasya, the Chchandas, Diksha, the Yagnas, Dakshina, the Agnis, the Havis poured in sacrifices, and all the elements of the yagnas, all standing there in their embodied forms.

All the Lokapalas, all the Nadis, all the Nagas, the Parvatas, the divine Matrikas, all the Devastris and Devaputris, millions of sannyasis were seen to bow down to Him who is the soul of serenity. The mountains, the oceans and the cardinal directions also did the same, while the Gandharvas and the Apsaras sang in divine voices the praises of the ineffable Siva. The Vidyadharas, the Danavas, the Guhyakas, the Rakshasas, and all created beings, mobile and immobile, adored him in thought, word and deed.

Before me, that Lord of all the Devas appeared, seated in all his glory.

Seeing that Isana had showed himself to me by being seated before my eyes, the whole universe, along with Brahma and Indra, looked at me. I, however, had not the power to look at Mahadeva.

Siva then said to me, "Look at me, Krishna, and speak to me. You have worshipped me hundreds and thousands of times. There is no one in the three worlds that is dearer to me than you."

After I had bowed to him, Devi Uma became pleased with me. I then spoke these words to Him whose praises are sung by all the Devas.'

Krishna continues, 'I bowed to Mahadeva, saying, "Salutations to you, you that are the eternal origin of all things. The Rishis say that you are the Lord of the Vedas. The righteous say that you are tapasya, you are sattva, you are rajas, you are tamas, and you are satya. You are Brahma, you are Rudra, you are Varuna, you are Agni, you are Manu, you are Bhava, you are Dhatri, you are Tvashtri, you are Vidhatri, you are the puissant master of all things, and you are everywhere.

All beings, mobile and unmoving, have sprung from you. This threefold world with all its entities has been created by you. The Rishis say that you are superior to the senses, the mind, the vital breaths, the seven sacrificial fires, all others that have their refuge in the all-pervading Soul, and all the deities that are adored and worthy of adoration. You, O illustrious one, are the Vedas, the yagnas, Soma, Dakshina, Pavaka, Havi, and all other components of sacrifice. The punya obtained through sacrifices, gifts made to others, the study of the Vedas, vratas, rules of restraint, modesty, fame, prosperity, splendour, contentment and success, all exist for the one purpose of leading to you. Desire, anger, fear, greed, pride, stupor, and malice, pain and disease, are your children.

You are the actions of all creatures, you are the joy and sorrow that flow from those deeds, you are the absence of joy and sorrow, you are that ignorance which is the indestructible seed of desire, you are the high origin of Manas, you are strength, and you are eternity.

You are the unmanifest, you are Pavana, you are inconceivable, you are the thousand-rayed sun, you are the effulgent Chit, you are the first of all the subjects, and you are the refuge of life. The use of words like

Mahat, Atman, Buddhi, Brahma, Brahmanda, Sambhu, and Swayambhu recurring in the Vedas show that your nature has been judged as identical with Mahat and Atman by men conversant with the Vedas. Verily, regarding you as all this, knowing Brahmanas overcome that ignorance which lies at the root of the world.

You dwell in the heart of all creatures, and you are adored by the Rishis as Kshetrajna. Your arms and feet extend to every place, and your eyes, head and face are everywhere. You hear everywhere in the universe, and you pervade all things. You are the fruit of all acts that are performed in the nimeshas and other divisions of time that occur on account of the sun.

You are the original brilliance of the supreme Chit. You are Purusha, and you live in the hearts of all things. You are the yogic attributes of success, subtlety and grossness, and fruition and supremacy, effulgence and immutability. Understanding and intelligence, and all the worlds, rest upon you.

They that are devoted to meditation, that are always engaged in yoga, that are devoted to satya and that have subjugated their passions, seek you and rely on you. They that know you to be immutable, the one that dwells in all hearts, the one that is endowed with supreme power, or the ancient Purusha, or pure gyana, or the effulgent Chit, or the highest refuge of all wise men, are certainly of great intelligence. Truly, such men transcend intelligence.

By understanding the seven subtle entities and the tanmatras, by comprehending your six attributes, of omniscience, contentment, knowledge without beginning, independence, flawless and infinite power, and being conversant with yoga freed from every falsity, the man of knowledge succeeds in entering into your great self."

After I had said these words to Bhava, the universe, both mobile and immobile, sent up a roar to show their approval of what I said. The countless Brahmanas present there, the Devas and the Asuras, the Nagas, the Pisachas, the Pitris, the Garudas, diverse Rakshasas, bhutas and pretas, and all the Maharishis, then bowed down before that Great

Deity. Showers of fragrant flowers showered down upon me and cool winds began to blow.

Siva looked at the Devi Uma and at Indra and at me and said, "Krishna, we know that you are devoted to us. Do what is for your good. My love for you is great. Ask for eight boons. I will grant them to you. Name what you wish for. However difficult to attain they may be, you will still have them."""

"**K**rishna said, 'Bowing my head to that mass of energy and radiance, I said, "Firmness in virtue, the slaying of enemies in battle, the highest renown, the greatest strength, devotion to yoga, your presence, and hundreds upon hundreds of children, these are the boons I ask of you."

"So be it", said Siva repeating the words I had uttered.

After this, Uma, the mother of the universe, the upholder and purifier of all things, that vast vessel of tapasya, said, "Mahadeva has granted you a son who shall be named Samba. Take from me another eight boons."

Bowing to her, I said, "From you I ask for peace with the Brahmanas, the blessings of my father, a hundred sons, the highest enjoyments, love for my family, and the grace of my mother, the attainment of tranquillity and peace, and intelligent action!"

Uma said, "They shall be yours. I never say what is untrue. You will have sixteen thousand wives. Your love for them and theirs for you shall be limitless. You will also receive the highest devotion from all your kinsmen. Your body shall be most beautiful. Seven thousand guests will dine every day at your palace."'

Krishna continued, 'Having granted me boons, Mahadeva and Uma along with their Ganas disappeared from sight. I narrated all those wonderful facts to Upamanyu, that Brahmana from whom I had obtained diksha before worshipping Mahadeva. Bowing down unto the great God,

Upamanyu said these words to me.

Upamanyu said, "There is no God like Sarva. There is no end or refuge like Sarva. There is none that can give so many or such boons. There is none that equals him in battle."'"

CANTO 16

"Krishna continues, 'Upamanyu said, "In the Krita yuga there lived a renowned Rishi named Tandi. With yoga-dhyana and great devotion he adored Siva for ten thousand years. Listen as I tell you about the fruits of such extraordinary devotion.

He succeeded in having a vision of Mahadeva and praised him by reciting great and holy mantras. With tapasya, meditating on him who is the Paramatman, immutable and unchanging, Tandi was filled with wonder, and said, 'I seek the refuge of Him whom the Samkhyas describe and the yogins think of as the Supreme, the Foremost, the Purusha, the Pervador of all things, and the master of all existence.

I seek the protection of him who, the learned say, is the cause of both the creation and the destruction of the universe, of him who is superior to all the Devas, the Asuras and the Munis, of him who has nothing higher, who is unborn, who is the Lord of all things, who has neither beginning nor end, and who is endowed with supreme power, possessed of the highest felicity, and who is irradiant and sinless.'

After he had said these words, Tandi beheld before him that ocean of tapasya, that Great Deity who is immutable and eternal, who is without equal, who is inconceivable, who is indivisible, who is whole, who is Brahman, who transcends all attributes being nirguna, and who is imbued with attributes being saguna, who is the highest ecstasy of yogins, who is imperishable, who is mukti, who is the refuge of Manas, of Indra, of Agni, of Vayu, of the entire universe, and of Pitamaha Brahma. Through Manas, Tandi saw him who is inconceivable, who is immutable, who is pure, who can be understood only through surrender and who is immaterial as the mind; who is hard to comprehend, who is immeasurable, who cannot be attained by those impure souls, who is the origin of the universe, and who transcends both the universe and the Tamoguna; who is ancient, who is Purusha, who is radiant, and who is higher than the highest.

Wanting to behold him who endowed with life-breaths, resides in what results from it, who is Jiva in the form of that effulgence which is called Manas, Rishi Tandi passed many years in the practice of the severest tapasya, and having succeeded in beholding Siva as the reward of that penance, eulogised Mahadeva in the following terms:

Tandi said, 'You are the most blessed of all that is sacred and the refuge of all. You are the fiercest among all kinds of tejas. You are the austerest of all tapasyas. You are the giver of blessings. You are the supreme truth.

Salutations to you, you of a thousand rays, O sanctuary of all felicity. You are the giver of that nirvana which Yatis strive for, who fear birth and death. Brahma, Indra, Vishnu, the Viswadevas and the Maharishis cannot comprehend you and your real nature. How then can we hope to fathom you?

From you flows everything. Upon you rests everything. You are called Kaala, you are called Purusha, and you are called Brahman. Devarishis who know the Puranas say that you have three bodies, that pertaining to Kaala, that pertaining to Purusha and that pertaining to Brahman, or the three forms of Brahma, Vishnu and Siva.

You are Adi-Purusha, occupying the physical frame from head to foot, you are Adhyatma, you are Adi-bhuta, and Adi-Daivata, and you are Adi-Loka, Adi-Vigyanam and Adi-Yagna. Men of wisdom, when they succeed in knowing you that dwells in them, and that cannot be known by the very Devas, become freed from all bonds and pass into a state of existence that transcends sorrow. They that do not wish to know you have to experience innumerable births and deaths.

You are the door of swarga and of mukti. You are he that projects all beings into existence and withdraws them again into yourself. You are the great giver. You are swarga, you are mukti; you are desire that is the seed of karma. You are the wrath that inspires creatures to action.

You are sattva, you are rajas, you are tamas; you are patala, and you are swarga. You are Brahma, you are Bhava, you are Vishnu, you are Skanda, you are Indra, you are Savitri, you are Yama, you are Varuna and Soma, you are Dhatri, you are Manu, you are Vidhatri and you are Kubera, the Lord of wealth.

You are Bhumi, you are Vayu, you are Jala, you are Agni, you are Akasa; you are speech, you are Buddhi, you are steadiness, you are intelligence; you are the kama of creatures, you are satya, you are asatya, you are existent and you are non-existent. You are the senses, you are that which transcends Prakriti, and you are unalterable.

You are superior to the universe of existent objects, you are superior to the universe of non-existent objects; you are capable of being conceived, you are inconceivable. That which is supreme Brahman, the highest entity, that which is the end of both the Samkhyas and the yogins, is, without doubt, identical with you.

Truly, today I have been rewarded by you as you have granted me a vision of yourself. I have attained the end which the righteous alone attain. I have been rewarded with that goal which is sought by those whose intellects have been purified by gyana.

Steeped in ignorance for so long, I was a mindless fool; I had no knowledge of you that are the Supreme Deity, you that are the only eternal One that only wise men can know. In the course of countless lives I have at last succeeded in acquiring that devotion towards you as a result of which you have shown yourself to me. You are ever inclined to extend your grace to those that are devoted to you.

He that succeeds in knowing you enjoys immortality. You are that which is ever a mystery with the Devas, the Asuras and the sannyasis. Brahman is concealed in the cave of the heart. Even the greatest sannyasis are unable to behold or know him.

You are he who is the doer of everything and whose face is turned towards every direction. You are the soul of all things, you see all things, you pervade all things, and you know all things. You create a body for yourself, and bear it. You are an embodied Being.

You enjoy a body, and you are the refuge of all embodied creatures. You are the Creator of the pranas, you possesses the life-breaths, you are one that is filled with the life-breaths, you are the giver of the pranas, and you are the refuge of all beings with prana. You are that Adhyatma which is the refuge of all righteous ones that are devoted to yoga-dhyana and conversant with the Atman and that are diligent in avoiding rebirth. You are that Supreme Lord identical with that refuge.

You give unto all creatures what ends become theirs, whether fraught with happiness or misery. You are he that ordains all created beings to birth and death. You are the mighty Lord who grants success to Rishis. Having created all the worlds beginning with Bhu, together with all the inhabitants of heaven, and uphold and cherish them all, you have divided yourself into your celebrated eight forms.

Everything flows from you. All things rest upon you. All things, again, disappear into you. You are the sole object that is eternal. You are that region of truth sought by the righteous and regarded by them as the highest. You are that cessation of individual existence which yogins seek. You are that Oneness which is sought by those conversant with the Soul.

Brahma and the Siddhas expounding the mantras have concealed you in a cave to prevent the Devas and Asuras and Manavas from seeing you. You live in the heart, yet you are concealed. Devas, Asuras and Manavas are all bewildered and unable to understand you truly and in all your aspects, O Bhava. You reveal yourself of your own accord to those that attain you after having cleansed themselves through bhakti.

By knowing you one can avoid both death and rebirth. You are the highest object of knowledge. By knowing you no higher object remains to be known. You are the greatest object of realisation. He that is truly wise, after attaining you, thinks there is no higher object to acquire. By reaching you that are subtle and the highest object of attainment, the wise become immortal and changeless.

The followers of the Samkhya system, who know their own philosophy and possess a knowledge of sattva, rajas and tamas and of those tattvas that are the subjects of enquiry, and those learned men who transcend the perishable by attaining to a knowledge of the subtle or indestructible by knowing you, succeed in liberating themselves from all bonds.

Those who know the Vedas regard you as the one object of knowledge, which has been expounded in those highest shastras. These men, devoted to pranayama, always meditate on you and enter into you as their final end.

Riding on the chariot made of AUM, those men enter into Maheswara. Of that which is called the Devayana, the path of the Devas, you are the door called Aditya. You are also the door called Chandramas, of that which is called the Pitriyana. You are Kashta, you are the cardinal directions of the horizon, you are the year, and you are the yugas. You are the sovereign of all the heavens and of the earth; you are Uttarayana and Dakshinayana, the northern and the southern declensions.

You who are called Nilalohita, in olden times Brahma sang your praises by reciting mantras and urged you to create living creatures. Regarding you as unattached to all things and divested of all forms, Brahmanas conversant with the Riks praise you by intoning those sacred Riks. Adhvaryus pour libations in yagnas, chanting Yajuses in honour of you that are the sole object of knowledge according to the three paths.

Men of pure intellects, who know the Samans, sing your praises with the Samans. Those Dvijas that know with the Atharvans, extol you as Rita, as truth, as the highest, and as Brahman. You are the highest cause, from which sacrifice has flowed. You are the Lord, and you are Supreme.

The night and day are your sense of hearing and sight. The fortnights and months are your head and arms. The seasons are your energy, tapasya is your patience, and the year is your anus, thighs and feet.

You are Mrityu. You are Yama, you are Hutasana, you are Kaala; you are swift in destruction, you are the original cause of time, and you are eternal Kaala. You are Chandramas and Aditya. With all the stars and planets and the atmosphere that fills space, you are Dhruva, the pole-star, you are the constellation called the Saptarishi, and you are the seven realms beginning with Bhu.

You are Pradhana and Mahat, you are unmanifest, and you are this world. You are the universe beginning with Brahman and ending with the lowest forms of vegetation. You are the beginning or origin of all creatures. You are the eight Prakritis. You are, again, above the eight Prakritis.

Everything that exists represents a portion of your divine self. You are that supreme felicity which is eternal. You are the end attained to by all things. You are that highest existence which is sought by the righteous. You are that state which is freed from every anxiety. You are eternal Brahman.

You are that highest state which constitutes the meditation of those knowers of the shastras and the Vedangas. You are the highest kashta, you are the highest Kaala. You are the highest success, and you are the highest refuge. You are the highest tranquillity. You are the highest cessation of existence. By attaining you, yogins think that they attain the highest success that is open to them.

You are contentment, you are success; you are the Sruti, and you are the Smriti. You are that refuge of the Atman which yogins strive for, and you are that indestructible Prapti which men of knowledge pursue. You are that goal sought by those who perform yagnas and offer sacrificial libations, and make ample gifts on such occasions.

You are that high end which is sought by those that waste and scorch their bodies with severe penances with ceaseless japa, with those rigid vows and fasts that pertain to their peaceful lives, and with other means of self-affliction. Eternal one, you are that end which is theirs that are detached from all things and that have renounced all action. You are that end which is theirs that wish to attain mukti from rebirth, that live aloof from all pleasures, and that desire the annihilation of the elements of Prakriti.

You are that high end, which is indescribable, which is stainless, which is the one beyond change, and which is theirs that are devoted to gyana and vigyana. These are the ends that have been affirmed in the Vedas and the Puranas and the other true shastras. It is through your grace that men attain to those ends or if they fail to attain to them, it is through the denial of your blessings to them.'

It was thus that tapodhana Tandi praised Isana. And he sang also that high Brahman which in ancient days was sung by Brahma in honour of Mahadeva."

Upamanyu continued, "Thus praised by Tandi, Mahadeva, who was accompanied by Uma, spoke. Tandi had further said, 'Neither Brahma, nor Indra nor Vishnu, nor the Viswdavas, nor the Maharishis know you.' Gratified at this, Siva said the following words.

The Holy One said, 'You will be indestructible and eternal. You will be freed from all sorrow. Great fame shall be yours. You will be full of tejas. Spiritual knowledge shall be yours. All the Rishis shall seek you, and through my grace your son shall be the author of profound Sutras. What can I give you today? Tell me, my son, what do you desire?'

At this, Tandi folded his hands and said, 'Let my devotion to you be unwavering.'"

Upamanyu continued, "Having given these boons to Tandi and having received the adorations of the Devas and the Rishis, Siva vanished. When he left with all his Ganas and other bhaktas, the Rishi came to my asrama and told me all that had happened to him. Listen now to all those celebrated names of Mahadeva that Tandi recited to me for your spiritual success.

Brahma had once recited ten thousand names that pertain to Mahadeva. In the shastras, Siva is known by a thousand names. These names are not known to all. In ancient times Brahma recounted these names to worship the high-souled deity. Having received them through the grace of Brahma, Tandi related them to me!'""

CANTO 17

"Krishna says, 'Yudhishtira, the regenerate Rishi Upamanyu, with hands joined together in reverence recited the names of Mahadeva, starting from the beginning.

Upamanyu said, "I shall adore that great deity who deserves the adorations of all creatures, by reciting those names that are celebrated over all the worlds, some of which were uttered by Brahma, some by the Rishis, and some of which occur in the Vedas and the Vedangas.

Those names have been used for Siva by renowned men. Those names, applied to Mahadeva by Tandi, who extracted them from Vedic lore with his devotion, are true and can surely bestow all the aims of the one who recites them.

Indeed, with those names that have been uttered by many righteousness men and by ascetics conversant with dharma, I shall adore him who is the foremost, who is the first, who leads to heaven, who grants boons to all creatures, and who is auspicious. These names have been heard everywhere in the universe, having spread from the realm of Brahma, where they were originally created. All of them are suffused with Truth.

With those names I shall adore him who is the Parabrahman, who has been declared unto the universe by the Vedas, and who is eternal. I shall now tell you, Lord of Yadu's vamsa. Hear them with rapt attention. You are a devoted bhakta of the Supreme Deity. Worship the illustrious

Bhava above all the Devas. And because you are devoted to him, I will recite those names in your hearing.

Mahadeva is Eternal Brahman. Even those endowed with yoga and its achievements are unable to grasp, even in a hundred years, the full glory and power of Siva. Truly, the beginning or middle or end of Mahadeva cannot be known by the very Devas. Then who can recite the attributes of Mahadeva in their entirety? For all that, through the grace of that illustrious and supreme God of perfect wisdom, granted to me for my devotion to him, I will recite his attributes summarised in a few words.

The Supreme Lord cannot be adored by anyone if he does not grant his leave to the devotee. As for me, it is only when I become fortunate enough to receive his blessing that I succeed in worshipping him.

I shall mention only a few names of that Mahadeva who is without birth and without death, who is the original cause of the universe, who has the highest Soul, and whose origin is unmanifest. Krishna, listen to these, a few names that were uttered by Brahma himself of that giver of boons, that adorable deity, that puissant one who has the universe for his form, and who is possessed of supreme wisdom.

These names that I shall recite are extracted from the ten thousand names, the Koti Rudriyam that Brahma recited in ancient times, even as ghee is extracted from butter. Just as gold represents the essence of rocky mountains, as honey represents the essence of flowers, as Manda represents the extract from ghrita, even so have these names been extracted from and represent the essence of those ten thousand names spoken by the Pitamaha Brahma.

This brief abstract of names can cleanse every sin, however heinous. It possesses the same punya as that in the four Vedas. It should be received with attention by spiritual aspirants and engraved on the memory. These auspicious names, great purifiers, leading to spiritual advancement, capable of destroying Rakshasas, should be imparted to only him that is devoted to Siva, to him that has faith, to him that believes.

Unto him that has no faith, him that is an unbeliever, him that has not subjugated his soul, it should never be communicated. That creature who harbours malice towards Mahadeva who is the original cause of everything, who is the Paramatman, and who is the great Lord, will certainly to go to naraka along with all his ancestors before and all his children after him. This abstract of names that I shall recite to you is regarded as yoga.

This is looked upon as the highest object of dhyana. This is that which one should constantly recite as japa. This is equivalent to gyana. This is the highest mystery. If one, even during his last moments, recites it or hears it recited, he will attain the supreme end.

This is holy. This is auspicious; this is filled with every kind of benefit. This is the best of all things. Brahma, the Pitamaha of all the universe, having composed it, assigned to it the foremost place among all excellent mantras. From that time, this chant to the greatness and glory of Mahadeva, which is held in the highest esteem by all the Devas, has come to be regarded as the king of all mantras.

This king of mantras was first passed down from the realm of Brahma to swarga. Tandi then obtained it from there. Hence is it known to be composed by Tandi. Tandi brought it from swarga to Bhumi. It is the most auspicious of all auspicious things, and is capable of purifying the heart of all sins however terrible.

Mahabaho, I will recite to you that best of all mantras. This sings of him who is the Veda of the Vedas, and the most ancient of all ancient objects, of him who is the energy of all energies, and the penance of all penances; of him who is the most calm of all peaceful creatures, and who is the splendour of all splendours.

It sings the praises of him who is looked upon as the most subtle of all subtle creatures, and him who is the intelligence of all intelligent creatures; of him who is looked upon as the Deity of all deities, and the Rishi of all Rishis; of him who is regarded as the sacrifice of all sacrifices and the most auspicious of all auspicious things.

It sings of him who is the Rudra of all Rudras and the effulgence of all things effulgent; of him who is the Yogin of all yogins, and the cause of all causes; of him from whom all the worlds come into existence, and unto whom all the worlds return when they cease to exist; of him who is the Soul of all existent creatures, and who is called Hara of immeasurable energy.

Hear me recite those thousand and eight names of the great Sarva. This is the Siva Sahasranama stotra[3]. Hearing these names, all your wishes will be fulfilled.

Aum! You are immobile, you are unchanging, you are powerful, you are terrifying, you are the foremost, you are boon-giving, and you are supreme. You are the Atman of all creatures, you are celebrated above all creatures, you are all things, you are the Creator of all, and you are Bhava.

You are the bearer of matted hair on your head. You wear animal skins for your garments. You wear a crown of matted hair on your head like the peacock. You are he who has the whole universe for your limbs. You are the creator of all things. You are Hara for you are the destroyer of all things.

You are he that has the eyes of the gazelle. You are the destroyer of all creatures. You are the supreme enjoyer of all things. You are Pravritti from which all actions flow. You are Nivritti or abstention from deeds. You keep fasts and vows, you are eternal, and you are unchangeable.

You are he that dwells in the cremation ground, you possess the six famed gunas of sovereignty, you live in the heart of every creature, you are he that enjoys all things with the senses, and you are the slayer of all sinful creatures.

You are he that deserves the salutations of all, you are of great feats, you are tapodhana, you create all the elements at your will, and you conceal your real nature by disguising yourself as a madman. You are the master of all the worlds and of all living creatures.

You are of immeasurable form, you are of vast body, you are of the form of righteousness, you are of great fame, you are of high soul, you are the Atman of all creatures, and you have the universe for your form. You have a great maw for you swallow the universe at the time of the

---

[3]The hymn of the 1008 names of Siva.

dissolution. You are the protector of all the lokas.

You are the soul residing in the inner heart and devoid of ahamkara originating from ignorance, one and undivided; you are ananda. Your chariot is borne by mules. You are he that protects Jiva from the thunderbolt of rebirth. You are adorable.

You are obtained by purity and self-restraint and vratas. You are again the refuge of all kinds of vows and observances including purity and self-restraint. You are the divine artist that knows every art. You are Swayambhu for no one has created you. You are the beginning of all creatures and things. You are Hiranyagarbha, the Creator of all things. You are inexhaustible puissance and felicity.

You have a hundred powerful eyes. You are Soma. You are he that makes all good creatures assume shapes of glory that shine in the sky. You are Chandramas, you are Surya, you are Sani, you are the waxing moon, you are the waning moon, you are Mangala, and you are Brihaspati and Sukra and Budha, you are the worshipper of Atri's wife, you are he who shot his arrow in anger at a sacrifice when Yagna fled from him in the form of a deer. You are sinless.

You possess tapasyas with the power to create the universe. You have tapasyas that empower you to annihilate the universe. You are high-minded and generous towards your devotees. You fulfill the wishes of all who surrender themselves to you.

You are the maker of the year for it is you who sets the wheel of Kaala revolving, by assuming the form of the sun and the planets. You are mantra in the form of Pranava and other sacred words and syllables. In the form of the Vedas and other shastras, you are the authority for all deeds. You are the highest penance. You are devoted to yoga.

You are he who merges himself in Brahman through yoga. You are the great seed, the cause of causes. You reveal what is unmanifest in the manifest form in which the universe exists. You possess infinite might. You are he whose seed is gold.

You are omniscient; you are all things and the great knower. You are the cause of all things. You are he that has the seed of action, ignorance and desire, for the means of moving from this world to the other and the other to this.

You have ten arms. Your unblinking eyes see at all times. You have a blue throat where you bear the poison that arose when the ocean was churned that would have otherwise destroyed the universe. You are the Lord of Uma. You are the origin of all the infinite forms that occur in the universe.

You are he whose authority is due to yourself. You are heroic because of such grand feats as the swift razing of the triple city of the Asuras. You are inert matter which cannot move unless it co-exists with the Atman. You are all the tattvas, subjects of enquiry of the Samkhyas. You are the ordainer and ruler of the tattvas. You are the chief of the Ganas who wait upon you.

You cover infinite space. You are Kama. You know the mantras, gyana being your tapasya. You are the highest mantra for you are that philosophy which defines the nature and attributes of the Soul and its distinction from the non-Soul. You are the cause of the universe as all that exists has sprung from your Atman. You are the universal destroyer and all that ceases to exist merges into you who are the unmanifest Brahman.

You bear the calabash in one of your hands, and the bow in another; in another hand you bear shafts and in yet another a skull. You bear the thunder-bolt. You are armed with the Satagni. You are armed with the sword. You wield the battle-axe. You are armed with the Sula. You are adorable. You hold the sacrificial ladle in one of your hands.

You are of beautiful form. You are endowed with abundant tejas. You generously give all that adorns those that are devoted to you. You wear a turban on your head. You are of a beautiful face. You are he who swells with splendour and power. You are he that is humble and modest. You are of great height. Your senses are your rays. You are the greatest of acharyas. You are Parabrahman, the state of pure blessed existence.

You are he that took the form of a jackal to console the Brahmana who had resolved to commit suicide when insulted by a rich Vaisya. You are he whose aims are achieved by themselves, without waiting for the power that derives from tapasya. You are one with the shaved head, a sign of the order of sannyasis.

You are the one who does good to all creatures. You are unborn. You have countless forms. Your body is covered with all kinds of fragrances. The matted locks on your head swallowed the river Ganga when she first descended from heaven, though you released the waters at the plea of King Bhagiratha. You are the giver of sovereignty.

You are a brahmacharin without ever having fallen away from the rigid vow of abstinence. You are renowned for your sexual restraint. You always lie on your back. You have your abode in puissance. You have three matted locks on your head. You are dressed in rags. You are the fierce Rudra.

You are the divine senapati, and you are all pervading. You are he that moves during the day. You are he that moves in the night. You are of fierce wrath. You possess a dazzling radiance that is born of Vedic study and tapasya.

You are the slayer of the mighty Asura who took the form of an enraged elephant to destroy your sacred city of Varanasi. You are the slayer of those Daityas who become the oppressors of the universe. You are Kaala, time which is the universal destroyer.

You are the supreme ordainer of the universe. You are a wealth of accomplishments. You are of the form of the lion and the tiger. You are he that is clad in the hide of an elephant. You are the yogin who deceives Kaala by transcending its irresistible influence. You are the original sound. You are the fruition of all desires. You are he that is adored in four ways.

You are a night-wanderer, like a Vetala. You are he that wanders in the company of spirits. You are he that wanders in the company of ghostly beings. You are the Supreme Lord of even Indra and the other Devas. You are he that has multiplied himself infinitely in the form of all existent and non-existent things.

You are the upholder of both Mahat and all the innumerable combinations of the five Mahabhutas. You are the primeval ignorance or tamas known as Rahu. You are without measure and infinite. You are the supreme end that is attained by the emancipated.

You love to dance. You are he that is always dancing. You are he that causes others to dance. You are the friend of the universe. You are he whose appearance is calm and gentle. Your penances endow you with power to create and destroy the universe. You are he who binds all creatures with the bonds of your maya. You are he that transcends death.

You are he who dwells on Kailasa. You transcend all bonds and, like space, you are detached from all things. You possess a thousand arms. You are victory. You are that perseverance which leads to success or victory. You are devoid of sloth or procrastination that hinders firm action.

You are fearless. You are fear. You are he who put a stop to Bali's sacrifice. You fulfill the desires of all your devotees. You are the destroyer of Daksha's yagna. You are good-natured. You are amiable. You are fierce and rob all creatures of their energy. You are the slayer of the Asura Bala.

You are always joyful. You are of the form of wealth which is coveted by all. You have never been defeated. There is none more adorable than you. You are he who, as the ocean, roars resoundingly. You are that space which is so deep that it cannot be measured. You are he whose power and the might of whose Ganas and Nandi have never been determined.

You are the tree of the world whose roots extend upwards and branches hang downwards. You are the banyan. You are he that sleeps on a human leaf when the universe, after dissolution, becomes one infinite expanse of water. You are he that shows compassion to all worshippers assuming the form of Hari or Hara or Ganesa or Arka or Agni or Vayu.

You have sharp teeth and you can masticate countless worlds even as one crunches and swallows nuts. In all your forms you are of vast dimensions. You have a mouth wide enough to swallow the universe in a moment. You are he whose forces are adored everywhere.

You are he who dispelled the fears of the Devas when the prince of elephants had to be captured. You are the seed of the universe. You are he whose bull is both your mount and the emblem on your banner in battle. You have Agni for your soul. You are Surya who has green steeds yoked to his chariot. You are the friend of the Jiva. You are he that knows with the proper time for the performance of all religious kriyas.

You are he whom Vishnu worshipped to obtain his celebrated chakra. You are yagna in the form of Vishnu. You are the ocean. You are the Varavanala horse's head that ranges within the ocean, ceaselessly heaving fire and drinking the salt waters as if they were sacrificial butter.

You are Vayu, the friend of Agni. You are of tranquil soul like the ocean when at rest and unstirred by the mildest wind. You are Agni that drinks the libations of ghee poured in yagnas with the help of mantras. You are he whom it is difficult to seek out. You are he whose lustre spreads over the infinite universe. You are ever skilful in battle. You well know the time when one should engage in battle so that victory may be achieved. You are that science of jyotisha, which treats of the movements of the stars and planets.

You take the form of jaya, of success or victory. You are he whose body is Kaala, never subject to death. You are a grihasta for you wear a tuft of hair on your head. You are a sannyasi for your head is shaven. You wear matted locks, as you are a vanaprastha.

You are distinguished for your fiery rays: the bright path on which the righteous walk is identical with you. You are he that appears in the sky within the heart in the body of every creature. You are he who enters into the skull of every creature. You bear the wrinkles of age.

You bear the bamboo flute. You also have the tabor. You bear the musical instrument called tali. You hold the wooden vessel used for husking grain. You are he who shrouds the illusion which covers Yama. You are an astrologer whose understanding is always directed towards the motion of the wheel of time made up of the stars in the sky.

You are Jiva whose understanding is directed to things that are the outcome of sattva, rajas and tamas. You are that in which all things merge when dissolution engulfs them. You are stable and fixed, there being nothing in you that is subject to change of any kind. You are the Lord of all creatures. Your arms extend all over the universe.

You reveal yourself in many forms that are but iotas of yourself. You pervade all things. You are he that has no mouth for you seek not to enjoy the objects of your creation. You are he who frees your creatures from the bonds of the world. You are easy to attain.

You are he that manifested himself with golden armour. You are he that appears in the linga. You are he that roams the forests in search of birds and animals. You are he that wanders across the earth. You are he that is omnipresent. You are the blast of all the conches blown in the three worlds. You are he that has all creatures for his kinsmen.

You have the form of a snake for you are identical with the mighty Sesha Naga. You are he that lives in mountain caves like Jaigishavya or other yogins. You are identical with Guha, the divine senapati. You wear garlands of flowers. You are he who enjoys the happiness that springs from the possession of worldly objects.

You are he from whom all creatures have derived their three states of birth, existence, and death. You are he that upholds all things that exist or occur in the three stages of Kaala—the past, the present and the future. You are he that frees creatures from the outcomes of all deeds of previous lives as well as those of the present life, and from all the bonds due to ignorance and desire.

You are he who binds the Asura lords. You are he who is the slayer of foes in battle. You are that can be attained through gyana alone. You are Durvasas. You are he who is served and adored by all the righteous. You are he who causes the fall of even Brahma. You are he that gives unto all creatures the just share of joy and sorrow that each deserves according to his actions.

You are he that is incomparable. You are conversant with the havis given and appropriated in yagnas. You dwell in every place. You range everywhere. You are he that wears simple garments. You are Vasava. You are immortal. You are identical with the Himavat Mountains. You are the maker of pure gold.

You are devoid of karma. You uphold in yourself the fruits of all karma. You are the foremost of those who sustain and uphold. You are he that has red eyes. You are he with a vision extending across the infinite universe. You are he that has a chariot whose wheels are ever victorious.

You are he that has vast learning. You are he that accepts your devotees as your servants. You are he that restrains and subdues your senses. You are he that acts. You wear clothes whose warp and woof are made of snakes. You are supreme. You are he who is the lowest of the celestials. You are he that is mature. You own the musical instrument called the kahala.

You grant all wishes. You are the embodiment of grace in all the three stages of time, the past, the present and the future. You have power that is well used. You are he who had assumed the form of Balarama, the elder brother of Krishna.

You are the foremost of all coveted things, being yourself mukti, the highest of all ends to which creatures attain. You are the giver of all things. Your face is turned in all directions. You are he from whom diverse creatures have sprung even as all forms have sprung from Akasa or are variations of that primal element. You are he who falls into the pit called deha or the body. You are he that is helpless; you fall into that pit and cannot transcend the sorrow that is your lot.

You live in the firmament of the heart. You are terribly fierce in form. You are the deity called Amsu. You are the companion of Amsu and are called Aditya. You radiate innumerable rays. You are of blinding effulgence.

You have the speed of the wind. You possess speed greater than that of the wind. You possess the speed of the mind. You are Nishachara since you enjoy all things filled with the night of avidya.

You dwell in every body. You dwell with prosperity as your companion. You are he that imparts knowledge and instruction. You are he who teaches in absolute silence. You are he that observes the vow of reticence for you teach with silence. You are he who leaves the body, gazing at the soul.

You are he that is well adored. You are the giver of treasures, for Kubera, the Lord of all the treasures, obtained his riches from you. You are the prince of birds, being Garuda, the son of Vinata and Kasyapa.

You are the friend that helps. Your radiance is like that of a million suns risen together. You are the master of all created beings.

You are he who rouses the appetites. You are Kamadeva. You are of the form of beautiful women that are coveted by all. You are the tree of the world. You are the Lord of wealth. You are the giver of fame. You are the God that distributes the fruits of actions, joy and sorrow to all creatures. You are yourself those rewards which you distribute.

You are the most ancient, having existed from a time when nothing else was. You can cover all the three worlds with a single step. You are Vamana who tricked the Asura king Bali; depriving him of his sovereignty you restored it to Indra. You are the yogi crowned with success, like Sanatkumara and others.

You are a Maharishi like Vasishta. You are one whose objects are always crowned with success like Rishabha or Dattatreya. You are a sannyasin like Yagnavalkya. You are he that is adorned with the marks of the mendicant. You are he that is without such markings. You are he that transcends the practices of the sannyasasrama.

You are he that protects all creatures from every fear. You are without any passions yourself so that glory and dishonour are alike to you. You are Kartikeya, the divine senapati. You are Visakha who was born from that senapati when Indra hurled his vajra at him. You are conversant with the sixty tattvas, the subjects of enquiry in the universe.

You are the Lord of the senses that achieve their respective functions guided by you. You are he that is armed with the thunder-bolt that rives mountains. You are infinite. You are the confounder of the Daitya ranks on the battlefield. You are he that drives his chariot in circles among his own ranks and that makes similar circles among the ranks of his enemies, returning safe after devastating them.

You are he that knows the lowest depth of the world's ocean because of your knowledge of Brahman. You are Madhu, the founder of the vamsa into which Krishna was born. Your eyes are honey-coloured. You are he that has been born after Brihaspati.

You are he that performs the karmas which Adhvaryus do in yagnas.

You are he who is always adored by men of all asramas. You are devoted to Brahman. You wander among the habitations of men in the world as a sannyasi. You are he that pervades all beings. You are he that is conversant with truth. You know and guide every heart. You are he that ranges over the whole universe.

You are he that gathers the good and bad deeds of all creatures in order to award them the fruits of their actions. You are he that lives during even the night that follows the Mahapralaya. You are the protector who wields the bow Pinaka. You dwell even among the Daityas that are the targets of your arrows. You are the source of prosperity.

You are the mighty Hanuman who helped Vishnu in his Rama avatara during his mission to slay Ravana. You are the lord of the Ganas. You are each of those diverse Ganas. You are he that gladdens all creatures. You enhance the joys of all.

You deprive even Indra of his sovereignty and prosperity. You are the universal destroyer in the form of death. You are he that resides in the sixty-four Kaalas. You are the very great. You are the Pitamaha, the father of Brahma. You are the supreme linga that is adored by both Devas and Asuras. You are of benign and beautiful countenance.

You are he who presides over the varied propensities for action and inaction. You are the Lord of sight. You are the Lord of yoga since you withdraw all the senses into the heart and unite them there. You are he that upholds the Krita and the other yugas by causing them to run ceaselessly. You are the Lord of seeds, giving the fruits of all virtuous and base actions. You are the original cause of such seeds.

You act in the ways that have been indicated in the shastras beginning with those that speak of the Atman. You are he in whom dwell rajas and the other gunas. You are the Mahabharata and other itihasas. You are the treatises called Mimamsa. You are Gautama, founder of the science of dialectics. You are the author of the great treatise on grammar named after the moon.

You are he who punishes his enemies. You are he whom none can chastise. You are he who is sincere in religious kriyas. You are he that becomes obedient to those that are devoted to you. You are he who inexorably subjugates all others. You are he who incites wars among the Devas and the Asuras.

You are he who has created the fourteen worlds beginning with Bhu. You are the protector of all beings beginning with Brahma and ending with the lowest forms of vegetation like grass and straw. You are the Creator of the very Panchamahabhutas.

You are he that never enjoys anything for you are always detached. You are free from decay. You are the highest form of felicity. You are a deity proud of his strength. You are Sakra. You are the punishment described in the shastras on dharma and meted out to offenders. You are of the form of that tyranny which prevails throughout the world.

You are of pure soul. You are unstained without any faults. You are worthy of adoration. You are the world that appears and disappears, endlessly. You are he whose grace is infinite. You are he that has good dreams. You are a mirror in which the universe is reflected. You are he that has subdued all internal and external enemies.

You are the Creator of the Vedas. You have made those declarations that are contained in the Tantras and the Puranas and that are embodied in language of humans. You are possessed of profound learning. You are a Parantapa in battle.

You are he that resides in the awesome clouds that appear at the time of the pralaya. You are most fierce as you bring about the dissolution of the universe. You are he who subdues all persons and all things. You are the great Destroyer. You are he that has fire for his energy. You are he whose tejas is mightier than fire. You are the yuga-fire that consumes all things.

You are he that is gratified with sacrificial libations. You are water and other liquids that are offered in yagnas along with the chanting mantras. You take the form of the Dharma, the deity of righteousness, the one who dispenses the fruits that attach to good and bad deeds. You are the giver of felicity. You are always endowed with light. You are of the form of fire. You are of the colour of the emerald. You are always present in the linga. You are the source of blessedness.

You cannot be confounded by anything in the pursuit of your goals. You are the giver of blessings. You are of the form of blessedness. You are he unto whom a share of the havis is always given. You are he who distributes unto each his share of that is offered in sacrifices. You are swift. You are he that is detached from all things. You are he that has the most powerful arms and legs. You are he that is ever engaged in the act of creation.

You are of a dark hue, being of the form of Vishnu. You are of a white colour being of the form of Samba, the son of Krishna. You are the senses of all embodied creatures. You possess enormous feet. You have mighty hands. You have a colossal body. You are widely renowned. You have a great head. You are of vast size.

You are of infinite vision. You are the home of the darkness of ignorance. You are the Destroyer of the destroyer. You are of immense age. You have huge ears. You have a vast mouth. You are he that has ample cheeks. You have a great nose. You have a tremendous throat. You have a gigantic neck. You are he that rends the bonds of the body. You have a deep and immense chest.

You are the inner soul which dwells in all creatures. You have a deer on your lap. You are he from whom countless worlds hang like fruits from a tree. You are he who opens his mouth at the time of the pralaya to swallow the universe. You are the ocean of milk.

You have enormous teeth. You have great vast jaws. You have a dense beard. You have hair of infinite length. You have a gigantic belly. You have matted locks of great length. You are ever cheerful. You are of the form of grace. You are of the form of belief. You are he whose bow and astras are the size of mountains.

You are he that is full of love for all creatures like a parent towards his children. You are he that has no love. You are unvanquished. You are devoted to yoga dhyana. You are of the form of the tree of life. You are he that is symbolised by the tree of the world.

You are never satiated when eating because you are of the form of fire which is never sated with its offerings. Identified with Agni, you are he that has Vayu for your vahana. You are he that ranges over hills and mountains. You are he that lives on the mountains of Meru. You are the king of the Devas.

You have the Atharvans for your head. You have the Samans for your mouth. You have the thousand Riks for your immeasurable eyes. You have the Yajuses for your feet and hands. You are the Upanishads. You are the entire body of rituals in the shastras.

You are all that moves. You are he whose desires are always fulfilled. You are he who is always inclined to grace. You are he of beautiful form. You are of the form of the good that one does to another. You are that which is beloved. You are he that always advances towards your devotees in the proportion as they advance to meet you.

You are gold and other precious metals that are treasured by all. Your radiance is like that of burnished gold. You are the navel of the universe. You are he that makes the fruits of sacrifices grow for the benefit of those that perform yagnas for your glory. You are of the form of that faith and devotion, which the righteous have for sacrifices. You are the Creator of the universe.

You are all that is unmoving in the form of mountains and other inert objects. You are the twelve stages of life through which a person passes. You are he that causes fear by assuming the intermediate states between the stated ten. You are the beginning of all things. You are he that unites the Jiva with Supreme Brahman through yoga. You are that yoga which causes such a union between the Jiva and the Parabrahman.

You are unmanifest, inspiring the deepest awe. You reign over the fourth yuga because of your association with lust, wrath, greed and other evil passions that flow from that Kali. You are eternal Kaala because of your form is that unending succession of births and deaths in the universe.

You are of the form of Kurma, the tortoise. You are worshipped by Yama himself. You live in the midst of your Ganas. You accept your devotees as your Ganas. Brahma himself drives your chariot. You sleep on ashes. You protect the universe with ashes. You are he whose body is made of ashes. You are the tree that grants all desires. You are of the form of those that are your Ganas.

You are the protector of the fourteen realms. You transcend all of them. You are complete without any imperfection. You are adored by all creatures. You are white, pure and stainless. You are he that has an untainted body, speech and mind. You are he who has attained to that purity of existence called mukti. You are he who cannot be sullied by any kind of impurity.

You are he who has been attained by the great ancient acharyas. You dwell in the form of dharma in all the four asramas. You are that dharma which is of the form of kriyas and yagnas. You have the power of the divine Creator of the universe. You are he who is adored as the primeval form of the universe.

You are Mahabaho, of mighty arms. Your lips are of a coppery hue. You are like the vast waters of the ocean. You are steadfast and firm as mountains. You are Kapila. You are brown. You are all the colours which when mixed produce white.

You are the span of life. You are ancient. You are recent. You are a Gandharva. You are the mother of the Devas in the form of Aditi, or the mother of all things in the form of Bhumi. You are Garuda, the prince of birds, also called Tarkshya, born of Vinata and Kasyapa.

You can be understood with ease. You are of excellent and agreeable speech. You are he that is armed with the battle-axe. You are he that is desirous of victory. You are he that helps others to achieve their goals. You are the greatest, closest and best friend.

You are he that bears a vina made of two hollow gourds. You are of terrifying wrath that you display at the time of the Apocalypse. Your children Brahma and Vishnu are beings higher than all Manavas and Devas. You are that form of Vishnu who floats upon the waters after the universal dissolution. You devour all things with great ferocity.

You are he that procreates. You are family and race, continuing from generation to generation. You are the venu nadam, the sound of a bamboo flute. You are faultless. Every limb of your body is beautiful. You are full of illusion. You do good to others without expecting any return.

You are Vayu. You are Agni. You are the bonds of the worlds which bind the Jiva. You are the Creator of those bonds. You are the render of such bonds. You are he that dwells with even the Daityas, the enemies of all sacrifices. You dwell with those that are the adversaries of all action, and with those that have abandoned all karma.

You have large teeth, and you have the mightiest astras. You are he that has been greatly reproached. You are he that astounded the Rishis dwelling in the Daruka forest. You are he that did good even to your detractors, those same Rishis living in the Daruka vana. You are he who dispels all fears and who, in doing so, bestowed mukti on those Rishis. You are he that has no riches as can be seen from your lack of clothes.

You are the Lord of the Devas. You are the greatest of them, being adored by even Indra and other high divinities. You are adored by even Vishnu. You are the slayer of the enemies of the Devas. You are he that, in the form of Sesha, lives in patala.

You are invisible but can be perceived, even as the wind which though invisible is felt by all. You are he whose knowledge extends to the roots of everything, and to whom all things, even in their hidden nature, are known. You are that which is enjoyed by him that enjoys it.

You are he among the eleven Rudras who is called Ajaikapat. You are the sovereign of the entire universe. You are of the form of all Jivas in the universe since you own the three gunas of sattva, rajas and tamas. You are he that is not subject to those three attributes. You are he that transcends all gunas and is a state of pure existence which cannot be described by any adjective that language can yield.

You are Dhanwantari, prince of physicians. You are a comet who brings calamities to the sinful. You are Skanda, the divine senapati. You are Kubera, king of the Yakshas, who is your inseparable companion and the Lord of all treasures in the world.

You are Dhatri. You are Sakra. You are Vishnu. You are Mitra. You are Tvashtri. You are the Dhruvatara. You are he that upholds all things.

You are he called Prabhava amongst the Vasus. You are the wind which goes everywhere, being the Sutratman that connects all things in the universe with a thread.

You are Aryaman. You are Savitri. You are Ravi. You are that ancient celebrated king known as Ushangu. You are he who protects all creatures in diverse ways. You are Mandhatri for you gratify all creatures. You are he from whom all creatures are born. You are he who exists in many forms. You are he who causes the various colours to exist in the universe. You are he who upholds all desires and all attributes because they originate from you.

You are he who has the lotus on your navel. You are he within whose womb are countless mighty creatures. You face is as beautiful as the moon. You are wind. You are fire. You are powerful. You are of serene soul. You are old. You are he that can be known through dharma.

You are Lakshmi. You create the very arena of actions, the karma kshetra through which persons worship the Supreme Deity. You are he who lives in the field of karma. You are the Soul of that field. You are the answer and the cause of the attributes of sovereignty. All things lie in you for, as the Srutis declare, all things becomes one in you, you being of the nature of that unconsciousness which reveals itself in dreamless sleep.

You are the Lord of all creatures endowed with prana. You are the God of the gods. You are he who is grace. In the form of cause you are Sat. In the form of effect you are Asat. You are he who possesses the best of all things. You are he who dwells on the mountains of Kailasa. You are he who repairs to the mountains of Himavat. You wash away all things near you like a mighty river washing away trees and other objects standing on its banks. You are the maker of Pushkara and other large lakes and water bodies.

You possess knowledge of infinite kinds. You are the giver of infinite blessings. You are a merchant who carries the goods of this land to another and brings the goods of that realm to this for the welfare of men. You are a carpenter.

You are the tree that provides the wood for your axe. You are the tree called bakula. You are the chandana, the sandalwood tree. You are the tree called chchanda.

You are he whose neck is powerful. You are he whose shoulders are vast. You are not restless; you are constant in all your actions that ensue from all your powers. You are the principal herbs and crops with their produce, rice, wheat and other grain.

You are he that helps men attain the objects of their desire. You are all the fitting end of the Vedas and Patanjali's grammar. You are he who roars like a lion. You have the fangs of the lion. To journey you ride a lion. Your chariot is drawn by a lion. You are he called the truth of truth.

You are the Destroyer of the universe. You always seek the welfare of the worlds. You are he who rescues all creatures from distress and lead them to moksha.

You are the bird called saranga. You are the young one of a swan. Like a cock or peacock you flaunt your beauty with the crest on your head.

You are he who protects the place where conclaves of the wise sit to dispense justice. You are the abode of all creatures. You are the cherisher of all creatures. You are day and night which are the constituent elements of eternity. You are he that is without fault and therefore never censured.

You are the upholder of all creatures. You are the refuge of all creatures. You are without birth. You exist. You are ever fruitful. You are imbued with dharana and dhyana and Samadhi. You are the steed Uchchaisravas. You are the giver of food. You are he who upholds the life-breaths of living creatures.

You are suffused with patience. You are possessed of fathomless intelligence. You are dexterous and energetic. You are honoured by all. You are the dispenser of the fruits of dharma and adharma. You are the senses and so they succeed in performing their respective functions since you preside over them.

You are the Lord of all the stars. You are all collections of objects. You are he whose garments are of leather. You are he who dispels the sorrow of his devotees. You have a golden arm. You protect the bodies of yogins who seek to enter their own selves. You are he who has reduced all his enemies to nothingness.

You are full of boundless joy. You are he who achieved victory over the irresistible Kamadeva. You are he who has subdued his senses. You are the gandhara in the musical scale. You are he who has a beautiful home which rests upon the delightful Mountain Kailasa. You are he who is ever attached to tapasya. You are of the form of happiness and contentment. You are infinite.

You are he in whose honour the best of mantras has been composed. You are he who dances in long strides and great leaps. You are he who is revered by the diverse tribes of Apsaras. You are he whose standard bears the emblem of the bull. You are the Meru Mountain. You are he who roves among all the peaks of that great mountain. You are so quick that it is difficult indeed to apprehend you.

You can be explained by gurus to their sishyas but cannot be described in words. You are of the form of that teaching which gurus impart to sishyas. You are he that can perceive all fragrances in an instant.

You take the form of the entrances to cities and palaces. You take the form of the moats and ditches that surround fortified towns and enable their besieged forces to be victorious. You are the wind. You take of the form of fortified cities and towns encompassed by walls and moats.

As Garuda, you are the ruler of all winged creatures. You proliferate creation by the union of the two sexes. You are the unsurpassed in dharma and gyana. You are superior to even him who is the first of all in goodness and knowledge. You transcend all morality and knowledge.

You are eternal and unchanging, as also dependent on just yourself. You are the master and protector of the Devas and Asuras. You are the master and protector of all creatures. You are he who wears a coat of armour. You are he whose arms can raze all enemies. You are an object of adoration for Suparvan in swarga.

You are he who grants the power to uphold all things. You are by yourself able to bear all things. You are unchanging and perfectly stable. You are white and perfectly pure, without any stain or blemish. You bear the trident that can destroy all things. You give physical forms to those that constantly revolve in the universe of births and deaths. You are more precious than wealth. As goodness and courteousness, you are the path of the righteous.

You are he who once tore off Brahma's fifth head, not out of anger but careful deliberation. You are he who is marked with all those auspicious marks that are spoken of in the sciences of palmistry and phrenology and other branches of knowledge that regard the physical frame as the indicator of mental attributes. You are the aksha, that wooden axle of a chariot and, therefore, are the one who is attached to the chariot of the body. You are attached to all things by pervading all things as their soul.

You are mighty, a Kshatriya of all Kshatriyas, a hero of heroes. You are the Veda. You are the Smritis, the itihasas, the Puranas, and other shastras. You are the illustrious deity of every sacred shrine. You are he who has the earth for his chariot. You are the inert elements in the composition of every creature. You are he who breathes life into every combination of those inert element. You are Pranava and other sacred mantras that instil life into dead matter.

You are he that casts serene glances everywhere. As the Destroyer, you are stern, even cruel. You are he who has countless precious attributes and possessions. You have a body that is red in colour. All the oceans are as so many pools filled for your drinking.

You are the root of the tree of the world. You are beautiful and shine with unsurpassed grandeur. You are of the form of amrita. You are both cause and effect. As a great yogi, you are an ocean of tapasya. You are he that desires to rise to the highest state of existence. You are he that has already attained to that state. You are he who is distinguished by the purity of his conduct, and his actions and observances. You are he who is renowned for the righteousness of his ways.

In the form of strength and courage, you are the jewel of armies. You are he who is adorned with celestial ornaments. You are Yoga. You are he from whom flows eternal time measured in yugas, manvantaras and kalpas. You are he who moves all creatures from place to place. You are of the form of dharma and adharma and their intermixing as can be seen in the successive yugas. You are great and formless.

You are he who killed the mighty Asura that attacked the sacred city of Varanasi in the form of an irate tusker. You are of the form of death. You grant the wishes of all creatures in accordance with their punya.

You are amiable. You are conversant with all things that are beyond the senses. You are conversant with the tattvas and hence unchanging. You are he who always radiates supernal beauty. You wear garlands that extend from your neck to your feet. You are that Hara who has the moon for his eye. You are the vast ocean.

You are the first three yugas—Krita, Treta and Dwapara. You are he whose appearance benefits others. The shastras, the guru and dhyana are your three eyes. You are he whose forms are very subtle for you are the subtle forms of the primal elements. You are he whose pierced ears are adorned with jewelled kundalas. You are the wearer of matted dreadlocks.

You are the bindu in the alphabet which indicates the nasal tone. You are the visarga, the two dots which denote the sound of the aspirated letters in Sanskrit. You have an incomparable face. You are the shaft that is shot by the warrior to destroy his enemy. You are all the astras used by great warriors.

You have limitless patience to bear all things. You are he whose knowledge has arisen from the cessation of all physical and mental activity. You are he who has become satya with the ending of all the other senses. You are the note which arises from the realm of Gandhara and is melodious to the ear.

You are he who is armed with the mighty bow, the Pinaka. You are he who is the understanding and the desires that exist in all creatures, and also the supreme upholder of all beings. You are he from whom all actions flow. You are that wind which rises at the time of the universal dissolution and which churns the entire universe even as the rod in the hands of the gopis churns the milk in the earthen pot.

You are he that is full. You are he that sees all things. You are the sound that arises from clapping one hand against another other. You are he whose palm serves as the plate from which to eat. You are he who has a body of steel. You are inconceivably great. You are of the form of the chatra, a parasol. You are he who carries a parasol. You are celebrated to be identical with all creatures. You are he who covered the universe with two steps and wanted space for the third one. You are he whose head is without hair. You are he whose form is ugly and fierce. You are he who has undergone infinite modifications and become all things in the universe.

You are he who bears the danda, the sign of sannyasa. You are he who has a kundala. You are he who cannot be attained with deeds. You are he who is identical with the lion, the green-eyed king of beasts. You are of the form of all the points of the compass. You are he who is armed with the thunderbolt. You are he who has a hundred tongues. You are he who has a thousand feet and a thousand heads.

You are the Lord of the Devas. You are he that is comprised of all the Devas. You are the Great Master. You are he who has a thousand arms. You are he who can grant all wishes. You are he whose protection is sought by everyone. You are he who is the Creator of all the worlds. You are he who purifies all from every kind of sin, in the form of shrines and sacred waters. You are he who has three high mantras.

You are the youngest son of Aditi and Kasyapa, the dwarf Upendra, who beguiled the Asura Bali and took from him his sovereignty of the three worlds and restored it to Indra. You are both black and incarnadine, in the form known as Hari-Hara. You are the maker of the Brahmana's danda. You are armed with the satagni, the paasa, and the astra. You are he that was born within the primeval lotus.

You are he who has a cavernous womb. You are he who has the Vedas in his womb. You are he who rises the infinite waters, the Ekarnava which succeeds the Pralaya. You are he who radiates brilliant light. You are the creator of the Vedas. You are he who studies the Vedas. You are he who knows the meaning of the Vedas.

You are devoted to Brahman. You are the refuge of all devoted to Brahman. You are of infinite forms. You host many bodies. You are filled with compelling prowess. You are the Soul that transcends the three universal gunas of sattva, rajas and tamas. You are the Lord of all Jivas.

You have the speed of the wind. You possess the swiftness of the mind. You are always smeared with sandalwood-paste. You are the tip of the stalk of the primeval lotus. You are he who caused the divine cow Surabhi to fall from her superior position by cursing her. You are that Brahma who was unable to see your end, the tip of the first linga of flames.

You are adorned with a large wreath of karnikara flowers. You are adorned with a crown of blue jewels. You are the wielder of the Pinaka. You are the master of that knowledge which deals with Brahman. You are he who has subdued his senses with your knowledge of Brahman. You are he who bears the Ganga on your head.

You are the husband of Uma, the daughter of Himavat. You are powerful, having assumed the form of the Varaha to lift up the submerged earth. You are he who protects the universe by assuming various incarnations. You are worthy of adoration. You are that primeval Being with the equine head who recited the Vedas in a thundering voice. You are he of great felicity.

You are the great conqueror. You are he who has slain all his enemies in the form of passions. You are both white and tawny being as you are half-male and half-female. The colour of your body is like that of gold. You are he that is of the form of pure joy, being, as you are, above the five layers of the Jiva, the anna-maya, the prana-maya, the mano-maya, the vigyana-maya, and the ananda-maya. You are of a restrained soul.

You are the foundation upon which rests that ignorance known as pradhana and which, consisting of the three gunas of sattva, rajas and tamas, is the cause of the emergence of the universe. You are he whose faces are turned in every direction. You are he who has three eyes in the forms of the sun, the moon and fire. You are he who is superior to all creatures in your vast righteousness. You are the Soul of all mobile beings. You are of the form of the subtle soul which cannot be perceived. You are the giver of immortality in the form of mukti as the fruit of all virtuous deeds achieved by creatures without desire of rewards.

You are the acharya of even those that are the Gods of the gods. You are Vasu, the son of Aditi. You are he who is filled with countless rays of light, who brings forth the universe, and who is the Soma which is drunk at yagnas. You are Vyasa, author of the Puranas and other sacred itihasas. Being identical with the Puranas and other itihasas, both long and short, you are the creations of Vyasa's mind. You are the sum of all Jivas.

You are the season. You are the year. You are the month. You are the fortnight. You are those sacred days that end these periods. You are the kaalas. You are the kashtas. You are the lavas. You are the matras. You are the muhurtas and days and nights. You are the kshanas.

You are the soil upon which the tree of the universe stands. You are the seed of all creatures being of the form of that Avyakta Chaitanya, unmanifest consciousness, imbued with maya from which all creatures spring. You are Mahatattva. Being the form of Chit, which appears after Mahatattva, you are the beginning of the jiva. You are Sat or cause. You are Asat or effect. You are manifest, able to be grasped by the senses.

You are the father. You are the mother. You are the Pitamaha. You are the door to swarga because of your tapasya. Because you are desire, you are the beginning of the generation of all creatures. And because you are the absence of desire, which alone leads to uniting with Brahman, you are the door to moksha. You are those acts of dharma which lead to the felicity of heaven. You are nirvana, that cessation of individual or distinct existence, which is mukti.

You give joy to every creature. You are that realm of satya which the righteous attain. You are superior to even that realm of truth. You are he who is the Creator of both the Devas and the Asuras. You are he who is the refuge of both the Devas and the Asuras. You are the guru of both the Devas and the Asuras, being as you are both Brihaspati and Sukra.

You are he who is ever victorious. You are he who is ever worshipped by the Devas and the Asuras. You are he who guides the Devas and the Asuras even as the mahamatra guides the elephant. You are the refuge of all the Devas and the Asuras, You are he who is the Lord of both the

Devas and the Asuras being both Indra and Virochana. You lead both the Devas and the Asuras in battle, being both Kartikeya and Kesi who lead their armies.

You are he who transcends the senses and excels by himself. You take the form of the Devarishis like Narada and the others. As Brahma and Rudra you grant boons to the Devas and Asuras. You are he who rules the hearts of the Devas and the Asuras. You are he into whom the universe enters when it is dissolved. Thus you are the refuge of even he who rules over the hearts of both the Devas and the Asuras. You are he whose body is made up of all the deities.

No being is superior to you. You are he who is the inner soul of the gods. You are he who has sprung from his own self. You are of the form of immobile things. You are he who covers the three worlds with three strides. You possess vast knowledge. You are without blemish. You are he who is freed from rajas. You are he who transcends destruction.

You are he in whose honour mantras must be chanted. You are the master of the inexorable elephant represented by Kaala. You are that Lord of tigers who is worshipped in the kingdom of the Kalingas. On account of your great strength, you are he who is called the lion among the gods. You are he who is the foremost among men.

You are filled with great wisdom. You are he who takes the first share of the offerings at yagnas. You are invisible. You are the sum of all the Devas. You are he in whom penances prevail. You always excel in yoga. You are auspicious. You are armed with the vajra. You are the source of the origin of the astras called paasas, the nooses. You are he whom your devotees attain to in diverse ways. You are Guha. You are the supreme limit of grace.

You are identical with your creation. You are he who rescues all creatures from death by liberating them. You purify all, including Brahma himself. You take the form of bulls and other horned animals. You are he who delights in mountain peaks. You are the planet Sani. You are Kubera, Lord of the Yakshas. You are perfection without flaw.

You are he who inspires happiness. You are all the gods united. You are the cessation of all things. You are all the duties of all the asramas. You are he who has an eye on his forehead. You are he who sports with the universe for his marble ball. You take the form of deer. You have the energy that is of the form of gyana and tapasya. As Himavat and Meru you are the Lord of all immobile things.

You are he who has subdued his senses with rules and vows. You are he whose aims have all been fulfilled. You are identical with mukti. You are different from him whom we worship. You have truth for your penances. Your heart is pure.

You are he who presides over all vratas and upavasas, being the giver of their fruits. You are the highest as you take the form of Turiya. You are Brahman. You are the highest refuge of devotees. You are he who transcends all bonds. You are freed from the linga sarira. You are filled with every kind of prosperity. You are he who enhances the wealth of your devotees. You are that which changes unceasingly.'

Krishna, I have now sung the praises of the illustrious deity, reciting his names in the order of their importance. Who is there that can sing the praises of the Lord of the universe, that great Lord of all who deserves our adorations and worship and reverence, whom the very gods with Brahma at their head are unable to adequately praise and whom the Rishis also fail to extol.

With my devotion and his leave, I have praised that Lord of sacrifices, that Supreme Deity, that wisest of all creatures. By reciting these auspicious names of the great and blessed One, a worshipper of devoted soul and pure heart succeeds in attaining his own Atman.

These names constitute a mantra that is the best means of attaining Brahman. With these one is sure to attain mukti. The Rishis and the Devas all praise the Highest Deity with this mantra. Sung by men of restrained soul, Mahadeva is pleased with them.

The illustrious deity is always full of compassion towards his devotees. He is omnipotent and grants moksha to those that worship him. So also the best among men, that possess faith and devotion, hear and recite for others and utter with reverence the praises of that highest and eternal

Isana, in all their successive lives and adore him in thought, word and deed, and adoring him thus at all times, while lying or seated or walking or awake or while opening their eyes or shutting them, and thinking of him repeatedly, come to be revered by other men and derive great gratification and happiness.

When a creature is cleansed of all his sins in the course of millions of births, in diverse varnas, it is then that devotion springs up in his heart for Mahadeva. It is through good fortune alone that undivided devotion to Bhava who is the original cause of the universe wells up in the heart of one that knows every way of worshipping him.

Such flawless and pure devotion to Rudra, which has singleness of purpose and that is irresistible in its course, is seldom to be found among even the Devas, and never among men. It is through the grace of Rudra that such devotion arises in the hearts of Manavas. As a result of such bhakti, identifying themselves wholly with Mahadeva, men attain to the highest success.

The illustrious deity who always blessed those that seek him with humility, and surrender themselves completely to him, rescues them from samsara. Except for him who frees creatures from rebirth, all other gods only efface men's tapasyas, for men are powerless before such great power.

In this manner, Tandi of tranquil soul, resembling Indra himself in splendour, praised the illustrious Lord of all existent and non-existent things, that great deity clad in animal skins. Indeed, Brahma once sung this hymn, the Siva Sahasranama in the presence of Sankara. You are a Brahmana for you are yourself conversant with Brahman and devoted to those conversant with Brahman. You will thus understand it well. This great stotra purifies, and washes away all sins. It confers yoga and mukti, and heaven and contentment.

He who recites this mantra with undivided devotion to Sankara succeeds in attaining to that high end which is theirs that are devoted to the doctrines of the Samkhya philosophy. That worshipper who recites this every day for one year with single-minded devotion succeeds in obtaining the end that he desires.

This hymn is a great mystery. It originally dwelt in the heart of Brahma. Brahma imparted it to Sakra. Sakra gave it to Mrityu. Mrityu imparted it unto the Rudras. From the Rudras, Tandi received it. Indeed Tandi acquired it in the realm of Brahma as reward for his severe austerities. Tandi gave it to Sukra, and Sukra of Bhrigu's race taught it to Gautama.

Gautama in his turn communicated it to Vaivaswata Manu. Manu communicated it to Narayana who was a sadhya and loved by him. The illustrious and glorious Narayana, gave it to Yama. Vaivaswata Yama communicated it to Nachiketa.

Nachiketa taught it to Markandeya. I had it as the reward for my vratas and upavasas from Markandeya. To you, O Parantapa, I give that mantra unheard by others. This mantra leads to swarga. It dispels sickness and bestows a long life. This is worthy of the highest praise, and is consistent with the Vedas.'"

Krishna continues, 'Arjuna, he who recites this awesome hymn with a pure heart while observing brahmacharya, and with his senses under control, consistently for a full year, succeeds in obtaining the fruits of an Aswamedha yagna. Danavas, Yakshas, Rakshasas, Pisachas, Yatudhanas, Guhyakas and Nagas cannot harm him.'"

Vaisampayana said, "After Krishna has finished, Mahayogi Vyasa says to Yudhishtira, 'My son, recite this mantra of the thousand and eight names of Mahadeva, and let Siva be gratified with you. In the past, I performed severe austerities on the mountains of Meru to have a son. I chanted this very mantra and my wish was granted. By doing the same, obtain from Sarva the fruition of all your wishes.'

After this, Kapila, the Rishi who spread the Samkhya doctrines, and who is honoured by the Devas themselves, says, 'I have worshipped Bhava with great bhakti for many lives. The illustrious deity was at last gratified with me and gave me the knowledge that enables men to free themselves from rebirth.'

The Rishi Charusirsa, who is Indra's loving friend, otherwise known as Alampana, says, 'In former days, I went to the Gokarna Mountains and performed a severe tapasya for a hundred years. As the reward for my penance, I had a hundred sons from Sarva, all of whom were born without sexual union with any woman; they were of restrained soul, righteous, possessed of great splendour, free from disease and sorrow, and endowed with lives of more than a hundred thousand years.'

The illustrious Valmiki says to Yudhishtira, 'Once upon a time, in course of a dialectical argument, some Rishis who possessed the homa fire accused me of killing a Brahmana. As soon as they had denounced me in this manner, the sin of Brahmahatya possessed me. To purify myself,

I sought the protection of the sinless Isana of overpowering tejas. I was cleansed of all my sins. That dispeller of sorrows, the destroyer of the triad city of the Asuras, said to me, 'Your fame shall be great in the world.'

Jamadagni's son Rama, foremost of all righteous men, shining like the sun in the midst of that gathering of Rishis, says to Yudhishtira, 'I was afflicted by the same sin for having killed my brothers who were all learned Brahmanas. To purify myself, I sought the protection of Mahadeva. I sang the praises of the great deity by reciting his names. Bhava became gratified with me and gave me a battle-axe and many other celestial astras.

And he said to me, "You will be freed from sin and invincible in battle; Yama himself shall not succeed in vanquishing you, for you will be freed from disease." Thus did the illustrious and crowned deity of auspicious form speak to me. Through his grace I obtained all that he had said.'

Viswamitra says, 'I was once a Kshatriya. I worshipped Bhava with the desire of becoming a Brahmana. Through the grace of that great deity I attained the high status of a Brahmarishi that is so difficult to obtain.'

The Rishi Asita-Devala says to the royal son of Pandu, 'Once, through the curse of Sakra, all the punya I had accumulated through my righteous deeds was destroyed. It was the puissant Mahadeva who gave me back that merit together with fame and a long life.'

The illustrious Rishi Gritsamada, also Indra's dear friend who resembled the Devaguru Brihaspati himself in splendour, says to Yudhishtira, 'In antique times Sakra performed a yagna extending over a thousand years. During that sacrifice, Sakra engaged me to recite the Samans.

Vasishta, the son of that Manu who sprung from the eyes of Brahma, came to that yagna and said to me, "Dvijottama, you are not singing the Rathantara properly. Do not find sin like this, and chant the Samans correctly. Ah, why do you commit such a sin as despoils the yagna?"

Having said these words, the Rishi Vasishta gave way to his anger and said to me, "I curse you to become an animal devoid of intelligence, always subject to grief, ever fearful, and an inhabitant of pathless forests without wind and water, and abandoned by other creatures. I condemn you to live thus for ten thousand years, and another eighteen hundred more. That forest in which you will pass this period will have no sacred trees and will be the haunt of Rurus and lions. You will have to become a cruel deer plunged into sorrow."

As soon as he had said these words, I was transformed into a deer. I then sought the protection of Maheswara. The great deity said to me, "You will be freed from all disease, and immortality shall be yours. You will never be afflicted by any anguish. Your friendship with Indra will remain unchanged, and may both Indra and your sacrifices multiply."

The puissant Mahadeva favours all creatures in this way. He is always the great dispenser and ordainer of the joy and sorrow of all living creatures. That illustrious God cannot be grasped by thought, word or deed. Best of warriors, through the grace of Mahadeva, there is none that is equal to me in learning.'

After this, Krishna speaks again, 'Mahadeva of golden eyes was gratified by my tapasya. Pleased he said to me, "Krishna, through my grace, you will be cherished more than wealth that is coveted by all. You will be invincible in battle. Your tejas will equal that of Agni's."

On that occasion, Mahadeva granted me thousands of other boons. In another former birth, I adored Mahadeva on the Manimanta Mountain for millions of years. Gratified, the illustrious deity said to me, "Blessed be you, ask me for any boons you desire."

Bowing to him, I said, "Isana, if the puissant Mahadeva has been gratified with me, then let my devotion to him be eternal! This is the boon that I ask." Mahadeva said to me, "Be it so", and disappeared.'

Jaigishavya says, 'Yudhishtira, once in the city of Varanasi, Mahadeva sought me and conferred upon me the eight attributes of sovereignty.'

Garga says, 'Son of Pandu, pleased with me because of a great mental sacrifice that I performed, Siva bestowed upon me, on the banks of the sacred Saraswati, that wonderful science, the knowledge of Kaala with its sixty-four branches. He also bestowed upon me a thousand sons, all with equal merit and all masters of the Vedas. Through his grace, our lives were expanded to ten million years.'

Parasara says, 'In a previous Manvantara, I gratified Sarva. At the time, I wanted a son with great ascetic punya, endowed with superior tejas, given to high yoga, who would earn world-wide fame, arrange the Vedas, and become a repository of prosperity; who would be devoted to the Vedas and the Brahmanas, and be distinguished for his compassion. Even such a son did I ask for from Maheswara.

Knowing that this was my heart's desire, Mahadeva said to me, "I will grant your wish and you will have a son named Krishna. In that Manvantara, which will be known as Savarni Manu, that son of yours will be reckoned among the seven Rishis. He will divide and re-arrange the Veda, and be the propagator of Kuru's race. In addition, he will be the author of the ancient itihasas and do great good to the universe. Blessed with austere tapasya, he will be a loving friend of Sakra. Free from diseases of every kind, that son of yours will be immortal."

Having said these words, the Great Deity vanished. Even such is the good, Yudhishtira, that I have obtained from that indestructible and immutable God, of the highest penances and supreme energy.'

Mandavya says, 'In former times, though I was not a thief, I was wrongly suspected of theft and was impaled on a stake on the orders of a king. I then worshipped Mahadeva who said to me, "You will soon be freed from this impalement and live for millions of years. Meanwhile, you will not experience any pain. You will also be freed from every kind of affliction and disease. And since your body has sprung from the fourth foot of Dharma, you will be unrivalled on earth. Make your life fruitful. Without any obstacles, you will be able to bathe in all the sacred tirthas of the earth. And after your body decays, I you will enjoy the pure felicity of swarga for all eternity."

Having said these words, Maheswara of unrivalled splendour and clad in animal skin, disappeared with all his Ganas.'

Galava says, 'Formerly, I studied at the feet of my guru Viswamitra. Taking his leave, I set out for home to see my father. But he had died and my sorrowing mother, weeping bitterly, said to me, "Alas, your father will never see his youthful son who, adorned with Vedic knowledge, filled with self-restraint, has been allowed by his guru to come home."

Hearing these words of my mother, I despaired of ever seeing my father again. I worshipped Maheswara with a rapt soul; He was gratified, revealed himself to me and said, "Your father, your mother, and you will all be freed from death. Go and enter your home without delay; you will find your father there."

Yudhishtira, hearing this from Siva and paying him homage, I left for home and saw my father appear before me after having completed his daily yagna. He came out bearing in his hands some homa, some kusa grass and some fallen fruits. And he seemed to have already eaten, for he had washed himself. Throwing down what he carried, shedding tears of joy, my father raised me up, for I had prostrated myself at his feet.

Embracing me he sniffed the top of my head and said, "It is my good fortune to see you again. You have returned, having acquired knowledge from the guru."'"

Vaisampayana continued, "Hearing of these wonderful feats of Mahadeva recited by the sannyasis, the son of Pandu is amazed. Then Krishna speaks once more to Yudhishtira, like Vishnu speaking to Puruhuta.

Krishna says, 'Upamanyu, who seemed to blaze with lustre like the sun, said to me, "Men that are stained with sin do not succeed in attaining to Isana. Their dispositions being tainted by rajas and tamas, they can never approach the Supreme Deity. It is only those evolved men of pure souls that succeed in attaining to him.

Even if a man lives in the enjoyment of every pleasure and luxury, he is regarded as equal to a vanaprastha of cleansed soul if he be devoted to the Supreme Deity. If Rudra be gratified with a person, he can confer upon him the states of Brahma or Krishna, or of Sakra above all the Devas, or the sovereignty of the three worlds. Men who worship Bhava even inwardly succeed in freeing themselves from all sins and attain a place in swarga with the Devas.

One who razes homes to the ground and destroys tanks and lakes, why, one who destroys the whole universe is not stained with sin if he adores and worships Mahadeva. One who is without any auspicious sign and is stained by every sin has all his sins washed away by meditating on Siva. Even worms, insects and birds that devote themselves to Mahadeva range fearlessly.

This is my firm conviction that those men who devote themselves to Mahadeva Siva are certainly liberated from rebirth.'"

After this, Krishna again says to Yudhishtira, 'Aditya, Chandra, Vayu, Agni, swarga, Bhumi, the Vasus, the Viswedevas, Dhatri, Aryaman, Sukra, Brihaspati, the Rudras, the Saddhyas, Varuna, Brahma, Sakra, Maruts, the Upanishads that deal with knowledge of Brahman, satya, the Vedas, the yagnas, dakshina given during sacrifices, Brahmanas reciting the Vedas, Soma, the Sacrificer, the havis of the Devas or ghee poured in yagnas, raksha, diksha, have all sprung from the Creator of all creatures.

All kinds of restraints in the form of vows and fasts and other rigid observances, swaha, vashat, the Brahmanas, the divine cow, the foremost acts of dharma, the wheel of Kaala, strength, fame, self-restraint, the steadfastness of all intelligent men, all deeds of goodness and their opposite, the Saptarishis, Buddhi, all kinds of excellent touch, the success of all religious acts, have emerged from him.

The diverse tribes of the Devas, those beings that drink Agni, those that are drinkers of Soma, clouds, Suyamas, Rishitas, all creatures having mantras for their bodies, Abhasuras, those beings that live upon just scent, those that live upon sight only, those that restrain their speech, those that restrain their minds, those that are pure, those that can assume diverse forms through yoga have been born from that Creator.

Those Devas that live on touch for their food, those that subsist on vision and those that subsist upon the ghee poured in sacrifices, those beings that can create with their wills whatever they want, they that are regarded as the foremost ones among the Devas, and all the other deities, the Suparnas, the Gandharvas, the Pisachas, the Danavas, Yakshas, the Charanas, and the Nagas have been born from him.

All that is gross and all that is subtle, all that is soft and all that is not, all sorrows and all joys, all sorrows that come after joy and all joy that comes after sorrow, the Samkhya philosophy, yoga, and that which transcends objects that are regarded as foremost and superior, all objects of veneration, all the Devas, and all the Viswadevas of the universe who, entering into the physical forces, sustain and uphold this ancient creation of that illustrious deity have sprung from that Creator of all creatures.

All this that I have said is grosser than that which the wise perceive with the help of tapasya. Indeed, that subtle Brahman is the source of life. I bow my head in reverence to It. Let that immutable and indestructible master, always adored by us, grant us desirable boons.

That man who, subduing his senses and purifying himself, recites this mantra, without interruption for one month, succeeds in acquiring the merit that is attached to an Aswamedha yagna. By reciting this the Brahmana succeeds in acquiring all the Vedas; the Kshatriya becomes crowned with victory, O son of Pritha; the Vaisya succeeds in gaining wealth and cleverness; and the Sudra, in winning happiness here and a good end hereafter.

Famed men, by reciting this prince among mantras, the Siva Sahasranama, the thousand and eight holy names of Mahadeva, sacred and able to purify all sins, set their hearts on Rudra. By chanting this best of mantras a man succeeds in living in swarga for as many years as there are pores on his body.'"

CANTO 19

"Yudhishtira says, 'Lord of the Bharata vamsa, what is the origin of the adage that, during the grihastasrama, when married, the husband and wife must perform all duties together? Does that saying refer to discharging all karmas together, due only to what is laid down by the great Rishis in ancient times, or does it refer to the duty of begetting children from religious motives, or has it reference only to carnal pleasure?

My mind is greatly troubled by this matter. In my opinion, what the Rishis have spoken of as joint duties is incorrect. That which in this world is called the union to discharge all duties together ceases with death and is not to be seen to continue in the next. This union to discharge all karmas together leads to swarga.

But swarga is attained by persons that are dead. Of a married couple it is seen that only one dies at a time. Where does the other remain? Do you tell me this.

Men attain to diverse kinds of fruits by practising diverse kinds of karmas. The occupations of men also are of many kinds. Diverse, again, are the narakas to which they go based on this diversity of dharma and karma. Women, in particular, the Rishis have said, are deceitful. When human beings are such, and when women in particular have been declared to be false, how can there be a union between the sexes for the purpose of discharging all duties together?

In the very Vedas one may read that women are untrue. The word dharma, as used in the Vedas, seems to have been coined in the first instance for general application. Hence applying that word to the rites and life of marriage, where it has no real relevance, is erroneous.

I cannot understand this although I constantly reflect upon it. Pitamaha, it is fitting for you to expound this to me in detail, clearly and according to what has been laid down in the Sruti. In fact, explain to me what its characteristics are, and the way in which it has come to be.'

Bhishma says, 'In this regard is cited the old story of the discourse between Ashtavakra and the woman known by the name Disa. In earlier days, Ashtavakra wished to marry and begged the Mahatman Rishi Vadanya for his daughter. Her name was Suprabha.

She was matchless in beauty. In virtues, dignity, conduct and manners, she was superior to all others. With a mere glance, she of the beautiful eyes had robbed him of his heart even as a delightful garden adorned with flowers does in spring.

The Rishi said to Ashtavakra, "Yes, I shall bestow my daughter on you. But first make a journey to the sacred north. You will see many things there."

Ashtavakra said, "Tell me what I shall see in that region. Indeed, I am ready to obey whatever command you give me."

Vadanya said, "Passing over the dominions of Kubera you will cross the Himavat Mountains. You will then behold the Kailasa Mountain on which Rudra dwells. It is inhabited by Siddhas and Charanas. It abounds with the Ganas of Mahadeva, of diverse forms, playful and lovers of dance.

It is also inhabited by many Pisachas of diverse forms and all covered with fragrant colourful powders, and dancing with joyful hearts accompanied by different kinds of instruments. Mahadeva dwells there, surrounded by these who move swiftly in the mazes of the dance or refrain at times altogether from forward, backward or transverse movement of every kind.

We have heard that he and his Ganas are always present in this delightful place on the Rudra Mountain. It was there that the goddess Uma performed the severest tapasya for the sake of acquiring Siva for her lord. Hence, it is said, that place is loved by both Mahadeva and Uma.

In ancient days, on the heights of the Mahaparswa Mountains, which lie to the north of these sacred mountains, many Devas and also the foremost of Manavas adored Mahadeva.

You will cross that realm on your northward journey. You will then see a beautiful blue forest resembling a mass of clouds. There, in that forest, you will see a beautiful female ascetic who looks like Sree herself. Venerable in age and highly blessed, she is in the observance of Diksha. When you see her, you must duly worship her.

After you have seen that Devi, you will return here and marry my daughter. If you are willing to do this, proceed on your journey and do as I have said."

Ashtavakra said, "So be it. I will do your bidding. I will go to that realm of which you speak. On your part, be true to your given word."

The illustrious Ashtavakra set out on his journey. He went towards the north and at last reached the Himavat Mountains peopled by Siddhas and Charanas. Arriving there, he came upon the sacred river Bahuda whose waters produce great punya. He bathed in one of its delightful tirthas in clear water, and worshipped the Devas with offerings of water.

His ablutions completed, he spread some kusa grass and lay down to rest awhile. Passing the night in this way, the Brahmana rose with the dawn. He once more performed his ablutions in the sacred waters of the Bahuda and then lit his homa fire and worshipped it with Vedic mantras.

He then worshipped both Rudra and Uma with appropriate kriyas, and rested for some more time on the shore of a lake in the Bahuda. Refreshed, he set off from there towards Kailasa.

He saw a golden gate ablaze with beauty. He saw also the Mandakini and the Nalini of the Mahatman Kubera. Seeing him arrive, all the Yakshas and Rakshasas with Manibhadra at their head, who protected that lake covered with unworldly lotuses, came out all together to welcome and honour the renowned traveller. In return the Rishi worshipped those beings of awesome strength and asked them to report his arrival to Kubera.

The Rakshasas said to him, "Without waiting for the news from us, King Vaisravana is coming into your presence of his own accord. He knows well the objective of your journey. Behold that blessed master, radiant with his own energy."

Then Kubera Vaisravana approached Ashtavakra and asked after his wellbeing. After these polite inquiries, the Lord of treasures said to the regenerate Rishi, "You are welcome here. Tell me what it is that you seek from me. I will do what you bid me to accomplish. Do you enter my abode as you like. Duly entertained by me, and after your business is complete, you may go without any hindrance."

Having said these words, Kubera led the Brahmana into his palace. He offered him his own throne and also padya to wash his feet and the customary arghya. After the two had taken their seats, the Yakshas of Kubera, led by Manibhadra, and many Gandharvas and Kinnaras, sat down before them.

After all of them had taken their seats, Kubera said, "Understanding what you desire, the Apsaras will dance for your pleasure. It is right for me to entertain you and you must be served with proper care."

Sannyasi Ashtavakra said in a sweet voice, "Let the dance begin."

Then Urvara and Misrakesi, Rambha and Urvasi, Alambusha and Ghritachi, Chitra, Chitrangada and Ruchi, and Manohara, Sukesi and Sumukhi, Hasini and Prabha, and Vidyuta, Prasami and Danta, and Vidyota and Rati, and many other exquisite Apsaras began to dance. And the Gandharvas present played on diverse musical instruments—music that made the heart soar and time stand still.

The Rishi Ashtavakra passed a full celestial year there in the abode of Lord Vaisravana and he never knew how much time had passed while he listened to that music and watched the dance.

Then Vaisravana said to the Rishi, "Learned Brahmana, behold, a little more than a year has passed since you came here. This music and dance, especially known as Gandharva, is a stealer of the heart and of time. Do as you wish or let this continue if that be your pleasure. You are my guest and, therefore, worthy of worship. This is my house. Command us. We are all bound to you."

Ashtavakra, greatly pleased, replied, "I have been duly honoured by you. I now wish to leave. I am pleased beyond all measure. All this befits you. Through your grace, and in accordance with Rishi Vadanya's command, I will now proceed to my journey's end. May you prosper, O Lord Kubera!"

Saying this, the Rishi left Kubera's abode and went northwards again. He crossed the Kailasa and the Mandara Mountains as also the golden Meru. Beyond those great mountains lay the realm where Mahadeva lived as a humble ascetic. With utmost concentration and reverence, the sage bowed and circled that place.

Descending again from that auspicious place, he now considered himself sanctified as he had seen that sacred abode of Mahadeva. Having circled that mountain three times, the Rishi, with his face still turned towards the north, went on with a joyful heart.

He saw another forest that was delightful in every respect. It was adorned with the fruits and roots of every season, and it resounded with the music of thousands of birds. There were many delightful groves throughout the forest. The illustrious Rishi then saw a pleasing hermitage.

Ashtavakra also saw many golden mountains in diverse forms, decked with precious stones. In the bejewelled earth he also saw many lakes and tanks. And he saw other marvels and, seeing these, his mind was filled with bliss.

He then saw a magnificent palace made of gold and adorned with jewels. It surpassed the place of Kubera himself in every way. Surrounding it were many mountains of precious stones. There were also many shimmering chariots and piles of jewels.

The Rishi saw the river Mandakini whose waters were strewn with countless mandara flowers. Luminous gemstones and especially diamonds were strewn everywhere across the grounds.

The palace contained many vast halls and chambers whose arches, too, were embellished with various kinds of precious stones. These were also adorned with filigree nets of pearls interspersed with many other fine jewels. Many unearthly sights that captivated the heart and the eye surrounded that palace. That delightful asrama was inhabited by numberless Rishis.

Beholding these sights all around, the Rishi began to think of where he would take shelter. He reached the palace gate and said, "Let those that live here know that a guest has come asking for shelter."

Hearing the Rishi's voice, many young girls came out together from that palace. Seven in number, they were of different kinds of beauty, each one lovelier than the next. Every one of those maidens stole the Rishi's heart. With his best efforts, the sage could not control his mind. Indeed, his heart lost all its serenity.

Observing himself succumbing to such wild emotions, the Rishi made a determined effort and, being wise, finally succeeded in controlling himself. The women said, "Let the illustrious one enter."

Curious about those maidens and about that palatial mansion, the regenerate Rishi entered as he was told. Going in, he saw an old woman in a state of decay, attired in white robes and adorned with every kind of ornament. The Rishi blessed her formally.

The old woman returned his good wishes in a fitting manner. She rose and offered him a seat. Having taken his seat, Ashtavakra said, "Let all the girls go to their chambers. Let only one stay here. That one who remains here must be wise and of tranquil heart. Let all the others leave."

Thus addressed, all of them circled the Rishi in pradakshina and then left the grand hall. Only the old woman remained there. The day quickly passed and night came. The Rishi, seated on a splendid bed, said to the old woman, "Blessed devi, the night deepens. You may go to sleep."

When the Rishi ended their conversation thus, the old woman laid herself down on an ample bed. But soon she rose from that bed and, pretending to shiver with cold she went to the bed of the Rishi. Ashtavakra courteously welcomed her. She stretched out her slender arms and tenderly embraced the Rishi.

Seeing him unmoved as a piece of wood, she was saddened and began to speak. "There is no pleasure, save that which waits upon Kama, which women can derive from a man. I am under the influence of desire and I seek you out. Do you embrace me in return. Be joyful and unite yourself with me. Embrace me, learned one, for I desire you greatly. This union with me is the reward of the stern tapasya that you have performed.

Even at first sight I wanted you. Do you also make love to me. All this wealth, and everything else that you see here, are mine. Along with my heart and body, you will become master of all this. I will satisfy all your wishes. Dally with me in these delightful forests that can fulfil every desire.

I will give you complete obedience in everything, and you can sport with me for your pleasure. We will enjoy every desire, human and divine.

There is no pleasure more agreeable to women than that which she derives from the companionship of a man. Indeed, sexual union with a man is the most delicious fruit of joy that we can reap. When urged by Kama, women become wanton and capricious. At such times, they do not feel any pain, even if they walk over a desert of burning sand."

Ashtavakra said, "'Blessed one, I never approach another's wife. Union with another man's wife is condemned by those conversant with the dharma shastras. I am a stranger to all kinds of pleasure. You should know that I want to marry in order to have children. I swear this by truth itself.

Through these children, righteously acquired, I will go to those realms of felicity which cannot be otherwise attained. Good devi, know what is consistent with dharma and do not attempt to seduce me."

The old woman said, "The very deities of wind and fire and water, or other divinities, are not as agreeable to women as Kama, the god of desire. Women are always drawn to sexual union. Among a thousand women, even among hundreds of thousands, only one may perhaps be found that is devoted to her husband. When under the influence of desire, they do not care for family, father, mother, brother, husband, sons or husband's brother but blindly pursue the path of lust.

Pursuing what they consider happiness, they destroy their families by birth and marriage even as many mighty rivers erode the banks that contain them. The Creator himself had observed these grave faults in women."

Determined to further know the good in women, the Rishi said, "Do not speak to me like this. Yearning springs from affection. Tell me what else I should do."

That woman said, "In time, you will see if I have anything good in me. Live here for some time and I shall regard myself abundantly rewarded."

Yudhishtira, thus addressed by her, the Rishi agreed, saying, "I will live with you in this place as long as I can."

The Rishi looked at the old woman and began to reflect on the matter. He was tortured by his very thoughts. His eyes derived no pleasure from any part of her body. On the other hand, he was repelled by the ugliness of her limbs.

"This woman is definitely the goddess of this palace. Has she been rendered ugly through some curse? I will gradually discover the cause of this." Reflecting thus within himself, and beside himself with curiosity, Ashtavakra passed the next day in some anxiety.

The woman then said to him, "Illustrious one, look at the evening clouds reddened by the setting sun. What can I do for you?"

The Rishi said, "Bring water for my ablutions. Having bathed, I will do my sandhya vandana, restraining my speech and my senses."

CANTO 20

"Bhishma says, 'Thus commanded, the woman said, "Be it so." She brought oil with which to rub the Rishi's body and a piece of cloth for him to wear during the ablutions. Allowed by the ascetic, she rubbed every part of his body with the fragrant oil she had brought. Gently was the Rishi massaged, and when that was over, he went to the room kept for his ablutions. There he sat upon a new and splendid asana.

After Ashtavakra sat, the old woman began to wash his body with her soft hands and tender fingers. One by one, in correct order, she served the Rishi in his ablutions. Between the warm water with which he was washed, and the soft hands that washed him, the Rishi did not realise that the whole night had passed.

Rising from the bath he was astounded. He saw that the sun had risen above the horizon in the east. He asked himself in some amazement, "Is this real or an illusion?" Ashtavakra duly worshipped Surya Deva. This done, he asked the woman what he should do next.

The old woman cooked some food for the sage that was like amrita itself. So delicious was that food that the Rishi could not eat much of it. In partaking that little, the day passed and evening arrived. The old woman asked the Rishi to go to bed and sleep. A marvellous bed was assigned to him and she lay on another one.

At first the Rishi and the old woman lay on different beds, but at midnight she left her own bed and came to his. And lo, now she was young and beautiful in her face and every limb.

Ashtavakra said, "My mind rejects sexual union with one who is another's wife. Leave my bed. Blessed are you; refrain from this of your own accord."

Thus dissuaded by that Brahmana of self-restraint, the woman said to him, "I am my own mistress. You will not earn any sin by taking me."

Ashtavakra said, "Women can never be their own mistresses. It is the opinion of Brahma himself that a woman never deserves to be independent."

The woman said, "Learned Brahmana, I am tormented by desire. You have seen my devotion to you. You incur sin by refusing to meet me lovingly."

Ashtavakra said, "Diverse faults drag away the man that does as he likes. As for myself, I am able to control my desire. O good devi, return to your own bed."

The woman said, "Look, I bow to you, bending my head. It becomes you to show me your grace. O sinless one, I prostrate myself before you; do you become my refuge. If indeed you see such sin in congress with one that is not your wife, I yield myself to you. Do you, O Dvija, take my hand in marriage. You will incur no sin. I tell you truly. Know that I am my own mistress, and if there be any sin in this let it be mine alone. My heart is devoted to you. I am my own mistress. Do you accept me."

Ashtavakra said, "How is it that you are your own mistress? Tell me the reason for this. There is not a single woman in the three worlds that deserves to be regarded as her own mistress. The father protects her while she is a girl. The husband protects her while she is in her youth. Sons protect her when she is old. Women can never be independent as long as they live."

The woman said, "Since my childhood I have adopted the vow of brahmacharya. Do not doubt it. I am still a virgin. Make me your wife, Brahmana, do not destroy my devotion for you."

Ashtavakra said, "As you are inclined to me, so am I inclined to you.

There is this question, however, that should be settled. Can it be that by yielding to my desire I will not break my word given to the Rishi Vadanya? All that here is wonderful. Yet, will it lead to what is truly beneficial? Here is a maiden adorned with fine ornaments and garments. She is exceptionally beautiful. Why did decay cloak her beauty for so long? Now suddenly she looks like a young and most lovely maiden. But there is no knowing what form she may take later.

I shall never swerve from the control which I have over desire and the other passions, or from my contentment with what I already have. It cannot lead to any good if I do so. I will keep myself united with the truth!"

CANTO 21

"Yudhishtira says, 'Tell me why, despite his great tejas, did that woman not fear Ashtavakra's curse? Also, how did Ashtavakra succeed in returning from that place?'

Bhishma says, 'Ashtavakra asked her "How do you change your form as you please? I want to know this and you must not lie to me. Speak truly before a Brahmana."

The woman said, "Best of Brahmanas, wherever you may be, in heaven or on earth, this desire for sexual union is to be found. Now listen with attention to what I have to say. I devised this trial to test you. You have conquered all the worlds for being true to your resolve.

Know that I am the embodiment of the north. You have seen the fickleness of woman. Even old women are tormented by the desire for sexual union. Brahma himself and all the Devas along with Indra have been pleased with you. I know the reason why you have come here.

You have been sent by the Rishi Vadanya, the father of your bride, in order that I may instruct you. In accordance with his wishes, I have already done so. You will return home safely. Your journey back will not be arduous.

You will have the girl you have chosen for your wife. She will bear you a son. I had sought you through desire and you answered me well. The desire for sexual union cannot be transcended in any of the three worlds. But you have achieved that punya; return now to your home.

What else do you wish to hear from me? Ashtavakra, I will tell you anything truthfully. The Rishi Vadanya worshipped me for your sake. I have said all this to you to honour him."

After receiving many further instructions from her, Ashtavakra joined his hands in reverence. He then asked the wonderful woman for her permission to return. Taking her leave, he came back to his own asrama. Resting there for a while, he sought the leave of his kinsmen and friends and went to the Brahmana Vadanya.

Welcomed by Vadanya, the Rishi Ashtavakra narrated all that he had seen during course of his sojourn in the north. He said, "Commanded by you I went to the mountains of Gandhamadana. North of these mountains, I found a devi, who welcomed me courteously. She mentioned you and also instructed me in various matters. Having listened to her I have now returned.

The learned Vadanya said to the Rishi, "Take my daughter's hand with the proper rites and under the proper constellations. You are the best husband I can choose for her."

Ashtavakra said, "So be it" and took the hand of Vadanya's daughter in marriage. Indeed the Rishi was overjoyed. Having taken that beautiful woman for his wife he continued to live in his own asrama, freed from passion of every kind.'"

CANTO 22

"Yudhishtira says, 'Whom do the eternal Brahmanas that keep strict vratas regard as worthy of receiving gifts? Is a Brahmana that bears the signs of a brahmachari regarded as such or even one who does keep brahmacharya?'

Bhishma says, 'Rajan, it has been said that gifts should be made to a Brahmana that observes his svadharma, the duties of his own varna, whether he bears the signs of a brahmachari or not, for both are without blemish.'

Yudhishtira says, 'What blame does an impure man incur, if he makes gifts of sacrificial butter or food with great devotion to Brahmanas?'

Bhishma says, 'Even one without self-restraint becomes, without doubt, cleansed by devotion. Such a man is purified in every act and not with regard to making gifts alone.'

Yudhishtira says, 'It has been said that a Brahmana who is engaged in worshipping the Devas must never be scrutinised. The learned, however, say that a Brahmana's behaviour and ability must be examined with respect to such actions as have reference to the Pitris.'

Bhishma says, 'The actions karmas that have reference to the Devas bear fruit not as a result of the Brahmana who performs the deeds but through the grace of the Devas themselves. Without doubt, those who perform yagnas obtain the punya of those actions through the blessing of the gods. Brahmanas are always devoted to Brahman. The

Rishi Markandeya, one of the greatest Rishis endowed with intelligence in all the worlds, said this in ancient times.'

Yudhishtira says, 'Pitamaha, why are these five types of men regarded highly: he that is a stranger, he that has knowledge of the duties of his varna, he that is connected by marriage, he that is rich in tapasya, and he performs yagnas?'

Bhishma says, 'The first three—strangers, relatives and ascetics, when pure of birth, devoted to religious acts, learning, compassion, modesty, sincerity and honesty, are regarded as fitting. The other two, men of learning and those devoted to sacrifices, when endowed with five of these attributes—purity of birth, compassion, modesty, sincerity and truthfulness, are also held in high regard.

Listen now to me as I tell you the opinions of Bhumi Devi, the Rishi Kasyapa, Agni and the sannyasi Markandeya.

Bhumi said, "As a lump of mud quickly dissolves when cast into the sea, even so every kind of sin disappears in the three high attributes of presiding at yagnas, teaching and receiving dakshina."

Kasyapa said, "The Vedas with their six branches, the Samkhya philosophy, the Puranas and high birth, all fail to save a Brahmana person if he falls away from good conduct."

Agni said, "If a Brahmana who regards himself as learned and is engaged in study seeks to destroy the reputation of others using that knowledge, he falls from dharma, and is regarded as being untruthful. A man of such destructive ways can never attain the realms of grace."

Markandeya said, "If a thousand Aswamedha yagnas and satya were weighed in the balance, I do not know if the former would weigh even half as much as the latter."'

Bhishma continues, 'Having spoken these words, those four, Bhumi Devi, Kasyapa, Agni and Markandeya, each invested with great tejas, left.'

Yudhishtira says, 'If Brahmanas observant of the brahmacharya vrata seek the offerings one makes to one's deceased ancestors in Sraddhas, will the Sraddha be regarded as properly performed, if those offerings are made to such Brahmanas.'

Bhishma says, 'Even if this brahmacharya vrata is practised for the prescribed period of twelve years and a Brahmana has mastered the Vedas and their angas, if a Brahmana himself seeks such offering and eats the same, he is regarded to fall away from his vow. The Sraddha itself, however, is not regarded as tainted in any way.'

Yudhishtira says, 'The wise have said that dharma has many ends and many doors. Pitamaha, tell me what are the definite conclusions in this matter.'

Bhishma says, 'Abstention from injury to others, truthfulness, forgiveness, compassion, self-restraint, and sincerity are the indications of dharma. There are men who roam the earth praising righteousness, but without practising what they preach and engaged all the while in sin.

He who gives gold, jewels or horses to such men has to sink into naraka and to live there for ten years, eating the faeces of those who subsist upon the flesh of dead cows and buffaloes, of base men called Pukkasas, of others that live on the outskirts of cities and villages, of untouchables, and of men that proclaim, under the influence of wrath and folly, the actions and the omissions of others. Those foolish men who do give the offerings made in Sraddhas to a Brahmana observant of the vow of brahmacharya have to descend into realms of untold misery.'

Yudhishtira says, 'Tell me what is superior to brahmacharya? What is the highest indication of virtue? What is the highest kind of purity?'

Bhishma says, 'I say to you that abstention from honey and meat is superior even to brahmacharya. Dharma consists of self-restraint; the best indication of righteousness is renunciation, which is also the highest kind of purity.'

Yudhishtira says, 'When should one practise dharma? When should artha be sought? When should kama be enjoyed? Pitamaha, tell me this.'

Bhishma says, 'One should earn wealth in the first part of one's life. Then should one earn righteousness, and then enjoy pleasure. One should not, however, attach oneself to any of these. One should honour the Brahmanas, worship one's guru and one's elders, show compassion for all creatures, and be of mild disposition and amiable speech. To utter a lie in a court of justice, to behave deceitfully towards the king, to act falsely towards teachers and elders, are considered to be as heinous as killing a Brahmana. One should never be violent towards a king. Nor should one ever strike a cow. Both these offences are equivalent to the sin of foeticide.

One should never abandon one's homa fire. One should also never disregard one's study of the Vedas. One should never attack a Brahmana in word or deed. All these offences are equivalent to Brahmahatya.'

Yudhishtira says, 'What kind of Brahmanas should be regarded as good? What kind of Brahmanas should one make gifts to in order to acquire great punya? What kind of Brahmanas must one feed? Tell me all this, Pitamaha!'

Bhishma says, 'Those Brahmanas that are free from anger, devoted to acts of righteousness, firm in truth, and that practise self-restraint are regarded as good. By making gifts unto them one acquires punya. One wins great merit by making gifts unto Brahmanas who are free from pride, capable of bearing everything, firm in the pursuit of their aims, with a mastery over their senses, devoted to the good of all creatures, and friendly towards all.

One earns punya by making gifts to Brahmanas who are free from greed, are pure of heart and conduct, who possess learning and modesty, are truthful in speech and observant of their svadharma as laid down in the shastras. The Rishis have declared that Brahmana to be deserving of dakshina who studies the four Vedas with all their angas and is devoted to the six duties laid down in the shastras. One acquires great punya by making gifts to Brahmanas possessing these qualities.

The man who makes gifts to a deserving Brahmana multiplies his merit a thousand-fold. A single righteous Brahmana with wisdom and Vedic lore, observant of the dharma and kartavyas laid down in the shastras, distinguished by purity of behaviour, is competent to save a whole vamsa.

One should make gifts of cows, horses, wealth and food to such a Brahmana. By making such gifts one earns great felicity and happiness in the next world. As I have already told you, even one such Brahmana can save the entire vamsa of the giver. What then can I say about the punya of making gifts to many Brahmanas of such attributes?

In making gifts, therefore, one should always judiciously choose the one to whom the gifts are to be made. Hearing of a Brahmana with the proper attributes and respected by all good people, one should invite him to one's home even if he lives far away, welcome him when he arrives and worship him with all one's means.'"

CANTO 23

"Yudhishtira says, 'Pitamaha, I want you to tell me about the laws that have been laid down with regard to the Devas and Pitris on occasions of Sraddhas.'

Bhishma says, 'Having purified oneself by bathing and performing the known auspicious rites, one should carry out all karmas relating to the Devas in the morning, and all those relating to the Pitris in the afternoon. What is given to men should be given at midday with love and reverence. An untimely gift will be appropriated by Rakshasas.

Gifts of articles that have been stepped over by anyone, or been licked or sucked, that which is not given gently or has been seen by menstruating women, do not produce any merit. Such gifts are regarded as the portion belonging to the Rakshasas. Gifts of things that have been announced before many people or from which a portion has been eaten by a Sudra, or that have been seen or licked by a dog, form portions for Rakshasas.

Food which is mixed with hair or in which there are worms, or which has been stained with saliva or which has been gazed at by a dog, or into which tear-drops have fallen or which has been trampled upon must be considered as forming the share of a Rakshasa. Food that has been eaten by one who cannot pronounce Pranava, the AUM, or that has been eaten by a person bearing arms, or that has been eaten by an evil man must be regarded as forming the portion of Rakshasas.

Food eaten by one from which a part has already been eaten by another, or which is eaten without a part being offered to Devas, guests and children, is appropriated by Rakshasas. Such tainted food, if offered to the Devas and Pitris is never accepted by them but is taken by Rakshasas. The food offered in Sraddhas by the three twice-born varnas, in which mantras are either not recited or recited incorrectly, and in which the niyamas laid down in the shastras about distributing to guests are not adhered to, is appropriated by Rakshasas.

Food distributed to guests without having been previously dedicated to the Devas or the Pitris with the aid of libations poured on the sacred fire, which has been stained in by a portion having been eaten by an evil or profane man, should be known to form the share of Rakshasas.

I have told you what the portions are of the Rakshasas. Listen now to me as I explain the rules for ascertaining the Brahmana deserving of dakshina. All Brahmanas that have become outcastes because of committing heinous sins, as also Brahmanas that are fools and madmen, do not deserve to be invited to Sraddhas in which offerings are made to either the Devas or the Pitris. That Brahmana who is afflicted with leukoderma, or he that is lacking in virility, or he that has leprosy, or he that has got phthisis or he that is epileptic with sensory delusions, or he that is blind, must not be welcomed.

Brahmanas that are physicians, those that receive regular pay for worshipping the images of deities established by the rich, or live upon the service of the Devas, those that observe vratas out of pride or other false motives, and those that sell Soma, do not deserve to be invited. Brahmanas that recite the shastras aloud without regard for time or place, or are singers, dancers or players of instruments, or warriors and athletes, do not deserve to be invited.

Brahmanas who pour libations on the sacred fire for Sudras, or who are teachers of Sudras, or are servants of Sudra masters, do not merit an invitation. That Brahmana who is paid for his services as teacher, or who, as a sishya, attends the talks of a guru because of some allowance that is made to him, does not deserve to be invited, for both of them are regarded as merchants of Vedic knowledge. The Brahmana who has been induced to accept the gift of food in a Sraddha at the very start, as also he who has married a Sudra woman, even if he possesses of every kind of knowledge, does not deserve to be invited.

Brahmanas without garhapatya, domestic fire, and they that attend upon corpses, they that are thieves, and they that have otherwise sinned should not be invited to Sraddhas. Brahmanas whose antecedents are not known or are base, and they that are Putrika-putras, do not deserve to be invited on occasions of Sraddhas.

Rajan, that Brahmana who loans money, or he who lives upon the interest of the loans given by him, or he who lives by selling living creatures, does not deserve invitation. Men who have been subordinated by their wives, or they who live by becoming the lovers of unchaste women, or they who abstain from their morning and evening prayers do not deserve to be invited to Sraddhas.

Listen now to me as I tell you about the Brahmana that has been ordained for revering the Devas and the Pitris. Indeed, I will tell you about those merits because of which one may become a giver or a receiver of gifts in Sraddhas, despite all these faults.

Brahmanas that observe of the rites and ceremonies laid down in the shastras, or they that possess punya, or they that chant the Gayatri mantra, or they that are observant of the nitya karmas of Brahmanas, even if they take to farming for a living, can be invited to Sraddhas. If a Brahmana happens to be high-born, he deserves to be invited to Sraddhas even if he is a soldier fighting another's battle.

That Brahmana who takes to trade for a living should be rejected even if he possesses punya. The Brahmana who pours libations every day on the sacred fire, or who dwells in a fixed place, who is not a thief and who is hospitable to guests who arrive at his house, deserves to be invited to Sraddhas. The Brahmana who recites the Savitri mantra morning, noon and night, or who lives on charity, who is observant of the rites and ceremonies laid down in the shastras for those of his varna, deserves to be invited to Sraddhas.

That Brahmana who having earned wealth in the morning becomes poor in the afternoon, or who poor in the morning becomes wealthy in the evening, or who is lacking in malice, or is stained only by a minor fault, deserves to be welcomed at Sraddhas. That Brahmana who is without pride or sin, who is not given to empty argument, or who subsists upon alms obtained as he roams from house to house, deserves to be invited to sacrifices.

One who does not observe vratas, or who is addicted to falsehood in both speech and conduct, who is a thief, or who lives by selling living creatures or by trade in general, only becomes worthy of invitation to Sraddhas if he happens to offer all to the Devas first and subsequently drink Soma. That man who having acquired wealth by dishonest or cruel means but subsequently spends it in adoring the Devas and fulfilling the duties of hospitality, becomes worthy of being invited to Sraddhas.

The wealth that one has acquired by selling Vedic knowledge, or which has been earned by women, or which has been gained by deceit like giving false evidence in a court of law should never be given to Brahmanas or spent in making offerings to the Pitris. That Brahmana, who upon completing a Sraddha refuses to utter the words Astu Swadha, incurs the sin of taking a false oath in a suit for land.

Yudhishtira, the time for performing a Sraddha is when one finds a good Brahmana, and curds and ghrita, and the sacred day of the new moon, and the meat of wild animals such as deer.

Upon the completion of a Sraddha performed by a Brahmana the word Swadha should be uttered. If performed by a Kshatriya the words that should be uttered are: Let your Pitris be gratified. Upon the completion of a Sraddha performed by a Vaisya the words that should be spoken are: Let everything become inexhaustible. Similarly, upon the conclusion of a Sraddha performed by a Sudra, the word that should be uttered is Swasti.

In respect of a Brahmana, the declaration regarding Punyaham should be accompanied with the chanting of AUM. In the case of a Kshatriya, such declaration should be without the chanting of AUM. In the kriyas performed by a Vaisya, instead of AUM, the words that should be uttered are: Let the Devas be gratified.

Listen now to me as I tell you the rites that should be performed for all the varnas. All the karmas called Jatakarma are necessary for the three twice-born varnas. All these rites, Yudhishtira, in the case of Brahmanas, Kshatriyas and Vaisyas, are to be performed using mantras.

The girdle of a Brahmana must be made of munja grass. That of a Kshatriya should be a bowstring. The Vaisya's must be made of the valwaji grass. This is what has been laid down in the shastras.

Listen now as I explain to you what constitutes the merits and faults of both givers and recipients of gifts. A Brahmana becomes guilty of a dereliction of duty by telling lies. Such an act on his part is sinful. A Kshatriya incurs four times and a Vaisya eight times the sin that a Brahmana incurs by uttering a falsehood.

Having been earlier invited by another Brahmana, a Brahmana should not eat elsewhere. By eating at the house of one such, he becomes inferior and even incurs the sin that attaches to the slaughter of an animal on occasions other than those of yagnas.

Also if he eats elsewhere after having been invited by a Kshatriya or Vaisya, he falls from his position and incurs half the sin that attaches to the slaughter of an animal on occasions other than those of sacrifices. That Brahmana who eats on occasions of such rites as are performed in honour of the Devas or the Pitris by Brahmanas and Kshatriyas and Vaisyas, without having performed his ablutions, incurs the sin of uttering a lie about a cow.

That Brahmana who is tempted into eating on occasions of similar rites performed by persons belonging to the three higher varnas, at a time when he is impure as a result of either a birth or a death in his family, knowing well that he is impure, incurs the same sin. He who lives upon wealth obtained under false pretences, like that of pilgrimages to sacred places, or who solicits another for money pretending that he would spend it in religious acts, incurs the sin of lying.

A man who belongs to any of the three higher varnas incurs sin if he distributes food with the help of mantras at Sraddhas to such Brahmanas who do not study the Vedas, or who do not keep vratas, or are impure in their conduct.'

Yudhishtira says, 'Pitamaha, I want to know to whom one should give the offerings dedicated to the Devas and the Pitris in order to earn abundant rewards.'

Bhishma says, 'Yudhishtira, feed those Brahmanas whose wives wait for the leftover food from their husbands' plates, like farmers waiting in reverence for timely showers of rain. One earns great punya by making gifts to those Brahmanas that are always pure in conduct, that are emaciated through abstaining from all luxuries and even full meals, that are devoted to the observances of such vratas that lead to the emaciation of their bodies, and that approach givers with the desire of receiving gifts.

By giving dakshina to such Brahmanas who regard conduct in this light of food, as regard conduct in the light of spouses and children, as regard conduct in the light of strength, as regard conduct in the light of their refuge for crossing this samsara and attaining to felicity in the next, and as seek wealth only when wealth is absolutely needed, one earns great merit. By making gifts to those men who approach you on account of having lost everything to thieves or oppressors, one acquires great punya.

One earns great merit by making gifts unto such Brahmanas who ask for food from the hands of an even poorer person of their varna who has just received something from others. One acquires great punya by making gifts to such Brahmanas who beg for alms after having lost everything in times of universal suffering.

By making gifts to Brahmanas who keep vows, and subject themselves freely to painful rules and practices, are respectful in their conduct to the laws laid down in the Vedas, and seek wealth for spending it upon the karmas necessary to complete their vratas and other observances, one earns great punya. By making gifts to Brahmanas who keep their distance from the ways of the sinful and the evil, are weak and without sufficient support, and are poor in material possessions, one earns great punya.

One earns great merit by making gifts to such Brahmanas who have been robbed of all their possessions by powerful men, and who desire to fill their stomachs with any food without heed for its quality. One earns great punya by making gifts to such Brahmanas who beg on behalf of others that perform tapasya and are satisfied with even small gifts.

You have now listened to the declarations in the shastras in respect of the acquisition of great merit by the giving of gifts. Listen now to those acts that lead to hell or heaven. Yudhishtira, they that lie on occasions other than those when such an untruth is needed to serve the guru or assure the safety of one who fears for his life, sink into naraka.

They who lust after other people's spouses, or have sexual union with them, or assist in such wrongdoing, sink into hell. They who rob others of their wealth, destroy the wealth and possessions of others, or proclaim the faults of others, sink into naraka. They who destroy the troughs of water used by cows to quench their thirst, damage buildings used for public meetings, who destroy bridges and roads, and raze the homes of people, must sink down to hell.

They who deceive helpless women, girls, or old women, or women who have been frightened, find hell for themselves. They who destroy the livelihood of men, they who raze men's homes, they who steal others' wives; they who sow dissension among friends, and they who devastate the hopes of others, fall into naraka. They who declare the faults of others, they who demolish bridges or roads, they who live by doing work not allowed to them, and they who are ungrateful to their friends for help given, have to descend into hell.

They who have no faith in the Vedas and show no reverence for them, they who violate their own vratas or force others into breaking theirs, and they who fall away from their positions through sin, fall into naraka. They who behave improperly, they who are usurious, and they who make unduly large profits on sales, will find hell.

They who gamble or unscrupulously indulge in other depravity, and they who are given to the slaughter of living creatures, have to sink into naraka. They who incite masters to dismiss loyal servants that hope for rewards, or are needy or are earning due wages or are waiting for rewards for valuable services rendered, have to plunge into hell.

They who themselves eat without offering portions to their spouse, their sacred fires, their servants or their guests, and they who abstain from performing the rites laid down in the shastras to honour the Pitris and Devas, have to sink into naraka. They who sell the Vedas, they who find fault with the Vedas, and they who commit the Vedas into writing, have all to descend into hell.

They who are outside the four varnas, they who take to practices forbidden by the Srutis and the Smritis, and they who live by immoral deeds or that do not belong to the varna of their birth, have to sink into naraka. They who live by selling hair, poisons, or milk must go down into hell. They who put obstacles in the path of Brahmanas, cows and women, Yudhishtira, have to descend into hell.

They who sell weapons, they who forge weapons, they who make arrows, and they who make bows, have all to find hell for themselves. They who obstruct paths and roads with stones and thorns and pits must sink into naraka. They who desert teachers and servants and loyal followers for no offence fall into naraka.

They who set young bulls to work, they who pierce the noses of bulls and other animals to control them while they work, and they who always keep animals tied, go to hell. Kings that do not protect their subjects while forcibly taking from them a sixth share of the produce of their fields, and they who, though able and rich, do not give gifts, find hell.

They who reject men who are imbued with forgiveness, self-restraint and wisdom, or those with whom they have associated for many years, when these are no longer of use to them, will surely sink into naraka. Men who eat without giving portions of the food to children, the aged and servants, inexorably descend into hell.

All such men have to go to hell. Listen now to me as I tell you who those men are that ascend into heaven. The man who transgresses against a Brahmana by impeding the rituals with which he worships the Devas is afflicted with the loss of all his children and animals. They who do not transgress against Brahmanas by obstructing their religious rites ascend into swarga.

Men who follow their svadharma laid down for them in the shastras and practise the virtues of charity, self-restraint and truthfulness, find heaven. Men who having acquired knowledge by rendering obedient service to their gurus, and observing austere tapasya are not greedy for gifts, rise into swarga. Men through whom others are saved from fear and sin, poverty and disease, and the difficulties that lie in their path go into heaven.

Men who have a forgiving nature, who are patient, who are prompt in performing all righteous deeds, and who are of auspicious conduct, succeed in gaining swarga. Men who abstain from honey and meat, who abstain from sexual union with the wives of other men, and who abstain from wines and spirits, ascend into heaven.

Men that help establish asramas for sannyasis, who become founders of families, who open up new lands for habitation, and lay out towns and cities, rise into swarga. Men who give away clothes and ornaments, food and drink, and who assist in marriage ceremonies, ascend to heaven.

Men that have abstained from any kind of harm to all creatures, who can endure everything, and who have made themselves the refuge of all creatures, ascend into swarga. Men who humbly serve their fathers and mothers, who have subdued their senses, and who love their brothers, succeed in gaining swarga. Men that control their senses despite being rich in worldly goods, enjoying their youth and power, ascend to heaven.

Men that are kind even towards those that offend against them that have a calm temperament, who have a liking for all who are peaceable, and that contribute to the happiness of others by serving them with humility, surely succeed in finding swarga. Those that protect thousands of people, that make gifts to thousands of people, and that rescue thousands of people from distress, find heaven.

Those who make gifts of gold and of cows, and of chariots and animals, gain swarga. Those who make gifts of articles needed in marriages, and serve men and women, and give clothes and robes, succeed in acquiring heaven.

Men who make public pleasure-houses and gardens and wells, resting houses and halls for public meetings, and tanks for cows and men to quench their thirst, and fields for cultivation, succeed in gaining swarga. Those who make gifts of houses and fields and populated villages to those who want them, do indeed find heaven.

Men who having made sweet and tasty drinks offer them to others, as also seeds and rice, find swarga for themselves. Men, whether born into high or low families, bear hundreds of children and live long lives practising compassion and keeping anger under complete control, succeed in ascending to heaven.

Bhaarata, I have expounded to you the rites in honour of the Devas and the Pitris which are performed for the sake of the other world. I have explained what the laws are for making gifts, and the views of the ancient Rishis with respect to both the items of gift and the manner of giving them.'"

CANTO 24

"Yudhishtira says, 'Bharatarishabha, it is fitting that you answer my next question truly and in detail. What are those circumstances under which a man may become guilty of Brahmahatya without actually killing a Brahmana?'

Bhishma says, 'Rajan, I once asked Vyasa to explain this very subject to me. Listen closely to what Vyasa said to me.

Once, repairing to the presence of Vyasa, I said to him "Maharishi, you are the fourth in descent from Vasishta. Do you explain to me what those circumstances are under which one becomes guilty of Brahmahatya without actually killing a Brahmana."

Vyasa gave me an excellent and assured reply, "You should know a man to be guilty of Brahmahatya who, having invited a Brahmana of righteous conduct to his house to give him alms, subsequently refuses to give anything to him on the pretence of there being nothing in the house. You should know that man as guilty of Brahmahatya who destroys the livelihood of a Brahmana learned in the Vedas and their angas, and who is free of attachments to worldly creatures and goods.

You should know that man to be guilty of Brahmahatya, who prevents thirsty cows from drinking water to quench that thirst. You should regard that man as guilty of Brahmahatya who, without studying the Srutis that have been transmitted from guru to sishya from age to age, finds fault with the Srutis or with those shastras that have been composed by the Rishis. You should know that man as guilty of Brahmahatya who does not give his beautiful and accomplished daughter to a suitable bridegroom.

You should know that foolish and sinful man to be guilty of Brahmahatya who inflicts such grief upon Brahmanas as wound the very core of their hearts. You should know that man to be guilty of Brahmahatya who robs the blind, the lame and fools. You should know that man to be guilty of Brahmahatya who burns down the asramas of sannyasis, or forests, villages or towns."

CANTO 25

"Yudhishtira says, 'It has been said that pilgrimages to sacred rivers are filled with punya; that bathing in such waters is meritorious; and that listening to the cadence of these waters is also most worthy. Pitamaha, I want to hear you speak on this subject. It befits you to tell me about such rivers on this earth.'

Bhishma says, 'Maharishi Angiras has spoken about the sacred tirthas of the earth. If you listen to what he said you will earn great punya.

Once, Gautama approached the great and learned Rishi while he was living in a forest and said to him, "Illustrious one, I have some questions about the merits of sacred waters and shrines. I want to hear you discourse on that subject. Speak to me of this. By bathing in sacred waters on earth, what punya is earned with regard to the next world? Do you expound to me this truly and according to the ordinance."

Angiras said, "A man who bathes for seven days in succession in the Chandrabhaga or the Vitasta, whose waters dance in waves, observing a fast the while, is sure to be cleansed of all his sins and suffused with the punya of a sannyasi. The many rivers that flow through Kasmira plunge into the great river Sindhu. By bathing in these rivers one is sure to become endowed with good character and to rise into swarga after leaving this world.

By bathing in Pushkara, and Prabhasa, and Naimisa, and the ocean, and Devika, and Indramarga, and Swarnabindu, one is sure to fly into swarga in a celestial chariot, filled with joy at the adorations of Apsaras. By diving in the waters of Hiranyabindu with concentration, and revering that sacred stream, and bathing next at Kusesaya and Devendra, one becomes cleansed of all one's sins.

Repairing to Indratoya close to the Gandhamadana Mountains and near Karatoya in the kingdom of Kuranga, one should fast for three days and then bathe in those sacred waters with a contemplative heart and pure body. By doing this, one is sure to acquire the punya of an Aswamedha yagna. Bathing in Gangadwara and Kusavarta and Bilwaka in the Nita Mountains, as also in Kankahala, one is sure to become cleansed of all one's sins and then ascend into heaven.

If one becomes a brahmacharin and subdues one's anger, devotes oneself to truth and practises compassion towards all creatures, and then bathes in the Jala pada, one is sure to acquire the punya of an Aswamedha yagna. The Bhagirathi-Ganga flows in a northward direction from the sangama of swarga, Bhumi and patala.

Fasting for one month and bathing in that sacred tirtha which is known to be loved by Maheswara, allows one to behold the Devas. Even if one has to be reborn, he who gives offerings of water to his Pitris at Saptaganga and Triganga and Indramarga obtains amrita for food. The man who in a pure state of body and mind attends to his daily agnihotra, and observes a fast for one month and then bathes in Mahasrama, is sure to attain success within one month.

By bathing in the Bhrigu Kunda, after an upavasa of three days and purifying the mind of all evil passions, one becomes purified of even the sin of killing a Brahmana. By bathing in Kanyakupa and performing one's ablutions in Balaka, one acquires great fame among the very Devas and shines in glory. Bathing in Devika and the lake known as Sundarika, as also in the tirtha called Aswini, one acquires great beauty in one's next life.

By fasting for a fortnight, and bathing in the Mahaganga and Krittikangaraka, one is cleansed of all one's sins and ascends into swarga. Bathing in Vaimanika and Kinkinika, one acquires the power of going everywhere at will and is highly respected in the celestial realm of the Apsaras. If a man controls his anger, observes the vow of brahmacharya for three days, and bathes in the river Vipasa at the Kalika asrama, he succeeds in transcending rebirth.

Bathing in the grove that is sacred to the Krittikas and offering oblations of water to the Pitris, and then gratifying Mahadeva, one becomes pure in body and mind and rises into heaven. If, observing a fast for three days with a purified body and mind, one bathes in the Mahapura, one is freed from the fear of all mobile and immobile animals as also of all animals having two legs. By bathing in the Devadaru forest and offering oblations of water to the Pitris and dwelling there for seven nights with a pure body and mind, one attains swarga.

Bathing in the waterfalls at Sarastambha and Kusastambha and Dronasarmapada, one is sure to attain to the realm of the Apsaras where they will dutifully serve that man. If one observes a fast and bathes at Chitrakuta and Janasthana and the waters of the Mandakini one is sure to become rich.

By repairing to the Samyasrama, living there for a fortnight and bathing in the sacred river there, one acquires the power of disappearing at will, delighting in the joy that has been ordained for the Gandharvas. Going to the Kausiki tirtha, living there with a pure heart and abstaining from all food and water for three days, one acquires the power of dwelling in the realm of the Gandharvas in one's next life.

Bathing in the delightful tirtha that goes by the name of Gandhataraka and living there for one month, abstaining all the while from food and water, one acquires the power of vanishing at will and then of ascending into swarga after twenty-one days. He that bathes in the Matanga Lake is sure to attain to success in a single night. He that bathes in Analamba or in eternal Andhaka, or in Naimisa, or the tirtha called swarga, and offers oblations of water to the Pitris, while subduing his senses, acquires the punya of a human sacrifice.

Bathing in Gangahrada and the Utpalavana tirtha, and daily offering oblations of water there for a full month to the Pitris, one acquires the punya of an Aswamedha yagna. Bathing in the confluence of the Ganga and the Yamuna as also at the tirtha in the Kalanjara Mountains and offering every day oblations of water to the Pitris for a month, one acquires the punya of ten Aswamedha yagnas. Bathing in the Sashti Lake one acquires merit much greater than what is attached to the gift of food.

Ten thousand tirthas and thirty million other tirthas come to Prayaga at the confluence of the Ganga and the Yamuna in the month of Magha. He who bathes in Prayaga, with a restrained soul and observing rigid vows, in the month of Magha, is purified of all his sins and attains swarga.

Bathing in the tirtha that is sacred to the Maruts, as also in that which is located in the asrama of the Pitris, and also in that which is known by the name Vaivaswata, one becomes cleansed of all one's sins and becomes oneself as pure and sanctified as a tirtha. Going to Brahmasaras as also to the Bhagirathi and bathing there and offering oblations to the Pitris every day for a full month, while abstaining from all food, one is sure to attain to the realm of Soma Deva.

Bathing in Utpataka and then in Ashtavakra and offering oblations of water to the Pitris every day for twelve days in succession, abstaining the while from food, one acquires the punya of an Aswamedha yagna. Bathing in Gaya, in Asmaprishtha and the Niravinda Mountains and Kraunchapadi, one is purified of the sin of Brahmahatya. A bath in the first place cleanses one of a single Brahmahatya; a bath in the second cleanses one of two such evil doings; and a bath in the third cleanses one of three.

Bathing in Kaalapinga, one acquires a large volume of sacred water for use in the next world. By bathing in the city of Agni, a man acquires such merit as entitles him to live during his next birth in the city of Agni's daughter. Bathing in Visala in Karavirapura and offering oblations of water to one's Pitris, and performing one's ablutions in Devahrada too, one becomes identified with Brahma and shines in splendour.

Bathing in Punaravarta-nanda as also Mahananda, a man of restrained senses and universal compassion repairs to Indra's garden, the Nandana, and is waited upon by Apsaras of many kinds. Bathing with concentrated soul in the tirtha named after Urvasi, in the river Lohitya, on the day of full moon of the month of Kartika, one attains to the punya of the Pundarika yagna.

Bathing in Ramahrada and offering oblations of water to the Pitris in the river Vipasa, and observing a fast for twelve days, one becomes cleansed of all sins. Bathing in the Mahahrada tirtha with a pure heart and after observing a fast for one month, one is sure to attain to the end which was that of the Rishi Jamadagni. By exposing oneself to the sun in the tirtha called Vindhya, one devoted to truth and humility, and filled with love for all creatures, should perform austere tapasya.

By so doing, he is sure to attain to ascetic success in the course of a month. Bathing in the Narmada as also in the Surparaka tirtha, observing a fast for a full fortnight, one is sure to become a royal prince in one's next birth. If one goes to the tirtha known as Jambumarga one is sure to attain to success in a single day and night.

By repairing to Chandalikasrama and bathing in the tirtha called Kokamukha, having lived on herbs alone and worn rags for clothes, one is sure to acquire ten beautiful girls for wives. One who lives near the tirtha known as Kanya-hrada will never go to the realms of Yama. Such a man is sure to ascend to the regions of felicity that belong to the Devas.

Mahabaho, he who bathes on the day of the new moon in the Prabhasa tirtha is sure of attaining success and immortality. Bathing in the tirtha known as Ujjanaka in the asrama of Arshtisena's son, and next in the tirtha in the asrama of Pinga, one is cleansed of all one's paapa. Observing a fast for three days and bathing in the tirtha known as Kulya and reciting the sacred Aghamarsana mantras one attains the punya of an Aswamedha yagna.

Observing a fast for one night and bathing in Pindaraka, one becomes purified on the dawn of the next day and attains to the merit of an Agnishtoma yagna. He who goes to Brahmasaras, which is adorned by the forests of Dharmaranya, is purified and attains to the punya of the

Pundarika yagna. Bathing in the waters of the Mainaka Mountain, and saying one's morning and evening prayers there, and living there for a month, subduing one's desires, one attains to the merit of all the great yagnas.

Setting out for Kalolaka and Nandikunda and Uttara-manasa, and reaching a place a hundred yojanas away from them, one becomes cleansed of the sin of killing an embryo in its mother's womb. One who succeeds in obtaining a glimpse of the image of Nandiswara, is cleansed of all paapa. Bathing in the tirtha called Swargamarga one is sure to reach Brahman.

The celebrated Himavat is sacred. That prince of mountains is the father-in-law of Sankara. He is a mine of all jewels and is the home of the Siddhas and Charanas. That twice-born one who is fully conversant with the Vedas and who, regarding this life to be transient, casts off his body on those mountains, while abstaining from all food and water in accordance with the rites laid down in the shastras, after having worshipped the Devas and the Rishis, is sure to attain the eternal Brahman.

Subduing his passions and anger, everything can be attained by him who dwells in a tirtha. In order to journey to all the tirthas in the world, one should think of those that are almost inaccessible or those that are filled with overwhelming difficulties.

Tirtha yatras produce the punya of yagnas. They can purify anyone of sin. Truly excellent, they lead straight to swarga. This subject is a great mystery. The very Devas should bathe in tirthas. They too will be purified."

This discourse on tirthas should be imparted to Brahmanas, and to righteous men who strive to achieve what is truly for their own good. It should also be recited in the hearing of one's well-wishers, friends and devoted disciples. Angiras possessed of great ascetic merit imparted this knowledge to Gautama.

Angiras himself had obtained it from Kasyapa. The great Rishis regard this discourse as worthy of constant repetition. It is the foremost of all purifying things. If one recites it regularly every day, one is sure to be cleansed of every sin and to ascend into heaven after this life. One who listens to it, this great mystery, is sure to be born into a good family in one's next life and, what is more, he will be endowed with a clear memory of his previous life.'"

CANTO 26

Vaisampayana said, "Equal to Brihaspati in intelligence and Brahma himself in forgiveness, resembling Sakra in prowess and Surya in energy, Bhishma, the son of Ganga, of vast power, had been overthrown in battle by Arjuna. Accompanied by his brothers and many other people, King Yudhishtira asks him these questions. The aged warrior lies on a bed of arrows, such as Kshatriyas covet, waiting for that auspicious time when he can leave his physical body.

Many great Rishis have come there to see that foremost one of Bharata's vamsa. Amongst them are Atri and Vasishta, Bhrigu and Pulastya, and Pulaha and Kratu. There are also Angiras and Gotama and Agastya and Sumati, and Viswamitra and Sthulasiras and Samvarta and Pramati and Dama. There, are also Brihaspati and Usanas, and Vyasa and Chyavana and Kasyapa and Dhruva, and Durvasas and Jamadagni and Markandeya and Galava, and Bharadwaja and Raibhya and Yavakrita and Trita.

Sthulaksha and Savalaksha and Kanwa and Medhatithi are present, and Krisa and Narada and Parvata and Sudhanwa and Ekata and Dwita. Nitambhu and Bhuvana and Dhaumya and Satananda and Akritavrana and Rama, son of Jamadagni, and Kacha have come. All these high-souled Maharishis Rishis have come there to Bhishma lying on his bed of arrows.

Yudhishtira, with his brothers, duly worships those Mahatman Rishis, one after another in proper order. Receiving that worship, those Rishis sit on the ground and begin to talk to one another. Their conversation relates to Bhishma, and is sweet and agreeable to all the senses and the mind.

Hearing them speak of him, Bhishma is filled with delight and regards himself to be already in swarga. Then, having taken Bhishma's leave and that of the Pandava princes, those Rishis vanish in a moment from the sight of all the beholders. Even after they have disappeared, the Pandavas repeatedly bow and offer their adorations to those most blessed sages.

They then wait on Bhishma, even as Brahmanas well-versed in mantras wait with reverence upon the rising sun. The Pandavas see the cardinal directions blaze with splendour because of the tejas of the Munis' tapasya and are filled with wonder at the sight. Thinking of the blessedness and puissance of those Rishis, the Pandavas begin to speak again to their Pitamaha. Yudhishtira touches Bhishma's feet with his head and then continues asking his questions about dharma.

Yudhishtira says, 'Pitamaha, which kingdoms, which provinces, which asramas, which mountains, and which rivers are the most holy?'

Bhishma says, 'Listen to the old story of a conversation between a Brahmana who was observing the Sila and the Unccha vratas and a Rishi crowned with hermetic success. Once upon a time, a man who had roamed all the earth arrived at the house of a grihastha who was observing the Sila vrata. The grihastha welcomed his atithi with all the due rites. Received with such hospitality, the happy Rishi spent the night in his host's home.

The next morning the Brahmana completed all his morning ablutions and worship, and having purified himself, cheerfully approached the Rishi. Meeting with each other and seated at their ease, the two began to talk about pleasing subjects connected with the Vedas and the Upanishads.

Towards the end of the discourse, the Brahmana respectfully addressed the Rishi. He asked this very question which you, Yudhishtira, have put to me.

The poor Brahmana said, "What kingdoms, what provinces, what asramas, what mountains, and what rivers should be regarded as the most sacred? Discourse to me on this."

The Rishi said, "Those kingdoms, those provinces, those asramas and those mountains through or near which the Bhagirathi flows are the most sacred. Only by living beside the Bhagirathi and bathing in her blessed waters can a man achieve the goals that can be attained by brahmacharya, by tapasya, by yagnas or by practising vairagya, renunciation. Those creatures whose bodies have been sprinkled with the sacred waters of the Bhagirathi or whose bones have been laid in the bed of that holy river will never fall from swarga. Those men who use the waters of the Bhagirathi surely ascend into heaven after leaving this world. Even those men who have sinned during the first part of their lives can attain to a superior end if in their later years they take to living on the banks of the Ganga. Hundreds of yagnas cannot produce that punya that men obtain by bathing in the sacred waters of the Ganga.

A man is treated with respect and worshipped in heaven for as long as his bones lie in the Ganga. Even as the rising sun blazes forth in splendour, having dispelled the shadows of night, in the same way the man that has bathed in the waters of the Ganga, cleansed of all his sins, shines brilliantly. Those kingdoms and realms that are empty of the sacred waters of the Ganga are like nights without the moon or like trees without flowers.

A world without the Ganga is like the varnas and the asramas without dharma or like yagnas without Soma. Without doubt, kingdoms and places without the Ganga are like the sky without the sun, or the earth without mountains, or without air. If offered the sacred waters of the Ganga, all the creatures in the three worlds are filled with joy unlike any other.

He who drinks Ganga jala that has been heated by the sun derives punya greater than that which attaches to the vrata of subsisting upon the wheat or other grains retrieved from cowdung. It cannot be said which is superior: he who performs a thousand Chandrayana rites to purify his body or he who drinks the water of the Ganga. It cannot be said whether the two are equal or not: one who stands for a thousand years on one foot and one who lives for only a month beside the Ganga.

One who lives permanently by the side of the Ganga is superior in merit to one who stays for ten thousand yugas suspended head down. As thread burns and vanishes without trace when set on fire, so are the sins of a man that bathes in the Ganga consumed. There is no end higher than the Ganga for those who, afflicted by sorrow, seek to attain that which could dispel their sorrow.

As snakes lose their poison at the very sight of Garuda, even so is one cleansed of all one's sins at the very sight of the sacred Ganga. They that are without renown and sinful in deeds have the Ganga for their fame, their protection, their means of liberation or their refuge. Many wretches among men, who are afflicted with heinous sins, and about to sink into naraka, are, despite all their sins, rescued by the Ganga in the next world if they seek her help and sanctuary.

They who bathe every day in the sacred waters of the Ganga become equals of Mahamunis and the very Devas with Vasava at their head. Brahmana, those wretches among men that are sinners without any trace of humility or shame become righteous and good by placing themselves before the Ganga. As amrita is to the Devas, as swadha is to the Pitris, as sudha is to the Nagas, even so is Ganga jala to the Manavas.

As children afflicted with hunger ask their mothers for food, in the same manner do those desiring their highest good seek out the Ganga. As the realm of Svayambhuva Brahma is said to be the foremost of all places, even so is the Ganga said to be best of all rivers. As the earth and the cow are said to be the main sustenance of the Devas, even so is the Ganga the main sustenance of all living creatures.

As the Devas nourish themselves upon the amrita that occurs in the sun and the moon and that is offered in yagnas, even so do humans sustain themselves with Ganga water. One smeared with the sand taken from the banks of the Ganga regards oneself as an inhabitant of swarga adorned with celestial liniments. He who bears on his head the mud taken from the banks of the Ganga presents an effulgence equal to that of Surya himself, who dispels the surrounding darkness.

When that wind that is moistened with drops of Ganga water touches one's body, it purifies him immediately of every sin. A man afflicted and weighed down by calamities, finds all his misfortunes dispelled by the very joy which wells up in his heart on seeing that sacred river. With the calls and songs of the swans and kokas and other water fowls that play on her breast, the Ganga challenges the very Gandharvas, and with her high banks the very mountains of the earth.

Heaven, too, is humbled beholding her surface teeming with swans and diverse other birds. The bliss which one enjoys by dwelling on the banks of the Ganga is greater than that of living in Swargaloka.

I have no doubt that he who is afflicted with impurity of speech, thought and deed is cleansed at the very sight of the Ganga. By holding that sacred river, touching it, and bathing in its waters, one purifies one's ancestors to the seventh generation, one's descendants to the seventh generation, and other ancestors and descendants as well. By hearing of the Ganga, by wishing to go to that river, by drinking its waters, by touching its waters, and by bathing in them a man saves both his paternal and maternal families.

By seeing, touching and drinking the waters of the Ganga, or even by praising her, hundreds and thousands of sinful men are washed of all their sins. They who wish to make their birth, life and learning fruitful, should repair to the Ganga and gratify the Pitris and the Devas by offering them tarpana of water. The punya that one earns by bathing in the Ganga cannot be earned through the acquisition of sons or wealth, or the performance of good deeds.

Those who are physically able but do not seek out the auspicious Ganga can be compared to those who are blind or those that are dead or those that are lame. What man is there that would not revere this sacred river that is adored by Maharishis that know the present, the past and the future, as also by the very Devas with Indra at their head? What man is there that would not seek the protection of the Ganga whose protection is sought by sannyasis and grihastas, and by Yatis and brahmacharins?

The man of righteous conduct who, with rapt soul, thinks of the

Ganga at the time of his dying, succeeds in attaining the highest end. That man who dwells by the side of the Ganga and worships her up to the time of his death, is freed from fear of every kind of calamity, of sin and of kings. When that blessed river plunged down from the sky, Maheswara bore her fall on his head. It is that very stream which is adored in swarga. Bhumi, swarga and patala are all adorned by the three streams of this sacred river. The man who uses her waters is crowned with success, material and of the spirit. As the sun's rays are to the Devas in heaven, as Chandramas is to the Pitris, as the king is to his subjects, even such is the Ganga to all rivers.

One who loses his mother or father, his sons or wives, or his wealth is not as grief-stricken as he that loses the Ganga. The joy that one gets from catching a glimpse of the Ganga one does not obtain through pious deeds that lead to Brahmaloka, or through such yagnas and kriyas that lead to swarga, or through sons or wealth.

The pleasure that men derive from seeing the Ganga is equal to what they derive from seeing the full moon. That man is cherished by the Ganga who adores her with deep devotion, with his mind wholly fixed upon her, with a reverence that is shared by no other object, with a feeling that there is nothing in the universe worthy of similar adoration, and with an absolute steadfastness.

Creatures that live on earth, in the sky, or in heaven, even the most superior beings, should always bathe in the Ganga. This is the first of all duties of the righteous. The fame of the Ganga's sanctity has spread across the entire universe since she revived all the sons of Sagara, whom Kapila reduced to ashes.

Men who are washed by the bright, beautiful, high, and swift waves of the Ganga, whipped up by the wind, are washed of all their sins and resemble the sun in its splendour. Men of tranquil souls that have cast off their bodies in the waters of the Ganga, whose sanctity is as great as that of the ghee and other oblations poured onto the fire in yagnas and which confer merits equal to those of the greatest of sacrifices, have certainly attained to a position equal to that of the Devas.

Ganga, with her fame and expanse, identical with the entire universe, and revered by the Devas, the Munis and men, can grant the wishes of even those that are blind, foolish and destitute. They that sought the refuge of the Ganga, that guardian of all the universe, she that flows in three streams, filled with sacred water, sweet as honey and powerful, succeed in attaining the blessings of swarga.

The man who dwells beside Ganga and beholds her every day, is purified by her sight and touch. The Devas grant him every kind of happiness in this world and the next. The Ganga can save every creature from sin and lead him to the felicity of swarga.

She is one with Prishni, the mother of Vishnu. She is the Vakdevi, Saraswati. She is aloof, and not easy to attain. She is the embodiment of auspiciousness and prosperity. She can bestow the six well-known attributes beginning with power. She is always generous with her grace.

She reveals all things in the universe, and she is the refuge of all creatures. Those who sought her protection in this life have surely attained heaven. The fame of the Ganga has spread all over the earth, the sky and swarga, and all the cardinal and subsidiary points of the horizon. Mortals use the waters of her streams to be crowned with success. He who, on beholding the Ganga, points her out to others, finds that she frees him from rebirth and confers mukti upon him.

The Ganga held the senapati of the Devas, Guha, in her womb. She also bears gold, the most precious of all metals, in her womb. They who bathe daily in her waters in the morning succeed in obtaining dharma, artha and kama. Her waters are as sacred as the ghrita that is poured into the sacrificial fire, while chanting mantras. Able to cleanse one from every sin, she has descended from swarga and is cherished by all.

The Ganga is the daughter of Himavat and Hara, and the jewel of both heaven and earth. She bestows everything auspicious, and grants the six renowned gunas beginning with puissance. Rajan, truly the Ganga is the one holy being in the three worlds and confers punya upon all.

The Ganga is righteousness in liquid form. She also is tejas that runs in liquid form over the earth. She is suffused with the beauty and power of the ghee that is poured along with mantras on the sacrificial fire. She is always adorned with high waves as also with Brahmanas who can be seen performing their ablutions in her waters at all times. Descending from swarga, she was contained by Siva on his head. The very mother of the heavens, she has sprung from the highest mountain and courses over the plains conferring the most precious benefits on all creatures of the earth. She is the highest cause of all things; she is perfectly pure. She is as subtle as Brahman.

She offers the best bed for the dying. She leads creatures to heaven. She carries an incalculable volume of water. She bestows great fame on all. She is the protector of the universe. She is identical with every form. She is greatly desired by those crowned with success. Indeed, for those who have bathed in her waters, the Ganga is the path to swarga.

The Brahmanas hold the Ganga as equal to the earth in forgiveness, and in the protection and upholding of those that live on her banks; further, as equal to Agni and Surya in energy and splendour; and also equal to Guha himself in bestowing favours upon the twice-born varna.

Men who seek, even in their minds, with all their souls, that ancient and sacred river praised by the Rishis, she that emerges from the feet of Vishnu, achieve the realms of Brahma. Men of subdued souls who want to attain Brahman, knowing that children and other possessions, and realms of felicity, are transient, always pay their adorations to the Ganga with that reverence and love that a son shows his mother.

Men of cleansed souls who wish for success should seek the protection of the Ganga who is like a cow that yields amrita instead of milk, who is prosperity itself, who is omniscient, who exists for all creatures, who is the source of all kinds of food, who is the mother of all mountains, who is the refuge of all righteous men, who is immeasurable in power and energy, and who enchants the heart of Brahma himself.

Having gratified all the Devas along with Vishnu with austere tapasya, Bhagiratha brought the Ganga down to the earth. Men go to her to free themselves from every kind of fear both here and in the next world. I have told you only some of the merits of the Ganga. My powers are not enough to speak of all the merits of the sacred river, or to measure her strength and blessedness.

With one's greatest powers, one may count the rocks in the mountains of Meru or measure the waters of the ocean, but one cannot determine the punya of the waters of the Ganga. Having listened to these merits of the Ganga, which I have described with great devotion, you should, in thought, word and deed, revere them with faith. Having listened to the merits that I have recited, you are sure to fill all the three realms with fame and attain great success and that is so difficult to have.

After that, you will sport in bliss created by the Ganga herself for those that worship her. The Ganga always extends her grace to those that are devoted to her with humility. She unites her devotees with every kind of happiness. I pray that the most blessed Ganga will always fill our hearts with righteous qualities.'"

Bhishma says, 'Having spoken to that poor Brahmana observing the Sila vrata on the infinite merits of the Ganga, the learned and enlightened Rishi rose into the sky. The Brahmana, awakened by his words, duly worshipped the Ganga and attained high success. Son of Kunti, seek the Ganga with great devotion, for then you, too, will be rewarded with excellent success.'"

Vaisampayana continued, "Hearing this discourse on the punya of the Ganga from Bhishma, Yudhishtira with his brothers are filled with rare and great delight. He who recites or hears this sacred discourse is purified of every sin."

CANTO 27

"Yudhishtira says, 'Pitamaha, you are old and wise, learned in the shastras, and marked by excellent gunas and unblemished conduct. You are celebrated above others by your gyana and tapasya. Foremost of all righteous men, I now ask you about dharma.

There is not another man in all the worlds, who is worthier of being questioned on such subjects. How can a Kshatriya, a Vaisya or a Sudra succeed in acquiring the status of a Brahmana? It is fitting that you tell me the means. Is it with austere tapasya or by religious kriyas, or through knowledge of the shastras that one belonging to any of the three lower varnas succeeds in acquiring the status of a Brahmana? Do tell me this.'

Bhishma says, 'Yudhishtira, the status of a Brahmana cannot be acquired by one belonging to any of the three other varnas. That is the highest condition for all creatures. After living through countless rebirths one is born finally as a Brahmana.

Listen to an ancient itihasa of a conversation between Matanga and a female donkey. Once, a Brahmana had a son who, though born of a woman of another varna, followed the laws laid down for Brahmanas in his childhood and youth. The child was named Matanga and possessed every accomplishment.

Wishing to perform a yagna, his father ordered him to collect the required articles. Having received his father's commands, Matanga set out on a swift chariot drawn by a donkey. It so happened that the donkey yoked to that chariot was young. Instead of obeying the reins, the animal ran with the chariot to his mother.

Matanga was angry and began to beat the animal on its nose with his goad. Seeing those marks of violence on her child's nose, full of compassion for him, the mother donkey said, "Do not grieve for his treatment, my child. This is a Chandala that is driving you. A Brahmana can never be so severe. The Brahmana is said to be the friend of all creatures. He is also the teacher and the master of all creatures. Can he punish any creature so cruelly?

This however is a sinful man. He has no compassion to show even to a being of such tender years as you. He is only reveals the varna of his birth by behaving in this way. The nature which he has inherited from his father prevents him from feeling the pity and kindness that are natural to the Brahmana."

Hearing these harsh words from the mother donkey, Matanga dismounted from his chariot and said to her, "Tell me by what fault is my mother stained? How do you know that I am a Chandala? Answer me at once. How do you know that I am a Chandala? How has my status as a Brahmana been lost? You of great wisdom, tell me all this in detail, from beginning to end."

The donkey said, "You were born to a Brahmana woman by a Sudra barber excited by desire. You are, therefore, a Chandala by birth. You do not enjoy the status of a Brahmana."

Thus addressed by the female donkey, Matanga returned home. Seeing him return, his father said, "I sent you on the difficult mission of gathering the requirements for my yagna. Why have you come back without having accomplished your task? Is all not right with you?"

Matanga said, "How can he who belongs to no definite varna, or an inferior varna, ever be regarded as well or happy? How can he whose mother is tainted be happy? Father, this female donkey, who seems to be more than a human being, tells me that I have been begotten upon a Brahmana woman by a Sudra. And for this reason, I will undergo the severest of penances."

Having said these words to his father, and firmly resolved upon what he had said, Matanga went to the great forest and sat in the most austere tapasya. He began to scorch the very Devas with the heat of his asceticism, undertaken to become a Brahmana.

While he sat unmoving in tapasya, Indra appeared and said, "Matanga, why do you pass your time in such grief, abstaining from all kinds of human enjoyment? I shall grant you boons. Name the boons you desire. Do not hesitate, but tell me what is in your heart. Even if it is unattainable, I will bestow it on you."

Matanga said, "I want to attain the status of a Brahmana with my tapasya. Only after becoming a true Brahmana will I go home. This is the boon I seek."

Indra said to him. "You cannot attain this status of a Brahmana which you desire. It is true you seek it, but it cannot be acquired by men who are born of those of uncleansed souls. Imprudent one, you are sure to meet with destruction if you persist in this pursuit.

Stop this vain endeavour at once. This object of your desire, of becoming a Brahmana, who is the foremost of all beings, cannot be achieved by tapasya. By craving this status, you will be only destroyed. One born as a Chandala can never attain to that status which is regarded as the most sacred among the Devas and Asuras and Manavas!"

CANTO 28

"Bhishma says, 'Matanga paid no heed to the counsels of Indra and stood on one foot for a hundred years, searing Devaloka even more.

Sakra appeared before him again and said, "The status of a Brahmana is unattainable. Although you covet it, it is impossible for you to acquire it. Matanga, by longing for that lofty condition you are sure to be destroyed. Do not be reckless. This cannot be a righteous path for you to follow.

You are foolish: it is impossible for you to become a Brahmana in this world. By craving that which is unattainable, you are sure to meet destruction. I repeatedly forbid you but you are intent on destroying yourself.

From the order of animal life one attains to the status of humanity. If born as a human being, he is first sure to be born as a Pukkasa or a Chandala. Having been born in this sinful order of existence one has to wander in it for a long time. After one thousand years in that varna, one next attains the status of a Sudra.

One has to live and die and be reborn in the Sudra varna for a long time. After thirty thousand years, one is born as a Vaisya. In that varna, a jiva again has to live for a long time. He is born a Kshatriya after sixty times the duration of his existence as a Sudra.

One has to pass a very long time in the Kshatriya varna. After a duration sixty times the previous length of time, one is born as a fallen Brahmana. One has to wander for a long time in this condition.

After two hundred times the previous length of time, one is born in the vamsa of a Brahmana who lives by fighting. In that one has to spend a great deal of time. After three hundred times the duration of his previous condition, one takes birth in the vamsa of a Brahmana that recites the Gayatri and other sacred mantras.

In that state also one has to remain for a long period. After a time measured by multiplying the last named period by four hundred, one takes birth into the family of a Brahmana conversant with all the Vedic shastras.

In that order again, one spends many a year. In that state of existence, joy and sorrow, desire and loathing, vanity and malicious speech try to enter into him and reduce him to wretchedness. If he succeeds in subduing those adversaries, he then attains a high end. If, on the other hand, those enemies triumph over him, he falls from that high state like one falling to the ground from a tall palm tree.

Knowing this for certain, I say to you, Matanga, ask for some other boon, for you who have been born a Chandala cannot dream of becoming a Brahmana!"

CANTO 29

"Bhishma said, 'Matanga still refused to accept Indra's advice. On the other hand, with regulated vows and a cleansed soul, he practised austere tapasya for a thousand years, standing on one foot and deep in dhyana. After a thousand years, Indra came again to him. The slayer of Bala and Vritra repeated the same advice.

Matanga said, "I have passed these thousand years standing on one foot in deep dhyana, observing of the brahmacharya vrata. Why is it that I have not yet succeeded in acquiring the status of a Brahmana?"

Indra said, "One born to a Chandala cannot become a Brahmana by any means. Therefore, name some boon so that all your efforts are not wasted."

Matanga was filled with grief. He journeyed to Prayaga, and lived there for a hundred years, standing all the while on just his toes. He became emaciated and his arteries and veins were swollen and visible. He was reduced to mere skin and bones. Indeed, while performing tapasya at Gaya, the Dharmatman Matanga collapsed from sheer exhaustion.

When Indra, who looks after the welfare of all creatures, saw him fall, the Lord and giver of boons came to that place and held him.

Indra said, "It seems, Matanga, that the status of a Brahmana which you seek is ill-suited to you. You cannot attain it. In fact, for you it is fraught with many dangers. One who worships a Brahmana finds happiness; abstaining from such worship, he finds sorrow.

For all creatures, the Brahmana is the giver of what they prize or covet and the protector of what they already have. It is through the Brahmanas that the Pitris and the Devas are gratified. The Brahmana is said to be foremost of all created beings. The Brahmana grants all objects of desire and in the way that they are desired.

Wandering through innumerable orders of being and undergoing repeated rebirths, one succeeds in some distant birth in being born as a Brahmana. Men of impure souls cannot obtain that condition. Give up this sinful and impossible ambition. Name some other boon. This boon cannot be granted to you."

Matanga said, "Already I am filled with anguish; Indra, why do you further torment me by what you say? You strike one that is already dead. I do not envy you for having acquired the status of a Brahmana; you fail to retain it for you show no compassion for one like me.

You of a hundred yagnas, you say that the status of a Brahmana cannot be attained by any of the three other varnas; yet, men that have succeeded in acquiring that high status through natural means do not adhere to it, for what sins do even Brahmanas not commit? Like wealth, the status of a Brahmana is difficult to acquire, and those who having acquired it do not seek to persevere with it by practising the necessary duties, must be regarded to be the lowest wretches in this world. Indeed, they are the most sinful of all creatures.

Without doubt, the status of a Brahmana is most difficult to attain, and once attained is difficult to maintain. It can dispel every kind of sorrow. Having attained to it, men do not always seek to maintain it by practising dharma and the duties attached to it. When even such men are regarded as Brahmanas, why is it that I, who am content with my own self, who am above all duality, who am detached from all worldly things, who am compassionate towards all creatures, and self-restrained in conduct, cannot be regarded as deserving of that status?

How unfortunate I am that through the fault of my mother I have been reduced to this condition, although I am not sinful in my behaviour. Without doubt, destiny cannot be avoided or conquered by individual exertion, since with all my efforts I am unable to acquire what I have set my heart upon. When such is the case, Indra, it is fitting for you to grant me some other boon if I have become worthy of your grace or if I have earned even a little punya.'"

Indra said to him, "Name the boon."

Matanga said, "Let me be possess the power of assuming any form at will, and moving through the skies, and let me enjoy whatever pleasures I may set my heart upon. And let me also have the willing adorations of both Brahmanas and Kshatriyas. I bow to you, great Sakra. Also ensure that my fame lives forever in the world."

Indra said, "You will be celebrated as the deity of a particular measure of verse and you will be worshipped by all women. Your fame will be unrivalled in the three worlds." Having granted him these boons, Indra vanished from sight. Matanga also cast off his life-breath and attained a high place.

Yudhishtira, you see that the status of a Brahmana is very high indeed. As the great Indra himself said, that condition of being cannot be acquired except by birth.'

"Yudhishtira says, 'I have now heard this great narrative. You have said that the status of a Brahmana is difficult to acquire. Yet, it has been said that in former times Viswamitra attained the status of a Brahmarishi. You, however, say that it cannot be obtained.

I have also heard that King Vitahavya in ancient times succeeded in obtaining Brahmatva. Pitamaha, I desire to hear the story of Vitahavya's advancement. With what deeds did that best of kings succeed in acquiring Brahmatva? Was it through some boon obtained from some powerful one or was it through the virtue of tapasya? Tell me everything.'

Bhishma says, 'Rajan, listen to how the famed Rajarishi Vitahavya succeeded in becoming a Brahmana, a condition that is so difficult to attain and that is held in such high reverence by all. While the high-souled Manu ruled his subjects wisely, he had a son of righteous soul who became renowned under the name of Saryati.

Two kings, Haihaya and Talajangha, were born into Saryati's vamsa. Both of them were sons of Vatsa. Haihaya had ten wives. Through them, a hundred sons, all great Kshatriyas, were born to him. All of them resembled one another in features and prowess. All of them were strong and all of them possessed great skill in battle. They all studied the Vedas and the science of weapons thoroughly.

In Kasi also there was a king who was the grandfather of Divodasa.

He was known by the name Haryaswa. The sons of King Haihaya, also known as Vitahavya, invaded the kingdom of Kasi and, advancing to the doab between the Ganga and Yamuna, fought a battle with King Haryaswa and killed him.

Having slain King Haryaswa, the sons of Haihaya, those daring Maharathikas, returned to their own delightful city in the kingdom of the Vatsas. Meanwhile Haryaswa's son Sudeva, who was like a god in splendour and who was a second Dharma Deva, was installed on the throne of Kasi as its ruler. The righteous prince had ruled his kingdom for a while when the hundred sons of Vitahavya once more invaded his dominions and defeated him in battle.

Having vanquished King Sudeva, the victors returned to their own city. After that Divodasa, the son of Sudeva, was crowned king of Kasi. Recognising the strength of the sons of Vitahavya, King Divodasa rebuilt and fortified the city of Varanasi at the command of Indra.

The kingdom of Divodasa was full of Brahmanas and Kshatriyas, and abounded with Vaisyas and Sudras. And they teemed with fine articles and provisions of every kind, and were adorned with shops and markets swelling with prosperity. Those territories stretched northwards from the banks of the Ganga to the southern banks of the Gomati, and resembled Amravati, the immortal city of Indra.

Bharta, the Haihayas once again attacked that tiger among kings. The splendid Divodasa sallied forth from his capital city and fought them. The battle between them was as fierce as that between the Devas and the Asuras in ancient times. King Divodasa fought the enemy for a thousand days becoming distraught at the vast number of his subjects and animals that were killed.

Having lost his army and exhausted his treasury, Divodasa fled his capital. Repairing to the delightful asrama of the wise Bharadwaja, the king humbly sought the Rishi's protection. Seeing the king before him, Bharadwaja, who was the king's purohita, said to him, "What is the reason for your coming here? Tell me everything, Rajan. I shall do what is agreeable to you without any hesitation."

The king said, "Holy one, the sons of Vitahavya have slain all the children and men of my house. I alone have escaped with my life, totally routed by the enemy. I seek your protection. Protect me with the love you bear for a sishya. Those sinful princes have slaughtered my entire vamsa, leaving only me alive."

To him who pleaded so piteously, Bharadwaja said, "Do not fear! Do not fear! Son of Sudeva, dismiss all your fears. I will perform a yagna which will give you a son through whom you will be able to annihilate thousands upon thousands of Vitahavya's forces."

After this, the Rishi performed a yagna in order to bestow a son on Divodasa. A son named Pratardana was born to Divodasa. On being born, he instantly grew into a boy of full thirteen years and quickly mastered all the Vedas and their angas.

Helped by his powers of yoga, Bharadwaja himself had entered into the prince. Gathering all the energies in the universe, Bharadwaja put them together in the body of Prince Pratardana. With shining armour and bow, Pratardana, his praises sung by Pauranikas and Devarishis, shone resplendent like the risen sun. Mounted on his chariot with his sword tied to his waist, he shone like a blazing fire. With his sword and shield whirling, he went to his father.

Seeing him, King Divodasa was filled with joy. Indeed, the old king considered the sons of his enemy Vitahavya as already slain. Divodasa installed his son Pratardana as the Yuvaraja, and regarding himself to be successful became exultant. He next commanded that parantapa, Prince Pratardana, to march against the sons of Vitahavya and destroy them in battle.

Pratardana, subduer of enemy cities, quickly crossed the Ganga on his chariot and rode against the city of the Vitahavyas. Hearing the clatter of his chariot's wheels, the sons of Vitahavya, riding on their own powerful chariots that looked like forts, came out of their city. Emerging from their capital, the sons of Vitahavya, all skilful warriors cased in mail, charged with weapons raised at Pratardana and enveloped him with fusillades of arrows.

Surrounding him with countless chariots, the Vitahavyas poured showers of astras upon Pratardana like clouds pouring torrents of rain on the breast of Himavat. Confounding their weapons with his own, mighty Pratardana killed them all with his shafts that resembled Indra's vajra. Beheaded by thousands of broad arrows, the bloodied bodies of the warriors of Vitahavya lay scattered like kimsuka trees felled by woodcutters with their axes.

After all his warriors and sons had fallen in battle, King Vitahavya fled from his capital to the asrama of Rishi Bhrigu. There the royal fugitive sought the protection of the sage. Bhrigu assured the defeated king of his protection. Pratardana followed Vitahavya.

Reaching the Rishi's asrama, the son of Divodasa said in a loud voice, "Listen, all you disciples of the Mahatman Bhrigu, I wish to see the sage. Go and inform him of this."

Recognising that it was Pratardana who had come, Bhrigu himself came out of his asrama and worshipped that best of kings with the due rites. The Rishi said, "Tell me, Rajan, what is it that you want." The king told the Rishi the reason for his presence.

The king said, "Brahmana, Vitahavya has come here. Surrender him to me. His sons destroyed my very vamsa. They laid waste the territories and the wealth of the kingdom of Kasi. I have slain a hundred sons of this proud king. By killing that king himself I will today pay the debt I owe my father."

The compassionate Maharishi Bhrigu replied, "There is no Kshatriya in this asrama. Here they are all Brahmanas."

Accepting Bhrigu's words to be true, Pratardana touched the Rishi's feet and, filled with delight, said, "Without doubt, on account of my prowess, I am now crowned with success, since this king has been abandoned by the very varna of his birth. Brahmana, allow me to leave you, and let me ask you to pray for my welfare. Because of my might, Vitahavya has been compelled to leave the very varna of his birth."

Dismissed by Bhrigu, Pratardana returned from the Rishi's asrama to his kingdom, even as a snake vomits out its real poison. Thus did

King Vitahavya attain the status of a Brahmana sage—purely by virtue of Bhrigu's words. He also acquired a complete mastery over all the Vedas in the same manner.

Vitahavya had a son named Gritsamada who was as handsome as Indra. Once, the Daityas harassed him greatly, believing him to be none other than Indra. With regard to that Rishi, one of the greatest srutis in the Riks says, "He with whom Gritsamada stays, Brahmana, is held in high regard by all Brahmanas."

Observing brahmacharya, the wise Gritsamada become a true Dvijottama, a twice-born sage. Gritsamada had a son named Sutejas. Sutejas had a son called Varchas, and the son of Varchas was known by the name Vihavya. Vihavya had a son named Vitatya and Vitatya had a son named Satya. Satya had a son named Santa. Santa's son was the Rishi Sravas.

Sravas begot a son named Tama. Tama had a son named Prakasa, who was a most superior Brahmana. Prakasa had a son named Vagindra who was the foremost of all silent reciters of sacred mantras.

To Vagindra was born a son named Pramati who was a complete master of all the Vedas and their angas. The Apsara Ghritachi bore Pramati a son who was named Ruru. Ruru had a son through his wife Pramadvara. That son was the great Rishi Sunaka. Sunaka gave birth to Saunaka.

It was thus that King Vitahavya, though a Kshatriya by birth, acquired the status of a Brahmana through the grace of Bhrigu. I have also told you the genealogy of the vamsa that sprung from Gritsamada. What else would you like to ask?'"

CANTO 31

"Yudhishtira says, 'Bharatarishabha, which men are worthy of reverence in the three worlds? Tell me this in detail. I am never satiated with hearing you discourse on these subjects.'

Bhishma says, 'Hear the ancient story of the discourse between Narada and Krishna. Seeing Narada once worshipping many excellent Brahmanas, Krishna said to him, "Whom do you worship? Whom among these Brahmanas do you worship with such great reverence? If it is something that I can be told, I wish to hear it. Foremost of righteous men, tell me."

Narada said, "Listen to the names of those whom I worship. Krishna, who else in this world deserves to hear this? I worship the Brahmanas who always worship Varuna and Vayu and Aditya and Parjanya and Agni, and Sthanu and Skanda and Lakshmi and Vishnu and the Brahmanas, and the Lord of speech, and Chandramas, and the waters and the earth and Devi Saraswati.

I always revere those Brahmanas that are imbued with tapasya, that are conversant with the Vedas, that are always devoted to Vedic study, and that possess high worth. I bow my head before those who are free of pride, who perform the rites in honour of the Devas while fasting, who are always content with what they have and who are forgiving. I adore them that perform yagnas, who are of a forgiving nature, and self-restrained, that are masters of their own senses, that worship truth and righteousness, and that give away land and cows to virtuous Brahmanas.

I bow unto them that are devoted to the observance of tapasya, that dwell in forests, that live upon fruits and roots, that never store anything for the next day, and that are observant of all the kriyas and karmas laid down in the shastras. I bow to them that feed and cherish their servants, that are always hospitable to guests, and that eat only the leftovers of what is offered to the gods.

I worship them that have become formidable by studying the Vedas, that are eloquent in discoursing on the shastras, that are observant of the brahmacharya vrata, and that are always devoted to the duties of presiding at others' yagnas and of teaching sishyas.

I worship them that are compassionate towards all creatures, and that study the Vedas all day. I bow to them that strive to obtain the grace of their gurus, that labour in their learning of the Vedas, that are firm in the observance of vows, that obediently wait upon their teachers and elders, and that are free from hatred and envy. I bow to them that observe excellent vratas, that practise mowna, that have knowledge of Brahman, that are resolute in truth, that offer libations of ghee and offerings of meat.

I bow to them that live upon alms, that are emaciated for want of adequate food and drink, that have lived in their gurus' homes, that are detached from all enjoyments, and that are poor in material goods. I bow to them that have no love for material wealth, that have no quarrel with others, that do not clothe themselves, that have no wants, that have become powerful through the acquisition of the Vedas, that are eloquent in the teaching of dharma, and that speak of Brahman.

I bow before those that are compassionate towards all creatures, firm in the observance of truth, self-restrained, and calm in their behaviour. Yadava, I bow to them devoted to the worship of Devas and Atithis, that belong to grihasta asrama, and that follow the way of pigeons in their manner of living. I always bow to those whose actions are marked by the triguna, without being weakened, and who are observant of truth and righteous conduct.

I bow unto them who are conversant with Brahman, who are endowed with knowledge of the Vedas, who are attentive in the pursuit of dharma, artha and kama, that are free of greed, and that are righteous. I bow unto them that survive only upon water, or upon air alone, or upon the leftovers of the food that is offered to gods and guests, and that observe diverse kinds of excellent vratas. I always worship those who have taken the vow of celibacy, who have wives and the domestic fire, that are the refuge of the Vedas, and that are the loving sanctuary of all creatures in the universe.

Krishna, I always bow to those Rishis that are the Creators of the universe, that are the elders of the universe, that are the eldest of the vamsa or the family, that dispel tamas, and that are the most righteous and most learned in the universe. For these reasons, you too, must worship those twice-born ones of whom I speak every day.

Deserving of reverence, they will, when worshipped, bestow happiness on you. Those of whom I speak always grant happiness in this world as well as in the next. Revered by all, they roam about in this world, and, if worshipped by you, are sure to grant you bliss.

They who are hospitable to all that come to them as guests, and who are always devoted to Brahmanas and cows, as also to truth in words and deeds, succeed in overcoming all calamities and obstacles. They who are always devoted to peace, as also they who are free from malice and envy, and they who are always attentive to the study of the Vedas, succeed in conquering all misfortunes and difficulties. They who bow before all the Devas without showing a preference for any, they who take refuge in any one Veda, they who are steadfast and self-restrained, prevail over all hardships and impediments.

They who worship the foremost of Brahmanas with reverence, are firm in the observance of vratas and practise the virtue of charity, overcome all calamities and obstacles. They who are engaged in the practice of tapasya, who are always observant of the vow of celibacy, and whose souls have been cleansed by tapasya, overcome all calamities and obstacles. They who are devoted to the worship of the Devas and atithis and Parvivara, dependents, as also of the Pitris, and they who eat the remnants of the food that is offered to Devas, Pitris, guests and dependents, conquer all problems and obstructions.

They who, having lit the domestic fire, duly keep it burning and worship it with reverence and they who duly pour libations in Soma yagnas, succeed in overcoming all difficulties. Krishna, they who behave as you do towards their mothers and fathers and gurus and elders triumph over all obstacles." Having said these words, the Devarishi fell silent.'

Bhishma continues, 'For these reasons, you must also always worship with great reverence the Devas, the Pitris, the Brahmanas and atithis who arrive at your palace, and as a result of such conduct you, too, will attain a lofty and desirable end.'"

CANTO 32

"**Y**udhishtira says, 'Wise Pitamaha conversant with all branches of knowledge, I want to hear you discourse on subjects related to kartavya and dharma, duty and righteousness. Tell me what are the merits are of those that grant protection to living creatures of all the four varnas when they entreat it?'

Bhishma says, 'Dharmaputra, listen to this ancient history on the great merit of granting protection to others when it is humbly sought. Long ago, a beautiful pigeon, pursued by a hawk, flew down from the skies and sought the protection of the king, Usinara Vrishadarbha.

The king comforted the terrified pigeon, saying, "Be reassured; do not fear. What has frightened you so much? What have you done and where, that you have lost your senses in fear and are more dead than alive? Your colour, beautiful bird, resembles that of a newly bloomed blue lotus. Your eyes are the colour of the pomegranate or the Asoka flower.

Do not be frightened. Set your mind at rest. When you have sought refuge with me, know that no one will have the courage to even think of harming you. For your sake, I will give up the very kingdom of Kasi and, if needed, my life too. Be comforted and feel no fear."

The hawk said to the king, "This bird has been ordained to be my food. It does not befit you to shelter him from me. I have hunted and overpowered this bird with great effort. His flesh and blood and marrow and fat will make good food for me. This bird will gratify me. Rajan, do not place yourself between him and me.

The thirst that tortures me is fierce, and hunger gnaws at my stomach. Release the bird and let me have him. I cannot bear the pains of hunger any longer. I pursued him as my prey. Look at his body, bruised and torn by my wings and talons. Look, how his breath has turned weak. It is not just for you to protect him from me.

In the exercise of that power which rightly belongs to you, you may intervene to protect men when other men try to kill them. You cannot, however, claim any power over a flying bird afflicted with thirst. Your power may extend over your enemies, your servants, your relatives, and the disputes that take place between your subjects. Indeed, it may extend over every part of your dominions and also over your own senses. Your power, however, does not extend to the sky.

Displaying your prowess over your enemies, you can establish your dominion over them. Your rule, however, does not extend over the birds that range the sky. Indeed, if you wish to earn punya by protecting this pigeon, it is your duty to also consider me and help me appease my hunger and save my life."'

Bhishma continues, 'Hearing the hawk's words, the royal sage was filled with some wonder. Wanting to heed these words and comfort the hawk, the king spoke to him.

The king said, "Let a bull, a boar, a deer or a buffalo be cooked for you today. Today appease your hunger on that food. I have taken a vow never to abandon anyone that seeks my protection. This bird will not leave my lap."

The hawk said, "I do not eat the flesh of the boar or the bull, the deer or the buffalo. What need have I of such food? My concern is only with that food which has been ordained for beings of my order? Hawks feed on pigeons, this is the eternal law. Sinless Usinara, if you feel such love for this pigeon, then give me flesh from your own body, equal in weight to that of this pigeon."

The king said, "You have shown me great respect by saying this to me. Yes, I shall do what you command."

Saying this, the king began to cut off his own flesh and weigh it in a balance against the pigeon.

Meanwhile, in the inner rooms of the palace, the wives of the king, adorned with jewels, heard what was happening, and came out grief-stricken and lamenting. Their cries, and those of the ministers and servants, rose in the palace like thunder. The clear sky was suddenly enveloped with dense clouds on every side. The earth began to quake because of the king's virtuous act.

Usinara continued to cut the flesh from his sides, from his arms, and from his thighs, and to fill one side of the scales to weigh it against the pigeon. Even after he had cut away a great deal of his flesh, the pigeon continued to weigh heavier. When at last the king was reduced to a fleshless skeleton of bones, covered with blood, he desired to give up his whole body, and climbed on to the scale in which he had placed his flesh.

At that moment, the three worlds, led by Indra, arrived there to see him. Celestial drums began to roll, played upon by spirits of the sky. King Vrishadarbha was bathed in a shower of amrita that was poured upon him. Garlands of heavenly flowers, of wonderful fragrance and texture, also rained down on him.

The Devas, Gandharvas and Apsaras began to sing and dance around him even as they do around Brahma. King Usinara ascended a celestial chariot that was more grand and beautiful than a palace made of gold; its arches were encrusted with gemstones and adorned with columns made of lapis lazuli. In this manner, the royal sage Usinara, also known as the great Sibi, went to swarga through his righteous act.

Yudhishtira, you too, must treat those that seek your protection in the same way. He who protects those that are devoted to him, those that are devoted to him, and those that depend upon him, and who has compassion for all creatures, attains great felicity in the next world. A virtuous king who is honest and honourable acquires every worthy reward by his actions.

The Rajarishi Sibi, of pure soul and great wisdom and indomitable prowess, the ruler of the kingdom of Kasi, became celebrated throughout the three worlds for his righteous deeds. He who protects one who seeks refuge in the same way will certainly attain the same happy end as Sibi did. He who narrates this history of Vrishadarbha is sure to be purified of every sin, and he who hears it recited is sure to attain to the same end.'"

CANTO 33

"Yudhishtira says, 'Pitamaha, what is the best conduct out of all those that have been established for a king? By doing what is a king able to enjoy both this world and the next?'

Bhishma says, 'The foremost dharma that has been laid down for a duly consecrated king, if he desires to obtain great happiness, is the worship of Brahmanas. This is what the best of all kings should do. Bharatarishabha, know this well. The king should always revere all righteous Brahmanas who possess Vedic knowledge.

The king must worship all learned Brahmanas living in his city or kingdom, with bowed head, elevating words, and gifts of all things of enjoyment. This is the foremost of all kartavyas laid down for the king. Indeed, the king must always be focused on this. He should protect and cherish the Brahmanas, even as he does himself or his own children. With even greater reverence the king must worship those Brahmanas who are learned and righteous.

When such men are free of all worries, the whole kingdom is ablaze with grace and beauty. Such men are worthy of adoration. The king must bow his head before them. They must be honoured, even as one honours one's fathers and grandfathers. Even as the existence of all creatures depends upon Vasava, so does the conduct of men depend on such Brahmanas. So compelling are their powers and tejas that if angered such men can raze the entire kingdom to ashes merely by their will, or with mantras, or by other means acquired through tapasya. Nothing can destroy them. Their power appears to be boundless, stretching to the ends of the universe. When angry, their glances fall upon men like a blazing fire upon a forest. The bravest of men are terrified by them. Their virtues and powers are vast and extraordinary.

Some among them are like wells and holes with their mouths covered by grass and creepers, while others resemble the bright and cloudless sky. Some among them, like Durvasas, are of fierce dispositions. Some, like Gautama, are as soft in nature as cotton. Some among them are cunning like Rishi Agastya who devoured the Asura Vatapi.

Some among them are devoted to the practice of tapasya; some are employed in farming like Uddalaka's guru; some are engaged in caring for cows as did Upamanyu, while attending on his guru. Some among them live on alms; some are even robbers like Valmiki in his early years and Viswamitra during a famine. Some, like Narada, enjoy inciting quarrels and disputes. Some, like Bharata, are actors and dancers.

Some can achieve all ordinary and extraordinary feats, like Agastya who swallowed the entire ocean as if it were a palmful of water. The Brahmanas are of diverse natures and behaviour. One must always sing the praises of the Brahmanas who are conversant with all duties, who are of righteous behaviour, who are devoted to virtuous deeds of many kinds, and who are seen to derive their sustenance from diverse kinds of occupations.

The Brahmanas who are older in origin than the Pitris, the Devas, men of the other three varnas, the Nagas and the Rakshasas are the most highly blessed. These regenerate men cannot be defeated by the Devas or the Pitris, the Gandharvas or the Rakshasas, the Asuras or the Pisachas. The Brahmanas can make one who is not a deity into one. They can also divest a Deva of his position.

He whom they wish to make a king becomes one. He whom they do not love or favour, on the other hand, is degraded. Rajan, I tell you truly that those foolish men who dishonour the Brahmanas meet with destruction. Skilled in praise and censure, and themselves the cause of other men's fame and disgrace, Brahmanas are always angered by those that seek to harm others.

That man whom the Brahmanas praise grows in prosperity. The man who is censured and cast off by the Brahmanas is disgraced. As a result of the absence of Brahmanas from among them, the Sakas, the Yavanas, the Kambojas and other Kshatriya tribes have fallen and devolved into Sudras. Similarly, the Dravidas, the Kalingas, the Pulindas, the Usinaras, the Kolisarpas, the Mahishakas and other Kshatriyas have become Sudras because of the absence of Brahmanas from among them.

Defeat at their hands is better than victory over them. The killing of a single Brahmana is a more heinous sin than the slaying all other living creatures in the world. The great Rishis have said that Brahmahatya is the worst sin. One must never humiliate or defame the Brahmanas. Where such condemnation of Brahmanas is pronounced, one should hang one's head in shame or leave that place in order to avoid both the speaker and his words.

That man has not as yet been, nor will be, born in this world who has been or will be able to pass his life in happiness after falling out with the Brahmanas. One cannot seize the wind in one's hands. One cannot touch the moon with one's hand. One cannot support the earth on one's arms. Similarly, one cannot vanquish the Brahmanas in this world.'"

CANTO 34

"Bhishma says, 'One must always offer the most respectful worship to the Brahmanas. Soma is their king, and they confer happiness and sorrow upon others. They must always be loved and protected as one loves and protects one's own fathers and grandsires, and they should be adored with reverence, gifts of food and ornaments, and other articles of enjoyment and desire.

The peace and happiness of the kingdom flow from such respect shown to Brahmanas, even as the peace and happiness of all living creatures flow from Indra. Let pure and radiant Brahmanas be born in a kingdom. Let Kshatriyas that are splendid maharathikas able to scorch all enemies, settle in a kingdom. Narada said this to me.

Rajan, there is nothing better than having a Brahmana of good birth, with a knowledge of neeti and dharma, morality and righteousness, and resolute in the observance of excellent vratas reside in one's palace. This will confer every kind of blessing. The sacrificial offerings given to Brahmanas reach the very Devas who accept them. Brahmanas are the fathers of all creatures. There is nothing higher than a Brahmana.

Aditya, Chandramas, Vayu, Jala, Bhumi, Akasa and the Diks, the cardinal directions, all enter the body of the Brahmana and partake of what the Brahmana eats. In that house where Brahmanas do not eat, the Pitris refuse to eat. The Devas also never eat in the house of the wretch who hates the Brahmanas. When Brahmanas are gratified, the Pitris also are gratified. There is no doubt about this.

They that give away the sacrificial ghrita to Brahmanas are themselves gratified in this and the other world. Such men can never be destroyed. They succeed in attaining to lofty ends. Those particular offerings in yagnas with which one gratifies the Brahmanas go to gratify both the Pitris and the Devas.

The Brahmana is the cause of that sacrifice from which all creation has sprung. The Brahmana knows that from which this universe has materialised and that to which, when apparently destroyed, it returns. The Brahmana knows the path that leads to swarga and the one that leads to naraka. The Brahmana is conversant with what has happened and what will happen.

The Brahmana is the foremost of all men. The Brahmana is fully acquainted with the dharma that has been laid down for his varna. Those that follow the Brahmanas are never destroyed. Even when they leave from this world, they never meet with death. They always triumph. Those Mahatmans, those that have subdued their souls, who accept the words spoken by the Brahmanas, are never defeated. They always prevail.

The tejas and shakti of Kshatriyas who scorch everything are impotent when they encounter the energy and power of Brahmanas. The Bhrigus conquered the Talajanghas. The son of Angiras conquered the Nipas. Bharadwaja conquered the Vitahavyas and the Ailas. Though all these Kshatriyas were masters of diverse kinds of astras, those Brahmanas, with only black deer skins for their emblems, overcame them decisively.

Bestowing the earth upon the Brahmanas and illuminating both the worlds with the splendour of such a deed, one must do that by which one may attain the end of all things. Like fire hidden within wood, everything that is said, heard or read in this world lies latent in the Brahmana. Listen to the itihasa of the conversation between Krishna and Bhumi Devi.

Krishna asked, "Mother of all creatures, auspicious Devi, I want to ask you to dispel a doubt. By what karma does a grihasta succeed in purifying himself of all his sins?"

Bhumi Devi replied, "One must serve the Brahmanas. This conduct is cleansing and excellent. If a man serves Brahmanas with reverence all his impurities are washed away. Prosperity arises from such behaviour; fame stems from this. And from this springs forth Atmagyana, the knowledge of the Soul. Through such conduct a Kshatriya becomes a maharathika and a parantapa, and acquires great renown.

This is what Narada said to me: if one desires many kinds of prosperity, one must always revere a Brahmana that is well-born, of firm vows and conversant with the shastras. He who is praised by Brahmanas, who are higher than all other men, grows in riches. He who speaks ill of the Brahmanas is soon disgraced, even as a lump of unbaked earth is destroyed when cast into the sea.

In the same manner, any cruelty to the Brahmanas is sure to bring shame and ruin. Behold the dark spots on the moon and the salty waters of the sea. The great Indra, too, had once been marked all over with a thousand phalluses. It was through the power of the Brahmanas that those penises were transformed into a thousand eyes.

Krishna, look at how all those events transpired. Desiring fame and prosperity and diverse realms of felicity in the next world, a man of pure conduct and soul must live in accordance with the dictates of the Brahmanas."

Bhishma continues, 'Hearing these words of the Devi, Krishna exclaimed, "Uttamam! Uttamam!" and duly worshipped her. Son of Pritha, having heard this discourse between Bhumi Devi and Madhava, you too, must always worship all superior Brahmanas with a rapt soul. Doing this, you will surely obtain what is highly beneficial for you!"'

CANTO 35

"Bhishma says, 'Brahmanas, by birth alone, become beings adored by all creatures, and as guests are entitled to eat the first portion of all cooked food. From them flow the great Purusharthas, the goals of life: dharma, artha, kama and moksha. They are the friends of all creatures in the universe. They are also the mouths of the Devas for food placed into Brahmanas' mouths is eaten by the gods.

Worshipped with reverence, they bless us with prosperity by uttering auspicious words. Scorned by our enemies, may the enraged Brahmanas curse them. Those who know ancient history recite the following Riks of how Brahma, after having created the Brahmanas, ordained their duties:

A Brahmana must never do anything other than what has been established for him. Protected, they should protect others. By conducting themselves in this way, they are sure to attain what is beneficial for them. By doing what has been ordained for them, they are sure to acquire spiritual wealth. They will be both the high standards for all creatures to aspire to, and the reins for restraining them. A learned Brahmana must never do that which is laid down for Sudras. By such a deed, a Brahmana loses merit.

With Vedic study he is sure to obtain prosperity and intelligence, and energy and puissance to overcome all enemies, as also glory of the most exalted kind. By offering oblations of ghrita to the Devas, the Brahmanas are blessed and become so worthy that they take precedence over even children in the matter of all kinds of cooked food.

Suffused with faith, marked by compassion towards all creatures, and devoted to self-restraint and the study of the Vedas, all your wishes will be fulfilled. Whatever exists in the world of Manavas, whatever occurs in the realm of the Devas, can all be acquired with through tapasya and gyana, and the observance of vratas and subduing the senses.

I have thus recited to you the verses that were sung by Brahma himself, moved by his deep love for the Brahmanas and his great wisdom. The power of those devoted to tapasya is equal to the power of kings.

They are compelling, fierce, and as swift as lightning in what they do. Among them are those with the strength of lions and then those that possess the might of tigers. Some of them have the power of boars, some with that of the great stag, and others with that of crocodiles. Some among them have the lash and venom of poisonous snakes, and the bite of some resembles that of sharks.

Some of them can decimate their enemies with words, while others can destroy with a mere glance of their eyes. While some are like snakes of virulent poison, some of them have gentle natures. The dispositions of the Brahmanas are of diverse kinds.

The Mekalas, the Dravidas, the Lathas, the Paundras, the Konwasiras, the Saundikas, the Daradas, the Darvas, the Chauras, the Savaras, the Varvaras, the Kiratas, the Yavanas, and numerous other tribes of Kshatriyas have become Sudras by the wrath of Brahmanas. By disdain of the Brahmanas, the Asuras were forced to take refuge in the depths of the ocean. Through the grace of the Brahmanas, the Devas have become Swargavasis.

Akasa cannot be touched. The Himavat Mountains cannot be moved from their place. The flow of Ganga cannot be checked by a dam. The Brahmanas cannot be subjugated. Kshatriyas cannot rule the earth without seeking the favour of the Brahmanas.

The Brahmanas are high-souled beings. They are the gods of the very Devas. If you wish to enjoy the sovereignty over the earth and her seas, worship them with gifts and dutiful service. When they accept a gift, their fierce energy and power abates. Rajan, you must protect your vamsa from those Brahmanas that do not want to accept gifts.'"

ACKNOWLEDGEMENTS

I am grateful to Ramesh Menon, my editor, for guiding my learning in this journey.

And to Jayashree Kumar, my friend, for drawing me into its joys and struggles and staying by my metaphorical side.

And to Roshan Ghose and Sheila Menon, my gurus, for instructing me in the ways vital for understanding the world of this compelling epic.

www.ingramcontent.com/pod-product-compliance
Lightning Source LLC
Chambersburg PA
CBHW030923020726
47498CB00001B/91